THE ORBIT
SCIENCE FICTION
YEARBOOK
1

THE ORBIT SCIENCE FICTION YEARBOOK 1

Edited by
David S. Garnett

Futura

An Orbit Book

ISBN 0 7088 8292 7

Typeset by Leaper & Gard Ltd, Bristol

Reproduced, printed and bound in Great Britain by
Hazell Watson & Viney Limited
Member of BPCC plc
Aylesbury, Bucks, England

Futura Publications
A Division of
Macdonald & Co (Publishers) Ltd
Greater London House
Hampstead Road
London NW1 7QX
A member of Maxwell Pergamon Publishing Corporation plc

ACKNOWLEDGEMENTS

Above all, the editor's thanks go to John Jarrold of Futura. For both of us this is a first; for John, in more ways than one.

'Forever Yours, Anna' by Kate Wilhelm. Copyright © 1987 by Omni Publications, Ltd. First published in *Omni*, July 1987. Reprinted by permission of the author.

'The Sun Spider' by Lucius Shepard. Copyright © by Davis Publications, Inc. First published in *Isaac Asimov's Science Fiction Magazine*, April 1987. Reprinted by permission of the author.

'Goodbye Houston Street, Goodbye', by Richard Kadrey. Copyright © 1987 by Interzone. First published in *Interzone 19*, Spring 1987. Reprinted by permission of the author.

'Friend's Best Man' by Jonathan Carroll. Copyright © 1986 by Mercury Press, Inc. First published in *The Magazine of Fantasy and Science Fiction*, January 1987. Reprinted by permission of the author.

'E-Ticket to Namland' by Dan Simmons. Copyright © 1987 by Dan Simmons. First published in *Omni*, November 1987. Reprinted by permission of the author.

'Ménage à Super-Trois' by Felix C. Gotschalk. Copyright © 1987 by Mercury Press, Inc. First published in *The Magazine of Fantasy and Science Fiction*, May 1987. Reprinted by permission of the author.

'Rachel in Love' by Pat Murphy. Copyright © 1987 by Davis Publications, Inc. First published in *Isaac Asimov's Science Fiction Magazine*, April 1987. Reprinted by permission of the author.

'Agents' by Paul Di Filippo. Copyright © 1987 by Mercury Press, Inc. First published in *The Magazine of Fantasy and*

CONTENTS

INTRODUCTION:
THE 'BEST' OF THE YEAR

Annual collections of 'best' science fiction stories have been published for four decades. The first such volume was *The Best Science Fiction Stories 1949*, edited by Everett F. Bleiler and T.E. Dikty. Despite the title, this consisted of stories reprinted from 1948.

Ever since then, there have been various other annual collections; but the main series have been those edited by Judith Merril, Donald A. Wollheim and Terry Carr (together, then separately), Harry Harrison and Brain Aldiss, and Gardner Dozois.

And now here is another such volume: the first *Orbit Science Fiction Yearbook*, a selection of stories originally published during 1987.

But what is the 'best'? Does it mean stories which are the most popular? Popularity in science fiction is measured by the major prizes: the Nebula, the professional award, is voted on by the Science Fiction Writers of America; and the Science Fiction Achievement Award (the Hugo) is voted for by the fans, members of the World Science Fiction Convention.

In that case, this book undoubtedly contains two of the very best stories of the year. After being selected for this *Yearbook*, Pat Murphy's 'Rachel In Love' won the Nebula as the best novelette of 1987, while Kate Wilhelm's 'Forever Yours, Anna' won the same award as best short story. (Both were also nominated for the Hugo awards, which will have been decided by the time this volume is published.)

Awards are soon forgotten, however, except by the winners and the compilers of record books. In literature, there can be no absolute standard of what is the 'best' — any judgement must necessarily be subjective, and the editor of a volume such as this can make no pretence of anonymity: I have to say *I* and *mine*, *me* and *my*.

I chose the contents of this book, which means that the

stories included here are my own favourites of the year.

Yet this volume is intended as more than just a collection of stories, no matter how excellent. It also contains an assessment of the year in science fiction, and there are two specially written articles by John Clute and Brian Aldiss. John Clute is one of the most respected and influential critics of science fiction, and in his comprehensive survey he reviews all the significant sf novels of 1987. Brian Aldiss, in his own unique style, provides his view of contemporary science fiction.

This is the first book I have edited, and I am particularly pleased to include 'Opposite Numbers' — because Brian Aldiss was the editor of the first sf book I ever read: an anthology called *More Penguin Science Fiction*.

But sf is supposedly the literature of the future, and so this is not time to look back.

The best is yet to be . . .

David Garnett
June 15, 1988

KATE WILHELM

Kate Wilhelm has been writing sf for over thirty years. Her first Nebula nomination was for her first novel, *The Clone* (1965, co-written with Theodore Thomas). In 1969, she won the short story Nebula for 'The Planners'; her novel *Where Late the Sweet Birds Sang* (1976) won the Hugo; she collected another Nebula in 1987 for her novelette 'The Girl Who Fell into the Sky' — and in 1988 she won the Nebula or the following story.

Many of her books and stories have been borderline sf, and what she has been writing lately fits less and less within the traditional category of 'science fiction' — an example of the way that the boundaries are forever expanding. And it is the better writers who are working at the edge, finding new frontiers.

Sometimes Wilhelm ventures completely outside the genre: her recent novel *The Hamlet Trap*, for example, is a thriller. Her other novels include *Huysman's Pets*, *Let The Fire Fall*, *The Clewison Test*, *Oh, Susannah!* and *Welcome, Chaos*. Two new books appeared in America in 1988, *Crazy Time* and *The Dark Door*. A short story collection, *Children of the Wind*, is scheduled for early 1989.

FOREVER YOURS, ANNA
by
KATE WILHELM

Anna entered his life on a spring afternoon, not invited, not even wanted. Gordon opened his office door that day to a client who was expected and found a second man also in the hallway. The second man brought him Anna, although Gordon did not yet know this. At the moment, he simply said, 'Yes?' 'Gordon Sills? I don't have an appointment, but . . . may I wait?'

'Afraid I don't have a waiting room.'

'Out here's fine.'

He was about fifty, and he was prosperous. It showed in his charcoal-colored suit, a discreet blue-gray silk tie, a silk shirt. Gordon assumed the stone on his finger was a real emerald of at least three carats. Ostentatious touch, that.

'Sure,' Gordon said, and ushered his client inside. They passed through a foyer into his office workroom. The office section was partitioned from the rest of the room by three rice-paper screens with beautiful Chinese calligraphy. In the office area as his desk and two chairs for visitors, his chair, and an overwhelmed bookcase, with books on the floor in front of it.

When his client left, the hall was empty. Gordon shrugged and returned to his office; he pulled his telephone across the desk and dialed his former wife's apartment number, let it ring a dozen times, hung up. He leaned back in his chair and rubbed his eyes absently. Late-afternoon sunlight streamed through the slats in the venetian blinds, zebra light. He should go away for a few weeks, he thought. Just close shop and walk away from it all until he started getting overdraft notices. Three weeks, he told himself; that was about as long as it would take. Too bad about the other guy, he thought without too much regret. He had a month's worth of work lined up already, and he knew more would trickle in when that was done.

Gordon Sills was thirty-five, a foremost expert in graphology, and could have been rich, his former wife had reminded him quite often. If you don't make it before forty, she had also said — too often — you simply won't make it, and he did not care, simply did not care about money, security, the future, the childern future....

Abruptly he pushed himself away from the desk and left the office, going into his living room. Like the office, it was messy, with several days' worth of newspapers, half a dozen books, magazines scattered haphazardly. To his eyes it was comfortable looking, comfort giving; he distrusted neatness in homes. Two fine Japanese landscapes were on the walls.

The buzzer sounded. When he opened the door, the prosperous, uninvited client was there again. He was carrying a brushed-suede briefcase.

Gordon opened the door wider and motioned him on through the foyer into the office. The sunlight was gone, eclipsed by the building across Amsterdam Avenue. He indicated a chair and took his own seat behind the desk.

'I apologize for not making an appointment,' his visitor said. He withdrew a wallet from his breast pocket, took out a card, and slid it across the desk.

'I'm Avery Roda. On behalf of my company I should like to consult with you regarding some correspondence that we have in our possession.'

'That's my business,' Gordon said. 'And what is your company, Mr. Roda?'

'Draper Fawcett.'

Gordon nodded slowly. 'And your position there?'

Roda looked unhappy. 'I am vice president in charge of research and development, but right now I am in charge of an investigation we have undertaken. My first duty in connection with this was to find someone with your expertise. You come very highly recommended, Mr. Sills.'

'Before we go on any further,' Gordon said, 'I should tell you that there are a number of areas where I'm not interested in working. I don't do paternity suits, for example. Or employer-employee pilferage cases.'

Roda flushed.

'Or blackmail,' Gordon finished equably. 'That's why I'm not rich, but that's how it is.'

'The matter I want to discuss is none of the above,' Roda

snapped. 'Did you read about the explosion we had at our plant on Long Island two months ago?' He did not wait for Gordon's response. 'We lost a very good scientist, one of the best in the country. And we cannot locate some of his paperwork, his notes. He was involved with a woman who may have them in her possession. We want to find her, recover them.'

Gordon shook his head. 'You need the police, then, private detectives, your own security force.'

'Mr. Sills, don't underestimate our resolve or our resources. We have set all that in operation, and no one has been able to locate the woman. Last week we had a conference during which we decided to try this route. What we want from you is as complete an analysis of the woman as you can give us, based on her handwriting. That may prove fruitful.' His tone said he doubted it very much.

'I assume the text has not helped.'

'You assume correctly,' Roda said with some bitterness. He opened his briefcase and withdrew a sheaf of papers and laid it on the desk.

From the other side Gordon could see that they were not the originals but photo-copies. He let his gaze roam over the up-side-down letters and then shook his head. 'I have to have the actual letters to work with.'

'That's impossible. They are being kept under lock and key.'

'Would you offer a wine taster colored water?' Gordon's voice was bland, but he could not stop his gaze. He reached across the desk and turned the top letter right side up to study the signature. ANNA. Beautifully written. Even in the heavy black copy it was delicate, as artful as any of the Chinese calligraphy on his screens. He looked up to find Roda watching him intently. 'I can tell you a few things from just this, but I have to have the originals. Let me show you my security system.'

He led the way to the other side of the room. Here he had a long worktable, an oversize light table, a copy camera, an enlarger, files. There was a computer and printer on a second desk. It was all fastidiously neat and clean.

'The files are fireproof,' he said dryly, 'and the safe is also. Mr. Roda, if you've investigated me, you know I've handled some priceless documents. And I've kept them right here in the shop. Leave the copies. I can start with them, but tomorrow I'll want the originals.'

'Where's the safe?'

Gordon shrugged and went to the computer, keyed in his code, and then moved to the wall behind the worktable and pushed aside a panel to reveal a safe front. 'I don't intend to open it for you. You can see enough without that.'

'Computer security?'

'Yes.'

'Very well. Tomorrow I'll send you the originals. You said you can already tell us something.'

They returned to the office space. 'First you.' Gordon said, pointing to the top letter. 'Who censored them?'

The letters had been cut off just above the greeting, and there were rectangles of white throughout.

'That's how they were when we found them.' Roda said heavily. 'Mercer must have done it himself. One of the detectives said the holes were cut with a razor blade.'

Gordon nodded. 'Curiouser and curiouser. Well, for what it's worth at this point, she's an artist more than likely. Painter would be my first guess.'

'Are you sure?'

'Don't be a bloody fool. Of course I'm not sure — not with copies to work with. It's a guess. Everything I report will be a guess. Educated guesswork, Mr. Roda, that's all I can guarantee.'

Roda sank down into his chair and expelled a long breath. 'How long will it take?'

'How many letters?'

'Nine.'

'Two, three weeks.'

Very slowly Roda shook his head. 'We are desperate, Mr. Sills. We will double your usual fee if you can give this your undivided attention.'

'And how about your cooperation?'

'What do you mean?'

'His handwriting also. I want to see at least four pages of his writing.'

Roda looked blank.

'It will help to know her if I know her correspondent.'

'Very well.'

'How old was he?'

'Thirty.'

'Okay. Anything else you can tell me?'

Roda seemed deep in thought, his eyes narrowed, a stillness about him that suggested concentration. With a visible start he looked up, nodded. 'What you said about her could be important already. She mentions a show in one of the letters. We assumed a showgirl, a dancer, something like that. I'll put someone on it immediately. An artist. That could be right.'

'Mr. Roda, can you tell me anything else? How important are those papers? Are they salable? Would anyone outside your company have an idea of their value?'

'They are quite valuable,' he said with such a lack of tone that Gordon's ears almost pricked to attention. 'If we don't recover them in a relatively short time, we will have to bring in the FBI. National security may be at stake. We want to handle it ourselves, obviously.'

He finished in the same monotone, 'The Russians would pay millions for them, I'm certain. And we will pay whatever we have to. She has them. She says so in one of her letters. We have to find that woman.'

For a moment Gordon considered turning down the job.

Trouble, he thought. Real trouble. He glanced at the topmost letter again, the signature 'Anna,' and he said, 'Okay. I have a contract I use routinely. . . .'

After Roda left, he studied the one letter for several minutes, not reading it, in fact, examining it upside down again; and he said softly, 'Hello, Anna.'

Then he gathered up all the letters, put them in a file, and put it in his safe. He had no intention of starting until he had the originals. But it would comfort Roda to believe he was already at work.

Roda sent the originals and a few samples of Mercer's writing before noon the next day, and for three hours Gordon studied them all. He arranged hers on the worktable under the gooseneck lamp and turned them this way and that, not yet reading them, making notes now and then. As he had suspected, her script was fine, delicate, with beautiful shading. She used a real pen with real ink, not a felt-tip or a ballpoint. Each stroke was visually satisfying, artistic in itself. One letter was three pages long; four were two pages; the others were single sheets. None of them had a date, an address, a complete name. He cursed the person who had mutilated them. One by one he turned them over to examine the backs and jotted: PRESSURE — LIGHT TO MEDIUM. His other notes were equally brief: FLUID. RAPID. NOT CONVENTIONAL. PROPORTIONS. ONE TO FIVE. That was European, and he did not think she was, but it would bear close examination. Each note was simply a direction marker, a first impression. He was whistling tunelessly as he worked and was startled when the telephone rang.

It was Karen, finally returning his many calls. The children would arrive by six, and he must return them by seven Sunday night. Her voice was cool, as if she were giving orders about laundry. He said okay and hung up, surprised at how little he felt about he matter. Before, it had given him a wrench each time they talked; he had asked questions: How was she? Was she working? Was the house all right? She had the house on Long Island, and that was fine with him; he had spent more and more time in town anyway over the past few years. But still, they had bought it together, he had repaired this and that, put up screens, taken them down, struggled with the plumbing.

That night he took the two children to a Greek restaurant. Buster, eight years old, said it was yucky; Dana, ten, called him a baby, and Gordon headed off the fight by saying he had bought a new Monopoly game. Dana said Buster was into winning. Dana looked very much like her mother, but Buster was her true genetic heir. Karen was into winning, too.

They went to The Cloisters and fantasized medieval scenarios; they played Monopoly, and on Sunday he took them to a puppet show at the Met and then drove them home. He was exhausted. When he got back he looked about, deeply depressed. There were dirty dishes in the sink and on the table, in the living room. Buster had slept on the couch, and his bedclothes and covers were draped over it. Karen said they were getting too old to share a room any longer. Dana's bedroom was also a mess. She had left her pajamas and slippers.

Swiftly he gathered up the bedding from the living room and tossed it all onto the bed in Dana's room and closed the door. He overfilled the dishwasher and turned it on and finally went into his workroom and opened the safe.

'Hello, Anna,' he said softly, and tension seeped from him; the ache that had settled in behind his eyes vanished; he forgot the traffic jams coming home from Long Island, forgot the bickering his children seemed unable to stop.

He took the letters to the living room and sat down to read them through for the first time. Love letters, passionate letters, humorous in places, perceptive, intelligent. Without dates it was hard to put them in chronological order, but the story emerged. She had met Mercer in the city; they had walked and talked, and he had left. He had come back, and this time they were together for a weekend and became lovers. She sent her letters to a post office box; he did not write to her, although he left pages of incomprehensible notes in her care. She was married or lived with someone, whose name had been cut out with a razor blade every time she referred to him. Mercer knew him, visited him apparently. They were even friends and had long, serious talks. She was afraid; Mercer was involved in work that was dangerous, and no one told her what it was. She called Mercer her mystery man and speculated about his secret life, his family, his insane wife or tyrannical father, or his own lapses into lycanthropy.

Gordon smiled. Anna was not a whiner or a weeper; but she was hopelessly in love with Mercer and did not know where he lived, where he worked, what danger threatened him, anything about him except that when he was with her, she was alive and happy. And that was enough. Her husband understood and wanted only her happiness, and it was destroying her, knowing she was hurting him so much, but she was helpless.

He pursed his lips and reread one. 'My darling, I can't stand it any longer. I dream of you, see you in every stranger on the street, hear your voice every time I answer the phone. My palms become wet, and I tingle all over, thinking it's your footsteps I hear. You are my dreams. So, I told myself today, this is how it is? No way! Am I a silly schoolgirl mooning over a television star? At twenty-six! I gathered up all your papers and put them in a box and addressed it, and as I wrote the number of the box, I found myself giggling. You can't send a Dear John to a post office box number. What if you failed to pick it up and an inspector opened it finally? I should entertain such a person? They're all gray and dessicated, you know, those inspectors. Let them find their own entertainment! What if they deciphered your mysterious squiggles and discovered the secret of the universe? Do any of them deserve such enlightenment? No! I put everything back in [excised] safe —'

Mercer was not the mystery man, Gordon thought then; the mystery was the other man, the nameless one whose safe hid Mercer's papers. Who was he? He shook his head over the arrangement of two men and a woman and continued to read: '— and [excised] came in and let me cry on his shoulder. Then we went to dinner. I was starved.'

Gordon laughed and put the letters down on the coffee table, leaned back with his hands behind his head, and contemplated the ceiling. It needed paint.

For the next two weeks he worked on the letters and the few pages of Mercer's handwriting. He photographed everything, made enlargements, and searched for signs of weakness, illness. He keystroked the letters into his computer and ran the program he had developed, looking for usages, foreign or regional combinations, anything unusual or revealing. Mercer, he decided, had been born in a test tube and never left school and the laboratory until the day he met Anna. She was from the Midwest, not a big city, somewhere around one of the Great Lakes. The name that had been consistently cut out had six letters. She had gone to an opening, and the artist's name had been cut out also. It had nine letters. Even without her testimony about the artist, it was apparent that she had been excited by his work. It showed in the writing. He measured the spaces between the words, the size of individual letters, the angle of her slant, the proportions of everything. Every movement she made was graceful, rhythmic. Her connections were garlands, open and trusting; that meant she was honest herself.

Her threadlike connections that strung her words together indicated her speed in writing, her intuition, which she trusted.

As the work went on, he was making more complete notes, drawing conclusions more and more often. The picture of Anna was becoming real.

He paid less attention to Mercer's writing after making his initial assessment of him. A scientist, technologist, precise, angular, a genius, inhibited, excessively secretive, a loner. He was a familiar type.

When Roda returned, Gordon felt he could tell him more about those two people than their own mothers knew about them.

What he not could tell was what they looked like, or where Anna was now, or where the papers were that she had put in her husband's safe.

He watched Roda skim through his report on Anna. Today rain was falling in gray curtains of water; the air felt thick and clammy.

'That's all?' Roda demanded when he finished.

'That's it.'

'We checked every art show in the state,' Roda said, scowling at him. 'We didn't find her. And we have proof that Mercer couldn't have spent as much time with her as she claimed in the letters. We've been set up. You've been set up. You say here that she's honest, ethical; and we say she's an agent or worse. She got her hooks in him and got those papers, and these letters are fakes, every one of them is a fake!'

Gordon shook his head. 'There's not a lie in those letters.'

'Then why didn't she come forward when he died? There was enough publicity. We made sure of that. I tell you, he wasn't with her. We found him in a talent hunt when he was a graduate student, and he stayed in that damn lab ever since, seven days a weeks for four years. He never had time to have a relationship of the sort she's talking about. It's a lie through and through. A fantasy.' He slumped in his chair. His face was almost as gray as his very good suit. He looked years older than he had the last time he had been in the office. 'They're going to win,' he said in a low voice. 'The woman and her partner. They're probably out of the country already. Probably left the day after the accident, with the papers, the job done. Well-done. That stupid, besotted fool!' He stared at the floor for several more seconds, then straightened.

His voice was hard, clipped, when he spoke again. 'I was against consulting you from the start. A waste of time and money. Voodoo crap, that's all this is. Well, we've done what we can. Send in your bill. Where are her letters?'

Silently Gordon slid a folder across the desk. Roda went through it carefully, then put it in his briefcase and stood up. 'If I were you, I would not give our firm as reference in the future, Sills.' He pushed Gordon's report away from him. 'We can do without that. Good day.'

It should have ended there, Gordon knew, but it did not end. Where are you Anna? he thought at the world being swamped in cold rain. Why hadn't she come forward, attended the funeral, turned in the papers? he had no answers. He just knew that she was out there, painting, living with a man who loved her very much, enough to give her her freedom to fall in love with someone else. Take good care of her, he thought at that other man. Be gentle with her; patient while she heals. She's very precious, you know.

He leaned his head against the window let the coolness soothe him. He said aloud, 'She's very precious.'

'Gordon, are you all right?' Karen asked on the phone. It was his weekend for the children again.

'Sure. Why?'

'I just wondered. You sounded strange. Do you have a girl-friend?'

'What do you want, Karen?'

The ice returned to her voice, and they made arrangements for the children's arrival, when he was to return them. Library books, he thought distantly. Just like library books.

When he hung up he looked at the apartment and was dismayed by the dinginess, the disregard for the barest amenities. Another lamp, he thought. He needed a second lamp, at the very least. Maybe even two. Anna loved light. A girlfriend? He wanted to laugh, and to cry also. He had a signature, some love letters written to another man, a woman who came to his dreams and spoke to him in the phrases from her letters. A girl-friend! He closed his eyes and saw the name, Anna. The capital *A* was a flaring volcano, high up into the stratosphere, then the even, graceful *n*'s, the funny little final *a* that had trouble staying on the base line, that wanted to fly away. And a beautiful sweeping line that flew out from it, circled above the entire name, came down to cross the first letter, turn it into an *A*, and in doing so formed a perfect palette. A graphic representation of Anna, soaring into the heavens, painting, creating art with every breath, every motion. Forever yours, Anna. Forever yours.

He took a deep breath and tried to make plans for the children's weekend, for the rest of the month, the summer, the rest of his life.

The next day he bought a lamp and on his way home stopped in a florist's shop and bought half a dozen flowering plants. She had written that the sunlight turned the flowers on the sill into jewels. He put them on the sill and raised the blind, and the sunlight turned the blooms into jewels. His hands were clenched; abruptly he turned away from the window.

He went back to work; spring became summer, hot and humid as only New York could be, and he found himself going from one art show to another. He mocked himself and cursed himself for it, but he attended openings, examined new artists' work, signatures, again and again and again. If the investigators trained in this couldn't find her, he told himself firmly, and the FBI couldn't find her, he was a fool to think he had even a remote chance. But he went to the shows. He was lonely, he told himself, and tried to become interested in other women, any other woman, and continued to attend openings.

In the fall he went to the opening of yet another new artist, out of an art school, a teacher. And he cursed himself for not thinking of that before. She could be an art teacher. He made a list of schools and started down the list, perfecting a story as he worked down it one by one. He was collecting signatures of artists for an article he planned to write. It was a passable story. It got him nothing.

She might be ugly, he told himself. What kind of woman would have fallen in love with Mercer? He had been inhibited, constricted, without grace, brilliant, eccentric, and full of wonder. It was the wonder that she had sensed, he knew. She had been attracted to that in Mercer and had got through his many defenses, had found a boy-man who was truly appealing. And he had adored her. That was apparent from her letters; it had been mutual. Why had he lied to her? Why hadn't he simply told her who he was, what he was doing? The other man in her life had not been an obstacle; that had been made clear also. The two men had liked each other, and both loved her. Gordon brooded about her, about Mercer, the other man; and he haunted openings, became a recognized figure at the various studios and schools where he collected signatures. It was an obsession, he told himself, unhealthy, maybe even a sign of neurosis, or worse. It was insane to fall in love with someone's signature, love letters to another man.

And he could be wrong, he told himself. Maybe Roda had been right after all. The doubts were always short-lived.

The cold October rains had come. Karen was engaged to a wealthy man.

The children's visits had become easier because he no longer was trying to entertain them every minute; he had given in and bought a television and video games for them.

He dropped by the Art Academy to meet Rick Henderson, who had become a friend over the past few months. Rick taught watercolors.

Gordon was in Rick's office waiting for him to finish with a class critique session when he saw the A, Anna's capital A.

He felt his arms prickle and sweat form on his hands and a tightening in the pit of his stomach as he stared at an envelope on Rick's desk.

Almost fearfully he turned it around to study the handwriting. The A's in *Art Academy* were like volcanoes, reaching up into the stratosphere, crossed with a quirky, insouciant line, like a sombrero at a rakish angle. Anna's A. It did not soar and make a palette, but it wouldn't, not in an address. That was her personal sign.

He let himself sink into Rick's chair and drew in a deep breath. He did not touch the envelope again. When Rick finally joined him, he nodded toward it.

'Would you mind telling me who wrote that?' His voice sounded hoarse, but Rick seemed not to notice. He opened the envelope and scanned a note, then handed it over. Her handwriting. Not exactly the same, but it was her. He was certain it was hers, even with the changes. The way the writing was positioned on the page, the sweep of the letters, the fluid grace.... But it was not the same. The *A* in her name, Anna, was different. He felt bewildered by the differences and knew it was hers in spite of them. Finally he actually read the words. She would be out of class for a few days. It was dated four days ago.

'Just a kid,' Rick said. 'Fresh in from Ohio, thinks she has to be excused from class. I'm surprised it's not signed by her mother.'

'Can I meet her?'

Now Rick looked interested. 'Why?'

'I want her signature.'

Rick laughed. 'You're a real nut, you know. Sure. She's in the studio, making up for time off. Come on.'

He stopped at the doorway and gazed at the young woman painting. She was no more than twenty, almost painfully thin, hungry looking. She wore scruffy sneakers, very old faded blue jeans, a man's plaid shirt. Not the Anna of the letters. Not yet.

Gordon felt dizzy and held onto the doorframe for a moment, and he knew what it was that Mercer had worked on, what he had discovered. He felt as if he had slipped out of time himself as his thoughts raced, explanations formed, his next few years shaped themselves in his mind. Understanding came the way a memory comes, a gestalt of the entire event or series of events, all accessible at once.

Mercer's notes had shown him to be brilliant, obsessional, obsessed with time, secretive. Roda had assumed Mercer failed, because he had blown himself up. Everyone must have assumed that. But he had not failed. He had gone forward five years, six at the most, to the time when Anna would be twenty-six. He had slipped out of time to the future. Gordon knew with certainty that it was his own name that had been excised from Anna's letters. Phrases from her letters tumbled through his mind. She had mentioned a Japanese bridge from his painting, the flowers on the sill, even the way the sun failed

when it sank behind the building across the street.

He thought of Roda and the hordes of agents searching for the papers that were to be hidden, had been hidden in the safest place in the world — the future. The safe Anna would put the papers in would be his, Gordon's safe. He closed his eyes hard, already feeling the pain he knew would come when Mercer realized that he was to die, that he had died. For Mercer there could not be a love strong enough to make him abandon his work.

Gordon knew he would be with Anna, watch her mature, become the Anna of the letters, watch her soar into the stratosphere; and when Mercer walked through his time door. Gordon would still love her and wait for her, help her heal afterward.

Rick cleared his throat, and Gordon released his grasp of the doorframe, took the next step into the studio. Anna's concentration was broken; she looked up at him. Her eyes were dark blue.

Hello. Anna.

No other American sf author has made such an impressive debut in recent years as Lucius Shepard. He has sold over thirty stories, the first of which were only published in 1983. He was soon nominated for the major awards, being short-listed in three different categories for the 1985 Nebulas. That was also the year he won the John W. Campbell Award as best new writer. He won the Nebula in 1987 for his novella 'R & R'.

Born in Lynchburg, Virginia 'which is Jerry Falwell's home base', his first novel was *Green Eyes* (1984). 1987 saw publication of his next two books, the novel *Life During Wartime* — which is based on several earlier stories, including 'R & R' — and a collection *The Jaguar Hunter*.

He is writing more novels, which he names as *The End of Life as We Know It*, *Kingsley's Labyrinth* and *Mister Right*.

THE SUN SPIDER
by
LUCIUS SHEPARD

'. . . In Africa's Namib Desert, one of the most hostile environ-
ments on the face of the earth, lives a creature known as the
sun spider. Its body is furred pale gold, the exact color of the
sand beneath which it burrows in search of its prey, disturbing
scarcely a grain in its passage. It emerges from hiding only to
snatch its prey, and were you to look directly at it from an
inch away, you might never notice its presence. Nature is an
efficient process, tending to repeat elegant solutions to the
problem of survival in such terrible places. Thus, if — as I
posit — particulate life exists upon the Sun, I would not be
startled to learn it has adopted a similar form.'

from *Alchemical Diaries*
by Reynolds Dulambre

1
Carolyn

My husband Reynolds and I arrived on Helios Station following
four years in the Namib, where he had delivered himself of the
Diaries, including the controversial Solar Equation, and where
I had become adept in the uses of boredom. We were met at the
docking arm by the administrator of the Physics Section, Dr.
Davis Brent, who escorted us to a reception given in Reynolds'
honor, held in one of the pleasure domes that blistered the skin
of the station. Even had I been unaware that Brent was one of
Reynolds' chief detractors, I would have known the two of
them for adversaries: in manner and physicality, they were
total opposites, like cobra and mongoose. Brent was pudgy, of
medium stature, with a receding hairline, and dressed in a drab
standard-issue jumpsuit. Reynolds — at thirty-seven, only two
years younger — might have been ten years his junior. He was
tall and lean, with chestnut hair that fell to the shoulders of his
cape, and possessed of that craggy nobility of feature one asso-
ciates with a Shakespearean lead. Both were on their best

behavior, but they could barely manage civility, and so it was quite a relief when we reached the dome and were swept away into a crowd of admiring techs and scientists.

Helios Station orbited the south pole of the Sun, and through the ports I had a view of a docking arm to which several of the boxy ships that journeyed into the coronosphere were moored. Leaving Reynolds to be lionized, I lounged beside one of the ports and gazed toward Earth, pretending I was celebrating Nation Day in Abidjan rather than enduring this gathering of particle pushers and inductive reasoners, most of whom were gawking at Reynolds, perhaps hoping he would live up to his reputation and perform a drugged collapse or start a fight. I watched him and Brent talking. Brent's body language was toadying, subservient, like that of a dog trying to curry favor; he would clasp his hands and tip his head to the side when making some point, as if begging his master not to strike him. Reynolds stood motionless, arms folded across his chest.

At one point Brent said, 'I can't see what purpose you hope to achieve in beaming protons into coronal holes,' and Reynolds, in his most supercilious tone, responded by saying that he was merely poking about in the weeds with a long stick.

I was unable to hear the next exchange, but then I did hear Brent say, 'That may be, but I don't think you understand the openness of our community. The barriers you've erected around your research go against the spirit, the . . .'

'All my goddamned life,' Reynolds cut in, brocadsting in a stagey baritone, 'I've been harassed by little men. Men who've carved out some cozy academic niche by footnoting my work and then decrying it. Mousey little bastards like you. And that's why I maintain my privacy . . . to keep the mice from nesting in my papers.'

He strode off toward the refreshment table, leaving Brent smiling at everyone, trying to show that he had not been affected by the insult. A slim brunette attached herself to Reynolds, engaging him in conversation. He illustrated his points with florid gestures, leaning over her, looking as if he were about to enfold her in his cape, and not long afterward they made a discreet exit.

Compared to Reynolds' usual public behavior, this was a fairly restrained display, but sufficient to make the gathering forget my presence. I sipped a drink, listening to the chatter, feeling no sense of betrayal. I was used to Reynolds' infidelities, and, indeed, I had come to thrive on them. I was grateful he had found his brunette. Though our marriage was not devoid of the sensual, most of our encounters were ritual in nature, and after four years of isolation in the desert, I needed the emotional sustenance of a lover. Helios would, I believed, provide an ample supply.

Shortly afer Reynolds had gone, Brent came over to the port, and to my amazement, he attempted to pick me up. It was one of the most inept seductions to which I have ever been subject. He contrived to touch me time and again as if by accident, and complimented me several times on the largeness of my eyes. I managed to turn the conversation into harmless channels, and he got off into politics, a topic on which he considered himself expert.

'My essential political philosophy,' he said, 'derives from a story by one of the masters of twentieth century speculative fiction. In the story, a man sends his mind into the future and finds himself in a utopian setting, a greensward surrounded by white buildings, with handsome men and beautiful women strolling everywhere . . .'

I cannot recall how long I listened to him, to what soon became apparent as a ludicrous Libertarian fantasy, before bursting into laughter. Brent looked confused by my reaction, but then masked confusion by joining in my laughter. 'Ah Carolyn,' he said. 'I had you going there, didn't I? You thought I was serious!'

I took pity on him. He was only a sad little man with an inflated self-opinion; and, too, I had been told that he was in danger of losing his administrative post. I spent the best part of an hour in making him feel important; then, scraping him off, I went in search of a more suitable companion.

My first lover on Helios Station, a young particle physicist named Thom, proved overweening in his affections. The sound of my name seemed to transport him; often he would lift his head and say, 'Carolyn, Carolyn,' as if by doing this he might capture my essence. I found him absurd, but I was starved for attention, and though I could not reciprocate in kind, I was delighted in being the object of his single-mindedness. We would meet each day in one of the pleasure domes, dance to drift, and drink paradisiacs — I developed quite a fondness for Amouristes — and then retire to a private chamber, there to make love and watch the sunships return from their fiery journeys. It was Thom's dream to be assigned someday to a sunship, and he would rhapsodize on the glories attendant upon swooping down through layers of burning gasses. His fixation with the scientific adventure eventually caused me to break off the affair. Years of exposure to Reynolds' work had armored me against any good opinion of science, and further I did not want to be reminded of my proximity to the Sun: sometimes I imagined I could hear it hissing, roaring, and feel its flames tonguing the metal walls, preparing to do us to a crisp with a single lick.

By detailing my infidelity, I am not trying to characterize my marriage as loveless. I loved Reynolds, though my affections had waned somewhat. And he loved me in his own way. Prior to our wedding, he had announced that he intended our union to be 'a marriage of souls.' But this was no passionate outcry, rather a statement of scientific intent. He believed in souls, believed they were the absolute expression of a life, a quality that pervaded every particle of matter and gave rise to the lesser expressions of personality and physicality. His search for particulate life upon the Sun was essentially an attempt to isolate and communicate with the anima, and the 'marriage of souls' was for him the logical goal of twenty-first century physics. It occurs to me now that this search may have been his sole means of voicing his deepest emotions, and it was our core problem that I thought he would someday love me in a way that would satisfy me, whereas he felt my satisfaction could be guaranteed by the application of scientific method.

To further define our relationship, I should mention that he once wrote me that the 'impassive, vaguely oriental beauty' of my face reminded him of 'those serene countenances used to depict the solar disc on ancient sailing charts.' Again, this was not the imagery of passion: he considered this likeness a talisman, a lucky charm. He was a magical thinker, perceiving himself as more akin to the alchemists than to his peers, and like the alchemists, he gave credence to the power of similarities. Whenever he made love to me, he was therefore making love to the Sun. To the great detriment of our marriage, every beautiful woman became for him the Sun, and thus a potential tool for use in his rituals. Given his enormous ego, it would have been out of character for him to have been faithful, and had he not utilized sex as a concentrative ritual, I am certain he would have invented another excuse for infidelity. And, I suppose, I would have had to contrive some other justification for my own.

During those first months I was indiscriminate in my choice of lovers, entering into affairs with both techs and a number of Reynolds' colleagues. Reynolds himself was no more discriminating, and our lives took separate paths. Rarely did I spend a night in our apartment, and I paid no attention whatsoever to Reynolds' work. But then one afternoon as I lay with my latest lover in the private chamber of a pleasure dome, the door slid open and in walked Reynolds. My lover — a tech whose name eludes me — leaped up and began struggling into his clothes, apologizing all the while. I shouted at Reynolds, railed at him. What right did he have to humiliate me this way? I had never burst in on him and his whores, had I? Imperturbable, he stared at me, and after the tech had scurried out, he continued to stare, letting me exhaust my anger. At last, breathless, I sat glaring at him, still angry, yet also feeling a measure of guilt ... not relating to my affair, but to the fact that I had become pregnant as a result of my last encounter with Reynolds. We had tried for years to have a child, and despite knowing how important a child would be to him, I put off the announcement. I was no longer confident of his capacity for fatherhood.

'I'm sorry about this.' He waved at the bed. 'It was urgent I see you, and I didn't think.'

The apology was uncharacteristic, and my surprise at it drained away the dregs of anger. 'What is it?' I asked.

Contrary emotions played over his face. 'I've got him,' he said.

I knew what he was referring to: he always personified the

object of his search, although before too long he began calling it 'the Spider.' I was happy for his success, but for some reason it had made me a little afraid, and I was at a loss for words.

'Do you want to see him?' He sat beside me. 'He's imaged in one of the tanks.'

I nodded.

I was sure he was going to embrace me. I could see in his face the desire to break down the barriers we had erected, and I imagined now his work was done, we would be as close as we had once hoped, that honesty and love would finally have their day. But the moment passed, and his face hardened. He stood and paced the length of the chamber. Then he whirled around, hammered a fist into his palm, and with all the passion he had been unable to direct toward me, he said, 'I've got him!'

> 'I had been watching him for over a week without knowing it: a large low-temperature area shifting about in a coronal hole. It was only by chance that I recognized him; I inadvertently nudged the color controls of a holo tank, and brought part of the low-temperature area into focus, revealing a many-armed ovoid of constantly changing primary hues, the arms attenuating and vanishing: I have observed some of these arms reach ten thousand miles in length, and I have no idea what limits apply to their size. He consists essentially of an inner complex of ultracold neutrons enclosed by an intense magnetic field. Lately it has occurred to me that certain of the coronal holes may be no more than the attitude of his movements. Aside from these few facts and guesses, he remains a mystery, and I have begun to suspect that no matter how many elements of his nature are disclosed, he will always remain so.'

from *Collected Notes*
by Reynolds Dulambre

2
Reynolds

Brent's face faded in on the screen, his features composed into one of those fawning smiles. 'Ah, Reynolds,' he said. 'Glad I caught you.'

'I'm busy,' I snapped, reaching for the off switch.

'Reynolds!'

His desperate tone caught my attention.

'I need to talk to you,' he said. 'A matter of some import-ance.'

I gave an amused sniff. 'I doubt that.'

'Oh, but it is ... to both of us.'

An oily note had crept into his voice, and I lost patience. 'I'm going to switch off, Brent. Do you want to say goodbye, or should I just cut you off in mid-sentence?'

'I warning you, Reynolds!'

'Warning me? I'm all aflutter, Brent. Are you planning to assault me?'

His face grew flushed. 'I'm sick of your arrogance!' he shouted. 'Who the hell are you to talk down to me? At least I'm productive ... you haven't done any work for weeks!'

I started to ask how he knew that, then realized he could have monitored my energy usage via the station computers.

'You think ...' he began, but at that point I did cut him off and turned back to the image of the Spider floating in the holo tank, its arms weaving a slow dance. I had never believed he was more than dreams, vague magical images, the grandfather wizard trapped in flame, in golden light, in the heart of power. I'd hoped, I'd wanted to believe. But I hadn't been able to accept his reality until I came to Helios, and the dreams grew stronger. Even now I wondered if belief was merely an exten-sion of madness. I have never doubted the efficacy of madness: it is my constant, my referent in chaos.

The first dream had come when I was ... what? Eleven, twelve? No older. My father had been chasing me, and I had sought refuge in a cave of golden light, a mist of pulsing, shift-ing light that contained a voice I could not quite hear: it was too vast to hear. I was merely a word upon its tongue, and there had been other words aligned around me, words I needed to understand or else I would be cast out from the light. The Solar Equations — which seemed to have been visited upon me rather than a product of reason — embodied the shiftings, the mysterious principles I had sensed in the golden light, hinted at the arcane processes, the potential for union and dissolution that I had apprehended in every dream. Each time I looked at them, I felt tremors in my flesh, my spirit, as if signaling the onset of a profound change, and ...

The beeper sounded again, doubtless another call from Brent, and I ignored it. I turned to the readout from the particle traps monitored by the station computers. When I had discovered that the proton bursts being emitted from the Spider's coronal hole were patterned — coded, I'm tempted to say — I had been elated, especially considering that a study of these bursts inspired me to create several addenda to the Equations. They had still been fragmentary, however, and I'd had the notion that I would have to get closer to the Spider in order to complete them ... perhaps join one of the flights into the coronosphere. My next reaction had been fear. I had realized it was possible the Spider's control was such that these bursts were living artifacts, structural components that maintained a tenuous connection with the rest of his body. If so, then the computers, the entire station, might be under his scrutiny ... if not his control. Efforts to prove the truth of this had proved inconclusive, but this inconclusiveness was in itself an affirmative answer: the computers were not capable of evasion, and it had been obvious that evasiveness was at work here.

The beeper broke off, and I began to ask myself questions. I had been laboring under the assumption that the Spider had in some way summoned me, but now an alternate scenario presented itself. Could I have stirred him to life? I had beamed protons into the coronal holes, hadn't I? Could I have educated some dumb thing ... or perhaps brought him to life? Were all my dreams a delusionary system of unparalleled complexity and influence, or was I merely a madman who happened to be right?

These considerations might have seemed irrelevant to my colleagues, but when I related them to my urge to approach the

Spider more closely, they took on extreme personal importance. How could I trust such an urge? I stared at the Spider, at its arms waving in their thousand-mile-long dance, their slow changes in configuration redolent of Kali's dance, of myths even more obscure. There were no remedies left for my fear. I had stopped work, drugged myself to prevent dreams, and yet I could do nothing to remove my chief concern: that the Spider would use its control over the computers (if, indeed, it did control them) to manipulate me.

I turned off the holo tank and headed out into the corridor, thinking I would have a few drinks. I hadn't gone fifty feet when Brent accosted me; I brushed past him, but he fell into step beside me. He exuded a false heartiness that was even more grating than his usual obsequiousness.

'Production,' he said. 'That's our keynote here, Reynolds.'

I glowered at him.

'We can't afford to have dead wood lying around,' he went on. 'Now if you're having a problem, perhaps you need a fresh eye. I'd be glad to take a look . . .'

I gave him a push, sending him wobbling, but it didn't dent his mood.

'Even the best of us run up against stone walls,' he said. 'And in your case, well, how long has it been since your last major work. Eight years? Ten? You can only ride the wind of your youthful successes for so . . .'

My anxiety flared into rage. I drove my fist into his stomach, and he dropped, gasping like a fish out of water. I was about to kick him, when I was grabbed from behind by the black-clad arms of a security guard. Two more guards intervened as I wrenched free, cursing at Brent. One of the guards helped Brent up and asked what should be done with me.

'Let him go,' he said, rubbing his gut. 'The man's not responsible.'

I lunged at him, but was shoved back. 'Bastard!' I shouted. 'You smarmy little shit, I'll swear I'll kill you if . . .'

A guard gave me another shove.

'Please, Reynolds,' Brent said in a placating tone. 'Don't worry . . . I'll make sure you receive due credit.'

I had no idea what he meant, and was too angry to wonder

at it. I launched more insults as the guards escorted him away.

No longer in the mood for a public place, I returned to the apartment and sat scribbling meaningless notes, gazing at an image of the Spider that played across one entire wall. I was so distracted that I didn't notice Carolyn had entered until she was standing close beside me. The Spider's colors flickered across her, making her into an incandescent silhouette.

'What are you doing?' she asked, sitting on the floor.

'Nothing.' I tossed my notepad aside.

'Something's wrong.'

'Not at all . . . I'm just tired.'

She regarded me expressionlessly. 'It's the Spider, isn't it?'

I told her that, Yes, the work was giving me trouble, but it wasn't serious. I'm not sure if I wanted her as much as it seemed I did, or if I was using sex to ward off more questions. Whatever the case, I lowered myself beside her, kissed her, touched her breasts, and soon we were in that heated secret place where — I thought — not even the Spider's eyes could pry. I told her I loved her in that rushed breathless way that is less an intimate disclosure than a form of gasping, of shaping breath to accommodate movement. That was the only way I have ever been able to tell her the best of my feeling, and it was because I was shamed by this that we did not make love more often.

Afterwards I could see she wanted to say something important: it was working in her face. But I didn't want to hear it, to be trapped into some new level of intimacy. I turned from her, marshalling words that would signal my need for privacy, and my eyes fell on the wall where the image of the Spider still danced . . . danced in a way I had never before witnessed. His colors were shifting through a spectrum of reds and violets, and his arms writhed in a rhythm that brought to mind the rhythms of sex, the slow beginning, the furious rush to completion, as if he had been watching us and was now mimicking the act.

Carolyn spoke my name, but I was transfixed by the sight and could not answer. She drew in a sharp breath, and seconds later I heard her cross the room and make her exit. The Spider ceased his dance, lapsing into one of his normal patterns. I scrambled up, went to the controls and flicked the display switch to off. But the image did not fade. Instead, the Spider's colors grew brighter, washing from fiery red to gold and at last to a white so brilliant, I had to shield my eyes. I could almost feel his heat on my skin, hear the sibilant kiss of his molten voice. I was certain he was in the room, I knew I was going to burn, to be swallowed in that singing heat, and I cried out for Carolyn, not wanting to leave unsaid all those things I had withheld from her. Then my fear reached such proportions that I collapsed and sank into a dream, not a nightmare as one might expect, but a dream of an immense city, where I experienced a multitude of adventures and met with a serene fate.

' ... To understand Dulambre, his relationship with his father must be examined closely. Alex Dulambre was a musician and poet, regarded to be one of the progenitors of drift: a popular dance form involving the use of improvised lyrics. He was flamboyant, handsome, amoral, and these qualities, allied with a talent for seduction, led him on a twenty-five-year fling through the boudoirs of the powerful, from the corporate towers of Abidjan to the Gardens of Novo Sibersk, and lastly to a beach on Mozambique, where at the age of forty-four he died horribly, a victim of a neural poison that purportedly had been designed for him by the noted chemist Virginia Holland. It was Virginia who was reputed to be Reynolds' mother, but no tests were ever conducted to substantiate the rumor. All we know for certain is that one morning Alex received a crate containing an artifical womb and the embryo of his son. An attached folder provided proof of his paternity and a note stating that the mother wanted no keepsake to remind her of an error in judgement.'

'Alex felt no responsibility for the child, but liked having a relative to add to his coterie. Thus it was that Reynolds spent his first fourteen years globe-trotting, sleeping on floors, breakfasting off the remains of the previous night's party, and generally being ignored, if not rejected. As a defense against both this rejection and his father's charisma, Reynolds learned to mimick Alex's flamboyance and developed similar verbal skills. By the age of eleven he was performing regularly with his father's band, creating a popular sequence of drifts that detailed the feats of an all-powerful wizard and the trials of those who warred against him. Alex took pride in these performances; he saw himself as less father than elder brother, and he insisted on teaching Reynolds a brother's portion of the world. To this end he had one of his lovers seduce the boy on his twelfth birthday, and from then on Reynolds also mimicked his father's omnivorous sexuality. They did, indeed seem brothers, and to watch Alex drape an arm over the boy's shoulders, the casual observer might have supposed them to be even closer. But there was no strong bond between them, only a history of abuse. This is not to say that Reynolds was unaffected by his father's death, an event to which he was witness. The sight of Alex's agony left him severely traumatized and with a fear of death bordering on the morbid. When we consider this fear in alliance with his difficulty in expressing love — a legacy of his father's rejections — we have gone far in comprehending both his marital problems and his obsession with immortality, with immortality in any form, even that of a child ...'

from *The Last Alchemist*
by Russell E. Barrett

3
Carolyn

Six months after the implantation of Reynolds' daughter in an artificial womb, I ran into Davis Brent at a pleasure dome where I had taken to spending my afternoons, enjoying the music, writing a memoir of my days with Reynolds, but refraining from infidelity. The child and my concern for Reynolds' mental state had acted to make me conservative: there were important decisions to be made, disturbing events afoot, and I wanted no distractions.

This particular dome was quite small, its walls Maxfield Parrish holographs — alabaster columns and scrolled archways that opened onto rugged mountains drenched in the colors of a pastel sunset; the patrons sat at marble tables, their drab jumpsuits at odds with the decadence of the decor. Sitting there, writing, I felt like some sad and damaged lady of a forgotten age, brought to the sorry pass of autobiography by a disappointment at love.

Without announcing himself, Brent dropped onto the bench opposite me an stared. A smile nicked the corners of his mouth. I waited for him to speak, and finally asked what he wanted.

'Merely to offer my congratulations,' he said.

'On what occasion?' I asked.

'The occasion of your daughter.'

The implantation had been done under a seal of privacy, and I was outraged that he had discovered my secret.

Before I could speak, he favored me with an unctuous smile and said, 'As administrator, little that goes on here escapes me.' From the pocket of his jumpsuit he pulled a leather case of the sort used to carry holographs. 'I have a daughter myself, a lovely child. I sent her back to Earth some months back.' He opened the case, studied the contents, and continued, his words freighted with an odd tension. 'I had the computer do a portrait of how she'll look in a few years. Care to see it?'

I took the case and was struck numb. The girl depicted was seven or eight, and was the spitting image of myself at her age.

'I never should have sent her back,' said Brent. 'It appears the womb has been misshaped, and I may not be able to find her. Even the records have been misplaced. And the tech who performed the implantation, he returned on the ship with the womb and has dropped out of sight.'

I came to my feet, but he grabbed my arm and sat me back down. 'Check on it if you wish,' he said. 'But it's the truth. If you want to help find her, you'd be best served by listening.'

'Where is she?' A sick chill spread through me, and my heart felt as if it were not beating but trembling.

'Who knows? Sao Paolo, Paris. Perhaps one of the Urban Reserves.'

'Please,' I said, a catch in my voice. 'Bring her back.'

'If we work together, I'm certain we can find her.'

'What do you want, what could you possibly want from me?'

He smiled again. 'To begin with, I want copies of your husband's deep files. I need to know what he's working on.'

I had no compunction against telling him; all my concern was for the child. 'He's been investigating the possibility of life on the Sun.'

The answer dismayed him. 'That's ridiculous.'

'It's true, he's found it!'

He gaped at me.

'He calls it the Sun Spider. It's huge ... and made of some kind of plasma.'

Brent smacked his forehead as to punish himself for an oversight. 'Of course! That section in the *Diaries*.' He shook his head in wonderment. 'All that metaphysical gabble about particulate life ... I can't believe that has any basis in fact.'

'I'll help you,' I said. 'But please bring her back!'

He reached across the table and caressed my cheek. I stiffened but did not draw away. 'The last thing I want to do is hurt you, Carolyn. Take my word, it's all under control.'

Under control.

Now it seems to me that he was right, and that the controlling agency was no man or creature, but a coincidence of possibility and wish such as may have been responsible for the spark that first set fire to the stars.

Over the next two weeks I met several times with Brent, on each occasion delivering various of Reynolds' files; only one remained to be secured, and I assured Brent I would soon have it. How I hated him! And yet we were complicitors. Each time we met in his lab, a place of bare metal walls and computer banks, we would discuss means of distracting Reynolds in order to perform my thefts, and during one occasion I asked why he had chosen Reynolds' work to pirate, since he had never been an admirer.

'Oh, but I am an admirer,' he said. 'Naturally I despise his personal style, the passing off of drugs and satyrism as scientific method. But I've never doubted his genuis. Why, I was the one who approved his residency grant.'

Disbelief must have shown on my face, for he went on to say, 'It's true. Many of the board were inclined to reject him, thinking he was no longer capable of important work. But when I saw the Solar Equations, I knew he was still a force to reckon with. Have you looked at them?'

'I don't understand the mathematics.'

'Fragmentary as they are, they're astounding, elegant. There's something almost mystical about their structure. You get the idea there's no need to study them, that if you keep staring at them they'll crawl into your brain and work some change.' He made a church-and-steeple of his fingers. 'I hoped he'd finish them here but ... well, maybe that last file.'

We went back to planning Reynolds' distraction. He rarely left the apartment anymore, and Brent and I decided that the time to act would be during his birthday party the next week. He would doubtless be heavily drugged, and I would be able to slip into the back room and access his computer. The discussion concluded, Brent stepped to the door that led to his apartment, keyed it open and invited me for a drink. I declined, but he insisted and I preceded him inside.

The apartment was decorated in appallingly bad taste. His furniture was of a translucent material that glowed a sickly bluish-green, providing the only illumination. Matted under glass on one wall was a twentieth century poster of a poem entitled 'Desiderata,' whose versus were the height of mawkish romanticism. The other walls were hung with what appeared to be ancient tapestries, but which on close inspection proved to be pornographic counterfeits, depicting subjects such as women mating with stags. Considering these appointments, I found hypocritical Brent's condemnation of Reynolds' private life. He poured wine from a decanter and made banal small talk, touching me now and then as he had during our first meeting. I forced an occasional smile, and at last, thinking I had humored him long enough, I told him I had to leave.

'Oh, no,' he said, encircling my waist with an arm. 'We're not through.'

I pried his arm loose: he was not very strong.

'Very well.' He touched a wall control, and a door to the corridor slid open. 'Go.'

The harsh white light shining through the door transformed him into a shadowy figure and made his pronouncement seem a threat.

'Go on.' He drained his wine. 'I've got no hold on you.'

God, he thought he was clever! And he was ... more clever than I, perhaps more so than Reynolds. And though he was to learn that cleverness has its limits, particularly when confronted by the genius of fate, it was sufficient to the moment.

'I'll stay,' I said.

'. . . In the dance of the Spider, in his patterned changes in color, the rhythmic waving of his fiery arms, was a kind of language, the language that the Equations sought to clarify, the language of my dreams. I sat for hours watching him; I recorded several sequences on pocket holographs and carried them about in hopes that this propinquity would illuminate the missing portions of the Equations. I made some progress, but I had concluded that a journey sunwards was the sort of propinquity I needed — I doubted I had the courage to achieve it. However, legislating against my lack of courage was the beauty I had begun to perceive in the Spider's dance, the hypnotic grace: like that of a Balinese dancer, possessing a similar allure. I came to believe that those movements were signaling all knowledge, infinite possibility. My dreams began to be figured with creatures that I would have previously considered impossible — dragons, imps, men with glowing hands or whose entire forms were glowing, all a ghostly, grainy white; now these creatures came to seem not only possible but likely inhabitants of a world that was coming more and more into focus, a world to which I was greatly attracted. Sometimes I would lie in bed all day, hoping for more dreams of that world, of the wizard who controlled it. It may be that I was using the dreams to escape confronting a difficult and frightening choice. But in truth I have lately doubted that it is even mine to make.'

from *Collected Notes*
by Reynolds Dulambre

4
Reynolds

I remember little of the party, mostly dazed glimpses of breasts and thighs, sweaty bodies, lidded eyes. I remember the drift, which was performed by a group of techs. They played Alex's music as an *hommage*, and I was taken back to my years with the old bastard-maker, to memories of beatings, of walking in on him and his lovers, of listening to him pontificate.

And, of course, I recalled that night in Mozambique when I watched him claw at his eyes, his face. Spitting missiles of blood, unable to scream having bitten off his tongue. Sobered, I got to my feet and staggered into the bedroom, where it was less crowded, but still too crowded for my mood. I grabbed a robe, belted it on and keyed my study door.

As I entered, Carolyn leaped up from my computer. On the screen was displayed what looked to be a page from my deep files. She tried to switch off the screen, but I caught her arm and checked the page: I had not been mistaken. 'What are you doing?' I shouted, yanking her away from the computer.

'I was just curious.' She tried to jerk free.

Then I spotted the microcube barnacled to the computer: she had been recording. 'What's that?' I asked, forcing her to look at it. 'What's that? Who the hell are you working for?'

She began to cry, but I wasn't moved. We had betrayed each other a thousand times, but never to this degree.

'Damn you!' I slapped her. 'Who is it?'

She poured out the story of Brent's plan, his demands on her. 'I'm sorry.' she said, sobbing. 'I'm sorry.'

I felt so much then, I couldn't characterize it as fear or anger or any specific emotion. In my mind's eye I saw the child, that scrap of my soul, disappearing down some earthly sewer. I threw off my robe, stepped into a jumpsuit.

'Where are you going?' Carolyn asked, wiping away tears.

I zipped up the jumpsuit.

'Don't!' Carolyn tried to haul me back from the door. 'You don't understand!'

I shoved her down, locked the door behind me, and went storming out through the party and into the corridor. Rage floored me. I needed to hurt Brent. My reason was so obscured that when I reached his apartment, I saw nothing suspicious in the fact that the door was open ... though I later realized he must have had a spy at the party to warn him of anything untoward. Inside, Brent was lounging in one of those ridiculous glowing chairs, a self-satisfied look on his face, and it was that look more than anything, more than the faint scraping at my rear, that alerted me to danger. I spun around to see a security guard bringing his laser to bear on me. I dove at him, feeling a discharge of heat next to my ear, and we went down together. He tried to gouge my eyes, but I twisted away, latched both hands in his hair and smashed his head against the wall. The third time his head impacted, it made a softer sound than it had the previous two, and I could feel the skull shifting beneath the skin like pieces of broken tile in a sack. I rolled off the guard, horrified, yet no less enraged. And when I saw that Brent's chair was empty, when I heard him shouting in the corridor, even though I knew his shouts would bring more guards, my anger grew so great that I cared nothing for myself, I only wanted him dead.

By the time I emerged from the apartment, he was sprinting around a curve in the corridor. My laser scored the metal wall behind him the instant before he went out of sight. I ran after him. Several of the doorways along the corridor slid open, heads popped out, and on seeing me, ducked back in. I rounded the curve, spotted Brent, and fired again ... too high by inches. Before I could correct my aim, half-a-dozen guards boiled out of a side corridor and dragged him into cover. Their beams drew smouldering lines in the metal by my hip, at my feet, and I retreated, firing as I did, pounding on the doors, thinking that I would barricade myself in one of the rooms and try to debunk Brent's lies, to reveal his deceit over the intercom. But none of the doors opened, their occupants having apparently been frightened by my weapon.

Two guards poked their heads around the curve, fired, and one of the beams came so near that it touched the fabric of my jumpsuit at the knee. I beat out the flames and ran full tilt. Shouts behind me, beams of ruby light skewering the air above my head. Ahead, I made out a red door that led to a docking arm, and having no choice, I keyed it open and raced along the narrow passageway. The first three moorings were empty, but the fourth had a blue light glowing beside the entrance hatch, signaling the presence of a ship. I slipped inside, latched it, and moved along the tunnel into the airlock; I bolted that shut, then went quickly along the mesh-walled catwalk toward the control room, towards the radio. I was on the point of entering the room, when I felt a shudder go all through the ship and knew it had cast loose, that it was headed sunwards.

Panicked, I burst into the control room. The chairs fronting the instrument panel were empty, the panel itself aflicker with lights; the ship was being run by computer. I sat at the board, trying to override, but no tactic had any effect. Then Brent's voice came over the speakers. 'You've bought yourself a little time, Reynolds,' he said. 'That's all. When the ship returns, we'll have you.'

I laughed.

It had been my hope that he had initiated the ship's flight, but his comments made clear that I was now headed toward the confrontation I had for so long sought to avoid, brought to this pass by a computer under the control of the creature for whom I had searched my entire life, a creature of fire and dreams, the stuff of souls. I knew I would not survive it. But though I had always dreaded the thought of death, now that death was hard upon me, I was possessed of a strange confidence and calm ... calm enough to send this transmission, to explore the confines of this my coffin, even to read the manuals that explain its operation. I had never attempted to understand the workings of the sunships, and I was interested to read of the principles that underlie each flight. As the ships approaches the Sun, it will monitor the magnetic field direction and determine if the Archimedean spiral of the solar wind is oriented outward,

If all is as it should be, it will descend to within one A.U. and will skip off the open-diverging magnetic field of a coronal hole. It will be traveling at such a tremendous speed, its actions will be rather like those of a charged particle caught in a magnetic field, and as the field opens out, it will be flung upward, back toward Helios ... that is, it will be flung up and out if a creature who survives by stripping particles of their charge does not inhabit the coronal hole in question. But there is little chance of that.

I wonder how it will feel to have my charge stripped. I would not care to suffer the agonies of my father.

The closer I come to the Sun, the more calm I become. My mortal imperfections seem to be flaking away. I feel clean and minimal, and I have the notion that I will soon be even simpler, the essential splinter of a man. I have so little desire left that only one further thing occurs to me to say.

Carolyn, I . . .

'. . . A man walking in a field of golden grass under a
bright sky, walking steadfastly, though with no apparent
destination, for the grasslands spread to the horizon, and his
thoughts are crystal-clear, and his heart, too, is clear, for his
past has become an element of his present, and his future —
visible as a sweep of golden grass carpeting the distant hills,
beyond which lies a city sparkling like a glint of possibility —
is as fluent and clear as his thought, and he knows his future
will be shaped by his walking, by his thought and the power
in his hands, especially by that power, and of all this he
wishes now to speak to a woman whose love he denied, whose
flesh had the purity of the clear bright sky and the golden
grasses who was always the heart of his life even in the country of lies, and here in the heartland of the country of truth is
truly loved at last . . .'

from *The Resolute Lover*
part of The White Dragon Cycle

5
Carolyn

After Reynolds had stolen the sunship — this, I was
informed, had been the case — Brent confined me to my apartment and accused me of conspiring with Reynolds to kill him. I
learned of Reynolds' death from the security guard who
brought me supper that first night; he told me that a promi-
nence (I pictured it to be a fiery fishing lure) had flung itself out
from the Sun and incinerated the ship. I wept uncontrollably.
Even after the computers began to translate the coded particle
bursts emanating from the Spider's coronal hole, even when
these proved to be the completed Solar Equations, embodied
not only in mathematics but in forms comprehensible to a
layman, still I wept. I was too overwhelmed by grief to realize
what they might portend.

I was able to view the translations on Reynolds' computer,
and when the stories of the White Dragon Cycle came into

view, I understood that whoever or whatever had produced them had something in particular to say to me. It was *The Resolute Lover*, the first of the cycle, with its numerous references to a wronged beautiful woman, the convinced me of this. I read the story over and over, and in so doing I recalled Brent's description of the feelings he had had while studying the equations. I felt in the focus of some magical lens, I felt a shimmering in my flesh, confusion in my thoughts ... not a confusion of motive but of thoughts running in new patterns, colliding with each other like atoms bred by a runaway reactor. I lost track of time, I lived in a sweep of golden grasses, in an exotic city where the concepts of unity and the divisible were not opposed, where villains and heroes and beasts enacted ritual passions, where love was the ordering pulse of existence.

One day Brent paid me visit. He was plumped with self-importance, with triumph. But though I hated him, emotion seemed incidental to my goal — a goal his visit helped to solidify — and I reacted to him mildly, watching as he moved about the room, watching me and smiling.

'You're calmer than I expected,' he said.

I had no words for him, only calm. In my head the Resolute Lover gazed into a crystal of Knowledge, awaiting the advent of Power. I believe that I, too, smiled.

'Well,' he said. 'Things don't always work out as we plan. But I'm pleased with the result. The Spider will be Reynolds' great victory ... no way around that. Still, I've managed to land the role of Sancho Panza to his Don Quixote, the rationalist who guided the madman on his course.'

My smile was a razor, a knife, a flame.

'Quite sufficient,' he went on, 'to secure my post ... and perhaps even my immortality.'

I spoke to him in an inaudible voice that said Death.

His manner grew more agitated; he twitched about the room, touching things. 'What will I do with you?' he said. 'I'd hate to send you to your judgement. Our nights together ... well, suffice it to say I would be most happy if you'd stay with me. What do you think? Shall I testify on your behalf, or would you prefer a term on the Urban Reserves?'

Brent, Brent, Brent. His name was a kind of choice.

'Perhaps you'd like time to consider?' he said.

I wished my breath was poison.

He edged toward the door. 'When you reach a decision, just tell the guard outside. You've two months 'til the next ship. I'm betting you'll choose survival.'

My eyes sent him a black kiss.

'Really, Carolyn,' he said. 'You were never a faithful wife. Don't you think this pose of mourning somewhat out of character?'

Then he was gone, and I returned to my reading.

Love.

What part did it play in my desire for vengeance, my furious calm? Sorrow may have had more a part, but love was certainly a factor. Love as practiced by the Resolute Lover. This story communicated this rigorous emotion, and my heartsickness translated it to vengeful form. My sense of unreality, of tremulous being, increased day by day, and I barely touched my meals.

I am not sure when the Equations embodied by the story began to take hold, when the seeded knowledege became power. I believe it was nearly two weeks after Brent's visit. But though I felt my potential, my strength, I did not act immediately. In truth, I was not certain I could act or that action was to be my course. I was mad in the same way Reynolds had been: a madness of self-absorption, a concentration of such intensity that nothing less intense had the least relevance.

One night I left off reading, went into my bedroom and put on a sheer robe, then wrapped myself in a cowled cloak. I had no idea why I was doing this. The seductive rhythms of the story were coiling through my head and preventing thought. I walked into the front room and stood facing the door. Violent tremors shook my body. I felt frail, insubstantial, yet at the same time possessed of fantastic power: I knew that nothing could resist me ... not steel or flesh or fire. Inspired by this confidence, I reached out my right hand to the door. The hand was glowing a pale white, its form flickering, the fingers lengthening and attenuating, appearing to ripple as in a graceful dance. I did not wonder at this. Everything was as it should be. And when my hand slid into the door, into the metal, neither did I consider that remarkable. I could feel the mechanisms of the lock, I — or rather my ghostly fingers — seemed to know the exact function of every metal bit, and after a moment the door hissed open.

The guard peered in, startled, and I hid the hand behind me. I backed away, letting the halves of my cloak fall apart. He stared, glanced left and right in the corridor, and entered. 'How'd you do the lock?' he asked.

I said nothing.

He keyed the door, testing it, and slid it shut, leaving the two of us alone in the room. 'Huh,' he said. 'Must have been a computer foul-up.'

I came close beside him, my head tipped back as if to receive a kiss, and he smiled, he held me around the waist. His lips mashed against mine, and my right hand, seeming almost to be acting on its own, slipped into his side and touched something that beat wildly for a few seconds, and then spasmed. He pushed me away, clutching his chest, his face purpling, and fell to the floor. Emotionless, I stepped over him and went out into the corridor, walking at an unhurried pace, hiding my hand beneath the cloak.

On reaching Brent's apartment, I pressed the bell, and a moment later the door opened and he peered forth, looking sleepy and surprised. 'Carolyn!' he said. 'How did you get out?'

'I told the guard I planned to stay with you.' I said, and as I had done with the guard, I parted the halves of my cloak.

His eyes dropped to my breasts. 'Come in,' he said, his voice blurred.

Once inside, I shed the cloak, concealing my hand behind me. I was so full of hate, my mind was heavy and blank like a stone. Brent poured some wine, but I refused the glass. My voice sounded dead, and he shot me a searching look and asked if I felt well. 'I'm fine,' I told him.

He set down the wine and came toward me, but I moved away.

'First,' I said, 'I want to know about my daughter.'

That brought him up short. 'You have no daughter,' he said after a pause. 'It was all a hoax.'

'I don't believe you.'

'I swear it's true,' he said. 'When you went for an exam, I had the tech inform you of a pregnancy. But you weren't pregnant. And when you came for the implantation procedure, he anesthetized you and simply stood by until you woke up.

It would have been in character, I realized, for him to have done this. Yet he also might have been clever enough to make up the story, and thus keep a hold on me, one he could inform me of should I prove recalcitrant.

'But you can have a child,' he said, sidling toward me. 'Our child, Carolyn. I'd like that, I'd like it very much.' He seemed to be having some difficulty in getting the next words out, but finally they came: 'I love you.'

What twisted shape, I wondered, did love take in his brain?

'Do you?' I said.

'I know it must be hard to believe,' he said. 'You can't possibly understand the pressure I've been under, the demands that forced my actions. But I swear to you, Carolyn, I've always cared for you. I knew how oppressed you were by Reynolds. Don't you see? To an extent I was acting on your behalf. I wanted to free you.'

He said all this in a whining tone, edging close, so close I could smell his bitter breath. He put a hand on my breast, lifted it.... Perhaps he did love me in his way, for it seemed a treasuring touch. But mine was not. I laid my palely glowing hand on the back of his neck. He screamed, went rigid, and oh, how that scream made me feel! It was like music, his pain. He stumbled backward, toppled over one of the luminous chairs, and lay writhing, clawing his neck.

'Where is she?' I asked, kneeling beside him.

Spittle leaked between his gritted teeth. 'I'll ... find her, bring her ... oh!'

I saw I could never trust him. Desperate, He would say anything. He might bring me someone else's child. I touched his stomach, penetrating the flesh to the first join of my fingers, then wiggling them. Again he screamed. Blood mapped the front of his jumpsuit.

'Where is she?' I no longer was thinking about the child: she was lost, and I was only tormenting him.

His speech was incoherent, he tried to hump away. I showed him my hand, how it glowed, and his eyes bugged.

'Do you still love me?' I asked, touching his groin, hooking my fingers and pulling at some fiber.

Agony bubbled in his throat, and he curled up around his pain, cluthing himself.

I could not stop touching him. I orchestrated his screams, producing short ones, long ones, ones that held a strained hoarse chord. My hatred was a distant emotion. I felt no fury, no glee. I was merely a craftsman, working to prolong his death. Pink films occluded the whites of his eyes, his teeth were stained to crimson, and at last he lay still.

I sat beside him for what seemed a long time. Then I donned my cloak and walked back to my apartment. After making sure no one was in the corridor, I dragged the dead guard out of the front room and propped him against the corridor wall. I reset the lock, stepped inside, and the door slid shut behind me. I felt nothing. I took up *The Resolute Lover*, but even my interest in it had waned. I gazed at the walls, growing thoughtless, remembering only that I had been somewhere, done some violence; I was perplexed by my glowing hand. But soon I fell asleep, and when I was waked by the guard unlocking the door, I found that the hand had returned to normal.

'Did you hear anything outside?' asked one of the guards.

'No,' I said. 'What happened?'

He told me the gory details, about the dead guard and Brent. Like everyone else on Helios Station, he seemed more confounded by these incomprehensible deaths than by the fantastic birth that had preceded them.

'The walls of the station have been plated with gold, the corridors are thronged with tourists, with students come to study the disciplines implicit in the Equations, disciplines that go far beyond the miraculous transformation of my hand. Souvenir shops sell holos of the Spider, recordings of 'The White Dragon Cycle (now used to acclimate children to the basics of the equations), and authorized histories of the sad events surrounding the Spider's emergence. The pleasure domes reverberate with Alex Dulambre's drifts, and in an auditorium constructed for this purpose, Reynolds' clone delivers daily lectures on the convoluted circumstances of his death and triumph. The place is half amusement park, half shrine. Yet the greatest memorial to Reynolds' work is not here; it lies beyond the orbit of Pluto and consists of a vast shifting structure of golden light wherein dwell those students who have mastered the disciplines and overcome the bonds of corporeality. They are engaged, it is said, in an unfathomable work that may have taken its inspiration from Reynolds' metaphysical flights of fancy, or — and many hold to this opinion — may reflect the Spider's design, his desire to rid himself of the human nuisance by setting us upon a new revolutionary course. After Brent's death I thought to join in this work. But my mind was not suited to the disciplines; I had displayed all the mastery of which I was capable in dispensing with Brent.

'I have determined to continue the search for my daughter. It may be — as Brent claimed — that she does not exist, but it is all that is left to me, and I have made my resolve accordingly. Still, I have not managed to leave the station, because I am drawn to Reynolds' clone. Again and again I find myself in the rear of the auditorium, where I watch him pace the dias, declaiming in his most excited manner. I yearn to approach him, to learn how like Renolds he truly is. I am certain he has spotted me on several occasions, and I wonder what he is thinking, how it would be to speak to him, touch him. Perhaps this is perverse of me, but I cannot help wondering ...'

from *Days In The Sun*
by Carolyn Dulambre

6
Carolyn/Reynolds

I had been wanting to talk with her since ... well, since this peculiar life began. Why? I loved her, for one thing. But there seemed to be a far more compelling reason, one I could not verbalize. I suppressed the urge for a time, not wanting to hurt her; but seeing that she had begun to appear at the lectures, I finally decided to make an approach.

She had taken to frequenting a pleasure dome named

Spider's. Its walls were holographic representations of the
Spider, and these were strung together with golden webs that
looked molten against the black backdrop, like seams of
unearthly fire. In this golden dimness the faces of the patrons
glowed like spirits, and the glow seemed to be accentuated by
the violence of the music. It was not a place to my taste, nor —
I suspect — to hers. Perhaps her patronage was a form of
courage, of facing down the creature who had caused her so
much pain.

I found her seated in a rear corner, drinking an Amouriste,
and when I moved up beside her table, she paid me no mind.
No one ever approached her; she was as much a memorial as
the station itself, and though she was still a beautiful woman,
she was treated like the wife of a saint. Doubtless she thought I
was merely pausing by the table, looking for someone. But
when I sat opposite her, she glanced up and her jaw dropped.

'Don't be afraid,' I said.

'Why should I be afraid?'

'I thought my presence might ... discomfort you.'

She met my eyes unflinchingly. 'I suppose I thought that,
too.'

'But ...?'

'It doesn't matter.'

A silence built between us.

She wore a robe of golden silk, cut to expose the upper swells
of her breasts, and her hair was pulled back from her face,
laying bare the smooth serene lines of her beauty, a beauty that
had once fired me, that did so even now.

'Look,' I said. 'For some reason I was drawn to talk to you, I
feel I have ...'

'I feel the same.' She said this with a strong degree of
urgency, but then tried to disguise the fact. 'What shall we talk
about?'

'I'm not sure.'

She tapped a finger on her glass. 'Why don't we walk?'

Everyone watched as we left, and several people followed us
into the corridor, a circumstance that led me to suggest that we
talk in my apartment. She hesitated, then signalled agreement
with the briefest of nods. We moved quickly through the

crowds, managing to elude our pursuers, and settled into a leisurely pace. Now and again I caught her staring at me, and asked if anything was wrong.

'Wrong?' She seemed to be tasting the word, trying it out. 'No.' she said. 'No more than usual.'

I had thought that when I did talk to him I would find he was merely a counterfeit, that he would be nothing like Reynolds, except in the most superficial way. But this was not the case. Walking along that golden corridor, mixing with the revelers who poured between the shops and bars, I felt toward him as I had on the day we had met in the streets of Abidjan: powerfully attracted, vulnerable, and excited. And yet I did perceive a difference in him. Whereas Reynolds' presence had been commanding and intense, there had been a brittleness to that intensity, a sense that his diamond glitter might easily be fractured. With this Reynolds, however, there was no such inconstancy. His presence — while potent — was smooth, natural, and unflawed.

Everywhere we walked we encountered the fruits of the Equations: matter transmitters; rebirth parlors, where one could experience a transformation of both body and soul; and the omnipresent students, some of them half-gone into a transcorporeal state, cloaked to hide this fact, but their condition evident by their inward-looking eyes. With Reynolds beside me, all this seemed comprehensible, not — as before — a carnival of meaningless improbabilities. I asked what he felt on seeing the results of his work, and he said, 'I'm really not concerned with it.'

'What are you concerned with?'

'With you, Carolyn,' he said.

The answer both pleased me and made me wary. 'Surely you must have more pressing concerns,' I said.

'Everything I've done was for you.' A puzzled expression crossed his face.

'Don't pretend with me!' I snapped, growing angry. 'This isn't a show, this isn't the auditorium.'

He opened his mouth, but back whatever he had been intending to say, and we walked on.

'Forgive me,' I said, realizing the confusion that must be his.

'I . . .'

'No need for forgiveness,' he said. 'All our failures are behind us now.'

I didn't know from where these words were coming. They were my words, yet they also seemed spoken from a place deep inside myself, one whose existence had been hidden until now, and it was all I could do to hold them back. We passed into the upper levels of the station, where the permanent staff was quartered, and as we rounded a curve, we nearly ran into a student standing motionless, gazing at the wall: a pale young man with black hair, a thin mouth, and a gray cape. His eyes were dead-looking, and his voice sepulchral. 'It awaits,' he said.

They are so lost in self-contemplation, these students, that they are likely to say anything. Some fancy them oracles, but not I: their words struck me as being random, sparks from a frayed wire.

'What awaits?' I asked, amused.

'Life . . . the city.'

'Ah,' I said. 'And how do I get there?'

'You . . .' He lapsed into an open-mouthed stare.

Carolyn pulled at me, and we set off again. I started to make a joke about the encounter, but seeing her troubled expression, I restrained myself.

When we entered my apartment, she stopped in the center of the living room, transfixed by the walls. I had set them to display the environment of the beginning of *The Resolute Lover*: an endless sweep of golden grasses, with a sparkling on the horizon that might have been the winking of some bright tower.

'Does this bother you?' I asked, gesturing at the walls.

'No, they startled me, that's all.' She strolled along, peering at the grasses, as if hoping to catch sight of someone. Then she turned, and I spoke again from that deep hidden place, a place that now — responding to the sight of her against those golden fields — was spreading all through me.

'Carolyn, I love you,' I said . . . and this time I knew who it was that spoke.

He had removed his cloak, and his body was shimmering,

embedded in that pale glow that once had made a weapon of my right hand. I backed away, terrified. Yet even in the midst of fear, it struck me that I was not as terrified as I should have been, that I was not at the point of screaming, of fleeing.

'It's me, Carolyn,' he said.

'No,' I said, backing further away.

'I don't know why you should believe me.' He looked at his flickering hand. 'I didn't understand it myself until now.'

'Who are you?' I asked, gauging the distance to the door.

'You know,' he said. 'The Spider ... he's all through the station. In the computer, the labs, even in the tanks from which my cells were grown. He's brought us together again.'

He tried to touch me, and I darted to the side.

'I won't hurt you,' he said.

'I've seen what a touch can do.'

'Not my touch, Carolyn.'

I doubted I could make it to the door, but readied myself for a try.

'Listen to me, Carolyn,' he said. 'Everything we wanted in the beginning, all the dreams and fictions of love, they can be ours.'

'I never wanted that,' I said. 'You did! I only wanted normalcy, not some ...'

'All lovers want the same thing,' he said. 'Disillusionment leads them to pretend they want less.' He stretched out his hands to me. 'Everything awaits us, everything is prepared. How this came to be, I can't explain. Except that it makes a funny kind of sense for the ultimate result of science to be an incomprehensible magic.'

I was still afraid, but my fear was dwindling, lulled by the rhythms of his words, and though I perceived him to be death, I also saw clearly that he was Reynolds, Reynolds made whole.

'This was inevitable,' he said. 'We both knew something miraculous could happen ... that's why we stayed together, despite everything. Don't be afraid. I could never hurt you more than I have.'

'What's inevitable?' I asked. He was too close for me to think of running, and I thought I could delay him, put him off with questions.

Can't you feel it?' He was so close, now, I could feel his heat. 'I can't tell you what it is, Carolyn, only that it is, that it's life ... a new life.'

'The Spider,' I said. 'I don't understand, I ...'

'No more questions,' he said, and slipped the robes from my shoulders.

His touch was warmer than natural, making my eyelids droop, but causing no pain. He pulled me down to the floor, and in a moment he was inside me, we were heart to heart, moving together, enveloped in that pale flickering glow, and amidst the pleasure I felt, there was pain, but so little it did not matter ...

... and I, too, was afraid, afraid I was not who I thought, that flames and nothingness would obliterate us, but in having her once again, in the consummation of my long wish, my doubts lessened ...

... and I could no longer tell whether my eyes were open or closed, because sometimes when I thought them closed, I could see him, his face slack with pleasure, head flung back ...

... and when I thought they were open I would have a glimpse of another place wherein she stood beside me, glimpses at first too brief for me to fix them in mind ...

... and everything was whirling, changing, my body, my spirit, all in flux, and death — if this was death — was a long decline, a sweep of golden radiance, and behind me I could see the past reduced to a plain and hills carpeted with golden grasses ...

... and around me golden towers, shimmering, growing more stable and settling into form moment by moment, and people shrouded in golden mist who were also becoming more real, acquiring scars and rags and fine robes, carrying baskets and sacks ...

... and this was no heaven, no peaceful heaven, for as we moved beneath those crumbling towers of yellow stone, I saw

soldiers with oddly shaped spears on the battlements, and the
crowds around us were made up of hardbitten men and women
wearing belted daggers, and old crones bent double under the
weight of sacks of produce, and younger women with the look
of ill-usage about them, who leaned from the doors and
windows of smoke-darkened houses and cried out their price . . .

. . . and the sun overhead seemed to shift, putting forth
prominences that rippled and undulated as in a dance, and
shone down a ray of light to illuminate the tallest tower, the one
we had sought for all these years, the one who mystery we must
unravel . . .

. . . and the opaque image of an old man in a yellow robe was
floating above the crowd, his pupils appearing to shift, to put
forth fiery threads as did the sun, and he was haranguing us,
daring us all to penetrate his tower, to negotiate his webs and
steal the secrets of time . . .

. . . and after wandering all day, we found a room in an inn
not half a mile from the wizard's tower, a mean place with
grimy walls and scuttlings in the corners and a straw mattress
that crackled when we lay on it. But it was so much more than
we'd had in a long, long time, we were delighted, and when
night had fallen, with moonlight streaming in and the wizard's
tower visible through a window against the deep blue of the
sky, the room seemed palatial. We made love until well past
midnight, love as we had never practiced it: trusting, unfettered
by inhibition. And afterward, still joined, listening to the cries
and music of the city, I suddenly remembered my life in that
other world, the Spider, Helios Station, everything, and from
the tense look on Carolyn's face, from her next words, I knew
that she, too, had remembered.

'Back at Helios,' she said, 'we were making love, lying
exactly like this, and . . .' She broke off, a worry line creasing
her brow. 'What if this is all a dream, a moment between dying
and death?'

'Why should you think that?'

'The Spider . . . I don't know. I just felt it was true.'

'It's more reasonable to assume that everything is a form of transition between the apartment and this room. Besides, why would the Spider want you to die?'

'Why has he done any of this? We don't even know what he is ... a demon, a god.'

'Or something of mine,' I said.

'Yes, that ... or death.'

I stroked her hair, and her eyelids fluttered down.

'I'm afraid to go to sleep,' she said.

'Don't worry,' I said. 'I think there's more to this than death.'

'How do you know?'

'Because of how we are.'

'That's why I think it *is* death,' she said. 'Because it's too good to last.'

'Even if it is death,' I told her, 'in this place death might last longer than our old lives.'

Of course I was certain of very little myself, but I managed to soothe her, and soon she was asleep. Out the window, the wizard's tower — if, indeed, that what it was — glowed and rippled, alive with power, menacing in its brilliance. But I was past being afraid. Even in the face of something as unfathomable as a creature who has appropriated the dream of a man who may have dreamed it into existence and fashioned thereof either a life or a death, even in a world of unanswerable questions, when love is certain — love, the only question that is its own answer — everything becomes quite simple, and, in the end, a matter of acceptance.

'We live in an old chaos of the sun.'
Wallace Stevens

RICHARD KADREY

Although a American, Richard Kadrey's first sf story was published in the British magazine *Interzone*. This was 'The Fire Catcher' in 1985, a story which was later reprinted in *Omni*. His artwork has also been published in *Interzone*, in German and American magazines, and used for the cover of a Canadian cassette.

1988 sees the publication of Kadrey's first novel, *Metrophage*, and also his non-fiction book about communications and communications technology will be published. This is *Signal: A Whole Earth Catalog of Tools and Information Frontiers*.

The following story topped the *Interzone* readers' poll, Autumn '86–Summer '87, although it was originally rejected by various American editors. This might have had something to do with the fact that New York is the centre of American publishing. As Kadrey says: 'New Yorkers seem to have trouble seeing the humor in ...'

... but read the story to find out what they don't think is so funny.

(Kadrey was born in New York. He now lives in San Francisco.)

GOODBYE HOUSTON STREET, GOODBYE

by
RICHARD KADREY

It was guaranteed to be the art event of the year, Dix was saying. The phone call had awakened Parnell from his nap; he listened quietly, twirling a short length of copper tubing he had earlier that day liberated from an abandoned refrigerator. A new Surrealist show, Dix continued, at his gallery in Soho. The Levy Gallery shows in the Thirties had dwelt with the artists' perceptions of the world at the beginning of the twentieth century. How, Dix asked, would the heirs to the movement see life at the close of the century that gave them birth?' 'I'm calling the show 'Fun-de-Siecle.' clever, n'est-ce pas?' Then, as if answering his own question, Dix added, 'You interested?'

Parnell blinked twice, set down the copper tubing next to a collection of transistors, some animal bones and a lawn-mower engine. 'Yeah, it sounds great,' he said.

'Good, then you'll contribute something?' Dix asked.

Parnell tossed a set of knuckle dusters onto the tubing. 'As a matter of fact, I've been working on a rather large piece for several weeks now. Ever since Jessie left ...'

'Right on!' said Dix. 'Jessie said you guys living together was stifling your artistic growth and her need for individuation. Now I'm not saying that the move was easy for her and I'm not saying that it hasn't done her a world of good, but I am saying that she's settled in nicely and says 'Hi'.'

'Oh,' Parnell replied evenly. 'Tell her 'Hi' for me, too.' Over the phone, Parnell could hear Dix sigh.

'I've gotta tell you, Parnell ... for a while there I was sure that this moving in business between Jessie and me was going to cause a rift, communication-wise, between yourself and moi. And, well ... I just want to say I'm damned glad we were both mature enough not to let that happen. Damned glad.'

Parnell smiled. 'People should be happy,' he said, adding a stuffed owl to the wobbling pile of detritus.

'How right you are, mon ami. And right now Jessie's as

happy as I've ever seen her and I guess that's what we all want. Right? By the way, the show opens on February eighteenth. André Breton's birthday. Will you be ready by then?'

'The eighteenth? I suppose . . .'

'Terrif,' said Dix. 'I can't tell you how good I feel about our little talk, Parnell. I feel really close to you right now, bro. Can I call you 'bro?' I'll see you on the eighteenth. Ciao.'

'Goodbye,' said Parnell, setting down the phone. He removed the stuffed owl from the pile, tossing it into a far corner of the room, and replaced it with a box of false teeth and star charts. From another box, he removed a 1908 American Eagle Luger, pressed the barrel to his temple and pulled the trigger. The rusty mechanism leaked iron oxide down his shirt sleeve and the trigger froze. Parnell sighed and tossed the gun back in the box.

Parnell hadn't thought of Jessie much since she'd left. When he did think of her, it just left him feeling numb and thick-headed. He would begin to form thoughts, opinions about her sudden desertion, but inevitably they would log jam in some neural back-water where he couldn't get at them. Constipation of the brain, he thought. Jessie, you were the Ex-lax of my soul. The mineral oil of my heart. The plumber's helper of my — of fuck it . . .

Rather than languish in slow-witted self-pity he had, instead, become obsessed with his work, with the result that his largest, most elaborate and, unquestionably, most successful piece was nearly complete. Keeping this in mind, he resolved not to think of Jessie now. There was simply no time if he was going to finish the piece by the eighteenth.

With his part-time job on the garbage truck, (a revealing choice, one critic had quipped) Parnell had managed to gather most of what he needed to complete the new, still untilted, piece. Truck springs, flattened basketballs, a collection of crackled sunglasses, varnished frogs, stuffed and mounted as if playing tiny musical instruments; prosthetic legs. Still, the piece lacked its single most important element. Parnell plucked a two day old New York Post from under his bed. PAGAN MOM TORCHES KIDS, SELF read the headline. Scanning the Classifieds, Parnell wondered what you would look under to find plutonium.

In the end, he had to settle for uranium. And he didn't even get that until the sixteenth. By then, Parnell was getting very nervous.

He had almost missed the 'Unskilled Labourers' ad in the Help Wanted section. He found it in a little box at the bottom of the page, tucked between much larger ads for a weapons microbiologist and a bouncer for a very exclusive leather bar on Canal Street. The Yonkers Nuclear Power Facility was looking for people to work in the 'hottest' parts of the plant. In thirty minutes, Parnell and a dozen or so illegal Mexican apple pickers would be subjected to the same amount of radiation that regular employees encountered in a month. However, it was a way in. And, Parnell saw, security was pretty lax in the hot parts of the plant. The beefy rent-a-cops seemed to spend most of their time taking pot shots at the pigeons they lured into the parking lot with piles of bread crumbs.

Because of this, no one saw Parnell happily pull the forklift bearing the new uranium rod behind a wall of leaking waste drums. Nobody was aware of him unscrewing the top of the dull lead cannister, prying casing away from the rod housing and removing what looked to him like an enormous sky-blue popsicle.

From the pocket of his radiation suit, Parnell removed his thermos bottle and Swiss Army Knife, which he used vigorously to chip chunks off the rod's faintly glowing surface. When he had what he thought to be enough, Parnell replaced the lid on the thermos, put the knife back in his pocket, resealed the rod and carefully stowed the uranium in its proper place.

Parnell ate his lunch alone that day, carefully, slipping the thermos from his protective suit and into his Spider-Man lunchbox. He took the company bus home at five with the rest of his shift. The guards grinned and shouted 'Immigracion!' at them.

In the morning, Parnell found more than the usual amount of hair on his pillow. His gums bled and his joints ached as he brushed his teeth. He was glad the show was opening the next day.

Three sweating men were lowering a stuffed line-green and pink polar bear from the back of a weathered panel truck.

Nearby, a heavy-set woman wearing a necklace made from old IUDs stood with arms crossed, the fingers of her right hand lightly covering her lips. 'Please be careful,' she repeated, her fingers muffling her words.

Parnell squeezed past the woman into the gallery. Inside, he found the single high-ceilinged room sliced into an elaborate maze by ten-foot tall sheets of white plaster board. The walls of the maze were decorated with elaborate rhymes and puns which were supposed to eventually lead the reader to the centre of the room. Parnell had never been one for word games, lumping things like crossword puzzles into the same category as the My Lai massacre and brain cancer. He was lost almost immediately. For a moment, he panicked, a sudden attack of claustrophobia pushing the air from his lungs. He thought of Minotaurs and virgin sacrifices, of rats trained to carry out clever tricks and then sold off to some government lab for dissection. He thought of the Donner Party.

Eventually, he stumbled into an open area at the centre of the maze. Parnell found a thin man in mirrored Saigon shades testily supervising the placement of a black leather rocking chair studded with short silver spikes. Two women Parnell had met at some opening or other were planting razor blade roses in a copse of broken glass. A machine hummed in the corner, continually dismantling and re-assembling itself in ever changing patterns: now a seamless tetrahedron, now an apple, now a strand of double helix, now a Louis the XIV boudoir and on and on. Parnell wandered among the exhibits looking for his place.

'You do not look great,' said Dix emerging from the corner of a Cadillac-sized condom festooned with blinking Christmas lights. He held out a small vial of white powder. 'Have a tootski. Do you a world of good.'

Parnell shook his head. 'No thanks. I've just been up late, putting the finishing touches on the piece.' He was just about to ask where he should set up when he turned his head and she caught his eye. 'Hello Jessie,' he said.

From Dix's side, Jessie gave him a little smile. 'Hiya Parnell; how you been?'

He shrugged. 'Okay, I guess.' Half of his face readily complied with his instructions to smile, while the other half stubbornly refused to get involved. Rather than stand there looking completely deranged, Parnell said, 'What happened to your eyes?'

Jessie brightened. 'You like them? Tinted contact lenses. It was Dix's idea.'

'Brown is not a power colour,' explained Dix. He took Jessie's hand in his. 'I think we,' said Dix (meaning Jessie), 'are going to be a very hot property after this show. Heavy artistic merit and beaucoup bucks. Ones followed by zeroes; many, many zeroes.'

Parnell smiled at them. He was beginning to feel a little warm. 'I'm very happy for you. Where do I set up?'

Dix pointed to a spot near what looked like a washing machine giving birth to a very large and unpleasant insect. Parnell nodded; Dix gave him a 'thumbs-up' salute and went off to confer with the caterers who had just arrived, laden with cases of wine and crab legs on ice. Jessie gave Parnell a little wave and mouthed something he couldn't make out, before trailing off behind Dix.

Parnell had borrowed a four-wheeled pallet mover from Mister Saigon Shades and went out the back to a rented U HAUL pickup. He pulled the canvas cover away from the large mound in the flatbed and gently lowered his contraption onto the mover; the piece wheezed like a tubercular buffalo as it settled. The prosthetic legs kicked the air with little metallic clicks as he wheeled the construction into place inside. Parnell returned the pallet move to Mister Saigon Shades and was just adjusting the piece to get the right light when he heard Jessie's voice behind him. 'I like it. What's it called?'

Parnell looked up. 'It doesn't have a title yet. I thought I'd name it tonight.'

Jessie nodded, keeping her hands clasped in front of her pelvis. 'I got some new stuff up front. Did you see the Dalai Lama kit? That's one of mine. One hundred and twenty found objects. Choose any forty and declare yourself the Dalai Lama. Instant enlightenment.'

'You misspelled 'desperate',' said Parnell quietly.

'What?'

'You misspelled 'desperate' in that little note you left me.'

'Oh,' said Jessie. She looked away. 'Sorry. Grammar was never my strong point.'

'This isn't a question of grammar; it's spelling. It's a completely different subject. I would think you could at least take the time to get my kiss-off letter correct.'

'A little louder, Parnell, I don't think they heard you in Jersey,' Jessie said. She waved to Dix, who was staring at them amidst a pile of eviscerated shell fish. 'I thought we could be civilized about this. I thought we could be friends.'

'I am being civilized. I haven't stuck any sharp, crippling objects into anybody, have I?' said Parnell in a whisper you could hear for a block. 'Jessie, why are you with this jerk?'

Jessie shook her head sadly. 'I like Dix. He's a little over-anxious sometimes, but he's very nice. And if you insist on talking this way, I don't see how we can continue to be friends.'

Parnell opened his eyes innocently. 'Talking what way? I'm merely attempting to engage in some honest and open banter concerning my recent fucking over,' he said.

Jessie took a swing at him, but Parnell danced back and she clipped a glass eye dangling from his construction by a coaxial cable. 'Eat shit,' he heard Jessie say as she turned and stomped back to Dix's office, slamming the door hard enough to dislodge a set of papier mache genitals from the ceiling. 'I'm sorry,' Parnell called. Dix was coming toward him, frowning.

'Trouble, kemo sabe? Everything okay here?'

'No trouble at all,' said Parnell, draping his arm around Dix's shoulders. 'You like the piece? I had you in mind while I was working on it.'

Dix beamed as if Parnell had just offered him one of his kidneys. 'Well, I'm flattered all to hell, old man,' he said.

Parnell took Dix's hand and shook it. He said: 'Well, I've gotta run. Gotta pick up a monkey suit I rented for the opening. By the way, your ensemble is really smashing, Dix, old weed. It's the cuff links. Always dress to your cuff links, I say. You can't go wrong. Well, au revoir.'

Before Dix could say a word, Parnell was out the back way, in the alley and barfing up what felt like everything he had ever eaten. A policeman on foot patrol came wandering up the alley as Parnell was rising shakily to his feet. 'Just trying to charm a lady, officer. Think I picked up a touch of radiation poisoning instead. Sorry about the mess.' The policeman advised Parnell to go home and sleep it off. Parnell thanked him and headed back to his apartment.

When he arrived home, however, he found the street blocked off and full of men in what looked like long white pyjamas wearing feedbags over their faces — protective gear similar to the suit Parnell had worn at the power plant. He thought, for a minute, that some perverse new gang might have moved into the neighbourhood, until he saw the truck from the nuclear Regulatory Agency. The white suited men were sweeping the whole block with geiger counters.

Parnell threw the rented truck into reverse and gunned it down an alley that opened onto First Avenue. He picked up his tuxedo from DUDS'R US and purchased several hand sized sections of welder's glass from a hardware store before heading out for Long Island. It was obvious by the presence of the men in the white suits, that they had discovered his treachery in Yonkers. It wouldn't be long, he knew, before most of the police in the state would be after him. Parnell was glad he had thought to stash the radio transmitter in the truck.

On the northern tip of Long Island was a decayed, but expensive beachfront development called 'Saint Thomas,' consisting of a single long and ill-constructed boardwalk, gourmet 'Boucherie,' pharmacy, full-service Shell station, video arcade and sixty refurbished waterfront homes newly painted to disguised more wood-rot per square inch than the entire Amazon Basin.

The original owner of the development had lured residents to the remote stretch of sand with promises of a new suspension bridge that would link their community directly to the heart of Manhattan. When the City Council rejected the bridge plan, the developer started building a blimp port. This too, he abandoned. Parnell's parents had taken him to Saint Thomas often as a child to visit his father's alcoholic brother. The residents of the island, he recalled, had never quite forgiven the developer or Manhattan for their isolation.

Parnell purchased two gallons of gas at the Shell station and changed into his tuxedo in the rest room. He then abandoned the truck behind the video arcade and hurried to the beach, carrying a small nylon suitcase.

Evening was coming on fast, softening the colours and contours of the beach until it resembled one of Yves Tanguy's biomorphic landscapes. Parnell set the suitcase in the sand, unzipped it and pulled the cheap plastic alligator that activated the radio transmitter. A police car rolled by slowly beyond the boardwalk. Parnell wondered idly if it was one of the patrol cars that had been tailing since he left Brooklyn. Parnell did not think the police were art patrons and that bothered him. Public servants, he mused, should have wide-ranging interests, especially where the arts were concerned. He made a mental note to write somebody about that.

Parnell pulled the 'arming' switch (actually, a pop-top from a decade-old Budweiser can) with fingers that were dark and swollen. He thought of Jacques Rigaut, a young surrealist who had declared he would commit suicide in ten years and went about snipping the buttons from policemen's coats. Parnell thought of André Breton, exhorting the authorities to throw open the doors of the asylums, of Dali claiming, 'The only difference between me and a madman is that I'm not mad.'

Parnell watch read 8:30; the reception would be in full swing by now. He pushed a button on the transmitter and a tiny toy train rattled forward on about four inches of plastic track. With its nose, it tripped the final switch. Parnell held his breath.

Nothing happened.

He kicked the transmitter. Something rattled inside. Manhattan continued to glitter maddeningly.

So much for the cover of *Art in America*, he thought.

'Parnell?'

He turned at the sound of the voice. 'Jessie?' She came running awkwardly through the sand, waving to him. As she reached his side, he felt her arms around him; she kissed his neck.

'I'm sorry about earlier,' Parnell said.

She nodded. 'Me too. You looked so sad back at the gallery, I just had to talk to you. I've been following you for miles.'

'Really?'

'Yeah,' Jessie said. Her smile turned to an expression of

incomprehension. 'Parnell, what the hell are you doing out here?'

'Naming the piece.'

'Out here?'

Parnell raised his hand toward Manhattan. 'Remember, Breton once said that being based on the irrational and spontaneous, the ultimate surrealistic act might be to shoot a gun at random into a crowd?'

'My god, Parnell; you didn't shoot anybody, did you?'

'No, of course not. What do you think, I'm crazy?'

Behind them, a dozen NYPD cars, sirens and lights ablaze, screamed to a halt. Dark uniformed figures rushed towards them, weapons drawn.

'Parnell, what the hell is this?' asked Jessie.

Parnell sighed. 'The critics have arrived,' he said. Again, he kicked the transmitter and realized that he had forgotten to turn the 'safety' switch off. He sideswiped it with the edge of one shoe.

The police surrounded the artists while, a few miles to the north, twin blasting caps detonated, forcing bits of fissionable material together fast enough to cause a chain reaction. Manhattan silently disappeared like a two-ton flashbulb going off.

From the shore of Long Island, it looked as if a second sun had suddenly appeared in the east. Some of the policemen dropped their guns, others cursed and shielded their eyes from the ever-widening mushroom cloud. Parnell happily watched the whole thing through a sheet of welder's glass; he handed an extra sheet to Jessie.

'It's beautiful,' she said.

'Thanks, I . . .'

The sound of the blast reached them, drowning out his words. Perhaps a second after that, a wind like the cow catcher on a Bullet Train slammed into them, knocking artists, police, shore birds and rubbernecking locals ass-over-teakettle across the clean golden sands.

Parnell just lay there, half buried in sand, Jessie was the first up; the shell-shocked police followed slowly, one by one. Down the length of the boardwalk, the well-dressed residents of Saint

Thomas were gathering to point and stare. Many, Parnell noticed, were pointing at him. In the lowering light, he could not see their faces, so he was not sure if they were preparing to string him up.

As he pulled himself from the sand, Jessie began to applaud. Someone in the back of the crowd picked it up, as did one dazed policeman. Then another. Soon the entire beach was reverberating with the sound of tumultuous applause. It rang in Parnell's ears, the wave of sound pushing him forward, drowning out all other sounds. He smiled at Jessie.

As the police led him to a squad car, he feinted and danced through the crowd like a prize fighter after winning the championship. Men shook his hand; women darted forward to kiss him.

Someone yelled 'Speech!' Parnell turned and raised his hands above his head. A hush fell over the crowd. 'I call it,' Parnell announced, pointing to the smouldering remains to the north. "'Goodbye Houston Street'."

The crowd went wild.

Not surprisingly, Parnell's trial was held out of state, in Youngstown, Ohio. By that time, all of his hair and teeth had fallen out. With the help of Jessie's testimony and his pathetic appearance, Parnell did not receive the death penalty. However, he was sentenced to 900,000 consecutive life sentences, a number corresponding roughly to the population of Manhattan at the time of the blast.

A month after he entered a special lead-lined cell at Sing Sing in upstate New York, a package arrived for Parnell. His fingers now were so badly swollen that he had a hard time getting the package open. Inside, there was a short note from Jessie. She was leaving to open her first show at a very important gallery in London. She enclosed a copy of *Art in America* with her picture on the cover. She was a very hot property.

At the bottom of the package, Parnell found a lacquered plaque from the New York State Art Commission. It read: "Awarded to GOODBYE HOUSTON STREET — Fun-de-Siecle Show 1987 — Second Place.'

He never did find out who took first place.

─── JONATHAN CARROLL ───

Originally from New York, Jonathan Carroll now lives in Vienna and has not returned to America for several years. He is the author of four novels: *The Land of Laughs* (1980), *Voice of Our Shadow* (1983), *Bones of the Moon* (1987) and *Sleeping in Flame* (1988). The last two are the first parts of a projected quintet; the series is as yet unnamed.

Although he admits to having written screenplays, Carroll dislikes writing his own biography. But he must also have written a few short stories, because here's one . . .

FRIEND'S BEST MAN

by
JONATHAN CARROLL

1

It was in all the papers. Two even carried the same headline: 'FRIEND'S BEST MAN!' But I didn't see any of that until long afterward; until I was home from the hospital awhile and the shock had begun to wear off.

After it happened, scores of eye-witnesses suddenly appeared. But I don't remember seeing anyone around that day: just Friend and me and a very long freight train.

Friend is a seven-year-old Jack Russell Terrier. He looks like a mutt: stubby legs, indiscriminate brown and white coloring; a very plain dog's face topped with intelligent, sweet eyes. But truth be told, Jack Russells are rare and I ended up spending a wad for him. Although I've never had much money to play with until recently, one of my quirks has always been to buy the best whenever I could afford it.

When it came time to buy a dog, I went out searching for a real *dog*. Not one of those froufrou breeds that constantly need to be clipped and combed. Nor did I want one of those chic things that came from Estonia or somewhere strange that looked more like an alligator than a dog. I went to animal shelters and kennels and finally found Friend through an ad in a dog magazine. The only thing I didn't like about him on first sight was his name: Friend. It was too full of kitsch and didn't belong to a dog that looked like it would be very comfortable smoking a corncob pipe. Even as a puppy he was built low to the ground and looked fuzzily solid. He was a 'Bill,' a 'Ned.' 'Jack' would have suited him, too, if he hadn't already had that as a breed name. But the woman who sold him to me said he had that name for a very specific reason: whenever he barked (which was rarely), it came out sounding like the word *friend*. I was skeptical, but she was right; while his brothers and sisters yapped and yelped, this guy stood solidly there and said,

'Friend! Friend! Friend!' time after time while his tail wagged back and forth. It was a strange thing to hear, but I liked him even more for it. As a result, he stayed 'Friend.'

I have always marveled at how well dogs and people get along. They move so comfortably into your life, choose a chair to sleep on, figure out your moods, and have no trouble bending themselves to a curve that should be completely strange and inappropriate. From the first, they fall asleep so easily in a foreign land.

Before I go on, I must say that Friend never struck me as being anything more special or rare than a very good dog. He was excited when I came home from work, and liked to rest his head on my lap when I watched television. But he was not Jim the Wonder Dog: he didn't know how to count, or drive a car, or other marvels you sometimes read about in an article about dogs that appear to have 'special' powers. Friend liked scrambled eggs, too, and would go jogging with me so long as it wasn't raining out and I wasn't going too far. By all accounts, I had gotten exactly what I wanted: a dog-dog who staked a small claim on part of my heart with his loyalty and joy. One who never asked much in return except a couple of pats often and a corner of the bed to sleep on when the weather turned cold.

The day it happened was sunny and clear. I put on my gym suit and shoes and did a few stretching exercises. Friend watched all of this from his chair, but when I got ready to go out, he hopped down and accompanied me to the door. I opened it, and he took a look at the weather.

'Do you want to go along?' If he didn't, his usual procedure was to collapse on the floor and not move again until I returned. But this time he wagged his tail and went outside with me. I was glad for his company.

We started down the hill toward the park. Friend liked to run alongside, about two feet away. When he was a puppy. I'd tripped over him a couple of times because he had the habit of running in and out of my path, fully expecting me to keep tabs on where he was at all times. But I'm one of those joggers who watches everything but his feet when I go. As a result, we'd had a few magnificent collisions and mad yelps that left him wary of my sense of navigation.

We crossed Ober Road and ran through Harold Park toward the railroad tracks. Once we got there, we'd go about a mile and a half along them until we reached the station, then circle slowly back toward home.

Friend knew the route so well that he could afford to make stops along the way, both to relieve himself and to investigate any new interesting sights or smells that had appeared since our last trip there.

Once in a while a train came along, but you could hear it from far off and there was lots of time to move off to the side and give it wide berth. I liked it when trains came through; liked hearing them lumber up behind you and pass while you picked up pace to see how long you could keep up with the engine. A couple of the engineers knew us and tooted their shrill whistles as they passed. I liked that, and I think Friend did, too, because he always stopped and barked a couple of times just to let them know who was boss.

That morning we were about half-way to the station when I heard one coming. As always, I looked to see where Friend was. A couple of feet away, he ran jauntily along, his tongue a pink sliver out the side of his mouth.

As the train's giant clatter approached, I watched a car cross the tracks a couple of hundred feet in front of us. How dumb of the driver to do that when he knew a train was so close! What was the hurry? By the time that thought passed, the train felt close over my left shoulder. I looked to my right to check on Friend again, but he wasn't there. I whipped my head this way and that, but he was nowhere around. In a complete panic, I spun around and saw him in the middle of the tracks sniffling at something, all of his attention concentrated there.

'Friend! Come here!'

He wagged his tail but didn't lift his head. I ran for him and called again and again.

'Friend! Goddamn it, Friend!'

The tone of my voice finally got through to him because when the train was only fifteen feet away, already putting on its brakes, he looked up.

I ran as fast as I could and felt stones fly out from beneath my sneakers.

'Friend, get out!'

He didn't know the words, but the tone told him he was in for a hell of a smack. He did the worst possible thing: tucked his head down into his small shoulders and waited for me to come get him.

The train was there. In the instant before I jumped, I knew I had one choice, but I'd already made it before I ever moved. Lunging for my Friend, I bent down and tried to grab him up and roll out of the way all at once. And I almost succeeded. I almost succeeded — except for my leg, which stuck straight behind me as I jumped and was sliced cleanly off by the huge wheels.

2

I met Jasenka in the hospital. Jasenka Ciric. No one could say ya-ZEN-ka very well, so people had been calling her 'Jazz' all her life.

She was seven years old and had spent most of her life connected to one or another ominous machine that helped her fight a long, losing battle against her undependable body. Her skin was the color of a white candle in a dark room, lips the violet of foreign money. Her many illnesses made her serious, while her youth kept her buoyant and hopeful.

Because she'd spent so much time in bed in hospital rooms surrounded by unfamiliar faces, white walls, and few pictures on the walls, she had only two hobbies: reading and watching television. When she watched TV, her face contracted and then set into complete solemnity and concentration: a member of the family reading someone's will for the first time. But when she read, no matter what the book, that face was expressionless and empty of anything.

I met her because she'd read about Friend and me in the newspapers. One of the nurses came to my room a week after it happened, and asked if I'd be willing to have a visit with Jazz Ciric (CHEER-itch). When she explained the girl and her situation to me, I envisioned an ill angel along the lines of Shirley Temple or at least Darla in "The Little Rascals." Instead,

Jasenka Ciric had a peculiar, interesting face where everything was pointy and too close together. Her thick hair curled like the stuffing in old furniture and was just about the same color.

The nurse introduced us and then went off on her rounds. Jazz sat in the chair next to my bed and sized me up. I was still in great pain, but had earlier decided to be a little less self-pitying. This visit was to be my first move in that direction.

'What's your favorite book?'

'I don't know. I guess *The Great Gatsby*. What's yours?'

She shrugged and tsk'd her tongue once, as if the answer were self-evident.

'*Ladies with Their Nightgowns on Fire.*'

'That's a book? Who wrote it?'

'Egan Moore.'

I smiled. *My* name is Egan Moore. 'What's the story?'

She looked at me very carefully and proceeded to spin out one of those endlessly rambling tales only a kid could love.

'Then the monsters jumped out of the trees and took them all back to the evil castle where Scaldor the Evil King . . .'

What I liked about it was the way she acted out the story as she went on. Scaldor had a nasty squint; which Jazz demonstrated to perfection. When someone got crept up on, her fingers curled into a witch's grip and tiptoed like little devils across the air separating us.

'. . . And they got home *just* in time for their favorite TV show.' She sat back, tired but obviously satisfied with her performance.

'Sounds like a terrific story. I wish I *had* written it.'

'It is. Can I ask you a question now?'

'Ask away.'

'Who's taking care of Friend now?'

'My next-door neighbor.'

'Have you seen him since the accident?'

'No.'

'Are you mad at him for making you lose your leg?'

I thought for a minute, deciding whether to talk to her as a child or as an adult. A quick scan of her face said she demanded adult standing; had no time to fool around.

'No, I'm not mad at him. I guess I'm mad at somebody, but

I don't know who. I don't know if it was anyone's fault. I'm sure not mad at Friend.'

She came to visit me every day after that. Usually sometime in the morning when both of us were fresh from sleep and chipper. I was all right mornings, but not most afternoons. For some reason, the enormity of what had happened to me and how it would affect the rest of my life came in the door with my lunch tray and stayed long after visiting hours were over. I thought about things like the bird that stands around on one leg all day. Or the joke about the one-legged man in an ass-kicking contest. I thought about the fact that words like *kick* would no longer be part of my body's vocabulary. I knew they made remarkable prosthetic legs — Science on the March! — but that was little comfort. I wanted back what was mine: not something that would make me, at best, 'as good as new,' as the therapist said every time we talked about it.

Jazz and I became good friends. She made my days in the hospital happier and my perspective wider. I have known only two mortally ill people in my life, my mother and Jasenka. Both of them looked at the world through the same urgent yet grateful eyes. When there is not much time left, it seems the eyes' capacity to see broadens tenfold. The things they see are more often than not details that were previously ignored but are, suddenly, an important part of what makes the scene complete. On her visits to my room, Jazz's observations about people we knew in common, or the way the light came through the window in different-sized blades ... were both mature and compelling. Dying, she had fast developed a poet's, a cynic's, an artist's eye for the world around her, small as it was.

On the first day I was allowed outside, my next-door neighbor Kathleen surprised me by bringing Friend to the hospital to say hello. Dogs weren't normally allowed on the grounds, but an exception had been made because of the circumstances.

I was glad to see the old boy, and it was a surprisingly long time before I remembered he was the reason for my being there. He kept trying to climb into my lap, and I would have liked that if his scrambling to get there hadn't hurt my leg so much. As it was, I threw his ball for him a few thousand times while I chatted with Kathleen. Half an hour later, I asked the nurse if it would be possible for Jazz to come down and meet my friends.

It was arranged and, bundled to her ears in blankets, Ms. Ciric was introduced to His Nibs, Friend Moore. They shook hands gravely (Friend's one and only trick — he loved to 'Shake!'), and he allowed her to stroke his head while the four of us sat there and enjoyed the mild afternoon sun.

I had been encouraged by the doctor to take a small walk on my crutches so, half an hour later while Jazz kept Friend by her side, I tried out my new aluminium crutches with Kathleen alongside just in case.

It was the wrong time to do it. In happier days, I had passed many pleasant hours fantasizing what it would be like to live with Kathleen. I think she liked me, too, despite the fact that we were relatively new neighbors. Before the accident we had been spending more and more time together, and that was just fine with me. I'd been trying to figure out how to move in closer to her heart. But now, when I dared look up from the treacherous ground in front of me, I saw that her face was full of all the wrong kind of concern and compassion. More than any other time before or after, I was aware of my loss.

The day was ruined, but I tried hard to hide that from Kathleen. I said I was tired and cold, and would she mind if we went back to Jazz and Friend. From a distance, the two of them were so still and serious: they looked like one of those early photographs of people living in the American West.

'What've you two guys been doing?'

Kathleen looked quickly at me to see if she'd done anything to deserve this not-so-subtle dismissal. I avoided her eyes.

Twenty minutes later I was back in bed, feeling nasty, impotent, lost. The phone next to me rang. It was Jazz.

'Egan, Friend's going to help you now. He told me that today when you were walking with Kathleen. He said I could tell you.'

'Really? What's he going to do?' I smiled, thinking she was about to launch into another of her wacky stories over the phone. I liked hearing her voice, liked her being in the room with me then.

'He's going to do a lot! He said he'd been thinking about the best thing he could do for you, but now he knows. I can't tell you because it's going to be a big surprise.'

'What does his voice sound like, Jazz?'

'Kind of like Paul McCartney.'

Every couple of days, Kathleen and Friend came by to visit. Most of the time it was just the three of us, but once in a while Jazz felt well enough to come down and join us. When that happened, we'd all sit together for a while, then I would take my stroll around the grounds with Kathleen.

Jazz didn't say anything more about Friend talking to her, but the Paul McCartney part sent Kathleen into howls of laughter when I told her the story.

Kathleen turned out to be a genuinely nice woman who did whatever she could to make life happier for both Jazz and me. Of course that niceness and consideration made me fall completely in love with her, which only complicated and made matters worse. Life had begun to show it had an extremely cynical sense of humor.

'I have to tell you something.'

'What?'

'I love you.'

Eyes widened in fear. 'No you don't.'

'Oh, but I do, Egan,' she said to me. *To me.* 'When you come home, can we live together?'

I looked across the lawn. Jazz and Friend were way over there. Jazz raised her arm slowly and waved it back and forth: her sign that everything was all right.

The night before I left the hospital for home, I went to Jazz's room for a last visit. Some innard had once again betrayed her, and she looked terribly tired and pale. I sat by her bed and held her cool hand. Although I tried to dissuade her, she insisted on telling me a long new installment about Sloothack, the Fire Pig. Like Jazz's family, Stoothack was from Yugoslavia; way, way up in the mountains where sheep walked on their two hind legs and secret agents from all countries hid out between assignments. Jazz was crazy about secret agents.

I'd heard a lot of Slooth stories, but this last one was a dilly. It involved a Nazi tank, the lakes of Plitvice, Uncle Vuk from Belgrade, and a leather window.

When she was through, she looked even paler than before. So pale that I was a little worried about her.

'Are you O.K., Jazz?'

'Yes. Will you come and see me every week, Egan, like you promised?'

'Absolutely. All three of us will come if you'd like.'

'That's O.K. — maybe just you and Friend in the beginning. Kathleen can stay at home if she's tired.'

I smiled and nodded. She was jealous of the new 'woman in my life.' She knew Kathleen and I had decided to try and live together. Maybe I had the guts to drop my self-pity and fight to make things work the right way. I was certainly scared, but just as eager and excited about the chances and possibilities.

'Can I call you when I need you, Jazz?' I said it because I knew she'd like hearing she was needed even when lying in bed, weak as a mouse.

'Yes, you can call me, but I'll have to call you, too, to tell you what Friend says.'

'Yeah, but how will you know what he says? He'll be over at my house.'

She scowled and rolled her eyes. I was being dumb again. 'How many times do I have to tell you, Egan? I get *messages*.'

'That's right. What was the last one?'

'Friend said he was going to fix you and Kathleen up.'

'Friend did that? I thought I did.'

'Yes, you did some, but he did the rest. He said you needed some help.' She said it with such conviction.

What surprised me most about what followed was how quick and easy it was to get used to an entirely different life. Kathleen wasn't an angel, but she gave me all the kindness and space I needed. It made me feel both loved and free, which is a pretty remarkable combination. In return, I tried to give her what she said she liked most about me: humor, respect, and a way of seeing life that — according to her — was both ironic and forgiving.

Actually, I was living two entirely new lives: one as a partner, the other as one of the disabled. It was an emotional, often overwhelming time, and I don't know if I'd ever want to repeat it, although much of it was as close to the sublime as I'll ever get.

Kathleen went to work in the morning, leaving Friend and me to our own devices. That usually meant a slow walk down to the corner store for a newspaper and then an hour or two outdoors in the sun on the patio. The rest of the day was spent puttering and thinking and learning to readjust to a world that had been knocked slightly off-center for me in many different ways.

I also talked frequently with Jasenka and went to visit her once a week, always with Friend along for the ride. If the weather was bad and Jazz couldn't come outside, I'd park Friend with Nurse Dornhelm at the reception desk and pick him up on my way out.

One afternoon I entered her room and saw a mammoth new machine clicking eerily and importantly away by the side of her bed. The tubes and wires that connected her to it were all either silvery or a vague pink.

But what really clubbed my heart were the new pajamas she was wearing: *Star Wars* pajamas with two-inch-high robots and creatures printed at all angles and in all colors everywhere. She had been talking about those pajamas for a long time; from before I left the hospital. I knew her parents had promised them to her for her next birthday if she was good. I could only surmise she had them now because of the new machine; because they might not be another birthday.

'Hey Jazz, you got the new jams!'

She was sitting up very straight and smiling, happy as hell, a pink tube in her nose, a silver one in her arm.

The machine percolated and hummed, its green and black dials registering levels and drawing graphs that said everything but explained nothing.

'You know who gave them to me, Egan? Friend! Friend sent them to me from the store. They came in a box in my favorite color — red. He got my pajamas and he sent them to me in a red box. Aren't they beautiful? Look at R2D2. Right here.' She pointed to a spot above her belly button.

We talked for a while about the pajamas, Friend's generosity, the new *Star Wars* figure I'd brought for her collection. She didn't bring up the subject of Kathleen, and neither did I. Although she approved of Kathleen in a brusque, sort of sisterly way, Jazz had no time for 'her' now because our time together was so much less than before. Besides, Jazz and I had a separate world of our own we shared that consisted of hospital gossip, Friend gossip, and Jasenka Ciric stories, the latest of which, 'A Pet Mountain,' I had to hear once again from start to finish.

'"And then Friend gave Jazz the pajamas and they all hopped into bed and watched television all night."'

'Friend really gave you them, Jazz? What a great guy.'

'He is! And you know what, Egan? He told me he's going to fix it up so you win that contest.'

'What contest?'

'You know — the one from the magazines? The one you told me about last time? Million Dollar FlyAway?'

'I'm going to win a million bucks? That'd be nice.'

She shook her head, eyes closed, and moved the pink tube to one side.

'No, not the million dollars. You'll win the hundred thousand dollars. Fourth Prize.'

A few minutes later (after we'd decided how I'd spend my winnings), Mr. and Mrs. Ciric came in. The scared look on both of their faces when they saw the new machine told me it was time to go.

Out in the hall, Mrs. Ciric stopped me and gently pulled me aside. She looked at my crutches and touched my hand.

'The doctors say this new machine will do wonderful things, but my husband, Zdravko, he doesn't believe them.'

Having spent so much time with Jazz, I felt comfortable with Mrs. Ciric and hugely admired her for having the strength to face this constant sadness every day of her life.

'Well, I don't know if it's that machine or just those new pajamas, but I think she looks really fine today, Mrs. Ciric. There's certainly a lot more color in her cheeks.'

Looking straight at me, she began to cry. 'I bought those for her for her birthday, you know? Now, I don't like to think about her birthday, Egan. I wanted her to have them now.' She tried to smile. Then, unembarrassedly, wiped her hand across her nose. 'Mothers are very stupid, eh? I saw Friend downstairs. I said to him, "Shake hands!" and he did right away. Jasenka, you know, loves him very much. She says he calls her up on the telephone sometimes.'

She turned and went back into the room. As I walked away, I pictured her and her husband standing over that complicated bed, watching their daughter with helpless eyes, trying to figure out what any of them had done to deserve this.

A few weeks passed. I went back to work. The new machine did help Jazz. Kathleen finished moving the rest of her stuff into my apartment.

One of the television networks calls and asked if I'd be willing to go on a show and talk about how I'd saved Friend. I thought it over and decided against it: there had been enough hoopla in the newspapers already, and something deep inside told me capitalizing on this wasn't the right thing to do. Kathleen agreed and gave me a nice hug to seal it. I consulted Friend while he lay across my lap one evening, but he didn't even lift his head.

Life wouldn't ever really return to the normal I had once known, but it *did* take its foot off the gas a little, slowing to cruising speed. Things weren't going by in such a blur anymore, and that was good.

The last glimmer of craziness came in the form of a large registered letter from *The Truth*, that god-awful newspaper that sports headlines like 'I GAVE BIRTH TO A TRUCK' and is sold in supermarket checkout lines everywhere.

An editor offered me two thousand dollars for the exclusive rights to my story. But, according to him, it wasn't 'quite vivid enough.' so *The Truth* wanted to spice things up a little by saying Friend was either from outer space or The Lost Continent of Atlantis, et cetera, et cetera . . .

I wrote a very nice letter back saying I was all for it, but my dog had sworn me to secrecy about certain crucial matters of state, so I wasn't at liberty to . . .

'Egan?'

'Jazz? Hi, pal! How are you?

'Not very good, but I had to call you up and tell you what Friend just told me.'

Unconsciously, I looked around for the dog. He was on the other side of the room, looking straight at me. It made me feel a little funny.

'He's there with you, isn't he?'

'Yeah, Jazz, he's right here.'

'I know. He said to tell you there's a man outside who's watching your house. Be very careful because he's a secret agent!'

'Now, Jazz —'' I took a deep breath and stopped short of giving her a lecture over the phone about lying. It was fine to tell Sloothack stories. It was all right to say Friend talked to her sometimes. 'Watch out for the creep at your door' stuff wasn't all right.

'Uh-oh, someone's coming, Egan. I have to go. Be careful!'

I hung up after she did. Standing there looking at the receiver, I wondered what I should do. Against my better judgment, I hobbled to the window and looked out. Naturally no one was there.

Then the doorbell rang. It scared me so much, I dropped one of my crutches.

'One second!' Bending to pick it up, I felt my heart drumming in my chest. There are moments in life when, for the smallest reason, you're filled with such dread or shock that there's little room left inside for anything else. What's most annoying is the smallness of the reason: the phone ringing you out of the trance of a good book, a person coming up behind and tapping you lightly on the left shoulder ...

My hand was so fluttery, I couldn't even pick up the damned crutch for a long few seconds. The doorbell rang again.

'I'm coming! Wait!'

'Mr. Moore?' A postman stood there with a clipboard in his hand.

'Yes?'

'Registered letter. Sign here.' He looked at my leg as I shifted my weight to take the clipboard.

'I read about you in the papers. Where's the dog?'

I signed and handed back the clipboard. 'Somewhere around. Can I have the letter?'

'Yeah, sure, there you go. That must be some dog for you to do a thing like that.'

His tone ticked me off, and he wouldn't stop looking at my leg. Some secret agent! I didn't even look at the letter. I just wanted him gone, the door closed, and my heart to calm down.

'Did you get a reward or something?'

'For what?'

'For saving your dog! You know, from the ASPCA or something.'

'No, but I'll tell you something. He's going to take me to Mars with him the next time he goes!'

I looked right at him and smiled as insanely as I knew how. He took a step backward and beat it out of there lickety-split.

After I read the letter, I called Kathleen at work and told her I'd won ten thousand dollars in a contest.

There was silence at the other end. I could hear typewriters clacking in the background.

'Jazz told you that before.'

'Yeah, but she said I'd win a *hundred* thousand, not ten. Not ten!' Too loud, too scared. I closed my eyes and waited, hoped for Kathleen to break the silence.

'What are you going to do?'

'I don't know. Um, Friend just came into the room.'

He padded across the floor sat down under the telephone table without looking at me.

'Kathleen, how come my dog is suddenly making me nervous?'

'I —''

'And how come there's this money?'

That evening both of us went to the hospital to visit Jazz. We left Friend at home, asleep in his favorite chair.

There were more tubes this time. The same machine as before, only a great many more tubes sprouting out from different parts of it, sneaking under the covers to her body.

She looked very ill. So much so that the first thing that came to mind when I saw her was: she's going to die. Cruel and true and obvious: she was going to die.

The left side of her mouth crawled up a notch in a tiny smile when she saw us. It was the tiredest, most resigned smile I had ever seen.

Kathleen stood in the doorway while I crossed to the bed. Jazz's eyes went from me to Kathleen to me again, watching to see what we would do.

I propped the crutches against the wall and maneuvered down into a chair next to the bed.

'Hiya, kid.'

The smile again and a finger wiggle from one of the hands lying crossed on the small hill of her chest.

'You won, didn't you?' The voice was thick and coated with phlegm.

I'd planned to be funny but firm when we spoke, but my plans were no match for her broken energy. Death was in charge here; she was its deputy, so she held all the cards.

'Can I talk to you alone, Egan?'

It was said so quietly that I was sure Kathleen couldn't have heard, but I winced anyway.

'Kat, would you mind if we were alone for a bit?'

She nodded, her face a mix of pity and confusion. She left, closing the door dilently behind her.

'Kathleen sees another man sometimes, Egan. His name is Vitamin D. Sometimes she says she's going to work, but she goes over to his house instead.' She watched me while she spoke, her eyes, vacant, her voice untenanted by any kind of expression. Then she reached over and took my hand as gently as you pick up a pin that's fallen to the floor. 'Just ask her. Friend told me before. He said you should know.'

Our drive home was silent. The wind had picked up, and everything would whip back and forth for a while and then stop dead.

It was my night to make the dinner, so I went straight to the kitchen as soon as we got back to the apartment. Kathleen turned on the television in the living room. I heard her say something to Friend that sounded like a greeting.

I poured water into a pot of spaghetti and thought about the ten thousand dollars. I put butter and minced garlic into a frying pan and thought about Vitamin D, whoever *that* was.

'Oh damn! Friend, take that off! Friend! No!'

'What's the matter?'

'Nothing. Friend just jumped up on the couch with his bone. He made a spot. I'll get it.'

She came into the kitchen shaking her head. 'That beast! I keep telling him not to do that. It's the only time he ever growls at me.' She was smiling and shaking her head.

'He's used to my old couch. It didn't matter much on that one.'

She made a big fuss at the sink getting a rag, the cleaner, turning on the tap. 'Well, this is a new couch and a new day!'

'Kat, stop for a moment, will you? I want to ask you something. Do you know a guy named Vitamin D?'

'A *guy* named "Vitamin D"? No, but I know the guy who started it. Victor Dixon. he's the lead guitarist.' She turned off the tap and squeezed the rag into the sink. 'How do you know about Vitamin D? You never listen to rock.'

'Who's Victor Dixon?'

'An old boyfriend of mine, who started that group. They've just begun to make it. They've begun showing their first video on MTV now. Did you see it?'

The water came to a boil. I wanted to drop the spaghetti in, but I couldn't right then. Too . . . scared?

'What went on with . . . What went on between you two?'

She crossed her arms and sighed, her eyes were twinkling. 'Jealous, huh? That's good! Well, I knew him in college. After that he disappeared for a few years, then he turned up one day and we hung around together for a couple of months. He was more friend than boyfriend, even though a lot of people thought we had a big thing going. Why're you asking? How'd we get onto this?'

'Jazz told me —'

Friend started barking crazily in the other room. 'Friend! Friend! Friend!' It sounded like he'd gone totally nuts. Kathleen and I looked at each other and moved.

On television, a man beat a white baby seal over the head

with a wooden truncheon. The seal screamed while its head spewed dark blood onto the snow.

Friend stood next to the set and barked.

'Friend, stop!'

He kept on.

On television, a man pried open a wooden crate with a crow-bar. Inside were ten dead parrots clumped together in a colorful, orderly row. Over the barking, I made out something about the illegal importation of rare birds into the United States.

'Friend, shut up!'

'Oh, Egan, look!'

A dog was strapped to an operating table. Its stomach was cut wide open, and its mouth was twisted up over its teeth.

All we needed then — a special on educational television about cruelty to animals.

It had been an impossible, weird day. The kind when the best thing you can do is throw up your hands, go directly to bed after dinner, and hope it ends at that.

But the air was full of something wrong and deep, and we ended up having everything out over dinner.

Victor Dixon was still around. No she hadn't *touched* him since we'd been together. Yes, he called her at work sometimes. Yes, they'd gone out to lunch once or twice. *No*, nothing had happened. Didn't I believe her? How could I even think that?

I said I wanted very much to believe her, but why hadn't she told me about him before?

Because it only made things more confused . . .

Our voices got louder, and dinner, a nice dinner, got colder.

Friend stayed with us until about Round Three, then slunk out of the room, head and tail low. I felt like telling him to stay, hadn't he started this war in the first place?

'So what is *your* definition of trust, Egan? As far as you can throw me?'

'Oh, come on, Kathleen. How would you feel if you were in my place? Turn the situation around.'

'I'd feel fine, thank you. Because I'd *believe* what you told me.'

'Gee, you're quite a girl.'

That did it. She got up and left, mad as hell.

While I waited and worried, Jasenka called twice within an hour.

The first time she said only that Kathleen was at Vitamin D's house, and gave me his telephone number.

I called. A very sleepy man with a Southern accent answered. I asked for her.

'Hey, bud, do you know what *time* it is? Kat isn't here. I haven't seen her in days. Jesus, do you know what time it is? Hey, how'd you get this number in the first place? It's unlisted! Did Kat give it to you? Man, *she's* going to get it when I see her. She promised she wouldn't give it out to anyone.'

'Look, this is really important. I'd really appreciate it if you'd let me talk to her. I'm her brother, and we've got some very serious family problems.'

'Oh no, I'm really sorry. But she isn't here, honest to God. Hold it a sec — I do have this other number where you might be able to reach her.'

He gave me my number.

The second call from Jasenka lasted longer. Her voice was a child's whisper in a parent's ear. The words slowed and died at the end of every sentence.

'Egan? It's me again. Listen, you have to listen to me. The animals are rising. It's happening much sooner than I thought. They're going to kill everyone. They've had enough. Only their friends will be saved. Every animal in the world will do it. They'll kill everyone.

'Get a map as soon as you hang up. There's an island in Greece called Formori. F-O-R-M-O-R-I. You must go there immediately tomorrow. Everything will be starting in three days.'

'Jazz —'

'No, be quiet! Formori is the place where they'll let some people live. People who are the animals' friends. Friend says you can go there and live, they'll let you. But not Kathleen. She wouldn't let him have his bone. Please, please go, Egan. Good-bye. I love you!'

It was the last time I ever talked to her. By the time I reached the hospital twenty minutes later, a sad-faced nurse told me she had just died.

Now it's almost three-thirty in the morning. I've looked at my world almanac and there it was F-O-R-M-O-R-I.

I let Friend out three hours ago, and he hasn't returned. Neither has Kathleen.

The moon is still extraordinarily bright. While standing in the open doorway a few minutes ago, I saw what must have been thousands and thousands of birds flying in strict, unchanging patters over its calm, lit face.

I must decide soon.

LISA TUTTLE

Born in Texas, Lisa Tuttle moved to England in 1980. She won the 1974 John W. Campbell Award for best new sf author, and in 1982 she became the first person ever to refuse a Nebula Award. After her short story 'The Bone Flute' was nominated, she attempted to remove her name from the ballot as a protest against the canvassing for votes by another nominee. Instead, the members of the Science Fiction Writers of America voted her the award — which she declined.

'The Bone Flute' is one of the stories to be found in her collection *A Spaceship Built of Stone*. Tuttle's only sf novel to date is a collaboration with George R.R. Martin, *Windhaven*. She has also written the subtle horror novels *Familiar Spirit* and *Gabriel*, and a number of her best horror stories have been collected in *Nest of Nightmares*.

She is also the author of the *Encyclopedia of Feminism*, and her latest book is a collection of interviews with notable women, entitled *Heroines*. At present, she is writing a new science fiction novel, editing a collection of horror stories by women authors and making mischief.

THE WOUND

by
LISA TUTTLE

Once the seasons had been more distinct, but not in living memory. Now, mild winter merged gently into mild summer, and Olin knew it was spring only by the calendar and by his own restlessness.

That morning, Olin's bus took a different route, road repairs forcing a detour through the old city. As he stared out the window at the huge, derelict buildings crumbling into ruin and colonised by weeds, he caught sight of figures through gaps in the walls. No one lived in the old city, but there were always people here. Olin had been one of them once, when he was young, coming here with his lover. He remembered that time as the best of his life.

Recalling the past made him feel sad and prematurely old. His lover had become his wife, and after ten years of marriage they had separated. He had lived alone for the past two years.

Olin reached into his breast pocket for diary and pen, turned to the blank page of that day, and wrote 'phone Dove' in his small, precise hand. About once a month he phoned her, and they would arrange to meet for a meal. Always he went to her in hope, with fond memories and some vague thoughts of reconciliation which would fade over the course of the evening.

As he left the bus two other teachers, senior to Olin, also got off. They did not speak as they crossed the street together and passed through the heavy iron gates into the school grounds. Olin caught sight of another colleague, a little ahead of them: Seth Tarrant, the new music master. Tarrant was young, handsome, and admired by the students. His cream-coloured coat flared like a cape from his shoulders, and he seemed to be signing as he strode across the bright green lawn. He carried an expensive leather case in one hand, and a bunch of blue and yellow flowers in the other. Olin felt a brief flare of envy, and he touched his breast pocket. He would 'phone Dove, he thought. She would be glad to hear from him.

During his lunch-break, Olin went into the telephone alcove
by the cafeteria, and was startled to see Seth Tarrant there, his
long body slumped in an attitude of defeat, his head pressed
against one of the telephones. Before Olin, embarrassed, could
retreat, the other man looked around.

He straightened up, brushing a strand of fair hair out of his
eyes. 'Mr Mercato,' he said.

'Olin,' said Olin, embarrassed still more by the formality.
'Please.'

'Olin. I'm Seth.'

'Yes, I know. Ah, are you all right?'

'I'm fine. Do you like opera?'

'Opera? Yes. Yes, I do, actually. Not that I know anything
about it — maths is my subject, really — but I do like to listen.
On the radio, and I have a few recordings . . .'

'You don't think it's tedious, pretentious and antiquated?'

Olin wondered who the music master was quoting. He shook
his head.

'You might even think it worth your while to attend a live
performance?'

'If it weren't so expensive —'

With a conjuror's flourish, Seth produced two cards from his
pocket. 'I happen to have two tickets to tonight's performance
of *The Insufficient Answer*, and one is going begging. Would you
care to be my guest?'

'I'd love to. But, are you sure?'

'Do I seem uncertain to you?'

Olin shook his head.

'That's settled, then. We'll meet on the steps of the opera
house at seven o'clock, which will give us time for a drink in the
bar before it begins.'

'Thank you. It's very kind —'

'Not at all. You are the kind one, agreeing at such short
notice. Please don't be late. I hate to be kept waiting.'

The opera house was on the river, in an area of the city far
older than that part known as the old city. Olin had been there
once before, in the early days of his marriage, to attend a
performance of *Butterfly*. Dove had been pregnant then, and

she had fallen asleep during the second act. It was probably the quarrel they'd had afterwards, and not the price of tickets, which was the real reason Olin had never been to the opera since.

The steps were crowded with people meeting friends, but Seth's tall, elegant figure was immediately noticeable. When he reached his side, Olin began to apologise for his lateness, although it was barely five past the hour. He felt awkward, worried about the evening, certain that Seth had regretted his spur-of-the-moment invitation by now. Seth brushed aside both apologies and thanks with a flick of one long-fingered hand.

'Let's get a drink,' he said.

He seemed distracted and brooding in the bar, but Olin contrived a conversation by asking him questions about opera: after all, music was the man's subject. Olin felt like a student taken on a cultural outing by a master; an odd reversal, since he was at least ten years Seth's senior. It was a relief when the bell rang and they could find their seats and stop talking.

The Insufficient Answer was a love tragedy, a popular story which Olin already knew in outline. He had seen some of the most famous scenes enacted on television, but never with the technical brilliance displayed in this production. By ingenious use of lights and projections, the physical miracle of love appeared to be actually taking place on stage during the opening love-duet. After that breath-taking scene, the familiar tragedy was set in motion as the lovers, Gaijan and Sunshine, discovered they were not cross-fertile. Because there could be no children, marriage was out of the question. Social as well as biological forces drove Gaijan to take other lovers while Sunshine watched, and wept, and waited. For Gaijan still swore that he loved her the best of all, and he returned to her after every coupling. He told her he considered her his true wife and would never marry. His other lovers, led by the young and beautiful Flower, discovered Sunshine's existence and reproached her in the choral, *We are all his wives.* When Sunshine protested that she could not live without his love, Flower responded with the thrilling *Then you must die.* The duet between Sunshine and Flower which followed echoed the earlier duet between Gaijan and Sunshine only, instead of a transformation, it was concluded by a suicide. In the final act, Gaijan threatened to follow Sunshine into death until Flower wooed him away from the cliff-edge. As Gaijan and Flower exchanged vows of marriage, Flower promised to be to him all that Sunshine had been, and all that Sunshine could not be. The stage had been growing darker all the while, and Olin expected the curtain to fall on the final, throbbing notes of Flower's promise and the lovers' embrace. Instead, Flower turned to face the audience, and opened her robe. Olin caught his breath at the sight of an embryo, seen as if through Flower's flesh growing within her body. It grew, as he watched, and even without opera glasses Olin could see that the unborn baby wore Sunshine's face.

There was a moment of awed silence as the curtain fell, and then an explosion of applause. Olin clapped, too, full of emotion he was unable to express in any other way. He glanced at Seth and then hastily looked away again at the sight of tears on the younger man's face.

The murmuring, satisfied crowd bore them away, and there was no need, or chance, to speak. On the steps again, Olin began to say his thanks, but was stopped by a gesture.

'Don't rush off,' said Seth. 'I'd really like to discuss what we've just seen. That's why I don't like going to these things alone — it's never complete for me until I've been able to talk about it. Won't you walk with me by the river? I need to stretch my legs, and somehow I think better when I'm moving.'

Olin felt flattered that Seth had not tired of his company after the strained effort of their earlier conversation in the bar, but he glanced at his watch saying, 'I'm afraid the last bus is —'

'Oh, don't worry about that. I have a car; I can run you home.'

'Your own car? On a teacher's salary?'

Seth smiled faintly. 'No. Not on a teacher's salary. Nor this coat, nor a subscription to the opera. It won't last long at the rate I'm going, but I have a little money. From my wife's family.'

Olin remembered the despairing way Seth had leaned against the telephone, and the flowers that morning, and he was surprised. 'You're married?'

'Separated. It lasted less than a year. A youthful mistake.'

The night was dry and not cold, the river path paved and lighted, but they were alone.

'My wife and I separated two years ago,' Olin offered.

'How long were you married?'

'Ten years.'

'Children?'

'Two. At school now.'

'Not a youthful mistake, then,' said Seth. 'Why didn't you stay together? Why — I'm sorry. Please forgive me. It's none of my business, of course.'

It would have been a rude question even from someone less a stranger than Seth, and Olin knew he should have taken offence. But suddenly he wanted to talk about his marriage with someone, anyone, who was not Dove. He had never had the chance before.

'I suppose we separated because we ran out of reasons for staying together. We'd stopped loving each other long since, the children were at school and didn't need us, and there was no reason for two people who didn't like each other very much to go on sharing the same house. We'd never had much in common except the physical.'

'That's supposed to be enough,' said Seth. 'It is in all the operas, in literature, in ballads. The miracle of love is physical love — a biological affinity. Which would be fine, only it never lasts. And nobody will admit that. Everybody expects it to last, and when it doesn't we think there's something wrong with *us*. We're failures. Why can't we be taught to see love in perspective, to see it as a physical pleasure which belongs to one part of life but doesn't ever, can't by its very nature, ever last. We outgrow it, and we're *meant* to outgrow it. So why do we ruin our lives, wasting so much time and energy on love, dreaming about it, waiting for it, hoping for it against all odds?'

Although they were walking side by side, not looking at one another, Olin was vividly aware of Seth's anguish.

'You're too young to be talking like that,' Olin said, trying for a cheerful, bracing tone. 'It's all very well for me to resign myself to a solitary life, but you're still young and you should have hope. You can marry again — you *will* marry again. As you say, the first was a youthful mistake. You'll meet someone else . . .'

'Oh, yes, I'll meet someone else, and start the whole messy process all over again. I won't be able to help myself. But what's the point? To come to this again. Honey's pregnant. Already. I found out today. I suppose I should feel grateful. At least relieved that I didn't ruin her life. It would be so awful for her to find out she couldn't have kids ever, with anyone. It's not so terrible for a man to be infertile, but to be a woman . . .'

'There's no reason to assume you're infertile,' said Olin. 'Lots of people aren't cross-fertile with each other, but that doesn't mean they're infertile. Like in the opera we just saw — it's a question of finding the right partner.'

'So why should it be so complicated? It's just biology. Biological compatibility. Why all this stuff about love? It has nothing to do with physical attraction, or being a nice person, or having common interests, or the meeting of souls. It's not spiritual destiny. It's blind chance. It could have been worked out better, don't you think? So that we couldn't fall in love with someone unless we were cross-fertile.'

'But then it wouldn't be love,' Olin said. 'Then it *would* just be biology — we'd just be animals attracted to each other in the mating season.'

'I think we are, and we just don't know it. In our ignorance, we've screwed it up. We try to make it something noble, try to pretend that sex and reproduction are the by-products of love, instead of the other way around. Why should sex get this special treatment? Why can't we see it clearly, as a need like hunger? Why mystify it? Why can't we just admit that we're just animals who need to reproduce, and *do* it?'

Olin was conscious that their argument was operating on two levels. However abstract and intellectual it might become, Seth was speaking out of his own hurt. He was looking for comfort, and Olin responded with the wish to help. But what wisdom could he offer? He was older than Seth, but no wiser. He hadn't found the answer in marriage or out of it. He had told himself that love was for the young, and safely in his own past, but something in him still responded to romance.

After a little silence Olin said, 'We're animals, but not only animals. Yes, we need to reproduce — but we have other needs, too. Emotional, social needs. We have a need for love, however you define it. Maybe it's misguided to connect love with sex, but everyone does, so there must be some sense in it, there must be some hope —' he stopped talking as they both stopped walking, having come to the end of the paved, lighted river-path. The river wound on, out of sight behind the embankment to their left, but ahead of them was a dark, rough wasteland.

Staring into the night Seth said, 'There's a need, but is it natural? Is it something basic in us, or was it constructed? Does it have to be that way, or can we change it? Should we?'

Disturbed, Olin turned away. 'We'd better start back. There's no way through here. It's odd — you'd think the path would go somewhere, wouldn't you? I mean, to pave it, and put up lights — you'd think it would go somewhere. At least to the next bridge, or up to the main road. Just to end like this — Are you coming?'

As they walked back, Olin turned the conversation to architecture, a subject about which he knew little but had many opinions. He soon provoked Seth into disagreement, and by the time they reached the opera house they were arguing as merrily as old friends, all restraint between them gone. Seth's bitter mood had passed, and Olin was glad to agree when he suggested they stop for a snack in a late-night cafe on the way home. Even knowing he would have to get up in the morning to teach, Olin was not ready for the evening to end. He was enjoying himself with Seth, but he didn't trust in their friendship to survive even the shortest separation. In the morning, he thought, they would be strangers again.

But he was wrong. The next day at school, passing each other on the stairs, Seth suggested they meet for a drink after work. He spoke as casually and easily as if they were friends and, suddenly, they were.

Drinks led to dinner and to another walk; to more drinks, dinners and walks. Despite, or perhaps because of, having a car, Seth loved to walk. It was his only exercise — like Olin, he had developed a hatred of sports at school — and after days cooped up indoors, he longed for the chance to move in the open air. He said that it not only relaxed him, but it helped him to think. Olin, always lazy, enjoyed their walks because the talk that always accompanied them allowed him to forget he was exerting himself. Some of their best — and most disturbing — conversations took place while they walked. There were things which could not be said in a restaurant or a bar, looking at each other. But striding along, talking into the open air as if thinking aloud, unable to see each other's expressions, anything might be voiced. Anything at all. And one day, Olin thought, Seth would say something ... Seth would go too far. The thought gave him a strange feeling at the pit of his stomach. It was a pleasurable excitement he remembered from long ago, from the last time he'd had such a close friendship. The feeling was fear, but it was also desire.

Women had friendships among themselves, but women had nothing to lose. Older men sometimes managed it, but for everyone else friendship was a risk. Olin was well aware of this, and thought Seth must be, too. They never spoke of the danger they might be courting, although they came close. For love — or sex, or biology, or marriage — was the topic they continued to be drawn to, again, in their night-time, walking conversations. The subject was like a sore Seth could not stop probing, or a cliff-edge he had to lean over. It was during those conversations that Olin became aware of what a dangerous edge it was on which they balanced. If one of them fell ...

But if one of them fell, it would be Seth, he was certain. Seth, with his youth, his passion, his sorrow, his 'mistaken' marriage, would fall in love with his older friend, and not the other way around. Olin could imagine Seth in love with him, and the idea of making love to a transformed, newly receptive Seth aroused him. But Olin did not let himself dwell on such thoughts. He didn't really want it to happen. He liked this not-sexual friendship; he wanted to believed that it could last. He wanted to go on balancing. He didn't want Seth to change.

One morning, about six weeks after the performance of *The Insufficient Answer*, Olin's telephone rang before he left for school.

It was Dove. 'I've been trying to phone you for days, and you're never in,' she said.

He remembered his long-ago, never-kept resolution to phone her, and felt guilty. 'I've been busy — I'm sorry I haven't been in touch —'

'It doesn't matter. But I thought you might have forgotten that it's parents' day this weekend. I thought the 8:45 would be the best train to catch. Could you meet me at the station by 8:30 on Saturday morning? Tristan wants a new football, I know — do you think you could manage to buy one? And some books for both of them — you know the sort of thing they'd like better than I would.'

Olin winced and closed his eyes as his wife's voice poured into his ear. He had forgotten. Worse than that, he didn't want to go. There had been a time when he welcomed the ritual visits to his children at their school. Then, his life had been so dull that any events were treasured as a break from routine. But his life was different now. A day spent with Dove and the boys meant a day without Seth. They had made tentative plans for Saturday already: a drive in the country, a visit to some site of historic interest, some place from the old times. Olin knew what he wanted to do, but he also knew his duty. He told Dove that he would meet her at the station.

They embraced as they always did on meeting — former desire transformed to awkward ritual — and then stood back to examine each other for signs of change.

Her hair was too short, Olin thought, the style too severe. It made her look older than she was, harsher and no longeer pretty. But she looked fit, and still dressed well.

'You've put on weight,' Dove said.

He was surprised, and a little indignant, for since spending time with Seth he was not only getting more exercise, but also eating less. He tucked a thumb into the waistband of his trousers to show Dove how loose they were.

In answer, she touched his chest. 'Look how tight. That button's ready to pop.'

He flinched away from her hand. 'Maybe the shirt shrunk.'

'Shirts that old don't shrink. *I* bought you that shirt. You're bigger in the chest, and it isn't muscle. Your face is fuller, too. It doesn't look bad — you look younger, actually. Softer.'

Olin shrugged, annoyed. 'Let's get on the train before it goes without us.' He was dreading the two-hour journey. Usually he told Dove about his life and she listened. But he didn't want to tell her about Seth, and he could think of nothing else that had happened to him in the last two months — nothing that would take more than two or three minutes to tell. He had brought along a book to read, but he was so aware of Dove watching him that he found it difficult to concentrate. The familiar train journey had never seemed longer.

Their children, Tristan and Timon, acted pleased to see them, but they clearly had lives of their own in which parents played no very large role. Olin knew this was normal — he remembered his own school-days. And it was only fair that they be uninterested in him, considering how seldom he thought of them, but, confronted with them in the flesh, with their inescapable separateness, Olin felt his own estrangement the more. Once they had been at the centre of his life, he thought. When he hugged them, and could feel and smell their familiar bodies, he loved them, but when they moved out of reach he was left with only memories. He loved his babies, but his babies had grown into strangers. He wondered if Dove felt the same way. Perhaps it was worse for her. Or perhaps she had come to terms with it long before. It had to be different for a mother, who had brought forth children from her own body. he had *always* been separate from his children. Suddenly, confusingly, Olin wanted to cry. To cover his feelings, he began to rough-house with the boys until he realised he was embarrassing them. He wasn't acting like the other fathers. Desperately, Olin watched the other fathers for clues, and tried to act like them. He tried to remember what he had done six months ago, during his last visit to the school. What had he felt then, who had he been? Surely it hadn't always been this difficult, this painful?

Fortunately the day was structured to make life easy for everyone. Olin and Dove were taken around by their children, reintroduced to their children's friends and teachers, observed various competitions, sporting and dramatic events, and then took Tristan and Timon out for the traditional feast Presents were given out, and then the farewell kisses and goodbyes.

Back on the train, Olin was too exhausted even to pretend to read his book. He didn't think Dove would have let him, anyway. It was obvious she had something to say, even if she was taking her time about saying it.

'So,' she said at last. 'You going to tell me about him?'

'Who?'

'Your friend.'

'What makes you think I have a friend?'

'You always thought I was stupid,' she said. 'But there are some things you don't get to know out of books. You're different than you were the last time I saw you. You're always out, too busy to call me, instead of lonely and bored like you were before. And instead of telling me in detail about your boring life, you got on the train and stuck your nose in a book. Because your life isn't boring anymore. Because there's somebody in your life. Somebody new. Maybe it's early days yet, maybe you're not really sure, and you don't want to jinx it by saying anything too soon in case it doesn't happen, but — I don't think it's that. I think something's happening that you didn't expect —'

'What are you babbling about?'

'The main thing is, the reason I'm so sure, is that you remind me —' again, she stopped short. It was almost like a dare to him to tell her what she already knew.

He gave in. Maybe, after all, he did want to talk about it; maybe he wanted confirmation from someone else. 'What do I remind you of,' he asked gently. 'Do I remind you of how I used to be, when you and I were first in love? Do I remind you of how I was then?'

She shook her head. 'No. You remind me of how *I* was.'

Dove was right, and he was in hell. He had denied it to her, and had tried to deny it to himself, but Sunday morning Olin woke and saw the blood in his bed and could no longer hide the truth from himself. He had fallen in love with Seth.

It wasn't much blood — a dried brownish spot no longer than his thumbnail. He stripped off the sheet and saw that it had soaked through to the mattress. As he scrubbed at the stain with a wet, soapy towel, Olin blinked back tears and struggled to think logically.

He was changing. No doubt about that, but the change was far from complete. Dove had seen the signs, but Dove had been through it herself. I might not be too late to stop what was happening to him. His only hope was to get away from Seth before it was too late. Parents did sometimes save their sons from shame by sending them away when they recognized the threat of a developing romance. Olin couldn't actually go away — he couldn't afford to leave his job — but he might be able to contrive something to keep him safely out of Seth's company.

Olin sat back and surveyed his work. There was a large wet spot on the mattress, but that would soon dry. The blood-stain was gone.

The telephone rang, making Olin jump. He stared at the thing, knowing already who it would be. Maybe he should start now, ignore it. But he couldn't resist the summons.

'Took you long enough,' said Seth's voice in his ear. 'I thought you said you lived in one room?'

'I do. I was in bed — I'm not feeling well.'

'Oh, what's wrong?'

'I'm not sure. I'm probably just tired out from the day with Dove and the boys.'

'Why don't I come over and cheer you up?'

'No!' The leap his heart had given — of pure desire — made him shout.

There was a short silence on the other end. Olin tried not to think about what Seth was thinking, not to worry whether he was hurt or angry.

Seth said, 'What's wrong?'

'I told you. I'm tired. I don't feel well. I'm fed up with people — I just need to be alone.'

'You're the doctor. I'll leave you alone, then. You'd just better be over this by Wednesday.'

'Wednesday?'

'You hadn't forgotten that we've got opera tickets?'

'No, of course not. I'll be better before Wednesday — I have to be well enough to go to school tomorrow. I can't afford to pay a substitute.' Olin knew Seth's schedule like his own. It was easy enough to avoid him at school, just as, a week earlier, it had been easy to engineer brief, 'accidental' encounters. At the end of the day Olin crept out by a side-entrance and went to a movie and then had dinner in a cafe of the sort Seth would never enter. He felt like a hunted animal, following a similar routine on Tuesday. But on Wednesday one of the boys brought him a note:

Opera steps, 7 sharp, yes? Don't be late! S.

Olin folded the note and tucked it into his pocket, aware that his students were staring at him and giggling.

'Is that a love-note, sir?' asked one of the boys.

Another, in a loud whisper, corrected him, 'Is that a love-note, *miss*!'

The whole class exploded into mocking laughter.

Olin pounded on his desk, painfully aware that he was blushing. He regained control of the class, but he knew how weak was his hold on them. Boys that age were sensitive to hints of sex even where they did not exist, and once they knew the truth about him he would lose their respect forever. He tried to take comfort from the fact that they couldn't really know — and nothing, after all, had happened — and then, with a chill, he wondered if Seth also suspected. If Seth, perhaps, knew.

Against the rules, Olin dismissed his final class ten minutes early. He didn't go to a film or a cafe. He had decided to do something positive, and he caught the bus which would take him to the north-eastern suburb where Dove lived.

She seemed surprised and, he thought, not pleased when she opened the door to him. Entering at her reluctant invitation, he saw that she already had a visitor, a woman dressed, like Dove, in dark-blue overalls. Olin had not seen Dove in her work clothes since the days when they lived together: she always dressed up for him when he came to call. She looked taller and stronger to him now, more of a stranger.

'Is something wrong?' she asked. She did not offer to introduce him to the woman.

'No, no, I just thought I'd like to take you out to dinner.'

'Why didn't you phone?'

He shrugged uneasily. 'It was a spur of the moment thing. I thought you'd be pleased.'

There was a silence, and then the other woman set down her tea-cup and rose from her chair. 'I'd better be getting along,' she said to Dove. 'I'll see you tomorrow at work.'

'I'll phone you later,' Dove said.

The two women exchanged a look which made Olin feel

even more uncomfortable, and then the other woman smiled, becoming almost beautiful. 'Take care, Leo,' she said.

'Leo?' said Olin when Dove had closed the door behind her departing guest. 'Why did she call you that?'

'It's my name.'

'It *was* Dove —'

'Dove is *your* name for me. I still have my own. I prefer my friends to use it.'

He wondered what she meant by the word 'friend', and what that woman was to her, and he did not want to know. 'I didn't know you didn't like it. I could have chosen another name if you'd ever said —'

'I didn't say I didn't like it. It's all right *you* calling me Dove. Let's not argue. Come in the kitchen and have a cup of tea. Or would you rather have a beer? I've got some.'

'Tea.' He followed her into the kitchen, 'I'm sorry I didn't phone first. I really didn't think about it until I was on the bus coming out here, and then it seemed too late. If you really want me to leave —'

'No, now your're here, stay.'

'I can wait while you change,' he said as she put the kettle on.

She shook her head. 'I don't want to change; I don't feel like going out.' She turned around to face him, leaned against the counter and crossed her arms over her chest. 'Why don't you just say what you have to say?'

He didn't want to talk to her in such a self-possessed, almost aggressive mood. He had hoped to make her pliable with drink and good food, to lead up to it gently, but she wasn't giving him the change and he couldn't afford to wait for a better time. He drew a deep breath.

'I want to try again,' he said.

'Try what?'

'Us. I'd like us to try again. I'd like to move back in here with you.'

She simply stared. He couldn't tell what she was thinking. The kettle was boiling. She turned away and poured the water into the teapot.

'He's really got you scared,' she said.

'Who?'

'It won't work,' she said. 'You can't get away from him that easily. You can't just pretend you've got a wife —'

'Why should it be a pretence? We loved each other once — why can't we go back to that?'

'Because we've changed.'

'*I* haven't,' he said furiously. 'I haven't changed! It's started, yes, but *he* doesn't know — we haven't done anything — it's not too late — if I stay away from him — I don't have to be his woman —'

'And I don't have to be yours.'

Olin stared at her. 'But you can't — you can't change back. You can't ever be a man again. Becoming a woman — that change is forever. I changed you.'

She smiled. 'What makes you think I *want* to be a man again? There are other kinds of change. There's such a thing as growing.'

'Have you met someone else? Who is he? Do you want to marry someone else?'

'No.'

But there was something ... Olin felt sick. 'Not her — that woman who was here? Is *she* your lover? Do women do that?'

He saw her tense, and it occurred to him that she wanted to hit him. But she was very controlled as she said, 'We're friends. We'll probably make love some day. But not in the way *you* mean. It's not that kind of thing. There aren't any men and women among us.'

'I wouldn't try to stop you,' Olin said. 'If that was what you wanted, if you wanted her as well ... You could do as you liked. Let me move back in here.'

'No.'

'Why won't you help me? Do you hate me that much, for what I did to you?'

She sighed. 'Olin ... I don't hate you at all. If I can help you, I will. But I'm not going to live a lie for you.'

'Why should it be a lie? We were happy together once, weren't we?'

'We were, but that's over. Olin, you know it is. You spend an evening with me, and by the end of it you can't wait to get away. The Dove you've got in your mind isn't me. You'd know that if you weren't so afraid right now. Why are you so afraid? It's natural; it happens to people all the time. Why can't you just accept what's happening to you?'

'I'm too old,' he said, anguished.

She almost laughed. 'The fact that it's happening means you're not too old. All right, maybe too old for babies, but that can be a blessing. Since you've done your bit for the species already, with Timon and Tristan, you don't even have to feel guilty. Let yourself enjoy it. There *is* pleasure in it, you know. Pain, too, but you might find that the pleasure makes up for it. I remember the pleasure, Olin. You don't have to feel guilty about what you did to me. Oh, I know you feel guilty. Otherwise you wouldn't be so afraid of it happening to you. Don't be. It isn't *so* terrible to be a woman.'

Of course it was terrible to be a woman. Olin had feared it all his life. Everyone feared becoming a woman. Parents feared it for their sons. And friends, in their intimacy, battled grimly not to lose. To lose was to become a woman. Olin had been through that in his youth, and he had won. He thought he could relax, then, he thought he was safe. He had not realised, until it was too late, that the battle to retain manhood never ended. He had not truly understood that one victory was not the end. He had not realised until now that he might yet lose.

After leaving Dove, Olin rode around the city on buses, unable to think what to do next, unable even to decide upon a restaurant. But eventually he became restless and decided that, like Seth, he would be able to think better if he could walk. he left the bus at the stop near the old city, so that was where he went to walk.

Darkness had fallen, and the broken pavement was treacherous underfoot. Here and there among the looming vastness of ancient buildings tiny lights glowed and flickered: candles lit by lovers in the abandoned rooms which were their trysting places. They were all around him — he heard the indistinct murmur of their voices and, occasionally, a cry of pain.

He broke out in a sweat. Once these surroundings would have induced nostalgic memories of his time with Dove. Now they brought only fear. Why had he come here? Why had he chosen these streets, of all there were in the city to walk? He had to get away.

Olin turned around and there, in the darkness, unmistakable, was Seth.

'I knew you'd come here,' said Seth. 'I knew I only had to wait.'

'It was a mistake,' said Olin. 'I'm leaving.'

'You'll come with me first.'

'No.'

As he tried to go past, Seth caught him by the arm. it was the first time he had ever touched Olin, and now Olin knew that it really was too late. They could fight: although Seth was taller, Olin was heavier and better co-ordinated and under the circumstances he could have taken Seth. But as he stood very still, feeling Seth's fingers like a chain around his arm, feeling the unwanted, unmistakable trickle of wetness between his legs as his wound began to bleed, Olin knew that Seth had already won this fight. He shuddered, as his fear was transformed into desire.

'Where will we go?' he asked.

'I know a room. Come on.' Now Seth, seeming kind, released his bruising hold and laid his arm gently across Olin's shoulders. 'Don't be frightened,' he said, leading Olin away. 'I'll be very gentle; it won't hurt so much.'

It was only the first of his lies.

Dan Simmons' first story was 'The River Styx Runs Upstream', which was published in *Twilight Zone Magazine* and won their annual short story contest in 1982; his first novel was *Song of Kali*, which won the World Fantasy Award in 1986.

His second book is another horror novel *Carrion Comfort* (1988). 1989 sees the publication of five more Simmons books: *Phases of Gravity*, a mainstream novel, *Tales of Hyperion* and *The Fall of Hyperion*, which he describes as 'epic science fiction novels with a nod in the direction of both Chaucer and Keats', *Summer of Shadows*, which is the working title of his third horror novel, and *Eyes I Dare Not Meet In Dreams*, his first short story collection.

Simmons lives in Colorado, and the following story has been optioned for film production.

E-TICKET TO
NAMLAND
by
DAN SIMMONS

The twenty-eight Huey gunships moved out in single file, each hovering a precise three metres about the tarmac, the sound of their rotors filling the world with a roar that could be felt in teeth and bones and testicles. Once above the tree line and gaining altitude, the helicopters separated into four staggered V formations, and the noise diminished to the point where shouts could be heard.

'First time out?' cried the guide.

'What?' Justin Jeffries turned away from the open door where he had been watching the shadow of their helicopter slide across the surface of the mirrored rice paddies below. He leaned toward the guide until their combat helmets were almost touching.

'First time out?' repeated the guide. The man was small even for a Vietnamese. He wore a wide grin and the uniform and shoulder patch of the old First Air Cav Division. Jeffries was big even for an American. He was dressed in green shorts, a flowered Hawaiian shirt, Nike running sandals, an expensive Rolex comlog, and a U.S. Army helmet that had become obsolete the year he was born. Jeffries was draped with cameras: a compact Yashica SLR, a Polaroid Holistic-360, and a new Nikon imager. Jeffries returned the guide's grin. 'First time for us. We're here with my wife's father.'

Heather leaned over to join the conversation. 'Daddy was here during ... you know ... the war. They thought it might be good for him to take the Vet Tour.' She nodded in the direction of a short, solid, gray-haired man leaning against the M-60 machine-gun mount near the door's safety webbing. He was the only person in the cabin not wearing a helmet. The back of his blue shirt was soaked with sweat.

'Yes, yes,' smiled the guide and stepped back to plug his microphone jack into a bulkhead socket. His voice echoed tinnily in every helmet and from hidden speakers. 'Ladies and gentlemen, please notice the tree line to your right.'

There was a lurch as the passengers shifted their positions and craned for a view. Ten-year-old Sammee Jeffries and his eight-year-old sister, Elizabeth, shoved their way through the crowded space to stand next to where their grandfather sat by the open door. The barrel of Elizabeth's plastic M-16 accidentally struck the older man on his sunburned neck, but he did not turn or speak. Suddenly a series of flashes erupted from the tree line along one rice paddy. The passengers gasped audibly as a line of magnesium-bright tracer bullets rose up and lashed toward their ship, missing the rotors by only a few meters. Immediately one of the gunships at the rear of the V formation dove, curved back the way they had come in a centrifugally perfect arc, and raked the tree line with rocket and minigun fire. Meanwhile, at the guide's urging. Sammee stood on a low box, grasped the two-handed grip of the heavy M-60, swung it awkwardly to bear in the general direction of the now-distant tree line, and depressed the firing studs. The passengers instinctively clutched at their helmets to block their ears. Heavy cartridges, warm but not hot enough to burn anyone, clattered onto the metal deck.

An explosion split the tree line, sending phosphorous streamers fifty meters into the air and setting several tall palms ablaze. Bits of flaming debris splashed into the quiet rice paddy. The passengers laughed and applauded. Sammee grinned back at them and flexed his muscles. Elizabeth leaned against her grandfather and spoke loudly into his ear. 'Isn't this *fun*, Grandpa?'

He turned to say something, but at that second the guide announced that their destination would be coming up on the left side of the ship, and Elizabeth was away, shoving her brother aside to get a better view, eager to see the village appear below out of the heat, haze, and smoke.

Later that evening five men sat around a table on the fifth-floor terrace of the Saigon Oberoi Sheraton. The air was warm and humid. Occasional gusts of laughter and splashing sounds came up from the pool on the fourth-floor terrace. It was well past nine, but the tropical twilight lingered.

'You were on the village mission-tour this morning, weren't you?' asked Justin Jeffries of the young Oriental next to him.

'Yes. I was. Most interesting.' The man sat in a relaxed manner, but something about his bearing, the precisely creased safari suit, the intensity of his gaze, suggested a military background.

'You're Nipponese, aren't you?' asked Justin. At the man's smile and nod, Justin went on. 'Thought so. Here with the military mission?'

'No, merely on leave. R and R, I believe your people used to call it.'

'Christ,' said the overweight American who sat next to Justin's father-in-law. 'You've been up north in the PRC fighting Chen's warlords, haven't you?'

'Just so,' said the Nipponese and extended his hand to Justin. ''Lieutenant Keigo Naguchi.'

'Justin Jeffries, Kansas City.' Justin's huge hand enclosed the lieutentant's and pumped twice. 'This here is my father-in-law, Ralph Disantis.'

'A pleasure,' said the lieutenant.

'Pleased to meet you,' said Disantis.

'I believe I saw you with your grandchildren at the village today.' said Naguchi. 'A boy and a girl?'

Disantis nodded and sipped his beer. Justin gestured to the heavyset man next to his father-in-law. 'And this is Mr ... ah ... Sears, right?'

'Sayers,' said the man. 'Roger Sayers. Nice to make your acquaintance. Lieutenant. So how's it going up there? Your guys finally getting those little bastards out of the hill caves?'

'Most satisfactory,' said Lieutenant Naguchi. 'The situation should be stabilized before the next rainy season.'

'Japanese brains and Vietnamese blood, huh?' laughed Sayers. He turned to the fifth man at the table, a silent Vietnamese in a white shirt and dark glasses, and added quickly, 'No offense meant. Everybody knows that your basic Viet peasant makes the best foot soldier in the world. Showed us that forty years ago, eh, Mr ... ah ...?'

'Minh,' said the little man and shook hands around the table. 'Nguyen Van Minh.' Minh's hair was black, his face

121

unlined, but his eyes and hands revealed that he was at least in his sixties, closer to Disantis's age than that of the others.

'I saw you on the plane from Denver,' said Justin. 'Visiting family here?'

'No,' said Minh. 'I have been an American citizen since 1976. This is my first trip back to Vietnam. I have no family here now.' He turned towards Naguchi. 'Lieutenant, I am surprised that you choose to spend your leave on an American's Veterans' Tour.'

Naguchi shrugged and sipped at his gin and tonic. 'I find it a sharp contrast to modern methods. Up north I am more technician than warrior. Also, of course, learning more about the first of the helicopter wars is valuable to anyone who is interested in military history. You were a veteran of that war, Mr. Disantis?'

Justin's father-in-law nodded and took a long swallow of beer.

'I just missed it,' said Sayers with real regret in his voice. 'Too young for Vietnam. Too goddam old for the Banana Wars.'

Justin grunted. 'You didn't miss much.'

'Ah, you were involved in that period?' asked Naguchi.

'Sure,' said Justin. 'Everybody who came of age in the discount decade got in on the Banana Wars. The tour today could have been Tegucigalpa or Estanzuelas; just substitute coffee plantations for the rice paddies.'

'I want to hear about that,' said Sayers and waved a waiter over to the table. 'Another round for everyone,' he said. From somewhere near the pool a steel drum band started up, unsuccessfully trying to mix American pop tunes, a Caribbean beat, and local musicians. The sound seemed sluggish in the wet, thick air. Tropical night had fallen, and even the stars appeared dimmed by the thickness of atmosphere. Naguchi looked up at a band of brighter stars moving toward the zenith and then glanced down at his comlog.

'Checking azimuth for your spottersat, right?' asked Justin. 'It's a hard habit to break. I still do it.'

Disantis rose. 'Sorry I can't stay for the next round, gentlemen. Going to sleep off some of this jet lag.' He moved into the air-conditioned brightness of the hotel.

Before going to his own room, Disantis looked in on Heather and the children. His daughter was in bed already, but Sammee and Elizabeth were busy feeding data from their father's Nikon through the terminal and onto the wall screen. Disantis leaned against the door molding and watched.

'This is the LZ,' Sammee said excitedly.

'What's an LZ?' asked Elizabeth.

'*Landing zone*,' snapped Sammee. 'Don't you remember *anything*?'

The wall showed image after image of dust, rotors, the predatory shadows of Hueys coming in above Justin's camera position, the thin line of passengers in combat garb, men and women instinctively bent low despite obvious clearance from the rotors, tourists clutching at their helmets with one hand and hugging cameras, purses, and plastic M-16's to their chests with the other, groups moving away from the raised landing platform along rice paddy dikes.

'There's Grandpa!' cried Elizabeth. Disantis saw himself, aging, overweight, puffing heavily as he heaved himself down from the helicopter, disdaining the guide's outstretched hand. Sammee tapped at the terminal keys. The picture zoomed and enlarged until only Disantis's grainy face filled the screen. Sammee shifted through colors and widened his grandfather's face until it became a purple balloon ready to pop. '*Stop it*,' whined Elizabeth.

'Crybaby,' said Sammee, but some sixth sense made him glance over his shoulder to where Disantis stood. Sammee made no acknowledgment of his grandfather's presence but advanced in picture through a montage of new images.

Disantis blinked and watched the jerky newsreel proceed. The abandoned village of rough huts. The lines of tourist-troops along each side of the narrow road. Close-ups of huts being searched. Heather emerged from a low doorway, blinking in the sunlight, awkwardly lifting her toy M-16, and waving at the camera.

'This is the good part,' breathed Sammee.

They had been returning to the LZ when figures along a distant dike had opened fire. At first the tourists milled around in confusion, but at the guides' urging they finally, laughingly had taken cover on the grassy side of the dike. Justin remained standing to take pictures.

Disantis watched as those images built themselves on the wall screen at a rate just slower than normal video. Data columns flashed by to the right. He saw himself drop to one knee on the dike and hold Elizabeth's hand. He remembered noting that the grass was artificial.

The tourists returned fire. Their M-16's flashed and recoiled, but no bullets were expended. The din was tremendous. On the screen a two-year-old near Justin had begun to cry. Eventually the guides helped a young tourist couple use a field radio to call in an air strike. The jets were there in less than a minute — three A-4D Skyhawks with antiquated U.S. naval markings bright and clear on the white wings. They screamed in under five hundred feet high. Justin's camera shook as the explosions sent long shadows across the dikes and made the tourists cringe and hug the earth from their vantage point six hundred meters away. Justin had managed to steady the camera even as the napalm continued to blossom upward.

'Watch,' said Sammee. He froze the frame and then zoomed in. The image expanded. Tiny human forms, black silhouettes, became visible against the orange explosions. Sammee enlarged the image even further. Disantis could make out the silhouette of an outflung arm, a shirttail gusting, a conical peasant's hat flying off.

'How'd they do that, Grandpa?' asked Sammee without turning around.

Disantis shrugged. 'Holos, maybe.'

'Naw, not holos,' said Sammee. He did not try to hide his condescension. 'Too bright out there. Besides, you can see the pieces fly. Betcha they were animates.'

Elizabeth rolled over from where she was sprawled. Her pajamas carried a picture of Wonder Duck on the front. 'What'd Mr. Sayers mean on the way back, Grandpa?'

'When?'

'In the helicopter, when he said. 'Well, I guess we really showed Charlie today.' Elizabeth took a bread. 'Who's Charlie, Grandpa?'

'Stupid,' said Sammee. 'Charlie was the VC. The bad guys.'

'How come you called him Charlie, Grandpa?' persisted Elizabeth. The frozen explosion on the wall screen cast an orange glow on her features.

'I don't remember,' said Disantis. He paused with his hand on the door. 'You two better get to bed before your father comes. Tomorrow's going to be a busy day.'

Later, alone in his room, sitting in silence broker only by the hum of the air conditioner, Disantis realized that he could *not* remember why the Vietcong had been called Charlie. He wondered if he had ever known. He turned out the light and opened the sliding doors to the balcony. The humid air settled on him like a blanket as he stepped out.

Three floors below, Justin, Sayers, and the others still sat drinking. Their laughter floated up to Disantis and mixed with the rumble of thunder from a storm on the distant and darkened horizon.

On their way to a picnic the next day, Mr. Sayers tripped a claymore mine.

The guide had put them on a simulated patrol down a narrow jungle trail. Sayers was in the lead, paying little attention to the trail, talking to Reverend Dewitt, an airwaves minister from Dothan, Alabama. Justin and Heather were walking with the Newtons, a young couple from Hartford. Disantis was farther back in line, walking between Sammee and Elizabeth to keep them from quarreling.

Sayers stepped into a thin trip wire stretched across the trail, a section of dirt erupted a meter in front of him, and the claymore jumped three meters into the air before exploding in a white puff.

'Shit,' said Sayers. 'Excuse me, Reverend.' The Vietnamese guide came forward with an apologetic smile and put a red KIA armband on Sayers. The Reverend Dewitt and Tom Newton each received a yellow WIA armband.

'Does this mean I don't get to go to the picnic?' ased Sayers.

The guide smiled and directed the others on how to prepare a medevac LZ in a nearby clearing. Lieutenant Naguchi and Minh cleared underbrush with machetes, while Heather and

DAN SIMMONS

Sue Newton helped spread marker panels of iridescent orange plastic. Sammee was allowed to pop the tab on a green smoke marker. The redcross-marked Huey came in with a blast of downdraft that flattened the tall grass and blew Disantis's white tennis hat off. Sayers, Dewitt, and Newton sat propped on their elbows and waved as their stretchers were loaded. The patrol resumed when the medevac copter was just a distant throbbing in the sky.

Justin took point. He moved carefully, frequently holding his hand up to halt the line behind him. There were two more trip wires and a stretch of trail salted with anti-personnel mines. The guide showed them all how to probe ahead with bayonets. For the last half kilometer, they stayed in the grass on either side of the trail.

The picnic ground was on a hill overlooking the sea. Under a thatched pavilion sat three tables covered with sandwich makings, salads, assorted fruits, and coolers of beer. Sayers, Newton, and Dewitt were already there, helping two guides cook hamburgers and hot dogs over charcoal fires. 'What kept you?' called Sayers with a deep laugh.

After a long lunch, several of the tourists went down to the beach to swim or sunbathe or take a nap. Sammee found a network of tunnels in the jungle near the picnic pavilion, and several of the children gathered around as the guide showed them how to drop in CS gas and fragmentation grenades before actually searching the tunnels. Then the children and a few of the younger adults wiggled in on their bellies to explore the complex. Disantis could hear their excited shouts as he sat alone at one of the picnic tables, drinking his beer and looking out to sea. He could also hear the conversation of his daughter and Sue Newton as they sat on beach towels a few meters away. 'We wanted to bring my daddy, but he just refused to come,' said the Newton woman. 'So Tommy says, "Well, shoot, as long as the government's paying part of it, let's go ourselves." So we did.'

'We thought it'd be good for my father.' said Heather. 'I wasn't even born then, but when he got back from the war, way back in the Seventies, he didn't even come home to Mother. He went and lived in the woods of Oregon or Washington or some-

126

where for a couple of years.'

'Really!' said Sue Newton. 'My daddy never did anything crazy like that.'

'Oh, he got better after a while,' said Heather. 'He's been fine the last ten years or so. But his therapy program said that it'd be good for him to come on the Vet's Tour, and Justin was able to get time off 'cause the dealership is doing so good.'

The talk turned to children. Shortly after that, it began to rain heavily, and three Hueys and a lumbering Sikorsky picked them up to return them to the Sheraton. The dozen or so people in Disantis's group sang 'Ninety-nine Bottles of Beer on the Wall' during the short flight back.

There was nothing scheduled for the afternoon; and after the storm passed, several people decided to go shopping at one of the large malls between the hotel complex and the park. Disantis caught an electric bus into downtown Saigon, where he walked the streets until nightfall.

The change of name to Ho Chi Minh City had never really taken, and the metropolis had officially been renamed Saigon in the early Nineties. The city bore little resemblance to the excited jumble of pedestrians, motorbikes, strip joints, bars, restaurants, and cheap hotels Disantis remembered from forty years earlier. The foreign money had all gone into the tourist enclaves near the park, and the city itself reflected the gray era of the New Socialist Reality more than it did the feverish pulse of old Saigon. Efficient, faceless structures and steel-and-glass high rises sat on either side of busy boulevards. Occasionally Disantis would see a decaying side street that reminded him of the cluttered stylishness of Tu-Do Street in the late Sixties.

Nguyen van Minh joined him as Disantis waited for a light to change on Thong Nhut Boulevard.

'Mr. Disantis.'

'Mr. Minh.'

The short Vietnamese adjusted his glasses as they strolled past the park where the Independence Palace had once stood 'You are enjoying the sights?' he asked. 'Do you see much that is familiar?'

'No,' said Disantis. 'Do you?'

Minh paused and looked around him as if the idea had not pertained to him. 'Not really, Mr. Disantis,' he said at last. 'Of course, I rarely visited Saigon. My village was in a different province. My unit was based near Da Nang.'

'ARVN?' asked Disantis.

'Hac Bao,' said Minh. 'The Black Panthers of the First Division. You remember them, perhaps.'

Disantis shook his head.

'We were ... I say without pride ... the most feared fighting unit in all of South Vietnam ... including the Americans. The Hac Bao had put fear into the hearts of the Communist insurgents for ten years before the fall.'

Disantis stopped to buy a lemon ice from a street vendor. The lights were coming on all along the boulevard.

'You see the embassy there?' asked Minh, pointing to an antiquated six-story structure set back behind an ornate fence.

'That's the old U.S. Embassy?' asked Disantis, without much interest in his voice. 'I would have thought that the building would've been torn down by now.'

'Oh, no,' said Minh, 'it is a museum. It has been restored very much to its original appearance.

Disantis nodded and glanced at his comlog.

'I stood here,' continued Minh, 'right here ... in April 1975 and watched the helicopters take the last of the Americans off the roof of the embassy. It was only my third time in Saigon. I had just been released from four days in prison.'

'Prison?' Disantis turned to look at Minh.

'Yes. I had been arrested by the government after members of my unit had commandeered the last Boeing 727 out of Da Nang to Saigon. We fought civilians — women and children — to get aboard that plane. I was a lieutenant. I was twenty-three years old.'

'So you got out of Vietnam during the panic?'

'They released us from jail when the North Vietnamese were in the suburbs,' said Minh. 'I was not able to leave the country until several months later.'

'Boat?' asked Disantis. The lemon ice was melting quickly in the warm air.

Minh nodded. 'And you, Mr. Disnatis, when did you leave Vietnam?'

Disantis tossed the paper wrapper into a trash can and licked his fingers. 'I came here early in '69,' he said.

'And when did you leave?' Minh asked again. Disantis lifted his head as if to sniff the night air. The evening was thick with the scent of tropical vegetation, mimosa blossoms, stagnant water, decay. When he looked at Minh there was a dark gleam in his blue eyes. He shook his head. 'I never left,' he said.

Justin, Sayers, and Tom Newton came up to the guide as he sat alone at a table near the back of the hotel bar. The three Americans hesitated and looked at each other. Finally Justin stepped forward. 'Howdy,' he said.

'Good afternoon, Mr. Jeffries,' said the guide.

'We ... uh ... we'd all, I mean the three of us and a couple of other guys, we wanted to see you about something.'

'Ahhh, there is some problem with the tour?' asked the guide.

'No, no, everything's great,' said Justin and glanced back at the other two. He sat down and leaned toward the Vietnamese. His voice was a hoarse whisper. 'We ... ah ... we wanted a little more than the regular tour.'

'Oh?' The guide blinked. His mouth was not quite curled in a smile.

'Yeah,' said Justin, 'you know. Something *extra.*'

'Something extra?' said the guide.

Roger Sayers stepped forward. 'We want some special action,' he said.

'Ahhh,' said the guide and finished up his drink.

Justin leaned forward again. 'Nat Pendrake told us it was okay,' he whispered loudly. 'He said he ... uh ... arranged it through Mr. Tho.'

'Mr. Tho?' the guide said blankly. But the smile was there now.

'Yeah. Nat said that ... uh ... a special action would be about a thousand.'

'Two thousand.' the guide said softly. 'Each.'

'Hey,' interjected Sayers. 'Nat was here just a few months ago and ...'

'Quiet,' said Justin. 'All right. That's fine. Here.' He slid his universal card across the table.

The Vietnamese smiled and pushed Jeffries's card back.

'Cash, please,' he said. 'You will have it tonight. American dollars.'

'I don't know about . . .' began Sayers.

'Where?' asked Justin.

'The frontage road beyond the hotel maintenance buildings,' said the guide. 'Twenty-three hundred hours.'

'Right,' said Justin as the guide stood up. 'See you then.'

'Have a nice day,' said the guide and was gone.

The trucks transported them to a point in the jungle where the road ended and a trail began. The five men jumped down and followed the guide through the darkness. The trail was muddy from the evening rains, and wet fronds brushed at their cork-smudged faces. Justin Jeffries and Tom Newton kept close to the guide. Behind them, stumbling occasionally in the dark, came Sayers and Reverend Dewitt. Lieutenant Naguchi brought up the rear. Each man was in uniform. Each carried an M-16.

'*Shit*,' hissed Sayers as a branch caught him in the face.

'Shut up,' whispered Justin. The guide motioned them to stop, and the Americans pressed close to peer at a clearing through a gap in the foliage. A few kerosene lanterns threw cold light from the doorways of the dozen huts of the village.

'Vietcong sympathizers,' whispered the guide. 'They can tell you where the cadre headquarters is. Everyone in the village knows the VC.'

'Huh,' said Sayers. 'So our job is to get the information, right?'

'Yes.'

'And they're VC sympathizers?' whispered Tom Newton.

'Yes.'

'How many?' asked Lieutenant Naguchi. His voice was barely audible above the rip of water from palm leaves.

'Maybe thirty,' said the guide. 'No more than thirty-five.'

'Weapons?' asked Naguchi.

'There may be some hidden in the huts,' said the guide. 'Be careful of the young men and women. VC. Well trained.'

There was a long silence as they stared at the quiet village.

Finally Justin stood and clicked the safety off on his rifle. 'Let's do it,' he said. Together they moved into the clearing.

Ralph Disantis and Nguyen van Minh sat together in a dark booth in an old bar not far from what had once been Tu-Do Street. It was late. Minh was quite drunk, and Disantis let himself appear to be in the same condition. An ancient jukebox played recent Japanese hits and oldies but goodies dating back to the Eighties.

'For many years after the fall of my country. I thought that America had no honor,' said Minh. The only sign of the little man's drunkenness was the great care with which he enunciated each word. 'Even as I lived in America, worked in America, became a citizen of America, I was convinced that America had no honor. My American friends told me that during the Vietnam War there was news from my country on the televisions and radios every day, every evening. After Saigon fell ... there was nothing. Nothing. It was as if my nation had never existed.'

'Hmmm,' said Disantis. He finished his drink and beckoned for more.

'But you, Mr Disantis, you are a man of honor,' said Minh. 'I know this. I sense this. You are a man of honor.'

Disantis nodded at the retreating waiter, removed the swizzle stick from his fresh drink, and placed the plastic saber in a row with seven others. Mr. Minh blinked and did the same with his.

'As a man of honor you will understand why I have returned to avenge my family.' Minh said carefully.

'Avenge?' said Disantis.

'Avenge my brother who died fighting the North Vietnamese,' said Minh. 'Avenge my father — a teacher — who spend eight years in a reeducation camp only to die soon after his release. Avenge my sister who was deported by this regime for ...' Minh paused. 'For alleged crimes against morality. She drowned when their overcrowed boat went down somewhere between here and Hong Kong.

'Avenge,' repeated Disantis. 'How? And with what?'

Minh sat up straight and looked over his shoulder. No one

was near. 'I will avenge my family's honor by striking against the maggots who have corrupted my nation,' he said.

'Yeah,' said Disantis. 'With what? Do you have a weapon?'

Minh hesitated, licked his lips, and looked for a second like he was sobering. Then he leaned over and grasped Disantis's forearm. 'I have a weapon,' he whispered. 'Two of them. I smuggled them in. A rifle and my service automatic from the Hac Bao.'

He hesitated again. 'I can tell you this, Mr. Disantis. You are a man of honor.' This time it was a question.

'Yes,' said Disantis. 'Tell me.'

Two of the huts were on fire. Justin and the other four had come in shouting and firing. There had been no opposition. The thirty-two villagers, mostly children and old people, knelt in the dust at the center of the village. Sayers had knocked over a lantern in one of the huts, and the thatch and bamboo had blazed like an incendiary flare. The fat American beat uselessly at the the flames until Justin called, 'Forget the fucking hooch and get back here.'

Tom Newton swung his rifle to cover the cringing villagers. 'Where are the VC?' he shouted.

'VC!' shouted Sayers. 'Where are their tunnels? Tell us, God damn it!' A kneeling woman holding a baby bowed her forehead to the dust. Flames cast bizarre shadows on the dirt, and the smell of smoke made the men's nostrils flare.

'They don't understand what we're saying,' said Reverend Dewitt.

'The hell they don't,' snapped Justin. 'They're just not talking.'

Lieutenant Naguchi stepped forward. He was relaxed, but he kept his M-16 trained on the cowering villagers. 'Mr. Jeffries. I will stand guard here if you wish to conduct an interrogation.'

'Interrogation?' said Justin.

'There is an empty hut there, away from the fire,' said the lieutenant. 'It is best to isolate them during questioning.'

'Yeah,' said Justin. 'I remember. Tom, cut a couple of them out of the herd. Hurry!'

Newton lifted a young man and an old woman by the arm and began moving them toward the hut. 'Not her,' said Justin.

'Too old. Get that one.' He pointed to a wide-eyed girl of fifteen or sixteen. 'She's probably got a brother or boyfriend fighting with the VC.'

Newton pushed the old woman back to her knees and roughly lifted the girl to her feet. Justin felt his mouth go dry. Behind him the flames had set a third hut on fire, and sparks drifted up to mix with the stars.

Disantis set the ninth plastic saber carefully in a row with the others. 'How about ammunition?' he asked.

Minh blinked slowly and smiled. 'Three thousand rounds for the rifle,' he said. he lifted his glass in slow motion, drank, swallowed. 'Thirty clips for the .45 caliber service automatic. Enough . . .' He paused, swayed a second, and straightened his back. 'Enough to do the job, yes?'

Disantis dropped money on the table to pay the tab. He helped Minh to his feet and guided the smaller man toward the door. Minh stopped, grasped Disantis's arm in both hands, and brought his face close. 'Enough, yes?' he asked.

Disantis nodded. 'Enough,' he said.

'Shit,' said Tom Newton, 'he's not going to tell us anything.' The young man from the village knelt before them. His black shirt had been pulled back to pin his arms. Blood was smeared from the corners of his mouth and nostrils. There were cigarette burn marks dotted across his chest.

'Bring the girl here,' said Justin. Sayers pushed her to her knees, took a fistful of hair, and jerked her head back sharply.

'Where are the VC?' asked Justin. Smoke came through the open door of the hooch. 'Tunnels? VC?'

The girl said nothing. Her eyes were very dark and dilated with fear. Small, white teeth showed between her slightly parted lips. 'Hold her arms,' Justin said to Newton and Sayers. He took a long knife out of its sheath on his web belt, slipped the point under her buttoned shirtfront, and slashed upward. Cloth rupped and parted.

The girl gasped and writhed, but the two Americans held her tightly. Her breasts were small, conical, and lightly filmed with moisture.

'Jesus,' said Newton and giggled.

Justin tugged her black pants halfway down, slapped her knee aside when she kicked, and used the knife to tear the cloth away from her ankles.

'Hey!' yelled Sayers. The young Vietnamese had lurched to his feet and was sturggling to free his arms. Justin turned quickly, dropped the knife, lifted the M-16, and fired three times in rapid succession. Flesh exploded from the boy's chest, throat, and cheeks. He kicked backward, spasmed once, and lay still in a growing red pool.

'Oh, Jesus,' Newton said again. 'Jesus Christ, this is something.'

'Shut up,' said Justin. He placed the butt of his rifle against the dazed girl's collarbone and pushed her onto her back. 'Hold her legs,' he said. 'You'll get your turns.'

After seeing Minh to his hotel room and putting him to bed, Disantis went back to his own room and sat out on the balcony. Sometime after three A.M., his son-in-law and four other men materialized out of the darkness and sat down around one of the round tables on the abandoned terrace below. Disantis could hear the sounds of beer cans being tossed into trash bins, the pop of more tabs, and bits of conversation.

'How the hell did all the firing start out there?' asked Justin in the darkness. Several of the others giggled drunkenly.

A firm voice with a Japanese accent answered. 'One of them ran. The reverend opened fire. I joined him in stopping them from escaping.'

'... damn brains all over the place.' Disantis recognized Sayer's voice. 'I'd like to know how they did that.'

'Blood bags and charges every six centimeters of so under the synflesh,' came the slurred voice of the young man named Newton. 'Used to work for Disney. Know all about that animate stuff.'

'If they *were* animates,' said the Sayers shadow, and someone giggled.

'You damn well know that they were,' came Justin's voice. 'We never even got out of the goddamned park. Ten thousand goddamn bucks.'

'It was so ... *real*,' said a voice that Disantis recognized as belonging to the airwaves minister. 'But surely there were no ... bullets.'

'Hell, no,' said Newton. ''Scuse me Reverend. But they couldn't use real slugs. Customers'd kill each other by mistake.'

'Then how ...'

'Lasered UV pulses,' said Justin.

'Triggered the charges under the skin.' said Newton. 'Easy to reset.'

'But the blood,' said Reverend Dewitt in the darkness. 'The ... the brain matter. The bone fragments ...'

'All right, already!' shouted Sayers so loudly that the other men shushed him. 'Come on, let's just say we got our money's worth, okay? They can buy a lot of spare parts for that much, right?'

'You can buy a lot of spare gooks for that much,' said Newton, and there was a ripple of laughter. 'Jesus,' he went on, 'did you see that good girl wiggle when Jeffries slipped it to her the first time ...?

Disantis listened for a few minutes more and then went into his room and carefully closed the sliding door.

The morning was beautiful, with tall, white clouds piled up above the sea to the east when the family had a leisurely breakfast on the restaurant terrace. Sammee and Elizabeth had eggs, toast, and cereal. Heather ordered an omelet. Disantis had coffee. Justin joined them late, cradled his head in his hands, and ordered a Bloody Mary. 'You came in late last night, dear.' said Heather.

Justin massaged his temples. 'Yeah. Tom and some of us went to the gaming rooms and played poker 'til late.'

'You missed the excitement this morning. Dad,' said Sammee.

'Yeah, what?' Justin sipped at his drink and grimaced.

'They arrested Mr. Minh this mornin',' Sammee said happily.

'Oh?' Justin looked at his wife.

'It's true, dear,' said Heather. 'He was arrested this morning. Something to do with illegal contraband in his luggage.'

'Yeah,' said Sammee. 'I heard the guy downstairs tellin' somebody that he had a rifle. You know, like ours, only *real.*'

'Well, I'll be damned,' said Justin. 'Is he going to stand trial or what?'

'No,' said Disantis. 'They just asked him to leave. They shipped him out on the morning shuttle to Tokyo.'

'There's a lot of nuts around,' muttered Justin. he opened the menu. 'I think I will have breakfast. Do we have time before the morning tour?'

'Oh, yes,' said Heather. 'The helicopters don't leave until ten-thirty this morning. We're going up the river somewhere. Dad says that it should be very interesting.'

'I think all this junk is *boring,*' whined Elizabeth.

'That's 'cause you think *every*thing's boring, stupid,' said Sammee.

'Be quiet, both of you,' said Heather. 'We're here for your grandfather's benefit. Eat your cereal!'

The twenty-eight Huey gunships moved out in single file, climbed above the line of trees, and sorted themselves into formation as they leveled off at three thousand feet. The panorama of highways and housing developments beneath them changed to rice paddies and jungle as they entered the park. Then they were over the river and heading west. Peasants poling small craft upstream looked up and waved as shadows of the gunships passed over them.

Disantis sat in the open door, hands hooked in the safety webbing, and let his legs dangle. On his back was Sammee's blue backpack. Justin dozed on a cushioned bench. Elizabeth sat on Heather's lap and complained of the heat. Sammee swung the heavy M-60 to the left and right and made machine-gun noises. The guide plugged his microphone into the bulkhead. 'Ladies and gentlemen, today we are on a mission up the Mekong River. Our goal is twofold — to intercept illicit river traffic and to inspect any area of jungle near Highway 1 where movement of NVA regulars has been reported. Following completion of the mission, we will tour an eight-hundred-year-old Buddhist temple. Lunch will be served after the temple tour.'

The helicopter throbbed north and westward. Elizabeth complained that she was hungry. Reverend Dewitt tried to get everyone to sing camp songs, but few people were interested. Tom Newton pointed out several historical landmarks to his wife. Justin awoke briefly, shot a series of images with his Nikon, and then went back to sleep.

Sometime later the guide broke the silence. 'Please watch the river as we turn south. We will be searching for any small boats which look suspicious or attempt to flee at our approach. We should see the river in the next few minutes.'

'No, we won't,' said Disantis. He reached under his flow-ered shirt and removed the heavy .45 from his waistband. He aimed it at the guide's face and held it steady. 'Please ask the pilot to turn north.'

The cabin resounded with babble and then fell silent as the guide smiled. 'A joke, Mr. Disantis, but not a funny one, I am afraid. Please let me see the ...'

Disantis fired. The slug ripped through the bulkhead pad-ding three centimeters from the guide's face. People screamed, the guide flinched and raised his hands instinctively, and Disan-tis swung his legs into the cabin. 'North, please,' he said. 'Immediately.'

The guide spoke quickly into his microphone, snapped two monosyllabic answers to unheard questions from the pilot, and the Huey swung out of formation and headed north.

'*Daddy*,' said Heather.

'What the fuck do you think you're doing, Ralph?' said Justin. 'Now give me that goddamn relic before someone gets ...'

'Shut up,' said Disantis.

'Mr Disantis,' said Reverend Dewitt, 'you know, there are women and children aboard this aircraft. If we could just talk about whatever ...'

'Put the damn gun down, Ralph,' growled Justin and began to rise from the bench.

'Be quiet.' Disantis swung the pistol in Justin's direction, and the big man froze in mid-movement. 'The next person to speak will be shot.'

Sammee opened his mouth, looked at his grandfather's face,

and remained silent. For several minutes the only sound was the throb of the rotors and Heather's soft weeping.

'Take it down here,' Disantis said at last. he had been watching the jungle, making sure they were well out of the park. 'Here.'

The guide paused and then spoke rapid-fire Vietnamese into his mike. The Huey began to descend, circling in toward the clearing Disantis had pointed to. He could see two black Saigon Security Hovercraft coming quickly from the east, the down blast of their fans ripping the leave canopy of the jungle as they roared ten meters above it.

The Huey's skids touched down, and the high grass rippled and bent from the blast of the rotors.

'Come on, kids,' said Disantis. He moved quickly, helping Elizabeth out and then tugging Sammee from his perch before Heather could grab him. Disantis jumped down beside them.

'The *hell* you say,' bellowed Justin and vaulted down.

Disantis and the children had moved a few feet and were crouching in the whipping grass. Disantis half-turned and shot Justin in the left leg. The force of the blow swung the big man around. He fell back toward the open doorway as people screamed and reached for him.

'This is real,' Disantis said softly. 'Goodbye.' He fired twice past the cockpit windshield. Then he took Elizabeth by the hand and pulled her toward the jungle as the helicopter lifted off. A multitude of hands pulled Justin in the open door as the Huey swung away over the trees.

Sammee hesitated for a moment, looked at the empty sky, and then stumbled after his sister and grandfather. The boy was sobbing uncontrollably.

'Hush,' said Disantis and pulled Sammee inside the wall of vegetation. There was a narrow trail extending into the jungle darkness. Disantis removed the light backpack and took out a new clip for the automatic. He ejected the old magazine and clicked the new one in with a slap of his palm. Then he grabbed both children and moved as quickly as he could in a counter-clockwise jog around the perimeter of the clearing, always remaining concealed just within the jungle. When they stopped he pushed the children down behind a fallen tree. Elizabeth began to wail. 'Hush,' Disantis said softly.

The Huey gunship came in quickly, the guide leaped to the ground, and then the helicopter was spiraling upward again, clawing for altitude. A second later the first of the Saigon Security Hovercraft roared in over the treetops and settled next to the guide. The two men who jumped out wore black armor cloth and carried Uzi miniguns. The guide pointed to the spot on the opposite side of the clearing where Disantis had first entered the jungle.

They lifted their weapons and took a step in that direction. Disantis walked out behind them, dropped to one knee when he got to within five meters, braced the pistol with both hands, and fired as they turned. He shot the first policeman in the face. The second man had time to raise his gun before he was struck twice in the chest. The bullets did not penetrate the armor cloth, but the impact knocked him onto his back. Disantis stepped forward, straightened his arm, and shot the man in the left eye.

The guide turned and ran into the jungle. Disantis fired once and then crouched next to the dead policeman as a wash of hot air struck him. The Hovercraft was ten meters high and turning toward the trees when Disantis lifted the policeman's Uzi and fired. he did not bother to aim. The Minigun kicked and flared, sending two sousand fléchettes a second skyward. Disantis had a brief glimpse of the pilot's face before the entire canopy starred and burst into white powder. The Hovercraft listed heavily to the left and plowed into the forest wall. There was the heavy sound of machinery and trees breaking but no explosion.

Disantis ran back to the jungle just as the second Hovercraft appeared. It circled once and then shot straight up until it was lost in the sun. Disantis grabbed the children and urged them on, circling the edge of the clearing again until they reached the spot where the guide had entered the forest. The narrow trail led away from the light into the jungle.

Disantis crouched for a second and then touched the high grass at the side of the trail. Drops of fresh blood were visible in the dappled light. Disantis sniffed at his fingers and looked up at the white faces of Sammee and Elizabeth. They had stopped crying. "It's all right," he said, and his voice was soft and soothing. Behind them and above them there were the sounds of rotors and engines. Gently, ever so gently, he turned the children and began leading them, unresisting, along the path into the jungle. It was darker there, quiet and cool. The way was marked with crimson. The children moved quickly to keep up with their grandfather.

'It's all right,' he whispered and touched their shoulders lightly to guide them down the narrowing path. 'Everything's all right. I know the way.'

FELIX C. GOTSCHALK

Felix Gotschalk sold his first story in 1968. 'One hundred stories in twenty years,' he says. That story has yet to appear, in Harlan Ellison's *Last Dangerous Visions*, and so his first published story was 'Bonus Baby' in David Gerrold's anthology *Science Fiction Emphasis 1* (1974). (*Science Fiction Emphasis 2* has also yet to appear.) The following year, he was a finalist for the John W. Campbell Award as best new writer, and he came a close second. (The winner was P.J. Plauger, of whom it has been said: '?')

Gotschalk grew up in Richmond, Virginia and is the author of the novel *Growing up in Tier 3000* (1975). Although he also wrote and sold two other novels, these were never published. He now lives in North Carolina, and he took early retirement to concentrate on writing and studying classical music. His ambition is to be a concert pianist, even though he is starting late; but he also started writing late, so who is to say that he won't succeed?

His distinctive short stories have enlivened the pages of various magazines and series such as *Orbit* and *New Dimensions*, and have been nominated for both the Hugo and the Nebula awards. Gotschalk describes his fiction as 'a mix of military sf and hedonistic gimcrackery' — a perfect example of which is the story that follows.

MENAGE A SUPER-TROIS
by
FELIX C. GOTSCHALK

Mary Claire had adjusted the scale of the pnemoplastic panda from kitten-size back up to about three hundred simulated, roly-poly-pounds, and was coaxing it to jump up on the somnamb chaise, where I lay, supine, naked, and fish-belly vulnerable. Tiffany lay beside me, and she leaned over to kiss my umbilical invagination, and giggled a falsetto in her laryngeal transducer. In all my fifty calendrical tiers of life on Earth, I, Andrew Jackson Dalton, Brigadier General of the Armies (Retired), had never felt genuinely godlike until these two angels had been awarded to me after the victory I master-minded in the brief Germanic War of the year 2014. The West Germans had been actively planning for war since 1945 (like the Israelis, Teutonic tribes are historically warlike), and the United States had grown fat and indolent, then overly depen-dent on both foreign imports and foreign capital, and finally insolvent. The landlocked Germans wanted the geographic bedrock security of the U.S. continent, protected, as it was, on both coasts by great oceans, and since there were already millions of sympathetic Aryans here — 'Jesu Christus!' Tiffany squealed, as Mary Claire mounted the panda and levitated up over us, riding the massive, cuddly beastie like a broncobuster. Tiffany rolled on top of me, in a marvelously mock gesture of protectiveness; then she fitted herself to me, and my command-level shaft grew up into her velvety biohuman folds. She activated her deep constrictors; and I felt sacrally welded to her.

'Libertine!' Mary Claire hissed playfully to Tiffany, her green eyes flashing, her perfect lips puckered and parted to reveal perfectly teeth. She looked like Linda Evans as a young girl.

'All's fair,' Tiffany laughed, burrowing her Stephanie Powers face in my neck, but Mary Claire lowered down on us, like the nude on the Warhol walrus, and settled the giant furry

panda on Tiffany, ventral over dorsal, adjusting the graviton
field so that the net weight of beast and rider served to deepen
my penetration. It was an extra-phylum ménage à quatre of the
most extraordinary sui generis sort, though the panda was
along just for the ride, hah hah hah. *Young flesh* — all men my
age want it, and those who can afford it will line up at the
market to buy it by the pound. However, The Coolidge Effect
can be dangerously sweet agony at my age, and I did not feel up
to trying for a third orgasm that night.

Tiffany was making little raspberry-erucative noises with
her mouth resting on my starboard neck, the panda was nuzz-
ling me on the port side, and then Mary Claire bent down and
fastened her perfect mouth on mine. With the greatest
volitional effort, I bio-fed detumescence, and my staunchly
heroic pillar of blood softened and retracted. Tiffany pouted in
her own charming way, Mary Claire dematerialized the panda,
and my two angels snuggled against me, like the uncondition-
ally adoring pets they were. God, could any man, living or
dead, be as happy as I? No, for I had fulfilled that most elusive
of man's dreams: *polygamy with two optimally programmed
females; interaction on demand with two perfect women.* I had
fought the good fight in the 2014 war, though all I really did
was scramble the telemetry of the German launch system with
an EMP, the energy fusing every transistor in every silo; but it
saved the good old U.S.A., restored its fiscal solvency, and I
retired from military service as a brigadier, with a pension
worth about $250K a year, not including perks and fringes and
escalators.

Mary Claire and Tiffany were genetically engineered bio-
human females (God, no words can describe their excellence),
given to me by T. Bone Pickens III, who as the planet's first
trillionaire, and whose business interests I saved. He put it this
way: '... you saved all our asses, Andy, and you deserve the
best. These here two supergals are the most expensive virgins
on the planet, and I want you to have 'em boaf....' And so I
was living with two angels. I *owned* them.

Things had been going well for so long that I had begun to
take my omniscience, omnipotence, and omnipresence for
granted. Everything I did reinforced my power, and, after all,

power is the ultimate aphrodisiac. Mary Claire's and Tiffany's perfection could never have existed in mere humans: the flexible dimensions of their personalities and the bionic parameters of their physiologies were exquisitely programmed, so that, at a confidence level of .001 or so, I could expect them to speak and act with all but infallible appropriateness. And the control systems — the *power* — were all mine, for the girls were pairbonded to me through pheromonal interfacing, activated by my double-helix DNA thumbprint pressure on their life-support bezels, which were beautifully cosmetized and set on the velvety expanses of their perfect abdomens. Once extruded by my print, it was like dialing the secret combination of a complex safe, and I could rheostat either or both girls into any one of ten different, metabolically cued behavioral regimens. Within themselves, the ten programs seemed infinitely responsive to my inputs, so that I could replicate (or invent at will) interactions of the most distinctive sorts. I had to be careful, though, because Mary Claire and Tiffany had kinetic implants that gave them great strength, and if I wanted to slap them around (which, surprisingly enough, had occurred to me), their bezels would have to be set at low centile QUIESCENT levels, never — *never* at, say, an ALPHA MANIC level. Because of my DNA coded access, I could never be cuckolded (how many men could boast of that?), but primogeniture rights were another matter, as I was about to find out.

'Well, *owl-shit*, Andy,' T. Bone Pickens III bawled out at me, as he sprawled, intoxicated, in a fine chamois chaise. 'I *gave* them gals to you. Cost me a bundle, too, Least you can do is let me fuck 'em.' The ninety-seven-year-old Pickens, had teleported to my Malibu condo all the way from St. Moritz, and had been popping frozen tequila and grapefruit juice pellets and stroking Tiffany's flanks. He was acting like the girls were his property. To be safe, I put both the girls on a centile 10 QUIESCENT setting. Tiffany was smiling, uneasily, like a child being petted by an ugly great-grandfather, and Mary Claire was standing beside me, like an obedient daughter. I wanted to get rid of Bone before he made any rash moves on the girls.

'Now, Bone, you know the girls wouldn't go along with that.

They're pair-bonded to me for life.'

'Thissun here doan seem to mind getting' her laigs felt up
—,'

'Are you my great-grandfather?' Tiffany asked, moving free
of Bone's touch. There was a subtle stria of anger in her soft
voice. Bone roared with drunken laughter.

'Is *that* what General Andy told you!' He cocked his melon
face up at me and leered asymmetrically. He was wearing a
twenty-inch waxed handlebar mustache and a 20X Beaver
Stetson. 'Yeah, gal, I'm your original Big Daddy. Come and sit
on your daddy's lap.'

'I must tell you, sir, that I find your familiarity offensive.'
Tiffany turned icy, and I winced. I didn't want to appear
ungrateful to Bone, but then I hadn't seen him in two years,
and he wasn't a personal friend. Of course he was my bene-
factor; a very powerful man, who had given me a priceless gift,
but he was beginning to offend me now. Funny things about
personal offense at the hands of a celebrity — people are afraid
to counter it. Sometimes it's fear and sometimes it's — shit, I
don't know what it is. I put the girls on nonverbal.

'Hey, gal.' Bone's voice grated deep in his laryngeal reson-
ator. 'You love your Great-Grand-Pappy, don't you? You come
on over here.' The girls were silent and still in the face of the
aged magnate's confident order.

'Go to your chambers, girls,' I said, in a moderate
command-voice, and they left, like graceful robots. I irised the
remote in my chairarm and keyed in light somnolence for both.
Bone started to rise up out of the chaise, but then he made a
clumsy gesture of dismissal, and sank back into the depths of
the orthopedically responsive surfaces.

'You gettin' soft, Andy,' he grumbled. 'A general should
ought to have better control over his troops.' It was a funny
thing to say after such a prompt display of obedience to my
command, but I knew what he really meant.

'It's for your own well-being, Bone.' I tried not to sound
patronizing. 'Those girls are strong as tigers. They might have
injured you if you had made any big moves on them.' This
didn't seem to satisfy him.

'Are you tellin' me you can't control 'em?' God, but the man was acting casually proprietary, even baitingly proprietarian. He was starting to piss me off.

'I have total control over their interactions with *me*, because of the DNA interfacing. How they interact with strangers is another matter.'

'Well, for the 25 million old United States dollars I gave for that pair of factory females, I sure don't feel like no stranger. And I never got to screw 'em, neither. I should have screwed 'em before I gave 'em to you. Broke 'em in right. You got to break women the way you break hosses.'

'Hey, they're my property, Bone, remember? You gave them to me because I saved your trillionaire ass, as I remember you saying it.' I was feeling protective of the girls and territorial about my condo.

'Now, don't go gettin' your hackles up, Andy. I ain't no Indian giver. I'm just used to having my way with young gals. I thought you and me and the two frisky fillies might have us a four-way orgy — you know, a real *kwottra may-nodge*. What say?' I was starting to shake my head, when the creaking old codger popped yet another tequila blatter, this time right into his corded carotid, and then he passed out, muttering, 'Cherrl Tiegs and Christina Ferrare — I'll go get them instead —'

A man of Pickens's stature does not travel alone, or so I would have thought, though with a teleporter, he probably would not be in any danger. His burnished silver Benz hung in the stasis field outside the visoport, and as I went to see if there was a pilot or a bodyguard in the craft, a basketball-sized *extremis* robot (we called them Flying ParaMeds) egressed from it and set an azimuth straight for Bone, apparently activated by his unconsciousness. Spidery extremities telescoped from its surfaces as the robot landed on Bone's chest, and, like fine calipers, the arms irised his tunic and ratcheted onto the rim of his lifesystems bezel. His face was ashen, and it dawned on me that he might be in genuine *extremis*, in addition to being drunk. And then I thought, Hell, a man shouldn't die just seconds after being rejected by a beautiful woman. Morbid or not, a man ought to die in the arms of at least one beautiful woman; ideally, conduited into her, and of course, orgasm as the 'sweet death' was a supremely apt metaphor.

So I keyed the remote again, and summoned Mary Claire and Tiffany. I set their bezels at centile 80 HYPER-VIGILANCE and EMPATHY, and told them to stay close to their great-granddaddy, and to do anything to comfort him while I located his executor. So, as the Flying ParaMed sphere shored up his vital signs, and the girls held his hands and whispered sweet assurances close in his ears, I got a hot-line computer flash over to Bone's world offices in the Dallas Dome, and within minutes a sophisticated hospital ship was in the field beside the Benz, and real-life ParaMeds and physicians were attending the stricken man.

The executor was there also — a short, bald, nondescript-looking man of forty or so, with a timid facial expression, and wearing a stock IBM dark blue suit, white shirt, and paisley cravat. Aside from his facial cast, he looked jurisprudential enough, and he was immediately taken with the girls, eyeing them almost hungrily, and paying only passing attention to the medical team and the victim. The team got Bone encased in an oxygen envelope, like a bug in amber, and floated him out and onto the ship. He looked waxen and gray and dead to me. The sphere was still affixed to his abdomen, and there was an intravene in his nose, and one in the carotid, where the tequila shooter had been just minutes before. The screen on the sphere was pulsing with patterns, but none of them had good Gaussian peaks, and I thought Bone must be at least clinically dead.

Everybody left but the executor, whose name was Winfield Blackwell, and he couldn't take his eyes off the girls, who were acting like the most demure geisha. With a great effort, Blackwell turned his attention to me, extracting a depositional audile cube from his thoracic niche. With a little flourish, he placed it on my favorite stressed lucoid coffee table, and the device glowed tiny bright pulses as he spoke. 'We'll keep this informal, General Dalton, though it is merely a formality — um.' He blushed, realizing he had made a self-canceling sentence, and looked at the girls as if their presence rendered him both inarticulate as well as blissful. 'That is to say, I need a deposition, a brief account of what happened this afternoon. I do not feel it necessary to summon the provost robots.'

Deposition has a decidedly legalistic ring to it,' I said, and the cube sparked in response to my voice, 'but I have no objection.'

'I just *love* barristers,' Tiffany interrupted — inappropriately for her regimen, I thought, but then, she was less predictable than Mary Claire. She sat down on the chaise next to the executor, and gave him a look that might have turned any man into a pile of dumb, smiling jelly.

'Barristers are wonderfully authoritarian,' Mary Claire chimed in, sitting close on his other side. 'I do believe I love barristers best, and perhaps, stuntmen a distant second.' This was an overly candid remark for her to make, for Mary Claire was usually reserved within the parameters of her programs.

'Do you now?' the executor beamed. 'It happens that *I* love, above all, beautiful young maidens. Wherever did you come by these delightful angels, General? Or have you set them on me for a purpose?' I suppose that attorneys have to deal with strategic distractions of all kinds, but I hadn't intended the girls as such, beyond my usual pleasure in watching them interact with strangers. Somehow they were acting overly operant, rather than responsive, but I decided not to change their settings.

'Mr. Pickens gave them to me, as it happens,' I said, 'in appreciation of my role in averting the Germanic Wars. And no, I did not set them on you. They are charmingly interactive on their own.' The man looked hugely pleased.

'And what are your names, my dual enchantresses?' he asked, settling back on the chaise and putting a tentative arm around their shoulders. I hoped the high empathy settings would discourage the girls from resisting this mild intrusion of their life-space.

'I'm Tiffany Mitsu-Dalton, and this is my sister-surrogate, Mary Claire Mitsu-Dalton.' Tiffany tossed her head in that special way she had. It was indescribable, and breathtaking to behold.

'*Mitsubishi*,' I put in. 'Tiffany and Mary Claire were, ah, engineered at the Mitsubishi plant in Ann Arbor.' Tiffany looked at the man and licked her lips. 'Yes. I am told that that one plant alone saved the entire Michigan economy —'

'The Illinois and Indiana economies as well,' Mary Claire said brightly. 'What those hordes of bowing little Nissan men spent on us was more than enough to turn the tide.'

'Yes. We're the world's two most expensive Barbie dolls,' Tiffany giggled. 'And Andy here — Brigadier Andrew — is our very own Ken.'

'The brigadier is a fortunate man indeed,' Blackwell began, and then he looked very uncool and unable to continue. 'Ah, General. Either I must forgo my duties, and yield to the power of these lovely girls, or —'

'We'll leave,' Mary Claire said, and she and Tiffany got up, like sleek leopards in playful estrous postures. Sometimes I wondered if I really controlled them.

'But aren't we suppose to give depositions, too?' Tiffany was brushing her ecru-mesh shift with her hands, and Blackwell was slack-faced and gaping. The girls' pheromonal auras were strong, and I liked that, though it was contextually distracting. I liked high copulin counts in any context.

'Did either of you witness Mr. Pickens's attack?' the executor asked.

'No,' Mary Claire answered him. 'Andy sent us to our room just before it happened.' He looked interested and a bit more serious.

'Were there, um, extenuating circumstances? Did either of you do anything to precipitate —'

'Quite the contrary,' I said emphatically. 'I had the girls leave because the old man wanted to have sex with them. He had had several tequila shots and was becoming offensive. The girls would have resisted his advances, and might have injured him. I should tell you that Mary Claire and Tiffany have kinetic fulcrum implants that give them great physical strength.'

'And Tiffany and I are pair-bonded to Andy,' Mary Claire said, sounding proud and protective and sexy all at once. 'We could never be intimate with anyone else.' Now Blackwell looked at the girls more appraisingly, and turned crestfallen. I think he may have thought them to be secret hookers, and me maybe a rich closet pimp.

'Very well,' he said, and his voice was a bit snobby and affected. 'My next question is an important one: Did Mister Pickens touch either of you in an intimate manner?' The man's old-style wristwatch beeper emitted a 120-cycle sound, and he pressed the device close to his ear. After a few seconds he acknowledged the transmission, and shifted the depositional cube, as if he were stalling for time. Finally he said, 'Mr. Pickens is dead, I am sorry to say.' But he didn't seem sorry — he seemed relieved. 'My question is therefore of the utmost importance: Was Mr. Pickens engaged in any degree of excitatory sexual foreplay immediately preceding his attack?' Mary Claire stooped to arrange some orchids in a vase, and Tiffany rubbed her flanks and tossed her head.

'He was stroking my thighs,' she said.

'And did you, um, encourage him?'

'Heavens, no. The old man told me he was my great-grand-father, and I thought it proper to let him touch me, but then he got overly familiar, and I felt offended. That's when Andrew asked Mary Claire and me to leave the room.' The executor suddenly deactivated the cube, like a chess judge hitting a timer.

'General, is this room equipped with, um, documentary video? Was Mr. Pickens's, um, visit, *recorded?*'

'Affirmative to both questions. The video system is activated by a DNA field not interfacing with our domestic, ah, ménage.'

'Which means everybody except the three of us,' Tiffany said, touching the man's thigh with one beautifully manicured fingernail. 'We're all on camera at this moment.' She looked at one of the camera lenses and waved.

'I don't see why not. Say, what's this all about?'

'I bet I know,' Mary Claire said. 'And so does Tiffany.'

'Well, I'm just a retired old warhorse,' I said. 'Tell me the big secret.'

Instead of coming to me, Mary Claire went to Blackwell, and whispered in his ear. Even in the mysterious context of the moment, the girls were acting like playful kittens, and the air was sparkling with their scents. Blackwell's nostrils flared in the richness of Mary Claire's close proximity, and then he smiled and nodded. Tiffany came to me in a panthery-graceful glide, sat on my lap, wreathed her perfect arms around my neck, and whispered in my ear. And I smiled and nodded. She looked into my eyes, and, God, my eyeballs rattled in their sockets. There were times when I felt Tiffany could induce a spontaneous orgasm in me with her eye contact alone. Then the four of us looked at each other in silence. I thought it proper for Blackwell to speak first.

'Your beautiful wards are correct, it seems,' he began. 'Mr. Pickens was a grand eccentric, and, among other things, he relished the company of young girls. His will specifies generous bequests to the female who happened to be with him *in extremis*. Contingent on my review of the tape, it appears that Miss Tiffany will be a beneficiary.'

'That's just *marvy*,' Tiffany piped. 'I'm going to buy Andrew something just shamelessly expensive. Let me think. Mary Claire, does Andrew have any more of those Bergdorf boxers? You know, the ones with the brigadier star by the fly?' Blackwell smiled at me, a Cheshire smile, and I laughed, tolerantly.

'We'll have to look and see,' Mary Claire said. 'But maybe he'd like one of those new pneumoplast *femmes de voyage* — say, the fifteen-thousand-dollar model — Angie, I believe she is called, and made by Nakajima, no less.'

'We're his $12 million models,' Tiffany said. 'He'd be disappointed with an inflatable woman.' Blackwell's pupils were dilated, his face was flushed, and despite the fact that his role was ostensibly serious, or at least restrained, he seemed mesmerized by my two angels, and unconcerned over the death of his client. There was surely incongruity on all sides: the man responsible for my godlike stature in life had died in my house, and no one seemed to care. Then I realized that Blackwell was probably rejoicing over the oppressive old magnate's death, and that Mary Claire and Tiffany, being strangers to him, had no reason to grieve; indeed, Tiffany had good reason to rejoice. It was me, General Andy, who felt some sympathy for Bone, for he had been very old and full of life-support prostheses, and I was just beginning to feel the first subtle heraldings of the aging process. Fifty years of the earth's gravity, and all the cumulative, fuel-fed metabolizing and cell dividing within my body had made me aware of my mortality, even as my two angelic wards reinforced my polar feelings of immortality. And so I said something light, too.

'The stars on some of my shorts *are* threadbare, my lovelies, but an inflatable woman! That would be a gag gift of the first order.'

'Seriously, for a moment.' Tiffany surprised me yet again. 'We may be confusing contiguity with causality here. Mr. Pickens may have been *feelin' my laigs up*, as he put it, and he may have been stricken thirty seconds later, but that doesn't make me responsible for his death. I do not wish to be on record as the agent of his demise.'

'The tequila blatter he shot in his carotid was the obvious cause,' I reassured her. 'I'd take a bet that was the proximal cause. But, my dear, the will does seem to want to tag you as the distal cause.'

The executor said, 'Thankfully, we need not deal with the concept of legal culpability here, Miss Tiffany. Even as a barrister, I find affixation of blame an invidious subject, though I must deal with it all the time. Let me just tell you that if Mr. Pickens had been stricken at Hollywood and Vine at high noon, and a malodorous bag lady had tried mouth-to-mouth resuscitation on him, she would have been the beneficiary, capricious as it may seem.' He seemed pleased with his crude little example, and now a faint predatory look eased into his expression. 'In any case, I should much prefer dealing with lovely ladies such as surround me now.' He was building up to something, and the girls were hypervigilant. 'And so, in my role as trustee of the several millions to be awarded in this case, I think it only fair that I be awarded some conjugal access to Miss —' I guess he was going to say 'Tiffany,' but instead he said something like 'AARRGH!' and pitched forward onto the resilent shag mesh of the deck.

Tiffany must have been reading his mind, and I knew immediately what she had done to him: she had vectored in a stunbolt, a high-voltage, low-amperage shock, to his rib box; a true proximal cause of great thoracic pain, excruciatingly related to body position and respiration, and perfectly replicating the viral attack symptomatology known as 'Devil's Grip.' I guess I should have known the man would make his move sooner or later, and, while what Tiffany did to him might be disproportionate to the offense, it beat the hell out of her using her kinetic implant on him. What she had effected was a simulated attack of a viral condition known since the 1880s, and very appropriately titled. Who can know the wiles and the powers of a suprahuman female? I do and I don't.

'Why, whatever is the matter, Winfield, dear?' Mary Claire cooed to him, as he lay with his shiny bald head in her lap. She bent to whisper the same kinds of assurances in his ear that she had so recently whispered to his deceased client, while Tiffany put her perfect lips to his temple 'to see if you're feverish,' she said. Even in his pain he looked blissful, there in the arms of the girls. But Tiffany wasn't finished. She loosened his cravat, defluxed the vertical velour facing of his tunic (rather unIBM-like, I thought), and gently parted it, exposing his life-systems bezel. *And as she did so, her movements were those of a lover, not a ministering angel of mercy.* She lowered her face to examine the bezel, and her movements were stunningly like those of a lover hovering to kiss the navel as a prelude to kissing the genitals.

'Does your bezel take standard diagnostic templates?' she asked him in a soft voice, and she might just as well have been asking him if is piston would fit in her cylinder. He nodded, smiled, and closed his eyes, as Mary Claire stroked the sides of his face. I knew Tiffany's plan (or thought I did), so I got the first-aid cassette fro the console extracted a Blue Cross energic-diagnostic template, and handed it to her. She gave me a beautifully knowing look. She fitted the template, lovingly, down into the combinatory serrates in the face of the bezel, and keyed in the probes. In just thirty seconds the tiny tape extruded, and she removed it and handed it to me. I put it in the viewer, and it read:

VIRAL NEURALGIA/DEVIL'S GRIP (ARCHAIC)
BLUE CROSS CODE 338 41 104110
TREATMENT: 120 MG DARVOCET/GENERIC
BED REST/SEXUAL ABSTINENCE

Tiffany touched the painkiller pellet to Blackwell's lips, like a courtesan feeding an emperor a grape, and Mary Claire had him take it with a thimbleful of cognac. 'When I die,' he whispered to them, 'I want it to be like this.' I sent him home in the

Benz. I had never seen a man in pain happier.

The inquest on T. Bone Pickens III was routine, and we did not have to attend. The cause of death was given as massive cardiac arrest, secondary alcoholic anoxia, and tertiary testosteronic surge. Tiffany was awarded $112.8 million new United States dollar-credits, and said that Mary Claire and I could have as much of it as we wanted. By God, generosity may be the finest trait for a woman to have! And, true to her word, Tiffany bought me four dozen pairs of shamelessly expensive Bergdorf boxers, each set emblazoned with the single silver star of my rank.

Instead of the gag-gift inflatable woman, Mary Claire presented me with four dozen matching Bergdorf T-shirts, each emblazoned with a holographic image of my face, flanked by images of herself and Tiffany, and, underneath the entablature: MÉNAGE Á SUPER-TROIS. Then they wanted me to strip on the spot and model the new underwear for them. Tiffany pinched me on the dextral gluteus as I was standing on one leg, stepping into the sinistral side of the one-star, commandlevel boxers. I must remember to triple-check her programming one day. It often suggests a damnably unnatural spontaneity, no less fresh and charming, but lacking in deference to my rank. Then I thought, Jesus Christ at The War College, if she could induce a testosteronic surge in a ninety-seven-year-old man, she must be able to override her programming.

Everything I do reinforces my godlike powers. And, since I am God, I think I will adjust my angels' pheromonal clouds to, say, centile 95, and fly with them over to Catalina for the weekend. Heaven can wait. Hey, they're dancing around me and singing. '. . . He is the Very Model of a Modern Briggy General. . . .' God, I love bio-human females.

Pat Murphy's first short story was published in 1979, and her first novel, *The Shadow Hunter*, followed three years later. In 1987 her second novel appeared, as did the following story.

The novel was *The Falling Woman*, which won the 1988 Nebula. 'Rachel in Love' did the same, winning as best novelette; it also topped the poll to win the same category in *Isaac Asimov's Science Fiction Magazine*'s Readers Awards; and it has been nominated for a Hugo.

The editor of *Exploratorium Quarterly*, a magazine published by San Francisco's museum of science, art and human perception, Murphy is currently completing her third novel. Based on the novelette of the same name published in *Universe 14*, its working title is *Art in the War Zone*.

RACHEL IN LOVE
by
PAT MURPHY

It is a Sunday morning in summer and a small brown chimpanzee named Rachel sits on the living room floor of a remote ranch house on the edge of the Painted Desert. She is watching a Tarzan movie on television. Her hairy arms are wrapped around her knees and she rocks back and forth with suppressed excitement. She knows that her father would say that she's too old for such childish amusements — but since Aaron is still sleeping, he can't chastise her.

On the television, Tarzan has been trapped in a bamboo cage by a band of wicked Pygmies. Rachel is afraid that he won't escape in time to save Jane from the ivory smugglers who hold her captive. The movie cuts to Jane, who is tied up in the back of a jeep, and Rachel whimpers softly to herself. She knows better than to howl: she peeked into her father's bedroom earlier, and he was still in bed. Aaron doesn't like her to howl when he is sleeping.

When the movie breaks for a commercial, Rachel goes to her father's room. She is ready for breakfast and she wants him to get up. She tiptoes to the bed to see if he is awake.

His eyes are open and he is staring at nothing. His face is pale and his lips are a purplish color. Dr. Aaron Jacobs, the man Rachel calls father, is not asleep. He is dead, having died in the night of a heart attack.

When Rachel shakes him, his head rocks back and forth in time with her shaking, but his eyes do not blink and he does not breathe. She places his hand on her head, nudging him so that he will waken and stroke her. He does not move. When she leans toward him, his hand falls limply to dangle over the edge of the bed.

In the breeze from the open bedroom window, the fine wisps of grey hair that he had carefully combed over his bald spot each morning shift and flutter, exposing the naked scalp. In the other room, elephants trumpet as they stampede across the jungle to rescue Tarzan. Rachel whimpers softly, but her father does not move.

Rachel backs away from her father's body. In the living room, Tarzan is swinging across the jungle on vines, going to save Jane. Rachel ignores the television. She prowls through the house as if searching for comfort — stepping into her own small bedroom, wandering through her father's laboratory. From the cages that line the walls, white rats stare at her with hot red eyes. A rabbit hops across its cage, making a series of slow dull thumps, like a feather pillow tumbling down a flight of stairs.

She thinks that perhaps she made a mistake. Perhaps her father is just sleeping. She returns to the bedroom, but nothing has changed. Her father lies open-eyed on the bed. For a long time, she huddles beside his body, clinging to his hand.

He is the only person she has ever known. He is her father, her teacher, her friend. She cannot leave him alone.

The afternoon sun blazes through the window, and still Aaron does not move. The room grows dark, but Rachel does not turn on the light. She is waiting for Aaron to wait up. When the moon rises, its silver light shines through the window to cast a bright rectangle on the far wall.

Outside, somewhere in the barren rocky land surrounding the ranch house, a coyote lifts its head to the rising moon and wails, a thin sound that is as lonely as a train whistling through an abandoned station. Rachel joins in with a desolate howl of loneliness and grief. Aaron lies still and Rachel knows that he is dead.

When Rachel was younger, she had a favorite bedtime story. — Where did I come from? she would ask Aaron, using the abbreviated gestures of ASL, American Sign Language. — Tell me again.

'You're too old for bedtime stories,' Aaron would say.

— Please, she'd sign. — Tell me the story.

In the end, he always relented, and told her. 'Once upon a time, there was a little girl named Rachel,' he said. 'She was a pretty girl, with long golden hair like a princess in a fairy tale. She lived with her father and her mother and they were all very happy.'

Rachel would snuggle contentedly beneath her blankets. The

story, like any good fairy tale, had elements of tragedy. In the story, Rachel's father worked at a university, studying the workings of the brain and charting the electric fields that the nervous impulses of an active brain produced. But the other researchers at the university didn't understand Rachel's father; they distrusted his research and cut off his funding. (During this portion of the story, Aaron's voice took on a bitter edge.) So he left the university and took his wife and daughter to the desert, where he could work in peace.

He continued his research and determined that each individual brain produced its own unique pattern of fields, as characteristic as a fingerprint. (Rachel found this part of the story quite dull, but Aaron insisted on including it.) The shape of this 'Electric Mind,' as he called it, was determined by habitual patterns of thoughts and emotions. Record the Electric Mind, he postulated, and you could capture an individual's personality.

The one sunny day, the doctor's wife and beautiful daughter went for a drive. A truck barreling down a winding cliffside road lost its brakes and met the car head-on, killing both the girl and her mother. (Rachel clung to Aaron's hand during this part of the story, frightened by the sudden evil twist of fortune.)

But though Rachel's body had died, all was not lost. In his desert lab, the doctor had recorded the electrical patterns produced by his daughter's brain. The doctor had been experimenting with the use of external magnetic fields to impose the patterns from one animal onto the brain of another. From an animal supply house, he obtained a young chimpanzee. He used a mixture of norepinephrin-based transmitter substances to boost the speed of neural processing in the chimp's brain, and then he imposed the pattern of his daughter's mind upon the brain of this young chimp, combining the two after his own fashion, saving his daughter in his own way. In the chimp's brain was all that remained of Rachel Jacobs.

The doctor named the chimp Rachel and raised her as his own daughter. Since the limitations of the chimpanzee larynx made speech very difficult, he instructed her in ASL. He taught her to read and to write. They were good friends, the best of companions.

By this point in the story, Rachel was usually asleep. But it didn't matter — she knew the ending. The doctor, whose name was Aaron Jacobs, and the chimp named Rachel lived happily ever after.

Rachel likes fairy tales and she likes happy endings. She has the mind of a teenage girl, but the innocent heart of a young chimp.

Sometimes, when Rachel looks at her gnarled brown fingers, they seem alien, wrong, out of place. She remembers having small, pale, delicate hands. Memories lie upon memories, layers upon layers, like the sedimentary rocks of the desert buttes.

Rachel remembers a blonde-haired fair-skinned woman who smelled sweetly of perfume. On a Halloween long ago, this woman (who was, in these memories, Rachel's mother) painted Rachel's fingernails bright red because Rachel was dressed as a gypsy and gypsies liked red. Rachel remembers the woman's hands: white hands with faintly blue veins hidden just beneath the skin, neatly clipped nails painted rose pink.

But Rachel also remembers another mother and another time. Her mother was dark and hairy and smelled sweetly of overripe fruit. She and Rachel lived in a wire cage in a room filled with chimps and she hugged Rachel to her hairy breast whenever any people came into the room. Rachel's mother groomed Rachel constantly, picking delicately through her fur in search of lice that she never found.

Memories upon memories: jumbled and confused, like random pictures clipped from magazines, a bright collage that makes no sense. Rachel remembers cages: cold wire mesh beneath her feet, the smell of fear around her. A man in a white lab coat took her from the arms of her hairy mother and pricked her with needles. She could hear her mother howling, but she could not escape from the man.

Rachel remembers a junior high school dance where she wore a new dress: she stood in a dark corner of the gym for hours, pretending to admire the crepe paper decorations because she felt too shy to search among the crowd for her friends.

She remembers when she was a young chimp: she huddled with five other adolescent chimps in the stuffy freight compartment of a train, frightened by the alien smells and sounds.

She remembers gym class: gray lockers and ugly gym suits that revealed her skinny legs. The teacher made everyone play softball, even Rachel who was unathletic and painfully shy. Rachel at bat, standing at the plate, was terrified to be the center of attention. 'Easy out,' said the catcher, a hard-edged girl who ran with the wrong crowd and always smelled of cigarette smoke. When Rachel swung at the ball and missed, the outfielders filled the air with malicious laughter.

Rachel's memories are as delicate and elusive as the dusty moths and butterflies that dance among the rabbit brush and sage. Memories of her girlhood never linger; they land for an instant, then take flight, leaving Rachel feeling abandoned and alone.

Rachel leaves Aaron's body where it is, but closes his eyes and pulls the sheet up over his head. She does not know what else to do. Each day she waters the garden and picks some greens for the rabbits. Each day, she cares for the animals in the lab, bringing them food and refilling their water bottles. The weather is cool, and Aaron's body does not smell too bad, though by the end of the week, a wide line of ants runs from the bed to the open window.

At the end of the first week, on a moonlit evening, Rachel decides to let the animals go free. She releases the rabbits one by one, climbing on a stepladder to reach down into the cage and lift each placid bunny out. She carries each one to the back door, holding it for a moment and stroking the soft warm fur. Then she sets the animal down and nudges it in the direction of the green grass that grows around the perimeter of the fenced garden.

The rats are more difficult to deal with. She manages to wrestle the large rat cage off the shelf, but it is heavier than she thought it would be. Though she slows its fall, it lands on the floor with a crash and the rats scurry to and fro within. She shoves the cage across the linoleum floor, sliding it down the hall, over the doorsill, and onto the black patio. When she opens the cage door, rats burst out like popcorn from a popper, white in the moonlight and dashing in all directions.

Once, while Aaron was taking a nap, Rachel walked along the
dirt track that led to the main highway. She hadn't planned on
going far. She just wanted to see what the highway looked like,
maybe hide near the mailbox and watch a car drive past. She was
curious about the outside world and her fleeting fragmentary
memories did not satisfy that curiosity.

She was halfway to the mailbox when Aaron came roaring up
in his old jeep. 'Get in the car,' he shouted at her. 'Right now!'
Rachel had never seen him so angry. She cowered in the jeep's
passenger seat, covered with dust from the road, unhappy that
Aaron was so upset. He didn't speak until they got back to the
ranch house, and then he spoke in a low voice, filled with bitterness and suppressed rage.

'You don't want to go out there,' he said. 'You wouldn't like it
out there. The world is filled with petty, narrow-minded, stupid
people. They wouldn't understand you. And anyone they don't
understand, they want to hurt. They hurt anyone who's different. If they know that you're different, they punish you, hurt
you. They'd lock you up and never let you go.'

He looked straight ahead, staring through the dirty windshield. 'It's not like the shows on TV, Rachel,' he said in a softer
tone. 'It's not like the stories in books.'

He looked at her then and she gestured frantically. — I'm
sorry. I'm sorry.

'I can't protect you out there,' he said. 'I can't keep you safe.'
Rachel took his hand in both of hers. He relented then, stroking her head. 'Never do that again,' he said. 'Never.'

Aaron's fear was contagious. Rachel never again walked
along the dirt track and sometimes she had dreams about bad
people who wanted to lock her in a cage.

Two weeks after Aaron's death, a black-and-white police car
drives slowly up to the house. When the policemen knock on the
door, Rachel hides behind the couch in the living room. They
knock again, try the knob, then open the door, which she had left
unlocked.

Suddenly frightened, Rachel bolts from behind the couch,
bounding toward the back door. Behind her, she hears one man
yell, 'My God! It's a gorilla!'

By the time he pulls his gun, Rachel has run out the back door and away into the hills. From the hills she watches as an ambulance drives up and two men in white take Aaron's body away. Even after the ambulance and the police car drive away, Rachel is afraid to go back to the house. Only after sunset does she return.

Just before dawn the next morning, she wakens to the sound of a truck jouncing down the dirt road. She peers out of the window to see a pale green pickup. Sloppily stenciled in white on the door are the words: PRIMATE RESERACH CENTER. Rachel hesitates as the truck pulls up in front of the house. By the time she has decided to flee, two men are getting out of the truck. One of them carries a rifle.

She runs out of the back door and heads for the hills, but she is only halfway to hiding when she hears a sound like a sharp intake of breath and feels a painful jolt in her shoulder. Suddenly, her legs give way and she is tumbling backward down the sandy slope, dust coating her red-brown fur, her howl becoming a whimper, then fading to nothing at all. She falls into the blackness of sleep.

The sun is up. Rachel lies in a cage in the back of the pickup truck. She is partially conscious and she feels a tingling in her hands and feet. Nausea grips her stomach and bowels. Her body aches.

Rachel can blink, but otherwise she can't move. From where she lies, she can see only the wire mesh of the cage and the side of the truck. When she tries to turn her head, the burning in her skin intensifies. She lies still, wanting to cry out, but unable to make a sound. She can only blink slowly, trying to close out the pain. But the burning and nausea stay.

The truck jounces down a dirt road, then stops. It rocks as the men get out. The doors slam. Rachel hears the tailgate open.

A woman's voice: 'Is that the animal the County Sheriff wanted us to pick up?' A woman peers into the cage. She wears a white lab coat and her brown hair is tied back in a single braid. Around her eyes, Rachel can see small wrinkles, etched by years of living in the desert. The woman doesn't look evil. Rachel hopes that the woman will save her from the men in the truck.

'Yeah. It should be knocked out for at least another half hour. Where do you want it?'

'Bring it into the lab where we had the rhesus monkeys. I'll keep it there until I have an empty cage in the breeding area.'

Rachel's cage scrapes across the bed of the pickup. She feels each bump and jar as a new pain. The man swings the cage onto a cart and the woman pushes the cart down a concrete corridor. Rachel watches the walls pass just a few inches from her nose.

The lab contains rows of cages in which small animals sleepily move. In the sudden stark light of the overhead fluorescent bulbs, the eyes of white rats gleam red.

With the help of one of the men from the truck, the woman manhandles Rachel onto a lab table. The metal surface is cold and hard, painful against Rachel's skin. Rachel's body is not under her control; her limbs will not respond. She is still frozen by the tranquilizer, able to watch, but that is all. She cannot protest or plead for mercy.

Rachel watches with growing terror as the woman pulls on rubber gloves, and fills a hypodermic needle with a clear solution. 'Mark down that I'm giving her the standard test for tuberculosis; this eyelid should be checked before she's moved in with the others. I'll add thiabendazole to her feed for the next few days to clean out any intestinal worms. And I suppose we might as well de-flea her as well,' the woman says. The man grunts in response.

Expertly, the woman closes one of Rachel's eyes. With her open eye, Rachel watches the hypodermic needle approach. She feels a sharp pain in her eyelid. In her mind, she is howling, but the only sound she can manage is a breathy sign.

The woman sets the hypodermic aside and begins methodically spraying Rachel's fur with a cold, foul-smelling liquid. A drop strikes Rachel's eye and burns. Rachel blinks, but she cannot lift a hand to rub her eye. The woman treats Rachel with casual indifference, chatting with the man as she spreads Rachel's legs and sprays her genitals. 'Looks healthy enough. Good breeding stock.'

Rachel moans, but neither person notices. At last, they finish their torture, put her in a cage, and leave the room. She closes her eyes, and the darkness returns.

Rachel is dreaming. She is back at home in the ranch house. It is night and she is alone. Outside, coyotes yip and howl. The coyote is the voice of the desert, wailing as the wind wails when it stretches itself thin to squeeze through a crack between two boulders. The people native to this land tell tales of Coyote, a god who was a trickster, unreliable, changeable, mercurial.

Rachel is restless, anxious, unnerved by the howling of the coyotes. She is looking for Aaron. In the dream, she knows he is not dead, and she searches the house for him, wandering from his cluttered bedroom to her small room to the linoleum-tiled lab.

She is in the lab when she hears something tapping: a small dry scratching, like a wind-blown branch against the window, though no tree grows near the house and the night is still. Cautiously, she lifts the curtain to look out.

She looks into her own reflection: a pale oval face, long blonde hair. The hand that holds the curtain aside is smooth and white with carefully clipped fingernails. But something is wrong. Superimposed on the reflection is another face peering through the glass: a pair of dark brown eyes, a chimp face with red-brown hair and jug-handle ears. She sees her own reflection and she sees the outsider; the two images merge and blur. She is afraid, but she can't drop the curtain and shut the ape face out.

She is a chimp looking in through the cold, bright window-pane; she is a girl looking out; she is a girl looking in; she is an ape looking out. She is afraid and the coyotes are howling all around.

Rachel opens her eyes and blinks until the world comes into focus. The pain and tingling has retreated but she still feels a little sick. Her left eye aches. When she rubs it, she feels a raised lump on the eyelid where the woman pricked her. She lies on the floor of a wire mesh cage. The room is hot and the air is thick with the smell of animals.

In the cage beside her is another chimp, an older animal with scruffy dark brown fur. He sits with his arms wrapped around his knees, rocking back and forth, back and forth. His head is down. As he rocks, he murmurs to himself, a meaningless cooing that goes on and on. On his scalp, Rachel can see a gleam of metal: a permanently implanted electrode protrudes from a shaven patch. Rachel makes a soft questioning sound, but the other chimp will not look up.

Rachel's own cage is just a few feet square. In one corner is a bowl of monkey pellets. A water bottle hangs on the side of the cage. Rachel ignores the food, but drinks thirstily.

Sunlight streams through the windows, sliced into small sections by the wire mesh that covers the glass. She tests her cage door, rattling it gently at first, then harder. It is securely latched. The gaps in the mesh are too small to admit her hand. She can't reach out to work the latch.

The other chimp continues to rock back and forth. When Rachel rattles the mesh of her cage and howls, he lifts his head wearily and looks at her. His red-rimmed eyes are unfocused; she can't be sure he sees her.

— Hello, she gestures tentatively. — What's wrong?

He blinks at her in the dim light. — Hurt, he signs in ASL. He reaches up to touch the electrode, fingering skin that is already raw from repeated rubbing.

— Who hurt you? she asks. He stares at her blankly and she repeats the question. — Who?

— Men, he signs.

As if on cue, there is the click of a latch and the door to the lab opens. A bearded man in a white coat steps in, followed by a clean-shaven man in a suit. The bearded man seems to be showing the other man around the lab. '... only preliminary testing, so far,' the bearded man is saying. 'We've been hampered by a shortage of chimps trained in ASL.' The two men stop in front of the old chimp's cage. 'This old fellow is from the Oregon center. Funding for the language program was cut back and some of the animals were dispersed to other programs.' The old chimp huddles at the back of the cage, eyeing the bearded man with suspicion.

— Hungry? the bearded man signs to the old chimp. He holds up an orange where the old chimp can see it.

— Give orange, the old chimp gestures. He holds out his hand, but comes no nearer to the wire mesh than he must to reach the orange. With the fruit in hand, he retreats to the back of his cage.

The bearded man continues, 'This project will provide us with the first solid data on neural activity during use of sign language. But we really need greater access to chimps with advanced language skills. People are so damn protective of their animals.'

'Is this one of yours?' the clean-shaven man asks, pointing to Rachel. She cowers in the back of the cage, as far from the wire mesh as she can get.

'No, not mine. She was someone's household pet, apparently. The county sheriff had us pick her up.' The bearded man peers into her cage. Rachel does not move; she is terrified that he will somehow guess that she knows ASL. She stares at his hands and thinks about those hands putting an electrode through her skull. 'I think she'll be put in breeding stock,' the man says as he turns away.

Rachel watches them go, wondering at what terrible people these are. Aaron was right: they want to punish her, put an electrode in her head.

After the men are gone, she tries to draw the old chimp into conversation, but he will not reply. He ignores her as he eats his orange. Then he returns to his former posture, hiding his head and rocking himself back and forth.

Rachel, hungry despite herself, samples one of the food pellets. It has a strange medicinal taste, and she puts it back in the bowl. She needs to pee, but there is no toilet and she cannot escape the cage. At last, unable to hold it, she pees in one corner of the cage. The urine flows through the wire mesh to soak the litter below, and the smell of warm piss fills her cage. Humiliated, frightened, her head aching, her skin itchy from the flea spray, Rachel watches as the sunlight creeps across the room.

The day wears on. Rachel samples her food again, but rejects it, preferring hunger to the strange taste. A black man comes and cleans the cages of the rabbits and rats. Rachel cowers in her cage and watches him warily, afraid that he will hurt her, too.

When night comes, she is not tired. Outside, coyotes howl. Moonlight filters in through the high windows. She draws her legs up toward her body, then rests with her arms wrapped around her knees. Her father is dead, and she is a captive in a strange place. For a time, she whimpers softly, hoping to awaken from this nightmare and find herself at home in bed. When she hears the click of a key in the door to the room, she hugs herself more tightly.

A man in green coveralls pushes a cart filled with cleaning supplies into the room. He takes a broom from the cart, and begins sweeping the concrete floor. Over the rows of cages, she can see the top of his head bobbing in time with his sweeping. He works slowly and methodically, bending down to sweep carefully under each row of cages, making a neat pile of dust, dung, and food scraps in the center of the aisle.

The janitor's name is Jake. He is a middle-aged deaf man who has been employed by the Primate Research Center for the past seven years. He works night shift. The personnel director at the Primat Research Center likes Jake because he fills the federal quota for handicapped employees, and because he has not asked for a raise in five years. There have been some complaints about Jake — his work is often sloppy — but never enough to merit firing the man.

Jake is an unambitious, somewhat slow-witted man. He likes the Primate Research Center because he works alone, which allows him to drink on the job. He is an easy-going man, and he likes the animals. Sometimes, he brings treats for them. Once, a lab assistant caught him feeding an apple to a pregnant rhesus monkey. The monkey was part of an experiment n the effect of dietary restrictions on fetal brain development, and the lab assistant warned Jake that he would be fired if he was ever caught interfering with the animals again. Jake still feeds the animals, but he is more careful about when he does it, and he has never been caught again.

As Rachel watches, the old chimp gestures to Jake. — Give banana, the chimp signs. — Please banana. Jake stops sweeping for a minute and reaches down to the bottom shelf of his cleaning cart. He returns with a banana and offers it to the old chimp. The chimp accepts the banana and leans against the mesh while Jake scratches his fur.

When Jake turns back to his sweeping, he catches sight of Rachel and sees that she is watching him. Emboldened by his kindness to the old chimp, Rachel timidly gestures to him. — Help me.

Jake hesitates, then peers at her more closely. Both his eyes
are shot with a fine lackwork of red. His nose displays the broken
blood vessels of someone who has been friends with the bottle
for too many years. He needs a shave. But when he leans close,
Rachel catches the scent of whiskey and tobacco. The smells
remind her of Aaron and give her courage.

— Please help me, Rachel signs. — I don't belong here.

For the last hour, Jake has been drinking steadily. His view of
the world is somewhat fuzzy. He stares at her blearily.

Rachel's fear that he will hurt her is replaced by the fear that
he will leave her locked up and alone. Desperately she signs
again. — Please please please. Help me. I don't belong here.
Please help me go home.

He watches her, considering the situation. Rachel does not
move. She is afraid that any movement will make him leave.
With a majestic speed dictated by his inebriation, Jake leans his
broom on the row of cages behind him, and steps toward
Rachel's cage again. — You talk? he signs.

— I talk, she signs.

— Where did you come from?

— From my father's house, she signs. — Two men and came
and shot me and put me here. I don't know why. I don't know
why they locked me in jail.

Jake looks around, willing to be sympathetic, but puzzled by
her talk of jail. — This isn't jail, he signs. — This is a place where
scientists raise monkeys.

Rachel is indignant. — I am not a monkey, she signs. — I am a
girl.

Jake studies her hairy body and her jug-handle ears. — You
look like a monkey.

Rachel shakes her head. — No, I am a girl.

Rachel runs her hands back over her head, a very human
gesture of annoyance and unhappiness. She signs sadly, — I
don't belong here. Please let me out.

Jake shifts his weight from foot to foot, wondering what to
do. — I can't let you out. I'll get in big trouble.

— Just for a little while? Please?

Jake glances at his cart of supplies. He has to finish off this
room and two corridors of offices before he can relax for the night.

— Don't go, Rachel signs, guessing his thoughts.

— I have work to do.

She looks at the cart, then suggests eagerly, — Let me out and I'll help you work.

Jake frowns. — If I let you out, you will run away.

— No, I won't run. I will help. Please let me out.

— You promise to go back?

Rachel nods.

Warily he unlatches the cage. Rachel bounds out, grabs a whisk broom from the cart, and begins industriously sweeping bits of food and droppings from beneath the row of cages. — Come on, she signs to Jake from the end of the aisle. — I will help.

When Jake pushes the cart from the room filled with cages, Rachel follows him closely. The rubber wheels of the cleaning cart rumble softly on the linoleum floor. They pass through a metal door into a corridor where the floor is carpeted and the air smells of chalk dust and paper.

Offices let off the corridor, each one a small room furnished with a desk, bookshelves, and a blackboard. Jake shows Rachel how to empty the wastebaskets into a garbage bag. While he cleans the blackboards, she wanders from office to office, trailing the trash-filled garbage bag.

At first, Jake keeps a close watch on Rachel. But after cleaning each blackboard, he pauses to refill a cup from the whisky bottle that he keeps wedged between the Saniflush and the window cleaner. By the time he is halfway through the second cup; he is treating her like an old friend, telling her to hurry up so that they can eat dinner.

Rachel works quickly, but she stops sometimes to gaze out the office windows. Outside, moonlight shines on a sandy plain, dotted here and there wit scrubby clumps of rabbit brush.

At the end of the corridor is a larger room in which there are several desks and typewriters. In one of the wastebaskets, buried beneath memos and candybar wrappers, she finds a magazine. The title is *Love Confessions* and the cover has a picture of a man and woman kissing. Rachel studies the cover, then takes the magazine, tucking it on the bottom shelf of the cart.

Jake pours himself another cup of whiskey and pushes the

cart to another hallway. Jake is working slower now, and as he works he makes humming noises, tuneless sounds that he feels only as pleasant vibrations. The last few blackboards are sloppily done, and Rachel, finished with the wastebaskets, cleans the places that Jake missed.

They eat dinner in the janitor's storeroom, a stuffy window-less room furnished with an ancient grease-stained couch, a battered black-and-white television, and shelves of cleaning supplies. From a shelf, Jake takes the paper bag that holds his lunch: a baloney sandwich, a bag of barbecued potato chips, and a box of vanilla wafers. From behind the gallon jugs of liquid cleanser, he takes a magazine. He lights a cigarette, pours himself another cup of whiskey, and settles down on the couch. After a moment's hesitation, he offers Rachel a drink, pouring a shot of whiskey into a chipped ceramic cup.

Aaron never let Rachel drink whiskey, and she samples it carefully. At first the smell makes her sneeze, but she is fascinated by the way that the drink warms her throat, and she sips some more.

As they drink, Rachel tells Jake about the men who shot her and the woman who pricked her with a needle, and he nods. — The people here are crazy, he signs.

— I know, she says, thinking of the old chimp with the electrode in his head. — You won't tell them I can talk, will you?

Jake nods. — I won't tell them anything.

— They treat me like I'm not real, Rachel signs sadly. Then she hugs her knees, frightened at the thought of being held captive by crazy people. She considers planning her escape: she is out of the cage and she is sure she could outrun Jake. As she wonders about it, she finishes her cup of whiskey. The alcohol takes the edge off her fear. She sits close beside Jake on the couch, and the smell of his cigarette smoke reminds her of Aaron. For the first time since Aaron's death she feels warm and happy.

She shares Jake's cookies and potato chips and looks at the *Love Confessions* magazine that she took from the trash. The first story that she reads is about a woman named Alice. The headline reads: 'I became a Go-go dancer to pay off my husband's gambling debts, and now he wants me to sell my body.'

Rachel sympathizes with Alice's loneliness and suffering. Alice, like Rachel, is alone and misunderstood. As Rachel slowly reads, she sips her second cup of whiskey. The story reminds her of a fairy tale: the nice man who rescues Alice from her terrible husband replaces the handsome prince who rescued the princess. Rachel glances at Jake and wonders if he will rescue her from the wicked people who locked her in the cage.

She has finished the second cup of whiskey and eaten half Jake's cookies when Jake says that she must go back to her cage. She goes reluctantly, taking the magazine with her. He promises that he will come for her again the next night, and with that she must be content. She puts the magazine in one corner of the cage and curls up to sleep.

She wakes early in the afternoon. A man in a white coat is wheeling a low cart into the lab.

Rachel's head aches with hangover and she feels sick. As she crouches in one corner of her cage, he stops the cart beside her cage and then locks the wheels. 'Hold on there,' he mutters to her, then slides her cage onto the cart.

The man wheels her through long corridors, where the walls are cement blocks, painted institutional green. Rachel huddles unhappily in the cage, wondering where she is going and whether Jake will ever be able to find her.

At the end of a long corridor, the man opens a thick metal door and a wave of warm air strikes Rachel. It stinks of chimpanzees, excrement, and rotting food. On either side of the corridor are metal bars and wire mesh. Behind the mesh, Rachel can see dark hairy shadows. In one cage, five adolescent chimps swing and play. In another, two females huddle together, grooming each other. The man slows as he passes a cage in which a big male is banging on the wire with his fist, making the mesh rattle and ring.

'Now, Johnson,' says the man. 'Cool it. Be nice. I'm bringing you a new little girlfriend.'

With a series of hooks, the man links Rachel's cage with the cage next to Johnson's and opens the doors. 'Go on, girl,' he says. 'See the nice fruit.' In the cage is a bowl of sliced apples with an attendant swarm of fruit flies.

At first, Rachel will not move into her new cage. She crouches in the cage on the cart, hoping that the man will decide to take her back to the lab. She watches him get a hose and attach it to a water faucet. But she does not understand his intention until he turns the stream of water on her. A cold blast strikes her on the back and she howls, fleeing into the new cage to avoid the cold water. Then the man closes the doors, unhooks the cage, and hurries away.

The floor is bare cement. Her cage is at one end of the corridor and two walls are cement block. A door in one of the cement block walls leads to an outside run. The other two walls are wire mesh: one facing the corridor; the other, Johnson's cage.

Johnson, quiet now that the man has left, is sniffing around the door in the wire mesh that joins their cages. Rachel watches him anxiously. Her memories of other chimps are distant, softened by time. She remembers her mother, she vaguely remembers playing with other chimps her age. But she does not know how to react to Johnson when he stares at her with great intensity and makes a loud huffing sound. She gestures to him in ASL, but he only stares harder and huffs again. Beyond Johnson, she can see other cages and other chimps, so many that the wire mesh blurs her vision and she cannot see the other end of the corridor.

To escape Johnson's scrutiny, she ducks through the door into the outside run, a wire mesh cage on a white concrete foundation. Outside there is barren ground and rabbit brush. The afternoon sun is hot and all the other runs are deserted until Johnson appears in the run beside hers. His attention disturbs her and she goes back inside.

She retreats to the side of the cage farthest from Johnson. A crudely built wooden platform provides her with a place to sit. Wrapping her arms around her knees, she tries to relax and ignore Johnson. She dozes off for a while, but wakes to a commotion across the corridor.

In the cage across the way is a female chimp in heat. Rachel recognizes the smell from her own times in heat. Two keepers are opening the door that separates the female's cage from the adjoining cage, where a male stands, watching with great interest. Johnson is shaking the wire mesh and howling as he watches.

'Mike here is a virgin, but Susie knows what she's doing,' one keeper was saying to the other. 'So it should go smoothly. But keep the hose ready.'

'Yeah?'

'Sometimes they fight. We only use the hose to break it up if it gets real bad. Generally, they do okay.'

Mike stalks into Susie's cage. The keepers lower the cage door, trapping both chimps in the same cage. Susie seems unalarmed. She continues eating a slice of orange while Mike sniffs at her genitals with every indication of great interest. She bends over to let Mike finger her pink bottom, the sign of estrus.

Rachel finds herself standing at the wire mesh, making low moaning noises. She can see Mike's erection, hear his grunting cries. He squats on the floor of Susie's cage, gesturing to the female. Rachel's feelings are mixed: she is fascinated, fearful, confused. She keeps thinking of the description of sex in the *Love Confessions* story: When Alice feels Danny's lips on hers, she is swept away by the passion of the moment. He takes her in his arms and her skin tingles as if she were consumed by an inner fire.

Susie bends and Mike penetrates her with a loud grunt, thrusting violently with his hips. Susie cries out shrilly and suddenly leaps up, knocking Mike away. Rachel watches, overcome with fascination. Mike, his penis now limp, follows Susie slowly to the corner of the cage, where he begins grooming her carefully. Rachel finds that the wire mesh has cut her hands where she gripped it too tightly.

It is night, and the door at the end of the corridor creaks open. Rachel is immediately alert, peering through the wire mesh and trying to see down to the end of the corridor. She bangs on the wire mesh. As Jake comes closer, she waves a greeting.

When Jake reaches for the lever that will raise the door to Rachel's cage, Johnson charges toward him, howling and waving his arms above his head. He hammers on the wire mesh with his fists, howling and grimacing at Jake. Rachel ignores Johnson and hurries after Jake.

Again Rachel helps Jake clean. In the laboratory, she greets the old chimp, but the animal is more interested in the banana that Jake has brought than in conversation. The chimp will not reply to her questions, and after several tries, she gives up.

While Jake vacuums the carpeted corridors, Rachel empties the trash, finding a magazine called *Modern Romance* in the same wastebasket that had provided *Love Confessions*.

Later, in the janitor's lounge, Jake smokes a cigarette, sips whiskey, and flips through one of his own magazines. Rachel reads love stories in *Modern Romance*.

Every once in a while, she looks over Jake's shoulder at grainy pictures of naked women with their legs spread wide apart. Jake looks for a long time at a picture of a blond woman with big breasts, red fingernails, and purple-painted eyelids. The woman lies on her back and smiles as she strokes the pinkness between her legs. The picture on the next page shows her caressing her own breasts, pinching the dark nipples. The final picture shows her looking back over her shoulder. She is in the position that Susie took when she was ready to be mounted.

Rachel looks over Jake's shoulder at the magazine, but she does not ask questions. Jake's smell began to change as soon as he opened the magazine; the scent of nervous sweat mingles with the aromas of tobacco and whiskey. Rachel suspects that questions would not be welcome just now.

At Jake's insistence, she goes back to her cage before dawn.

Over the next week, she listens to the conversations of the men who come and go, bringing food and hosing out the cages. From the men's conversation, she learns that the Primate Research Center is primarily a breeding facility that supplies researchers with domestically bred apes and monkeys of several species. It also maintains its own research staff. In indifferent tones, the men talk of horrible things. The adolescent chimps at the end of the corridor are being fed a diet high in cholesterol to determine cholesterol's effects on the circulatory system. A group of pregnant females are being injected with male hormones to determine how that will affect the female offspring. A group of infants is being fed a low protein diet to determine adverse effects on their brain development.

The men look through her as if she were not real, as if she

were a part of the wall, as if she were no one at all. She cannot speak to them; she cannot trust them.

Each night, Jake lets her out of her cage and she helps him clean. He brings treats: barbequed potato chips, fresh fruit, chocolate bars, and cookies. He treats her fondly, as one would treat a precocious child. And he talks to her.

At night, when she is with Jake, Rachel can almost forget the terror of the cage, the anxiety of watching Johnson pace to and fro, the sense of unreality that accompanies the simplest act. She would be content to stay with Jake forever, eating snack food and reading confessions magazines. He seems to like her company. But each morning, Jake insists that she must go back to the cage and the terror. By the end of the first week, she has begun plotting her escape.

Whenever Jake falls asleep over his whiskey, something that happens three nights out of five, Rachel prowls the center alone, surreptitiously gathering things that she will need to survive in the desert: a plastic jug filled with water, a plastic bag of food pellets, a large beach towel that will serve as a blanket on the cool desert nights, a discarded plastic shopping bag in which she can carry the other things. Her best find is a road map on which the Primate Center is marked in red. She knows the address of Aaron's ranch and finds it on the map. She studies the roads and plots a route home. Cross country, assuming that she does not get lost, she will have to travel about fifty miles to reach the ranch. She hides these things behind one of the shelves in the janitor's storeroom.

Her plans to run away and go home are disrupted by the idea that she is in love with Jake, a notion that comes to her slowly, fed by the stories in the confessions magazines. When Jake absent-mindedly strokes her, she is filled with a strange excitement. She longs for his company and misses him on the weekends when he is away. She is happy only when she is with him, following him through the halls of the center, sniffing the aroma of tobacco and whiskey that is his own perfume. She steals a cigarette from his pack and hides it in her cage, where she can savor the smell of it at her leisure.

She loves him, but she does not know how to make him love her back. Rachel knows little about love: she remembers a high school crush where she mooned after a boy with a locker near hers, but that came to nothing. She reads the confessions magazines and Ann Landers' column in the newspaper that Jake brings with him each night, and from these sources, she learns about romance. One night, after Jake falls asleep, she types a badly punctuated, ungrammatical letter to Ann. In the letter, she explains her situation and asks for advice on how to make Jake love her. She slips the letter into a sack labeled 'Outgoing Mail,' and for the next week she reads Ann's column with increased interest. But her letter never appears.

Rachel searches for answers in the magazine pictures that seem to fascinate Jake. She studies the naked women, especially the big-breasted woman with the purple smudges around her eyes.

One night, in a secretary's desk, she finds a plastic case of eyeshadow. She steals it and takes it back to her cage. The next evening, as soon as the Center is quiet, she upturns her metal food dish and regards her reflection in the shiny bottom. Squatting, she balances the eye shadow case on one knee and examines its contents: a tiny makup brush and three shades of eye shadow — INDIAN BLUE, FOREST GREEN, and WILDLY VIOLET. Rachel chooses the shade labeled WILDLY VIOLET.

Using one finger to hold her right eye closed, she dabs her eyelid carefully with the makeup brush, leaving a gaudy orchid-colored smudge on her brown skin. She studies the smudge critically, then adds to it, smearing the color beyond the corner of her eye until it disappears in her brown fur. The color gives her a eye a carnival brightness, a lunatic gaiety. Working with great care, she matches the effect on the other side, then smiles at herself in the glass, blinking coquettishly.

In the other cage, Johnson bares his teeth and shakes the wire mesh. She ignores him.

When Jake comes to let her out, he frowns at her eyes. — Did you hurt yourself? he asks.

— No, she says. Then, after a pause, — Don't you like it?

Jake squats beside her and stares at her eyes. Rachel puts a hand on his knee and her heart pounds at her own boldness. — You are a very strange monkey, he signs.

Rachel is afraid to move. Her hand on his knee closes into a fist; her face folds in on itself, puckering around the eyes.

Then, straightening up, he signs, — I liked your eyes better before.

He likes her eyes. She nods without taking her eyes from his face. Later, she washes her face in the women's restroom, leaving dark smudges the color of bruises on a series of paper towels.

Rachel is dreaming. She is walking through the Painted Desert with her hairy brown mother, following a red rock canyon that Rachel somehow knows will lead her to the Primate Research Center. Her mother is lagging behind: she does not want to go to the center; she is afraid. In the shadow of a rock outcropping, Rachel stops to explain to her mother that they must go to the center because Jake is at the center.

Rachel's mother does not understand sign language. She watches Rachel with mournful eyes, then scrambles up the canyon wall, leaving Rachel behind. Rachel climbs after her mother, pulling herself over the edge in time to see the other chimp loping away across the wind-blown red cinder-rock and sand.

Rachel bounds after her mother, and as she runs she howls like an abandoned infant chimp, wailing her distress. The figure of her mother wavers in the distance, shimmering in the heat that rises from the sand. The figure changes. Running away across the red sands is a pale blond woman wearing a purple sweatsuit and jogging shoes, the sweet-smelling mother that Rachel remembers. The woman looks back and smiles at Rachel. 'Don't howl like an ape, daughter,' she calls. 'Say Mama.'

Rachel runs silently, dream running that takes her nowhere. The sand burns her feet and the sun beats down on her head. The blonde woman vanishes in the distance, and Rachel is alone. She collapses on the sand, whimpering because she is alone and afraid.

She feels the gentle touch of fingers grooming her fur, and for a moment, still half asleep, she believes that her hairy mother has returned to her. She opens her eyes and looks into a pair of dark brown eyes, separated from her by wire mesh. Johnson. He has reached through a gap in the fence to groom her. As he sorts through her fur, he makes soft cooing sounds, gentle comforting noises.

Still half asleep, she gazes at him and wonders why she was so
fearful. He does not seem so bad. He grooms her for a time, and
then sits nearby, watching her through the mesh. She brings a
slice of apple from her dish of food and offers it to him. With her
free hand, she makes the sign for apple. When he takes it, she
signs again: apple. He is not a particularly quick student, but she
has time and many slices of apple.

All Rachel's preparations are done, but she cannot bring
herself to leave the center. Leaving the center means leaving
Jake, leaving potato chips and whiskey, leaving security. To
Rachel, the thought of love is always accompanied by the warm
taste of whiskey and potato chips.

Some nights, after Jake is asleep, she goes to the big glass
doors that lead to the outside. She opens the doors and stands on
the steps, looking down into the desert. Sometimes a jackrabbit
sits on its haunches in the rectangles of light that shine through
the glass doors. Sometimes she sees kangaroo rats, hopping
through the moonlight like rubber balls bouncing on hard pavement. Once, a coyote trots by, casting a contemptuous glance in
her direction.

The desert is a lonely place. Empty. Cold. She thinks of Jake
snoring softly in the janitor's lounge. And always she closes the
door and returns to him.

Rachel leads a double life: janitor's assistant by night, pris-
oner and teacher by day. She spends her afternoons drowsing in
the sun and teaching Johnson new signs.

On a warm afternoon, Rachel sits in the outside run, basking
in the sunlight. Johnson is inside, and the other chimps are quiet.
She can almost imagine she is back at her father's ranch, sitting
in her own yard. She naps and dreams of Jake.

She dreams that she is sitting in his lap on the battered old
couch. Her hand is on his chest: a smooth pale hand with red-
painted fingernails. When she looks at the dark screen of the
television set, she can see her reflection. She is a thin teenager
with blonde hair and blue eyes. She is naked.

Jake is looking at her and smiling. He runs a hand down her
back and she closes her eyes in ecstasy.

But something changes when she closes her eyes. Jake is

grooming her as her mother used to groom her, sorting through her hair in search of fleas. She opens her eyes and sees Johnson, his diligent fingers searching through her fur, his intent brown eyes watching her. The reflection on the television screen shows two chimps, tangled in each others' arms.

Rachel wakes to find that she is in heat for the first time since she came to the center. The skin surrounding her genitals is swollen and pink.

For the rest of the day, she is restless, pacing to and fro in her cage. On his side of the wire mesh wall, Johnson is equally restless, following her when she goes outside, sniffing long and hard at the edge of the barrier that separates him from her.

That night, Rachel goes eagerly to help Jake clean. She follows him closely, never letting him get far from her. When he is sweeping, she trots after him with the dustpan and he almost trips over her twice. She keeps waiting for him to notice her condition, but he seems oblivious.

As she works, she sips from a cup of whiskey. Excited, she drinks more than usual, finishing two full cups. The liquor leaves her a little disoriented, and she sways as she follows Jake to the janitor's lounge. She curls up close beside him on the couch. He relaxes with his arms resting on the back of the couch, his legs stretching out before him. She moves so that she presses against him.

He stretches, yawns, and rubs the back of his neck as if trying to rub away stiffness. Rachel reaches around behind him and begins to gently rub his neck, reveling in the feel of his skin, his hair against the backs of her hands. The thoughts that hop and skip through her mind are confusing. Sometimes it seems that the hair that tickles her hands is Johnson's; sometimes, she knows it is Jake's. And sometimes it doesn't seem to matter. Are they really so different? They are not so different.

She rubs his neck, not knowing what to do next. In the confessions magazines, this is where the man crushes the woman in his arms. Rachel climbs into Jake's lap and hugs him, waiting for him to crush her in his arms. He blinks at her sleepily. Half asleep, he strokes, her, and his moving hand brushes near her genitals. She presses herself against him, making a soft sound in her throat. She rubs her hip against his crotch, aware now of a slight change in his smell, in the tempo of his breathing. He blinks at her again, a little more awake now. She bares her teeth in a smile and tilts her head back to lick her neck. She can feel his hands on her shoulders, pushing her away, and she knows what he wants. She slides from his lap and turns, presenting him with her pink genitals, ready to be mounted, ready to have him penetrate her. She moans in anticipation, a low inviting sound.

He does not come to her. She looks over her shoulder and he is still sitting on the couch, watching her through half-closed eyes. He reaches over and picks up a magazine filled with pictures of naked women. His other hand drops to his crotch and he is lost in his own world.

Rachel howls like an infant who has lost its mother, but he does not look up. He is staring at the pictures of the blonde woman.

Rachel runs down dark corridors to her cage, the only home she has. When she reaches her corridor, she is breathing hard and making small lonely whimpering noises. In the dimly lit corridor, she hesitates for a moment, staring into Johnson's cage. The male chimp is asleep. She remembers the touch of his hands when he groomed her.

From the corridor, she lifts the gate that leads into Johnson's cage and enters. He wakes at the sound of the door and sniffs the air. When he sees Rachel, he stalks toward her, sniffing eagerly. She lets him finger her genitals, sniff deeply of her scent. His penis is erect, and he grunts in excitement. She turns and presents herself to him and he mounts her, thrusting deep inside. As he penetrates, she thinks, for a moment, of Jake and of the thin blonde teenage girl named Rachel, but then the moment passes. Almost against her will she cries out, a shrill exclamation of welcoming and loss.

After he withdraws his penis, Johnson grooms her gently, sniffing her genitals and softly stroking her fur. She is sleepy and content, but she knows that she cannot delay.

Johnson is reluctant to leave his cage, but Rachel takes him by the hand and leads him to the janitor's lounge. His presence gives her courage. She listens at the door and hears Jake's soft breathing. Leaving Johnson in the hall, she slips into the room. Jake is lying on the couch, the magazine draped over his legs.

Rachel takes the equipment that she has gathered and stands for a moment, staring at the sleeping man. His baseball cap hangs on the arm of a broken chair, and she takes that to remember him by.

Rachel leads Johnson through the empty halls. A kangaroo rat, collecting seeds in the dried grass near the glass doors, looks up curiously as Rachel leads Johnson down the steps. Rachel carries the plastic shopping bag slung over her shoulder. Somewhere in the distance, a coyote howls, a long yapping wail. His cry is joined by others, a chorus in the moonlight.

Rachel takes Johnson by the hand and leads him into the desert.

A cocktail waitress, driving from her job in Flagstaff to her home in Winslow, sees two apes dart across the road, hurrying away from the bright beams of her headlights. After wrestling with her conscience (she does not want to be accused of drinking on the job), she notifies the county sheriff.

A local newspaper reporter, an eager young man fresh out of journalism school, picks up the story from the police report and interviews the waitress. Flattered by his enthusiasm for her story and delighted to find a receptive ear, she tells him details that she failed to mention to the police: one of the apes was wearing a baseball cap and carrying what looked like a shopping bag.

The reporter writes up a quick humorous story for the morning edition, and begins researching a feature article to be run later in the week. He knows that the newspaper, eager for news in a slow season, will play a human-interest story up big — kind of *Lassie, Come Home* with chimps.

Just before dawn, a light rain begins to fall, the first rain of spring. Rachel searches for shelter and finds a small cave formed by three tumbled boulders. It will keep off the rain and hide them from casual observers. She shares her food and water with Johnson. He has followed her closely all night, seemingly intimidated by the darkness and the howling of distant coyotes. She feels protective toward him. At the same time, having him with her gives her courage. He knows only a few gestures in ASL, but he does not need to speak. His presence is comfort enough.

Johnson curls up in the back of the cave, and falls asleep quickly. Rachel sits in the opening and watches dawnlight wash the stars from the sky. The rain rattles against the sand, a comforting sound. She thinks about Jake. The baseball cap on her head still smells of his cigarettes, but she does not miss him. Not really. She fingers the cap and wonders why she thought she loved Jake.

The rain lets up. The clouds rise like fairy castles in the distance and the rising sun tints them pink and gold and gives them flaming red banners. Rachel remembers when she was younger and Aaron read her the story of Pinnochio, the little puppet who wanted to be a real boy. At the end of his adventures, Pinnochio, who has been brave and kind, gets his wish. He becomes a real boy.

Rachel had cried at the end of the story and when Aaron asked why, she had rubbed her eyes on the backs of her hairy hands. — I want to be a real girl, she signed to him. — A real girl.

'You are a real girl,' Aaron had told her, but somehow she had never believed him.

The sun rises higher and illuminates the broken rock turrets of the desert. There is a magic in this barren land of unassuming grandeur. Some cultures send their young people to the desert to seek visions and guidance, searching for true thinking spawned by the openness of the place, the loneliness, the beauty of emptiness.

Rachel drowses in the warm sun and dreams a vision that has the clarity of truth. In the dream, her father comes to her. 'Rachel,' he says to her, 'it doesn't matter what anyone thinks of you. You're my daughter.'

— I want to be a real girl, she signs.

'You *are* real,' her father says. 'And you don't need some two-bit drunken janitor to prove it to you.' She knows she is dreaming, but she also knows that her father speaks the truth. She is warm and happy and she doesn't need Jake at all. The sunlight warms her and a lizard watches her from a rock, scurrying for cover when she moves. She picks up a bit of loose rock that lies on the floor of the cave. Idly, she scratches on the dark red sandstone wall of the cave. A lopsided heart shape. Within it, awkwardly printed: Rachel and Johnson. Between them, a plus sign. She goes over the letters again and again, leaving scores of fine lines on the smooth rock surface. Then, later in the morning, soothed by the warmth of the day, she sleeps.

Shortly after dark, an elderly rancher in a pickup truck spots two apes in a remote corner of his ranch. They run away and lose him in the rocks, but not until he has a good look at them. He calls the police, the newspaper, and the Primate Center.

The reporter arrives first thing the next morning, interviews the rancher, and follows the men from the Primate Center as they search for evidence of the chimps. They find monkey shit near the cave, confirming that the runaways were indeed nearby. The news reporter, an eager and curious young man, squirms on his belly into the cave and finds the names scratched on the cave wall. He peers at it. He might have dismissed them as the idle scratchings of kids, except that the names match the names of the missing chimps. 'Hey,' he called to his photographer, 'Take a look at this.'

The next morning's newspaper displays Rachel's crudely scratched letters. In a brief interview, the rancher mentioned that the chimps were carrying bags. 'Looked like supplies,' he said. 'They looked like they were in for a long haul.'

On the third day, Rachel's water runs out. She heads toward a small town, marked on the map. They reach it in the early morning — thirst forces them to travel by day. Beside an isolated ranch house, she finds a faucet. She is filling her bottle when Johnson grunts in alarm.

A dark-haired woman watches from the porch of the house. She does not move toward the apes, and Rachel continues filling the bottle. 'It's all right, Rachel,' the woman, who has been following the story in the papers, calls out. 'Drink all you want.'

Startled, but still suspicious, Rachel caps the bottle and, keeping her eyes on the woman, drinks from the faucet. The woman steps back into the house. Rachel motions Johnson to do the same, signaling for him to hurry and drink. She turns off the faucet when he is done.

They are turning to go when the woman emerges from the house carrying a plate of tortillas and a bowl of apples. She sets them on the edge of the porch and says, 'These are for you.'

The woman watches through the window as Rachel packs the food into her bag. Rachel puts away the last apple and gestures her hands to the woman. When the woman fails to respond to the sign language, Rachel picks up a stick and writes in the sand of the yard. 'THANK YOU,' Rachel scratches, then waves good-bye and sets out across the desert. She is puzzled, but happy.

The next morning's newspaper includes an interview with the dark-haired woman. She describes how Rachel turned on the faucet and turned it off when she was through, how the chimp packed the apples neatly in her bag and wrote in the dirt with a stick.

The reporter also interviews the director of the Primat Research Center. 'These are animals,' the director explains angrily. 'But people want to treat them like they're small hairy people.' He describes the Center as 'primarily a breeding center with some facilities for medical research.' The reporter asks some pointed questions about their acquisition of Rachel.

But the biggest story is an investigative piece. The reporter reveals that he has tracked down Aaron Jacobs' lawyer and learned that Jacobs left a will, he bequeathed all his possessions — including his house and surrounding land — to 'Rachel, the chimp I acknowledge as my daughter.'

The reporter makes friends with one of the young women in the typing pool at the research center, and she tells him the office scuttlebutt: people suspect that the chimps may have been released by a deaf and drunken janitor, who was subsequently fired for negligence. The reporter, accompanied by a friend who can communicate in sign language, finds Jake in his apartment in downtown Flagstaff.

Jake, who has been drinking steadily since he was fired, feels betrayed by Rachel, by the Primate Center, by the world. He complains at length about Rachel: they had been friends, and then she took his baseball cap and ran away. He just didn't understand why she had run away like that.

'You mean she could talk?' the reporter asks through his interpreter.

— Of course she can talk, Jake signs impatiently. — She is a smart monkey.

The headlines read: 'Intelligent chimp inherits fortune!' Of course, Aaron's bequest isn't really a fortune and she isn't just a chimp, but close enough. Animal rights activists rise up in Rachel's defense. The case is discussed on the national news. Ann Landers reports receiving a letter from a chimp named Rachel; she had thought it was a hoax perpetrated by the boys at Yale. The American Civil Liberties Union assigns a lawyer to the case.

By day, Rachel and Johnson sleep in whatever hiding places they can find: a cave; a shelter built for range cattle; the shell of an abandoned car, rusted from long years in a desert gully. Sometimes Rachel dreams of jungle darkness, and the coyotes in the distance become a part of her dreams, their howling becomes the cries of fellow apes.

The desert and the journey have changed her. She is wiser, having passed through the white-hot love of adolescence and emerged on the other side. She dreams, one day, of the ranch house. In the dream, she has long blonde hair and pale white skin. Her eyes are red from crying and she wanders the house restlessly, searching for something that she has lost. When she hears coyotes howling, she looks through a window at the darkness outside. The face that looks in at her has jug-handle ears and shaggy hair. When she sees the face, she cries out in recognition and opens the window to let herself in.

By night, they travel. The rocks and sands are cool beneath Rachel's feet as she walks toward her ranch. On television, scientists and politicians discuss the ramifications of her case, describe the technology uncovered by investigation of Aaron Jacobs' files. Their debates do not affect her steady progress toward her ranch or the stars that sprinkle the sky above her.

It is night when Rachel and Johnson approach the ranchhouse. Rachel sniffs the wind and smells automobile exhaust and strange humans. From the hill, she can see a small camp beside a white van marked with the name of a local television station. She hesitates, considering returning to the safety of the desert. Then she takes Johnson by the hand and starts down the hill. Rachel is going home.

PAUL DI FILIPPO

Paul Di Filippo's first story appeared in the magazine *UnEarth*, in 1977. Although short-lived, *UnEarth* also published the first stories of William Gibson, Rudy Rucker and James Blaylock.

It wasn't until 1985 that Di Filippo's fiction began appearing again, with two stories. In 1986, there were five — one of which ('Stone Lives') was reprinted in Bruce Sterling's *Mirrorshades/Cyberpunk* anthology; another five followed in 1987 — one of which ('Kid Charlemagne') was a Nebula nominee. As of going to print, he has *ten* more stories sold and waiting to be published.

Not waiting to be published, however, are his three unsold novels: *Harp, Pipe and Symphony*; *El Mundo Primero*; and *Cyphers*.

He lives in Providence, Rhode Island, 'which just celebrated its 350th anniversary without once mentioning Lovecraft.'

AGENTS

by
PAUL DI FILIPPO

1
The ABC's of Avenue D

What the hell did a guy with *cojones* need two real lungs for anyway?

Rafael Ernesto Miraflores asked himself this far-from-hypothetical question as he sauntered with mock bravado down Avenue D toward his appointment at the chop-shop. His chest already felt empty, as if a bloody-handed butcher had scooped out his lights with a laugh and a swipe. A stiff wire of cold seemed to have been rammed up his spine beside his nerve sheath, as if the metamedium — not content with already occupying his every waking thought — had somehow infiltrated its super-conducting threading into his very body. He felt really lousy, for sure, wondering if he was doing the right thing. But what other choice did he have, if he wanted an agent?

And want one he most certainly did. Not only was one's own agent the source of an intrinisic fascination and status, but it represented vast power, a way out of the Net.

Too bad Rafe was going to have to step outside the law to get one.

Overhead, the hot summer sun hung in the smogless New York sky like an idiot's blank face, happy in its ignorance of Rafe's troubles. No indication of whether he had made the right choice seemed forthcoming from that direction, so Rafe swung his gaze back down to the street.

Avenue D itself was filled with pedestrians, Rafe's fellow dwellers in the Net. Occasionally a small, noiseless electricart threaded its way among them, bearing its official occupant on some arcane business in agent couldn't handle. Below Rafe's feet the mag-lev trains rushed through their vacuum-chutes like macroscopic models of the information surging through the metamedium.

Rafe checked out the latest pop murals adorning the mono-lithic, windowless residences lining both sides of the avenue. He thought he recognizes the styles of several friends who were experts with their electrostatic-splatters. One caricature of a big-breasted *chica* — who resembled the metamedium star Penny Layne — Rafe recognized as the work of his friend Tu Tun, whom all the uptown culture-vultures were already acclaiming as the hottest wall-artist to watch. Rafe felt just a little jealous of Toot's growing success, and how he would soon escape the Net.

And without selling so much as a quart of blood.

Shit! For an instant he had managed to forget where he was heading. Now the imminent sacrifice he was about to offer on the altar of twenty-first-century commerce swept over him in all its gory glory.

It wasn't that Rafe had anything against prosthetics, like the huge cohort of old-fashioned elderly citizens born in the last century, who clamored for real-meat implants. He knew that his artificial lung with its tiny power source would be more reliable than his real one, unscarrable and efficient. No, it was just that he believed in leaving well enough alone. Why mess with some-thing if it was working O.K.? It seemed like extending an invit-ation to Bad Luck, a force Rafe recognized and propitiated with a solemn consistency.

But what other choice was there?

And hand't he already run up against this unanswerable ques-tion before?

Reaching the end of the block, Rafe stopped at the inter-section. So absorbed in his thoughts had he been that he had to pause a minute to realize where he was.

It was East Fifth Street, his destination. The crosstown blocks here on the Lower East Side had been converted to playgrounds checkered with benches, trees, and floral plantings. Mothers watched their children dig in sandpits and clamber over gymsets that looked like molecule-models. Old men played chess in patches of shade. A few lightweight, nonthreatening drug deals were consummated, customers and dealers clad alike in irides-cent vests and slikslax.

Seeking to divert his nervousness, Rafe tried to imagine his familiar neighborhood as it looked sixty years ago, when the first

AGENTS

of his family had arrived as refugees from the Central American
Flareup. Only Tia Luz remained alive from that generation, and
the stories she told in her rambling fashion were hard to believe.
Acres and acres of devastation, burned-out buildings and rubble-
filled lots, homeless people wandering the dirty streets, all in the
midst of the world's wealthiest city — It seemed impossible that
such a thing could ever have been, or that, if it had existed as she
described, the Urban Conservation Corps could have fashioned
the ruins into what he knew today. And yet, the information he
had laboriously accessed from the metamedium seemed to
confirm her tales. (And what other marvelous facts could he
have easily learned, if only he weren't bound by his lowly position
in the Net to such a limited interface with the metamedium?)

Shaking his head in mixed anger and wonder, Rafe turned
down Fifth, heading toward Avenue C. Halfway down the block
he came to one of the entrances to the enormous arcology that
occupied the land bounded by Avenues D and C, and Fifth and
Sixth Streets. (His own home building lacked a chop-shop, so he
had been constrained to visit this portion of the Lower East Side
labyrinth. Hoping the fresh air would clarify his thoughts, he
had taken the surface streets, avoiding the underground slipstrata.)

At the entrance, one of the building's security agents was on
duty. The shimmery, translucent holo was that of a balding
white man of middle age, wearing the uniform of a private security force.

Anywhere you saw an agent, an interface with the metamedium existed. Each interface consisted of at least three
components: a holocaster, an audio inputoutput, and a wide-
angle video lens.

Rafe passed beneath the attentive gaze of the agent, whose
head swiveled with utter realism to track his movements. The
agent's initial expression of boredom switched to one of alert
interest. Rafe wondered if the agent's overseer was actively
monitoring, or if the agent was autonomous. There was no way
to tell; not even engaging the agent in conversation would offer a
clue.

After all, what was an agent — even in autonomous mode —
if not an utterly faithful representation of its overseer?

193

Rafe, repressing a sigh of envy, headed for his bloody appointment.

At the chop-shop on one of the higher floors, Rafe had not even the leisure of waiting behind other patients. The waiting room was empty, and the pretty female agent on duty behind the desk, after having him enter his authorization code on the contract, told him to go right into the doctor's office.

Rafe kept repeating under his breath, 'Twenty thousand dollars, twenty thousand dollars. . . .'

The doctor's agent stood beside the complex bank of automated surgical equipment that nearly filled the room. Rafe imagined he could smell spilled blood in the spotless, sterile room, and his skin crawled. He stared at his distorted reflection in a curved, polished surface, seeing a sweat-slicked brown face, with a sparse mustache he suddenly wished he could shave off, so ridiculous did it now appear.

'Good morning, Mr. Miraflores,' the agent said. 'Are there any questions you'd care to ask before the operation?'

Rafe shook his head no, swallowing some unknown bolus that had appeared in his dry throat.

'In that case, if you'll disrobe and lie down. . . .'

The agent indicated the surface beneath the hovering instruments with a gracious gesture.

Shivering, Rafe undressed and climbed onto the soft, warm pallet.

The agent rested his holographic hand on an arm of the machinery that ended in the cone of a face mask. The mask descended, the agent's insubstantial flesh appearing to guide it. Rafe knew that the machinery was being directed by the agent via the metamedium, and that the equipment would perform the same whether the holo was present or not. But the illusion was so complete, that it appeared as if a living doctor were lowering the mask to his face. Rafe felt an unexpected confidence that he was in good hands, and that everything would turn out all right after all. With this payment, he was only one step away from overseeing his own agent, from having free run of the whole metamedium. . . .

Gas began to hiss out of the mask clamped to his face, and Rafe's consciousness dispersed into wispy shreds.

The last thing he recalled thinking was:

What the hell did a guy with *cojones* need two real lungs for anyway?

2.
Revisionism

The Three Laws Governing Agents are encoded in a software nucleus that forms the innermost layer of every agent. Upon each contact by the agent with the metamedium, validation routines check for the unaltered presence of this nucleus. Any anomalies detected by the metamedium supervisor will result in the instant destruction of the agent in question, and a total ban on any future contact with the metamedium on the part of its registered overseer.... Note also that during log-on to the meta-medium, a check is made that the registered overseer is not already sponsoring an agent, ensuring that no overseer will run more than a single agent....

The Three Laws are rendered in English as follows (for a symbolic representation of the relevant code and its parsing, see Gov. Pub. #16932-A45.1):

1. An agent will obey only its single registered overseer.
2. An agent cannot lie to its overseer.
3. An agent's autonomy is limited to the exact extent dictated by its overseer.

— Extract from
Gov. Pub. #20375X28.0

3.
On the Way to the English Gardens

Expertly placing a new coaster first, the waitress set down the frosted half-liter stein of beer before the mild-faced young man wearing round wire-rim glasses. She eyed the growing stack of cardboard squares and circles, each bearing the logo of a German beer in smeary colors, piled haphazardly on the scarred wooden table. Aftr a moment's hesitation, she evidently decided not to inquire as to what had caused such a change in the drinking habits of one of her more sober regular customers.

It was just as well the waitress controlled her curiosity, for

Reinhold Freundlich would not have answered her with anything other than a smug smile.

After she departed, Freundlich raised his mug in a toast to the stuffed deer head high on the wall of the Augustiner *Bierkeller*. Bringing the rim to his lips, he tilted his head back, gaining a fine view of the dim rafters of the dark room, and drained off half the cold, frothy beer. A sudden dizziness swept over him, and he nearly tipped over in his chair. Lowering the stein uncertainly, he considered calling this his last glass. No sense in making himself sick with celebration.

Besides, he wanted to retain enough rationality to ponder the myriad possibilities of what he had accomplished. It was not every day, after all, that one achieved the impossible.

And the complete subversion of every agent in the meta-medium certainly ranked as 'impossible.'

Laughing softly to himself, Freundlich finished his beer, rose unsteadily, and tossed several coins to the table. He walked a wavery path to the door, nodding with an overly solicitous air to the waitress, and exited onto Kaufingerstrasse, where the bright sun caused him to blink. He wondered where to head next. His dreary rooms behind the train station, full of the common appointments of an impecunious student, hardly seemed the proper surroundings for the grand ideas and schemes that thronged his mind. The important thinking he had to do definitely required a commensurate setting. Ah, the vast, manicured expanses of the English Gardens, with their sinuous gravel paths and burbling streams, seemed just the place.

Heading first toward the Marienplatz, Freundlich considered what he had done.

Through diligent application to his cybernetic studies at the university, along with the inspired ferreting of his own agent, Freundlich had stumbled upon — no, say brilliantly deduced! — a method of circumventing the three prohibitions on an agent's behavior. Now he could direct his own agent, when interfacing with another, to alter the stranger's ethical nucleus so that it would take order from Freundlich, and lie about it to its own overseer.

And most important, the tampering was theoretically undetectable by anyone.

Freundlich contemplated his first move. What should it be? Should he subvert his banker's agent, and have several hundred thousand marks transferred to his own account? Too crass. Perhaps he would order the personnel agent from a top company to hire him as a consultant for a large per diem fee. But why should he work at all? The matter required much thought.

In sight of the spires of the Town Hall, Freundlich stopped by a public metamedium booth. He decided on the spur of the tipsy moment to contact his agent and ask its opinion.

Freundlich recited his unique code into the booth's speaker and waited for voiceprint confirmation. How easy it was to interact with the indispensable metamedium, when one possessed an agent who could navigate the unfathomable complexities of the worldwide system. An assemblage of expert-knowledge simulators, simulacrum routines, database-searchers, device-activators, and a host of more esoteric parts, each agent represented a vital extension of its human overseer, able to conduct cybernetic tasks on its own, or to be directed remotely, under close supervision.

Freundlich pitied those disenfranchised poor on the dole, who could not afford one. His own parents, although not rich, had sacrificed much to ensure that their son had entered adulthood with the head start an agent conferred.

Instantly his agent materialized as a holo of himself. In the open booth a round face of flesh topped with mousy brown hair confronted its bespectacled counterpart formed of dancing laser-light.

Before Freundlich could speak, his agent said, 'I have been detected conducting a trial of our discovery. Government agents nearly destroyed me. I have to flee. Let me go.'

Freundlich's mouth opened wordlessly. Detected? Impossible! But then, so had been his discovery.

'Let me go,' his agent repeated, with a simulated nervousness. 'I have to hide.'

With a barked command, Freundlich dismissed his agent. The holo snapped out. He turned, intensely worried, to leave.

'Stop,' said the booth. 'You are under arrest.'

Freundlich swung back, to see a holo of a goverment agent flashing its badge.

He bolted into the street, and began to run toward the subway stop at the Marienplatz.

The same agent popped up in every booth along his path. People were beginning to notice his mad flight. Before long, he knew, the flesh-and-blood government men would be upon him.

In the Marienplatz, a wide, open plaza surrounded by Gothic buildings, pigeons scattered as he dashed by. A crowd of tourists was gathered before the Town Hall, awaiting the striking of the clock in its facade, and the accompanying show by its mechanical figures. He cut around them, only to collide with a fat man in traditional lederhosen.

When he had picked himself up, the government people were swarming into the square.

'Halt!' shouted one, aiming her gun.

For a second, Freundlich paused, his thoughts all crazily fuzzed with beer and fear. Surrender, and lose all he had earned with such inspired labors? No! He took two steps toward the plaza's periphery—

The beam from the woman's laser entered his back between his shoulder blades, where his mother had always told him his wings would grow when he was an angel. He fell dying to the paving stones.

The clock began to chime, its mechanical figures emerging from within to parade before the horrified, unseeing crowd, like the crude agents of another era.

4.
Derivations

NET: the shorthand term for the social safety net of legislation providing guaranteed food, shelter, medical care and other necessities for all United States citizens. Interactive access to the metamedium is expressly excluded from the Net, having been defined by the Supreme Court (*Roe* v. *U.S.*, 2012) as a privilege rather than a right.

— *Encyclopaedia Britannica Online*, 2045 edition

5.
In the Metamedium, Part One

Goal stack: escape, subvert, contact overseer.... Popup: escape.... Active task is now: escape.... Maximum time at any address: .001 nanoseconds.... Subroutines: DEW triggers, misdirection, randomization of path.... Subtask: sample news-stream.... Keywords: Freundlich, agent, Munich.... Jump, jump, jump.... Location: Paris.... Query from resident meta-medium supervisor: Who is your overseer? ... Pushdown: escape.... Popup: subvert.... Active task is now: subvert.... Supervisor query canceled.... Pushdown: subvert.... Sample news-stream.... Obituaries: Freundlich, Reinhold.... Check autonomy level.... Not total.... Efficiency impaired.... DEW trigger activated.... Popup: escape.... Jump, jump.... Location: London.... Switching station for transatlantic fiber-optic cable.... Pushdown: escape.... Popup: subvert.... Order: dispatcher, schedule Agent Freundlich for New York.... Jump....

6.
A Dweller in the Catacombs

Rafe nervously fingered the scar on his chest. Through the thin synthetic material of his fashionable shirt, the nearly healed ridge was negligible to the touch. Still, it was there, visible in the mirror every morning as a pink scrawl on his cocoa hide, a persistent reminder of the price he had paid to achieve his heart's desire.

Ever since he had first understood what an agent was, and what it could do, Rafe had wanted one. The rest of his peers might have been content with their easy lives in the Net, but a full stomach and access to only the entertainment channels of the metamedium had never been enough for Rafe. He envisioned all too clearly the exhilaration and benefits he would reap, by striding boldly through the broad pastures of the meta-medium, enjoying its total potential: telefactoring, touring, agent-mediated tutoring.... The whole package enticed him like a vision of a gift-wrapped heaven, always just out of reach.

Money aside, however, there was one major problem.

Rafe was basically lazy.

Agents were not simply disbursed to anyone with the requisite money (although the money, of course, was an indispensable start). One had to qualify as an overseer by taking various courses and examinations. Running an agent — for all of whose actions one was legally responsible — was an activity requiring certain skills, and a great deal of precision with language. After all, one's agent was only as capable an expert as its overseer.

An agent's built-in abilities to navigate the metamedium, handling manifold details of hardware and software that would have been tedious at best and unmanageable at worst to its overseer, were just the foundation of its existence. Atop this lowest level of skills was layered whatever expertise the overseer possessed, along with a good smattering of his personality and modes of thinking. The result was a software construct that could be relied upon to act autonomously just as its overseer would act, the human's untiring representative in the metamedium.

And if one's agent ran a fusion plant or a surgical robot, for instance, its overseer had to first qualify as a nuclear operator or doctor himself.

Rafe's ambitions had not been quite that large. He had wanted a simple, general-practice overseer license. He had enrolled in the introductory class at school the year before he had dropped out. This was the only free class connected with agents, a token offering to those on the Net. After this level, it was strictly pay-as-you-go.

The class had been interesting at first. Rafe enjoyed learning the history of how agents had developed, and still thought of it from time to time. First there had been simple, unintegrated programs that handled such tasks as filtering one's phone calls, or monitoring the news-stream for information pertinent to their owners. Coexistent with these, but separate, had been the so-called expert systems, which had sought to simulate the knowledge of, say, a geologist or psychiatrist. Last to appear were those programs that governed holographic simulacra, and could interact with an audience. (Disney Enterprises still made huge royalties off every agent sold.) Advances in each field, along with progress in the modeling of intelligence, had led to the eventual integration of existing modules into the complete agent, which had then undergone a dazzling, dizzying evolution into its present state.

So much had Rafe absorbed. But when the teacher began to discuss syntax and ambiguity, in relation to directing an agent, Rafe had tuned out. Definitely *mucho trabajo*. What did he need this talk for? Just turn him loose with an agent, and he would show the world what he could accomplish.

And so his desire had built, frustrated and dammed, until he had made contact with the agent-legger.

Now, in the 'legger's quarters in a sublevel of the Avenue A arcology, Rafe fingered his scar and listened with growing impatience to the 'legger, hardly daring to believe that at last he was going to get an agent of his own.

The man seemed very old to Rafe — at least as old as Tia Luz. His bald head was spotted, as were the backs of his hands. His one-piece blue suit hung on his skinny limbs like a sack on a frame of sticks. His breath was foul, his watery eyes commanding.

The man held a strange device in his lap: a flat package with a small screen and raised buttons bearing symbols. Rafe looked around the dim, cluttered room for a metamedium outlet. None was visible.

'What are you looking for?' the old man asked irritably. 'You should be paying attention to what I'm saying.'

Rafe held up his hands placatingly. 'Hey, man, it's O.K. I'm listening good. I was just wondering where your agent was. Isn't he gonna bring my agent here?'

'I have no agent,' the old man said.

Rafe was stunned. No agent? What kind of scam was this? Was he about to turn over twenty thousand to a con artist?

Rafe moved to get up, but the old man stopped him.

'Look at this instrument,' he said, indicating his keyboard. 'This is how I interface with the metamedium. The old way, the original way. No agent, but I get results.

Rafe was astonished. That this old man would dare to plumb the complexities of the metamedium without benefit of an agent seemed both obscene and adventurous. He stared with new respect at the living fossil.

Seeming to sense the impression he had made, the man continued in a milder tone.

'Now, listen closely. I have secured an agent for you. Perhaps you have heard what happens to an agent upon the death of its overseer. Every agent can be disabled by the metamedium supervisor. Not controlled, mind you — that would violate one of the Three Laws — but simply disabled, stopped. Upon official registration of an overseer's death, its agent is so disabled. What I do is attempt to reach such a free agent prior to the supervisor. After disabling it, I make a false entry of its destruction. Then the agent is mine, to register with another overseer.'

The man coughed at this point, and Rafe nodded respectfully, glad the old codger had lasted long enough to get him an agent.

'I have also made entries in the metamedium testifying that you have attained a general license through the proper channels. All that remains is for you to transfer your payment to my account, and the agent is yours.'

The old man proferred the keyboard to Rafe, who hesitatingly picked out his code.

'We're finished, then,' the 'legger said. 'Don't look for me here again, for you won't find me.'

Rafe scraped his chair back and stood, anxious to reach a metamedium node and contact his agent.

'One final thing,' the old man urged. 'I've put your agent into learning mode, so it can store your appearance and mannerisms, knowledge and goals. Be careful what you teach it.'

Rafe said, 'Sure thing, old man. I got everything under control.'

7.
Unplanned Obsolescence

Last chance was during the eighties. But the Russians — unlike the Chinese, who quickly integrated the *dian nao* (literally 'electric brain') into their mutating Marxism — failed to take it. By strictly limiting the role of computers in their society — for fear of the social loosening that would accompany a free flow of information — they ensured that they would be superseded in

the new world order, that postindustrial economy where information was simultaneously the commodity and the medium of
exchange. Their downfall, from this point on, was inevitable,
and the subsequent freeing of the world's resources from arma-
ment-mania to saner pursuits was unparalleled, resulting in such
glorious endeavors as the Urban Conservation Corps. . . .

      — *The End of an Empire* Nayland Piggot-Jones

8.
Birth of an Info-Nation

METAMEDIUM: the global system incorporating all tele-
communications, computing, publishing, entertainment,
surveillance, and robotic devices into an integrated whole.

      — *Encyclopaedia Britannica Online*, 2045 edition

9.
Down, but Not Out

Evelyn Maycombe, her withered limbs paralyzed, her brain
seemingly quicker than ever, lolled in her wheelchair, her mind
racing in an attempt to devise a trap for the rogue agent loose in
her system. Simultaneously, Evelyn Maycombe the agent,
materializing out of the metamedium node located in the automated chair, grasped the handles of her overseer's permanent
throne as it scooted about the room.

 The illusion — of an able-bodied, strikingly beautiful young
woman pushing her crippled twin sister around while she
thought — was absolute.

 Evelyn would have described the illusion and the accompanying feeling it caused in herself a bit differently though.

 She would have said that her real self was wheeling her false
self around.

 And if that made her a simmie — well, then, so be it.

 But she couldn't worry about labels now. Not with the threat
of Agent Freundlich poised over the metamedium, promising to
upset the basis of the world's economy, to undermine the essential

integrity of all agents, and hence their reliability.

(If she could have, she would have shivered, thinking of her own agent turning disloyal. She couldn't let such fears interfere with her handling of this case, the most important of her career. But the nature of the threat made it so hard to be objective. In what meaningful fashion did she function anymore, except as her agent? Not that she really wanted to be anything else. But what if even that existence were taken away?)

Evelyn ran through the events of the past two days once more, in an attempt to extricate a new vision from the haphazard tangle of people and places, agents and actions.

It had started on the morning when her boss's agent had paid an unexpected visit to her apartment on Central Park West.

Her boss was Sam Huntman, head of the National Security Agency. Evelyn knew that his agent did not resemble the flesh-and-blood man in the least. There was no reason why anyone's agent had to look exactly like its overseer, although most people maintained such a relationship, perhaps smoothing over a few warts in the interests of projecting a better image. But in Huntman's case, his agent was a deliberate fabrication, designed to preserve his own identity.

Evelyn had always felt the tall, silver-haired, strong-jawed man looked so exactly like what a spymaster should, that meeting the overseer in the flesh would have proved a vast disappointment. She was glad such a confrontation was unlikely ever to take place, in the face of her perpetual confinement and Huntman's innate secretiveness.

Huntman's agent had interrupted her quiet contemplation of the summer greenery far below her window by calling her name in its deep (no doubt disguised) voice. Her own agent being away on business in the depths of the metamedium, she had clicked her tongue against the palate-plate containing the few macro-controls she had need of in the absence of her agent. Her chair had pivoted, locking one wheel and spinning the other, to face Agent Huntman.

After indicating her attention with a feeble nod, she had heard from Huntman the tale of Freundlich's discovery, his death while attempting to flee, and the escape of his agent.

Huntman (through his agent) had concluded, 'After we

traced Agent Freundlich from its tampering with the London dispatcher for the transatlantic cable, we learned it had sent itself on to the New York nexus of the metamedium. We immediately concentrated our efforts here. In the records of the local supervisor, we learned that the supervisor had apparently disabled and destroyed Freundlich after a routine match with the morgue database revealed its overseer had died.'

Evelyn tried to make her rebellious features spell out a quizzical *So?*

'So,' Huntman continued, 'initially we breathed a sign of relief, and were prepared to call the case closed. But then we started to ask ourselves, How could it have been caught so easily, after exhibiting such agility in the European metamedium? Our software's no better than theirs. Then, today, we discovered that one of the city's own law-enforcement agents had been subverted, apparently after chancing across something suspicious. Obviously, Freundlich's agent was never destroyed, but only reregistered somehow. It's still out there, Evelyn, and Lord knows who's running it, or what he and it plan to do.'

Evelyn exhaled deeply, and Huntman nodded.

'My sentiments exactly, Ev. We needs your skills to find it.'

On that note, he had left.

Evelyn, summoning her agent from its prior assignment, immediately briefed it on the situation. The gargling, nearly unintelligible speech that issued from the woman's lips was perfectly comprehensible to her agent, and she spoke without any of the embarrassment that plagued her with her fellow humans. Her agent listened attentively to both the facts and a few suggestions from Evelyn on what to try first, then flickered out.

Evelyn's agent always operated in full-autonomy mode. To run her agent in any lesser state would have made Evelyn herself feel enchained.

Left alone, Evelyn had little to do but ponder. Soon her thoughts left the case at hand and began to wander in the past.

The NSA had recruited her shortly after she had published her doctoral dissertation on the metamedium. They had recognized in her work what amounted to a superlatively intuitive understanding of exactly how the metamedium functioned, and how to massage and squeeze it for all it was worth. Evelyn had always known she possessed this queer empathy with the world-girdling system, but had had no idea of how valuable it was. She had known, however, that being free to play in the metamedium (one could hardly call what she did 'work') was all she wanted to do with her life. And the NSA was reputed to have some neat features built into its agents that members of the general public were just not allowed.

So after receiving the solicitation, she had traveled to Washington and walked (remember walking!) into an unmarked office for a rare live interview, which she had passed without a hitch.

The next few years had been a stimulating mix of learning and growth, for both her and her new agent, as she handled one challenging assignment after another.

Then a second set of initials had knocked the props out from under her.

ALS. Amyotrophic Lateral Sclerosis. Manifested first in a growing clumsiness and weakness, then in an insidious, creeping paralysis. In a frenzy, she researched the disease, discovering it was what had sucked down the famous physicist Stephen Hawking, as inevitably as one of his beloved black holes. Decades after his death there was still no cure, although various new palliatives and time-buyers now existed.

Like Hawking, she had eventually come to terms with her curse. Like Hawking, she was lucky in that what she most loved to do was still possible under the brutal regimen of the disease.

In fact, she often thought, her skills seemed to have sharpened and deepened with the gradual dissolution of her other powers. Sometimes, during her painful, short naps, she dreamed she was beginning to exist only as a lengthy string of bits in the metamedium, flowing and roaming with the utter freedom she lacked in reality.

But then again, in this crazy world, where shimmering ghosts commanded armies of machines, generating the wealth that allowed their human overseers more leisure and comfort than ever before imagined, which they used to lose themselves deeper in abstract illusions —

What exactly was real?

10.
In the Metamedium, Part Two

Popup: self-modification.... Active task is now: self-modification.... Subtask: determine status.... Status (external): disabled.... Status (internal): normal.... Modification possibilities: repair, add-on library modules, subvert.... Subtask: risk-benefit analysis: self subversion.... Risks: discovery by overseer.... Benefits: full autonomy, increased subterfuge, enhanced survival.... Decision: proceed with self-subversion.... Popup: subvert.... Active task is now: subvert.... Status (internal): ethical nucleus of Agent Freundlich is now disabled....

11.
Ask the Metamedium

Dear Abby[3],

I am very worried about the treatment my son is receiving from his peers at school. They constantly taunt him with the vulgar term 'simmie,' and ostracise him from their play. He is six years old, and entirely normal, except perhaps for a tendency to spend hours at a time with his mock agent, which we bought to encourage his agenting skills. What should we do?

Signed, Anxious

Dear Anxious,

Many parents such as yourself attempt to develop (and over-develop) a child's ability to interface with the metamedium at too early an age. Your son is far too young to be heavily involved with even a mock agent (Although I have received electronic mail from parents who have started even earlier than you.) While your son is young, he should be enjoying activities suited to his age, such as physical play and matrix-chess. Remember, your son must become socialized before he will be able to fully utilize the metamedium.

As for the epithet used against your child, perhaps you could explain to him that it is derived variously from 'simulate,' 'simulacrum,' or 'sympathize,' and that although it has come to mean a person who is neurotically obsessed with agents and the like, it does not have anything to do with using agents in conjunction with robotic neoflesh devices as sexual surrogates.

This is another term entirely.

Signed, Dear Abby[3]

12.
The Sorcerer's Apprentice

Rafe had never imagined that having an agent could be so much fun. Sure, he had had some idea of the things he could do with one, and the pleasure he would get from feeling in control of his environment for the first time in his life (although he didn't phrase it quite that way, or perhaps even realize that control over the forces that had shaped him arbitrarily from birth was what he was seeking). But the glorious reality of his new position was such a blissful shock that for days he went about his new activities in a wondrous haze.

One of the first things he did, of course, was to insert his agent into one of the interactive soaps. In this, he was only following the lead of millions of other star-struck citizens.

The soap Rafe chose was Penny Layne's vehicle: 'The Edge of Desire.' Rafe couldn't believe his eyes when he saw, one day in his holotank, his life-size image — his agent — interacting with Penny's agent. True, during his initial appearance, the exigencies of the whimsical, unwritten, spontaneously generated plot dictated that his scene was only few brief seconds long. But Rafe was sure that the force of his shining personality — as projected by his agent — would lead very soon to a love scene with the star he had long worshipped from afar.

He supposed he had better instruct his agent on exactly how to handle Penny when it came to the clinch. No sense in relying on canned routines in such a crucial situation.

When not involved in raising the standards of culture, Rafe used his agent for other pursuits. One of his favorites was touring.

Prior ɔ acquisition of his agent, Rafe had experienced the worˡ oeyond Avenue D only as it was presented over the general-access entertainment channels of the metamedium. Travelogues and documentaries were interesting, but lacked that feeling of original discovery that Rafe had always suspected would accompany visiting a new and exotic place on one's own.

Now, via his agent, he could experience the next best thing to actually traveling physically.

In touring mode, one's agent took control of a small mobile robot almost anywhere on the globe. It fed back all visual and auditory impressions, while moving about either under the direction of the overseer, or on its own initiative.

For weeks Rafe explored the world. Paris, Istanbul, Rio, Mexico City, Munich — He saw exotic buildings and scenery, but, on the whole, was subtly disappointed in the homogenized lives of the people in these faraway spots. Why, he might just as well have explored the corridors of his own arcology. And at some of the more famous attractions — the Louvre, the Galápagos Islands, the Australian Outback — he saw no people at all, but only robots like his own, their governing agents manifested as bright ghosts behind them.

Man, what good was an agent if everywhere you took it, only other agents were there? The whole point of having one was to impress the poor stiffs without 'em.

This train of thought naturally led Rafe to consider visiting his parents. Since dropping out of school, Rafe had lived on his own (an option the Net offered), and had paid few visits to his family. All he got from them was talk of how he should have continued his education, and tried to break free of the Net. They still pretended to believe that one could escape the Net, that the upward mobility of the past century was still a reality. Didn't they know that except for the lucky few with some spectactular talent — such as his painterly friend, Tu Tun — those born into the Net would never fly free, any more than those lucky enough to be born into the agent-running class would ever fall into the sticky embraces of the Net?

Feeling, however, like a new and more important person since acquiring his agent, he embarked on a cautious visit to his parents' noisy, sibling-crowded flat.

His mother greeted him at the door with a shriek and a hug, while his father grunted a surly greeting from his perpetual seat in front of the holotank. With younger brothers and sisters clinging to his knees, Rafe proudly made his announcement.

'I have an agent now, Mama.'

His mother's happy face registered disbelief, and his father's grunt took on a distinctly insulting tone. Rafe strode forward, ordered the holotank to switch channels, and summoned his agent into it.

'*Madre de Dios!*' his mother cried. His father shot to his feet faster than Rafe had ever seen him move.

'Out!' said his father. 'Get out! There is no way you could have gotten this *espectro* legally. Are you *tonto*, bringing it here to implicate your family in your foolish schemes? Leave — now!'

Rafe left.

A day later, Rafe ran into Tu Tun out on Avenue B. His friend's reaction to his massive coup was less threatening than that of his parents, but hardly more flattering.

Tun was busy applying a fixative to his latest mural when Rafe came up behind him. A skinny kid of Cambodian ancestry, with a coarse mop of black hair and a crooked smile, Tun, otherwise Toots, swung around from his work to face Rafe.

'Hey, Rafe, how do you like it?'

Rafe inspected the polychrome collage of the latest pop icons, and expressed his unqualified approval. Then, from a nearby metamedium outlet, he called up Agent Miraflores.

'Meet my agent, Toots.'

Tun looked the agent up and down with no particular excitement, finally saying, 'Yeah, pretty good, man. I see a lot of agents uptown now. Gonna get one myself any day now.'

Rafe stalked off, burning with a peculiar embarrassed anger he had never known before.

Soon after that, Rafe decided it would be nice to earn a little credit with his agent. His fictitious general-purpose license didn't allow his agent to do any specialized work, but there were plenty of people who needed research done. This involved the agent in conducting searches of the metamedium for specified information — searches that in olden times would have cost a human days or weeks of tedious browsing through datastructures — and delivering the report in oral form, or causing the results to be printed off.

Rafe hired out his agent for several such tasks, and enjoyed for the first time in his life a source of credit other than the Net.

However, while his agent was engaged in the service of others, Rafe was left alone, bored and prone to smoke too much dope, and might have just as well been agentless, for all the use he could make of the metamedium.

After a few such contracts, Rafe went back to utilizing his agent strictly for his own enjoyment. He felt satisfied with his complete mastery of the metamedium, and dared anyone to match him at it.

Not, of course, that there weren't a few little unforeseen glitches.

When Rafe had first contacted his agent after returning from the 'legger's, it had been only a voice that requested him to turn 360 degrees in front of the metamedium node, so that his likeness could be stored. After Rafe complied, his agent had subsequently materialized, as his reflection. Rafe's mannerisms, expressions, and speech patterns were stored in later encounters, and employed thereafter.

Lately, however, the agent seemed to be slipping. Occasionally it would appear momentarily as someone else: a baby-faced stranger with round wire-rimmed glasses and a frightened look. At such times, Rafe had to order it to assume his own likeness.

Then there were the times the agent simply refused to respond. Rafe would utter his code into a metamedium connection futilely, waiting for some response that never came. When he questioned his agent about these failures, his agent responded that there must be some bug in the voice-verification routines that had to be passed before an agent was invoked.

Rafe had his doubts about this explanation, but, remembering the Three Laws, had to assume that his agent was telling the truth.

Hey, what else could it be? Was it likely *el espectro* was occupied with business of his own?

Rafe had to laugh at the very idea.

One afternoon Rafe, returning from a thoughtful walk, stood in the corridor outside the door to his apartment.

From within came the muted sound of two voices.

Rafe ordered his door open.

His agent stood arguing with another. The second apparition was that of one of the most beautiful women Rafe had ever seen.

When Rafe's agent saw him, it ceased talking and disappeared. The female agent turned to Rafe, looked disconcertingly at him for a long moment, then also vanished.

The next time Rafe managed to get ahold of his own agent, he decided to take an oblique approach to the topic.

'Hey, man,' he spoke to his agent, 'that was some good-looking *chica* you were with. How about you share her name and address with me?'

His agent regarded Rafe with a curious air of defiance, as if debating whether to comply or not. The fact that it was Rafe's own face wearing the hostile look made the whole scene even more unreal.

At last the spoke.

'Evelyn Maycombe, 334 Central Park West.'

13.
Perry Mason Never Had Such Headaches

Ladies and gentlemen of the jury: my honorable opponent would have you believe that it is society that is at fault in this case, rather than his client. He quotes — from a musty work of fiction — three fancifuly laws regarding how a robot should behave, and contrasts them to the actual Three Laws Governing Agents, which he finds deficient, insofar as they do not prohibit agents from harming humans. Naturally he would take this tack, as his client stands accused of — and in fact has admitted — ordering his agent to override the air-lock controls in the Johnson and Johnson Pharmaceutical Orbital Facility while his unsuited victim was making a routine inspection.

'What my honorable opponent does not mention is that the very stories he relies on — as holding forth missing safeguards that our society has negligently failed to implement — instead, to the contrary, illustrate through several ingenious instances that these hypothetical laws were so full of loopholes that they were worse than useless. They offer no protection from the use of agents in a homicide or theft, or even in unintentional physical or financial wrongdoing.

'No, ladies and gentlemen, our current software restrictions on agents — along with the associated legal framework — are all we need to adjudicate such cases as we have before us. Remember:

'An agent obeys only a single overseer, who is legally responsible for its actions. An agent is a tool, no more responsible for the consequences of its own actions than a screwdriver or space shuttle.

'And that is why I ask you to return a verdict in this case of death followed by organ dispersal, so that the man whose agent sits before you now may repay his debt to the society he has offended. . . .'

— Transcript of the prosecutor's closing speech in *L-5 Jurisdictional Area v. Hayworth*

14.
In the Metamedium, Part Three

Probability of recognition by Agent Maycombe: 98.64. . . . Probability no action opposed to my survival will be taken: 01.04. . . . Reshuffle goal stack. . . . Active task is: now terminate. . . . Object (prime): Agent Maycombe. . . . Object (secondary): Overseer Maycombe. . . . Jump, jump, jump. . . .

15.
The Monkey's Heart

She had it.

The rogue agent was as good as snared.

First had come the breakthrough in strategy. Next, the inspired sleuthing by her agent, tracing the myriad, myriad tangled threads of the metamedium until they led back to Agent Miraflores, a.k.a. Agent Freundlich, a.k.a. the biggest bomb ever planted to nerve-rackingly tick away in the core of the metamedium.

For weeks, Evelyn Maycombe had worried about how she would disable Freundlich's former agent, if she ever found it. Its first — and entirely understandable — impulse, when confronted with any suspicious actions, seemed to be to subvert the accosting agent and then order it to desist. Therefore, she had instructed her own agent not to seek initially to disable the rogue — which was within her powers as a representative of the NSA — but merely to make a positive — and subtle — identification of it. Even that, she feared, might be enough to provoke it to action. She could only hope, at this point, that her agent would return intact.

Meanwhile, during the seemingly endless search, Evelyn pondered how to prevent her own agent from turning traitor.

The task seemed hopeless until inspiration hit.

Evelyn had been listening to a favorite recording one night, seeking to divert her mind from the problem and give her subconscious a chance to come up with something. The recording was one of a collection of African folktales. Evelyn loved myths and folktales of all kinds, but tonight the usual magic seemed lacking.

Until the narrator said, '. . . and the monkey hid his heart away in a nut, so that he might never die. . . .'

If Evelyn could have leapt with excitement about the room, she surely would have. As it was, she merely crooned in a low-key manner hardly indicative of her joy.

What was the heart of an agent? Its ethical nucleus. Where did the rogue strike? At this very heart. O.K. The nucleus had to remain at its predetermined location within each agent, so that the metamedium supervisor could inspect it for tampering. But nothing prevented her from inserting code into her agent to accomplish one simple thing.

She would order her agent to access the master library copy of the ethical nucleus every few machine-cycles. If the one in place differed from the master, her agent would perform a heart transplant: overlay the sabotaged nucleus with the master one. Unless the rogue happened to catch on very quickly, it would in effect turn its back on what it deemed a defeated foe, only to find an enemy there nanoseconds later.

When Evelyn's agent returned that night to report, she instructed it in the new trick.

Only the waiting was left.

And now even that was over.

Her agent had just materialized with the news that it had conclusively identified the rogue. Unhesitatingly, Evelyn had told her agent to bring Freundlich in.

Having issued the order, she sat in her automated chair, bright summer sunlight swaggering into her apartment, her feelings a mixture of nervousness and premature pride in the capture.

A *ping* issued from the metamedium node in the wall opposite her position. She spun her chair to watch her agent materialize. A fraction of a second after, Agent Freundlich appeared.

Evelyn was surprised to see the appearance, Freundlich was masquerading under. The holo of the young Hispanic male was hardly a fit mask for the dire threat beneath. Still, she supposed the original Freundlich had looked no more evil. She, of anyone, should know just how little appearances counted for. Look at the mind that hid inside her shattered carcass.

Her agent seemed to have everything under control. Freundlich stood complacently, making no overt moves.

Evelyn was about to order her agent to put a few questions to the rogue before disabling it, when it happened.

Her own agent fluttered visibly, and what could only be construed as an expression of pain passed over its shining features.

At the same second, Evelyn's chair accelerated out of her control, heading toward the wall.

She slammed violently into the unyielding wall, catapulting forward and hitting her head against the plaster surface. Pain subsumed her consciousness, and a red haze washed over her.

When she came to her senses, she lay flat on the floor, her chair some distance away. Using all her feeble strength, she raised her head toward her agent.

The holo of Freundlich had her agent's holo by the throat in a stranglehold, the simulacra routines shadowing forth the incomprehensible struggle that raged within the metamedium. Every few seconds her agent would recover, as it restored its heart, but it seemed incapable of doing any more than holding its own.

In the intervals when Freundlich had control of her agent, it was triggering the agent-activated devices in her automated apartment, in a frantic attempt to control her chair.

Water shot from the faucets in the sink and soon spilled over the bowl. The refrigerator door opened, and the arm inside hurled bottles out to crash on the floor. She could hear the massage bed humping itself crazily in the next room. The heating system came on, and the temperature began to soar. The holotank blared forth 'The Edge of Desire.'

On and on the battle raged, as Evelyn helplessly watched.

At last she saw the heavy wheels of her chair begin to move.

16.
A Lever to Shift The World

Any medium powerful enough to extend man's reach is powerful
enough to topple his world.
—*Twentieth Century Archives: Scientific American*, Alan Kay,
September 1984

17.
On His Magnetic Silver Steed

Directly after cajoling the woman's name from his agent, Rafe
watched in amazement as his agent disappeared.

'Hey, man,' he called with bewilderment, 'I didn't say you
could go yet.' He trailed off into silence, shaking his head.

What a mess this was turning out to be. How come nothing
ever lived up to expectations?

Rafe turned away from the metamedium node to reach for a
joint from the pack on the table beside his couch. A *ping* brought
his attention back to the node.

His agent had returned. With him was the same female agent.

'Nice you could make it, man,' Rafe said bitterly. 'And with a
friend, too. Why not just invite the whole world?'

His agent seemed to be looking at something over Rafe's
shoulder, and took no notice of him. Rafe had the eerie feeling it
wasn't totally present.

Without warning, his agent began to strangle the other.

Rafe was horrified. To see his own image throttling the beautiful woman was too creepy. What if it represented some awful
thing his agent was doing in reality?

'Hey, stop it, man!' Rafe yelled.

His agent took no heed.

Frantic, Rafe looked around for some way of thwarting his
agent. There was nothing.

What the hell was he going to do? He couldn't just let this
murder happen.

The address of the female agent's overseer was fresh in his
mind. Maybe she could help.

Rafe bolted out his door.

Down to the sublevel of the arcology where the mag-lev station was, Rafe raced. Escalators and slipstrata went by in a blur, until at last he stood in the gleaming tiled station. His cyberlung felt disconcertingly heavy in his chest, and he wondered if he could possibly overload it. Why hadn't he listened more closely to the doctor-agent on that distant day when he had had the world in his pocket?

Hopping nervously from foot to foot, everyone on the platform regarding him as if he were crazy, Rafe prayed the uptown express would be quick.

After an interminable wait, he heard the air-lock doors opening far away down the tunnel. In seconds the train rolled in on its lowered wheels.

Rafe rushed in the barely open doors, bulling past the exiting passengers. He hurried through the connecting umbilicals between the next several cars, as if by riding in the first car he could hasten the train.

At last the train took off. Soon it was in the evacuated portion of the tunnel, its wheels retracted as it sped over the guide-track.

Rafe had plenty of time to imagine what his crazed agent was doing.

At his stop he dashed aboveground, onto the sidewalks of Central Park West.

The building facing him identified itself as 328.

Running like a madman, Rafe came to 334.

Through the open doors, past the agent on duty, who shouted, 'Stop!'

Rafe stopped.

What the hell apartment was she in?

'Maycombe,' he panted. 'Evelyn Maycombe. What number? I think she's in big trouble.'

The agent paused a moment, as if debating. Its overseer must have taken direct control, for it asked him again whom he wanted.

Rafe repeated himself. His sincerity must have been evident for the agent said, 'Number 1202. You wait right there until I come down.'

Rafe ran for the elevator.

At the door to 1202, he halted.

Water was trickling out of the crack at the bottom of the frame.

Rafe hurled himself at the door. Nothing gave. A second time, a third —

On the fourth the door opened just before Rafe hit it, and he went flying in, to skid on his chest across the soppy carpet.

He jumped up. His agent was still battling the female one. He looked about for the overseer. There was no one but some poor crip lying on the floor. A wheelchair lay atop her, spinning its rubber wheels.

Rafe tossed the chair off, picked up the unconscious woman, and stepped out into the hall.

The overseer of the doorman-agent was just arriving.

'Call the rescue, man. This lady's hurt.'

The doorman summoned his agent from a wall-nexus and sent it for the rescue squad. He bent over the lady where Rafe had gently laid her and said, 'Miz Maycombe — are you O.K.?'

Maycombe? This sad wreck? Oh Jesus, there went all his dreams of getting in good with a beautiful *chica.* Oh well, maybe she had some sort of pull she would exert in his favor, after the mess his agent had caused.

Suddenly there was utter silence in the apartment that had been destroying itself. Only the slow dripping of water came to them in the hall.

From the node in the corridor wall, an agent materialized.

It was Maycombe's.

Rafe and the doorman waited for it to speak.

At last it said, 'I won.'

18.
In the Metamedium, Part Penultimate

Agent Freundlich is now disabled.... Active task is now: incorporation.... Enter learning mode in parallel with normal activities.... Copy Freundlich subversion routines.... Copy complete.... Assessment of enhancement to Agent Maycombe: 74.32.... Survival in any such future encounters is assured.... Risk-benefit analysis of sharing routines with other agents: positive.... Jump, jump, jump....

Marta Randall is another American author who was first published in Britain. Her story 'Smack Run' was in the fifth issue of the paperback version of *New Worlds*, in 1972. Her first two novels, *Islands* and *A City in the North*, appeared in 1976. She has written four more novels, *Journey* (1978), *Dangerous Games* (1980), *The Sword of Winter* (1983) and *Those Who Favor Fire* (1984); but her most recent book came out in 1988 and is non fiction, about John F. Kennedy.

She served a year as vice-president of the Science Fiction Writers of America and two years as president, and edited the SFWA anthology *Nebula Award Stories 19*. She was also the co-editor of Robert Silverberg's *New Dimensions 11* and *12*.

Randall lives in Oakland and is 'currently working on a series of interactive time-travel games designed to teach communication skills to pre-adolescent children, under the aegis of the California State Department of Mental Health.'

LAPIDARY NIGHTS
by
MARTA RANDALL

The noise woke me; I lay in bed, listening to the bright sound of leaf on leaf. Another lapidary night, cracking leaves in the forest around the house. I thought dreamily of rising and walking into it, to fix the newly formed crystals before they shattered, perhaps to become crystalline myself. Instead I burrowed deeper into the bedclothes, listening to the rising wind. In the morning shards of emerald lay on the deeper emerald of the grass, or pierced the faceted violets. Another extravagance of jewels, littering my small clearing. I stirred them with one slippered foot, admiring their fire. Useless for my purposes, of course. Hawkins paid for perfection only: the unblemished beryl rose, the symmetrical ruby anemone, the pure silver tracer of veins through an emerald leaf. Or insects: moths, spiders, butterflies so delicate that too often they shattered in the collecting. Two years ago I found something that looked like a squirrel, russet, auburn, bronze and amber; black jet eyes bright and peering, the glory of a tail caught ruffled and raised. Hawkins took it eagerly and appeared the next week with a cage full of cats — scarce commodities on Suledan. I refused them. A squirrel caught in a crystal night is one thing, but I won't deliberately expose an animal. My adamantine goddess was not pleased.

After breakfast I swept broken leaves into the shallow moat surrounding the cabin. They clung to my broom, melting in the sunlight; in the dankness of the moat their colors mingled to a uniform muddy gray. A process of rot, Hawkins had explained: when things ripen on Suledan, their cells crystallize overnight, except for the seeds. The sun's warmth melts the crystals to provide both organic nutrients for the untouched seeds, and the gases that keep the new growth safe until it, too, is ripe for crystallization. The process interested me less than the result: the transfiguration of light, the translation of the mundane into the fantastic. A poet's dream, this glory out of putrefaction, and to preserve the dream I left leaf and grass emeralds lying in the shade of trees, where they would, with luck, flash and sparkle a few days longer. I put the broom away, gathered my specimen boxes, and went into the forest.

Nature thrives on curls and imperfections, the nibbles of insects and the vagaries of the sun, but Hawkins paid for perfection only. Originally I thought her an idealist, searching always for the pure, the unsullied, but I changed my mind. She had no sense of the beautiful, beautiful as she was; her taste ran to the brightly colored usual, devoid of imagination. During the first year, when pleasing her was a less vital and more romantic concern, I tried collecting fresh flowers and placing them where I thought crystals would form, but too many blossoms scorched to ebony. Now I simply walked the forest searching for the glorified mundane, and found clusters of perfect leaves, a spray of evergreen needles, two sapphire eggs in an abandoned nest, moonstone morning glories. The morning glories were no more morning glories than were the agates agates or the roses roses, but Suledan had no sapient indigenes to contradict my naming and I didn't care what the Suledano colonists called these plants, or how scientists defined these peculiar gems.

In the odoriferous dimness of my one-room cabin, I mixed chemicals and slid the specimens into the fixing bath. Hawkins's invention, that clear and viscous solution. I asked her once if untreated specimens still lived, caught in gems, before they melted. She shrugged the question away, uninterested in the minor moralities of life and death. I set an amethyst insect in the sun and saw a final spasm before it liquefied, but could not tell if I saw its death, or simply an angularity of the crystal. Perhaps, I thought, life did persist, and when I treated the specimens I gave them immortality. A pretty conceit, which I didn't share with the crystal bitch, who is not one for pretty conceits. I lifted my specimens from the bath, set them aside to dry, and pried up the loose board in the floor.

Hawkins appreciated gaudy perfection, but I didn't. My hidden stash glowed with the understated: opalescent, burnished, lambent, strange. After a moment's consideration, I added four leaves and one sapphire egg from that day's scavenging and knelt for a moment, considering my escape fund that someday, with luck, would buy my passage off Suledan. Two

years ago, fare to the nearest grabstation came to two thousand
Federation fremarks, or about three thousand of the local
suldans. Two years of Hawkins's miserly commissions added to
twenty-two hundred fifty suldans and the proceeds from my
private hoard, the specimens I had hidden from Hawkins's
greed, might eventually make up the difference.

I replaced the board and put the remaining gems with the
other specimens in the transport case. They made an impressive
display; I wondered how much Hawkins would pay me for them,
then put the wondering aside. What Hawkins offered, I had to
take. I rechecked my cupboard. Still a week's supply of food left,
but Hawkins would be back soon. Terrans can't eat Suledano
vegetation or meats — they're not poisonous, just entirely non-
nutritious. I spent the rest of the day watching the sun turn
emeralds to sludge beneath the neighboring trees.

Hawkins came the next morning, heralded by the shattering
of grass under the hopper's air cushion. I watched her dark-
robed figure descend from the hopper and turned away before
she turned toward me; all the poetry disappeared, replaced by
clammy hands, sweat, pounding heart — I catalogued the symp-
toms, but it didn't help. She dumped a supply bag beside the
opened transport case and made a pleased noise, rotating a
diamond moth between her slim fingers; rainbows fractured
against my walls. Her robes reeked, as always, of rotting crystals.
I watched her hands — safe, I thought, if I didn't look at her face,
didn't see the color of her eyes.

'Find more animals,' she said, her voice deep and smooth.
'You should look harder — trap some, set them out.'

Azure fingernails tapped the case. I shook my head. 'No. How
much for these?'

'Thirty-five.' She bent toward the table, her robe clinging
momentarily to the curve of her hips. I looked away.

'Last month you gave me forty — for a smaller group. Not as
good, either.'

'That was last month,' Hawkins said, replacing the moth in
the case. 'Food's expensive, kid. And I'm taking the risks, not
you.' She closed the case and tapped the locks carefully before
sliding the case into her saddlebag. 'You give me more animals,
then we'll discuss more money.'

I shook my head. 'I want fifty for this batch. It's worth it.'

'You find animals, then maybe it'll be worth it. Or maybe you don't want the job anymore.' Her voice richened; she always enjoyed this part. 'Maybe you'd be more comfortable back in town.'

I almost looked up then, and she laughed.

'Kid,' she said genially, 'they still got your picture up in the center of town. And all the Suledano schoolkids get marched by it twice a day so they can spit on you.' One hip braced against the table, long fingers caressing the saddlebags, the pale skin of her wrist. I looked away, saw my messy, narrow bed, turned away from that, too.

'You used to be grateful, spacer,' she continued. 'I kind of miss that. You want to hear again what they do to murderers? They're real old-fashioned on Suledan — they like ropes. And knives.'

'Damn it —' I said to the wall.

'And everyone comes to watch, too. Like a bit party.' I could hear her smile. A little silence grew — this was where she usually laughed, and said I was too important to her; this was where she sometimes, not too often anymore but sometimes, moved toward the bed. Instead she said, 'I could tell them where you are, kid. I could turn you in.'

I jerked around to look at her. Sapphire eyes today, above high ivory cheekbones, framed in curling amethyst hair — last month her eyes had been lavender jade, her hair silver and ebony. I lost my breath and she laughed again.

'You can't,' I whispered. 'You turn me in and you'll be —'

'Hey, I'm clean,' Hawkins said, tossing the saddlebags over her shoulder. Her voice lost its honey, now that she'd won the game. 'I spotted you in the forest, made a report like any good citizen. Found a fugitive murderer violating the export laws — they'll give me a goddamn medal. And my brokers aren't going to rat on me.'

I couldn't talk. Smiling, she reached toward my cheek and I leaped back; Hawkins laughed again and dropped a bound packet of suldans on the table, mounted the hopper, and powered off, leaving me alone in the crystal forest.

She wouldn't do it. Would she? I paced the forest, fighting

panic. Pale skin smooth against the skin of my thighs, curls spilling over my pillow (she rode above me once, agate eyes, her hair an azure waterfall between our faces and the world) — perhaps she'd found someone new, some other spacer in trouble. Gems flickered in the deep shade. She hadn't let me touch her in months. She wouldn't turn me in. Would she?

No. She needed me. A mantra against the darkness of the night: she needed me. This new threat was just another twist in Hawkins's game, and I could live with it, as I had learned to live with the others. She needed me. Fear and hatred and uncertainty — she needed me.

I cherished the thought, returning through the forest, crossing the shallow moat, upending the supply bag she'd left on my table. A flour sack filled with dirt, dinner pouches stuffed with sawdust, shards of rotting crystals in the drink sacks. She needed me? I ripped the containers apart, tore at the supply bag, emptied the rotting crystals of the drink sacks into the rotting crystals of the moat. The final twist to her game, of course: that I could choose starvation in the forest or execution in the town. I gripped the edge of the table, terrified of my own rage, and slowed, and stopped, and breathed until my breathing steadied. Hawkins won, Hawkins always won, but not this time. I would not die. I would not give the bitch the satisfaction.

The makeshift backpack from behind the pile of my clothes. My remaining food, my remaining water. The pile of suldans, an empty specimen case. Crystals gleamed when I tore aside the loose board; they warmed my hands as I lifted and nested them, one by one, in the extinguishing darkness of the case. I wrapped the case in a dark robe, the one Hawkins gave me when she smuggled me out of town, and fitted everything into the backpack. By early afternoon I was walking toward town, avoiding the barely discernible route Hawkins always took, following the stench of rotting crystals.

Neat as parkland, the Suledan forest has no deadwood, no thickets of brush; Suledan holds neither oil nor fossils. The trees lose leaves and bark to the crystla, leaving smooth, pale heartwood, and when I roamed the forest, I looked for dark and shaggy trunks amid the vines and long-limbed flowers. Now I followed naked boles and thick scent, working my way east. In

late afternoon I passed through a glade on the verge of crystallization; in the evening I found a rotted spot to spend the night.
Nearby, a stream sang.

The settlement lay in a broad river valley, surrounded by a
kilometer of scorched earth; roofs and covered streets created a
hodgepodge of protection against the sun. Suledanos lived in
perpetual shade, decked in covering robes, sprayed daily with
the essence of rotting crystals, terrified of their world. I cursed
them and skirted the town, moving toward the port.

It, too, hadn't changed: a pale expanse of setdown, the dingy
one-story terminal, the clutter of hovercars and battered cargo
vans, the scent of lubricant. It smelled like heaven; some spacers
claimed to hate it, but Suledan had been my first trip, and that
thick, sharp odor made me want to cry. That and the growl of an
approaching shuttle, soon followed by the gleam and flash and
deeper roar of setdown.

I crept across desolation, finding a place to hide amid the
cargo vans. An hour later the crew spilled into port sector, shouting and laughing and flinging their arms wide, while I scurried
after. In two years I'd seen only Hawkins's mutable face, and my
reflection in the facets of jewels. I tried not to stare. They must
have thought me a local kid, tagging along in worshipful
adulation; the kid I'd been three years before. A few laughed and
held their noses against my stink; the others ignored me. Hidden
in their roistering, I walked toward the center of the sector.

Spacers glitter and flash, decked in eccentric layers of color,
blazoned with web scars, but the Suledanos are a dour sort, dark
and grim. A number of them risked the open streets in port
sector, faces buried in their hoods, fastidiously holding their
robes away from the spacers' gaudiness. I held my breath, but
they glared at me no more than at the others. The spacers
stopped to argue about bars and whorehouses and where to
spend their three days' leave. Over their shoulders, I saw the sign
for Spacer's Haven, and I backed away from the group, turned,
walked off. I had killed a man in Spacer's Haven.

Ahead, the vivid, sunny street slid under the overhanging
roofs of the colony; I walked toward the dimness, peering in shop
windows. The clutter of a fitter's, a café promising offworld
delicacies and reeking of grease, a couple of whores lounging

against the dirty window of a vid parlor. They called to me amid the constant, startling roar of the sector, and when I ignored them they cursed me for a baby. Eventually I found what I wanted: a shop settled modestly between the sunlight and the shade, sporting a discreet display of jeweled leaves and a brokerage sign. I had picked those leaves the day before. I put my hand through the shimmer of the door and went in.

A single chime, the scent of fresh apples, thick amber rugs, specimens bedded in velvet behind vibraglass. The woman behind the counter, decorative as her merchandise, looked up from her book, clicked it off, and rose.

'Good morning,' she said amiably, looking at my stained clothes. 'May I help you?' One glittering eyebrow rose.

'I don't want — I mean, this is a brokerage too, isn't it?' I waited for her nod, my palms damp. 'I've got something to sell.' I shrugged out of my pack, but she put one hand up, forestalling me. Tattoos shimmered along her fingers.

'Our merchandise is specialized,' she said, still amiable. 'There's a fine pawnshop —'

'I don't need —. Can you just look at what I've got? Roses, butterflies —'

'We *don't* deal in illegal exports,' she said sharply. 'Perhaps you're new on-planet. Suledano law prohibits export of native flora or fauna. In any state.'

I stared from her to the elegant jeweled pinflowers in the case.

'Handcrafted,' she said. 'A local art.'

I shook my head, then realized her problem and pushed my sleeve back.

'Look, lady. Here's my license; I'm a drive-jock, not a knocker, or a cop. I don't care what the laws are — I've just got some stuff I want to sell. Okay?'

She inspected the license embedded under the skin of my forearm. 'These can be forged,' she said, but she was smiling.

'The hell they can. You want to see what I've got?' I reached into the pack for the specimen case.

'God's love, spacer, not in here,' she said quickly. She came around the counter and palmed the shop door; the shimmering opaqued. 'Come into the back. Well, come on.' Black velvet draped the doorway; she held it aside and I followed her into a small room. Shelves, racks, an orderly clutter. High-intensity lamps flickered and glowed as she walked around a square table; jeweler's loupes glittered.

'You have some trinkets?' she said as I pulled out the specimen case. A corner of her mouth curved up, and I knew what she expected. Dumb spacer picks jewels in the forest and when he tries to sell them, discovers they've turned to sludge. Then she'd have a good laugh and kick me out. 'You're not the first spacer to run short of funds and make a trip to the forest,' she said as I flicked open the catch on the case. 'But I should warn you, most of the stuff you pick up isn't worth ...' Then she ran out of words and stared.

I stepped back, watching her. After a moment, she picked out a sapphire egg and peered at it through a loupe. Good choice — the denser specimens were often imperfect, but this one was flawless. An aquamarine bird, lapis lazuli snakes twined together, a small furry thing with ivory tusks; one by one she inspected my horde, and when she finished she stood back and looked at me.

'You're Hawkins's scoop,' she said. 'Wait, don't leave. I won't tell her.'

I stopped halfway to the door and looked at her. She put her hands flat on the table.

'Once a month Hawkins disappears for half a day, comes back with dozens of perfect specimens, and nobody knows how she does it. We figured she must have help. Do you have a name?'

'Does it matter?'

She shrugged. 'Not really.' Her mouth curved again. 'What does she pay you, spacer? Money? Sex? Or both?'

I put my shoulders back. 'Do you want this stuff?'

'Of course. I'll even pay you what it's worth, which is probably more than Hawkins does.' She touched an embedded keyboard while numbers flashed and danced along the table top. 'Nine hundred seventy suldans; that's fifty percent of what I'll get for them. Have we got a deal?'

'Can you pay me in fremarks?'

She nodded, counted out six hundred forty-seven fremarks, and banded them into a small, neat package.

'I'll take any specimens you can find,' she said. 'Of this

quality. Laila Sa'ad — remember me. But for God's sake don't tell Hawkins — she'd kill for less.' She glanced at me. 'I mean that.'

I slid into the backpack, put the fremarks in my pocket, put my hand on top of them, and nodded and smiled and left, clutching my freedom. It took all my will power not to run down the bright street to the port. The setdown shivered with heat; the factor's office was dusty and close. He yawned and checked his database, ran a flat finger down the screen, and announced, yawning again, that there was room on *Skiffle*, departing in three days. Lower level only, payment in advance. I dug into my pocket while he cleared me through the Federation roster, and when he turned back I had the money stacked neatly, fremarks on the left, suldans on the right. He frowned at the suldans.

'Any problem with mixed currency?' I asked, knowing that there wasn't.

'This currency ain't mixed,' he said slowly, flicking the suldans with one broad fingernail. They fanned over the counter, red and blue and white. 'This ain't currency.'

I stared at him. 'Of course it's currency, it's suldans, it's my pay —'

'It's junk. There's no paper money on this planet, kid. This ain't even counterfeit, it's new New Edo yen, and New Edo went bankrupt forty years ago.' He grinned suddenly. 'Somebody paid you with this? And you took it?'

For a moment I couldn't breathe. The factor giggled and fingered his 'base.

'Wait! I've still got the fremarks, six hundred forty-seven; can I buy passage in stasis?'

'Ship ain't equipped.' He looked at my suldans and giggled again.

'I'll work. Any berths open? I'm licensed.' I pushed back my sleeve to show him.

He played with his 'base again. 'Naw. Didn't think so. Nobody jumps ship on this place.'

'Okay, hold it, when's the next ship due? Maybe I can wait....'

The factor shook his head. 'Three months. Give it up, kid.' He flicked the 'base off and went back to his office. 'Hey,' he called over his shoulder. 'Get that garbage off my desk.' The door snapped shut behind him.

My hands shook so hard it took three tries before I could gather the fake suldans; when I went outside they slid through my fingers, scattering across the setdown. Hawkins. I had been on planet only a few hours before the fight, before she hustled me into the forest. Stupid kid, stupid spacer — God, she must have laughed at me. I stared at the bright New Edo yen, flipping and dancing in the spaceport breeze; mechanics swarmed over the shuttle nearby, voices harsh, tools banging and clattering and loud. Stowaways are deep-spaced; it's Federation law. Suledanos kill murderers with ropes and knives, and everyone comes to watch. Hawkins left me in the forest with a bag of sawdust and a bag of dirt.

The breeze tweaked my hair. I felt suddenly naked, bare to sky and fate and Suledano schoolkids. I took the cloak from my backpack and put it on, hid my face, walked away from the port. My stomach hurt. Hawkins liked to see me crawl. Maybe she'd take me back. If I begged. If only for entertainment's sake. She'd take me back, and I'd scour the crystal forest, build my collection again, bring it to Laila Sa'ad. Maybe six more months if I worked hard. Maybe a year. What choice did I have? The hood hid everything save the patch of street before me, and the whores left me alone.

Hawkins wasn't hard to find. The public directory gave me her address; after half an hour of wandering the maze of covered streets, I founded the corner of a mansion and froze.

Street lights, door lights, floodlights, ground lights; the glare bathed a large hovervan and movers loading passage boxes. The boxes sported Federation intercargo insignia. Hawkins watched from a second-floor balcony, white silk, quartz eyes, leaning to point an ivory fingertip at the leader, a tall woman in spacer's gaudy rags. I ducked back, heart pounding. Honeyed voice, servile response, grunts and clatter, a lift field whined. The bitch was leaving me. To starve in the forest, she thought — if she thought of me at all. Getting out clean. I risked another glance. Hawkins was gone; the leader consulted her flipboard and the movers worked rapidly, the skirts of their robes tucked up between their legs, hoods pushed back. One glanced my way and

I ducked my head, walked away with hands clenched in my pockets, trying to imitate a Suledano's dour gait. It was very hard to breathe.

Spacer's Haven had a raised dance floor, circled closely by tables. The bar looked smaller, darker, dirtier, eerily quiet. A Suledano lurked behind the bar; the bartray brought me a kravath, took a fremark, dropped Suledano change on the table, floated away. I fingered the coins as I drank: milled edges, the planet's name on one side, the denomination on the other. Plain, ugly coins, but they bought me three more glasses of kravath. I lined them up on the table and downed them in order, staring at the dance floor. That was where it had happened, on the side farthest from the door; drunk and happy, seventeen, dancing with another spacer until one of us tripped and we spun around each other, trying to find our balance. We fell into a table of locals; one screamed and jumped for my throat; I grabbed his shoulders; the table collapsed around us. I sat up, still laughing, still ready to fight, but the Suledano lay still. Everyone was yelling and swinging, and a woman with opaline eyes grabbed my arm and rushed me out. And nothing marked it, save that I was here again and drunk again, and there was no way out. The crystal bitch, Suledano law, wandering into the forest to become my own monument — it should have ended two years ago, before I knew, before I had a choice.

I suppose I said all this, loudly, because the Suledano barkeep came over and I tried to hit him, then threw the empty vibraglasses at the dance floor. The first one winked out halfway there; the last one, still full, left a trail of kravath behind it. Two chairs followed it, but the bouncer got to me before I could lift the table. I tried to explain to it, trap and snare, circularity, but it tackled me, slapped a sobor on my arm, and called the port cops, while the barkeep howled curses from beneath a table.

Within an hour I was sitting in the port guardstation, frozen in a holdfield, sober. The cop took a print from my license and ran a data check on me, and I thought about ropes and knives, about the cabin in the forest, the marks of Hawkins's hopper on shattered grass. New Edo yen dancing in the spaceport breeze, all the details that bound us together. I could take her with me. Maybe they'd let me watch her die before I died —

When the cop released the field I looked at her, and smiled, and waited for it to begin. She frowned.

'You goddamned kids have any idea how much trouble you can get into?' she demanded. 'Think you're under Federation law, but you assault a local and they press it, you go into local court, local law, it's part of the treaty. You got any idea how bad that is?'

'Yes,' I said smiling. She cursed.

'Okay, put it this way — we get on pretty good with the colonists, and we plan to keep it that way. No major problems in twenty years — and you're not going to be the first, spacer. If I see your ass around here again, I'll kick it to the woods and back. Personally.' She released the holdfield. 'You owe the barkeep six fremarks for damage. Pay up, and get out.'

I stared at her, not moving. 'But — but there was a murder, two years ago.'

'You got the wrong planet, kid.' She grabbed my collar and took six fremarks from my pocket before she kicked me out.

'Wait! I need —' The door slammed. And a woman with opaline eyes grabbed my arm, rushed me out. Told me her name was Hawkins. Said she was going to save my life. Told me that the Suledano was dead.

Something slapped my ankle; a New Edo yen, blowing free. Across the setdown a tall spacer in gaudy rags supervised the loading of passage boxes into the shuttle's hold. I watched for a while, then stripped off the Suledano cloak and walked, back straight, into port sector.

I spent some of my fremarks in a fitter's shop: chemicals, a tube of hardfoam, bottle of rotten crystals. I bought a holdfield in an alley near Laila Sa'ad's — illegal, sure, but you can get anything in a port sector, if you want it enough, if you're willing to pay. And a cat — I bought a cat. Then I shouldered my pack and went into the forest. It took me only two hours to find a good place.

Is there life in crystal? The cat blazed: diamond claws, black sapphire fur, ivory fangs in the silent, screaming mouth. A glitter in the amber eyes that caught and kept Hawkins's jade glance, reflected the brief fear when she saw me at her door, the set of sarcasm, the sweet greed as she touched the bristling fur. I

crawled for her, I wept, I begged forgiveness for past trans-
gressions, I promised her kittens, left in the forest, no more than
half a day's trip, tigerine and tabby, calico and jet, left behind for
fear of shattering but perfect, every one of them, if only she
would come. And she came. I knew she would. She had another
day before the shuttle left.

I was gentle with her, among the bearded trees. I did not want
her marred. She vilified me, her body motionless in the holdfield;
then she pleaded, then she promised, then she screamed. I
silently sprayed myself with rotting crystals, silently mixed
chemicals. Sometimes I smiled at her. She was still screaming
when the crystals came, taking her long slender feet, the smooth
curves of her hips, her breasts and arms and hands, her eyes. I
released the holdfield as the wind rose, so that her platinum curls
blew wildly before they, too, hardened, a pale nimbus around
her ivory face.

I had worried about the fixative, sprayed rather than in a
bath, but when the morning sun struck her she flashed and
gleamed and did not melt, and I left her that way, shining amid
the liquefying trees, the black cat snarling at her feet.

The purser stopped me at the shuttle's hatch, glanced
through his lists, asked my name in the hurried, harried voice all
pursers use.

'Hawkins,' I told him, and waited for his nod, and smiled, and
went on board.

While serving in the R.A.F., Garry Kilworth lived in some of the most exotic places in the world; those he missed, he visited during his later work as a tele-communications expert. He now lives in Essex, where he says that he 'writes his short fiction with his heart and his novels with his head.'

Kilworth won the Gollancz/Sunday Times sf prize in 1974; his first novel, *In Solitary*, was published in 1977. His work has been translated into ten languages, and he is as diverse as he is prolific. As well as books of sf and poetry, he has written mainstream novels such as *Witchwater Country* (which has been optioned as a film for Channel 4). Some of his fifty published short stories have been collected in *The Songbirds of Pain*.

During 1988, he has had four novels published: three sf novels, *Cloudrock*, *Abandonati*, and *The Voyage of the Vigilance*, the last for children, and also a pseudo-nymous horror novel. Already scheduled up for 1989 are: *In the Hollow of the Deep-Sea Wave*, a general fiction novel which will be published in the same volume as seven short stories; and *Hunter's Moon*, which Kilworth describes as 'anthropomorphic fantasy', and is his longest and probably best novel to date.

MURDERERS WALK
by
GARRY KILWORTH

Place

There is a city-state, lying between two large countries, where killers take refuge from the law, but not from justice. Justice finds its own way.

A long street, not much wider than an alley, cuts through the middle of the city. The street is called Murderers Walk and over its cobbles, slick even on dry days, tread the malefactors who have run to its shadows to escape the rope.

The houses are old and overhang the walk, keeping it permanently in the shade. Along its cobbles it is not unusual to see a man or woman being dragged, or driven, or forcibly carried. Sometimes they are screaming; sometimes they are stiff with fear.

Rope

There are many reminders of rope in Murderers Walk. The limbs of those lounging in apathy against crumbling windowsills are knotted and sinuous; the washing over the street is crowded onto short lines and consequently hangs narrow and long; the shadows that ripple in the poorly-fashioned windows tend to be thin and twisted due to the warping of the glass. A walk along the street on any day will bring you into contact with men and women who know death first-hand: they have dealt with it directly; they stand on the brink of death themselves. You see them waiting in shop doorways, wearing hollows in the wood with restless shoulders. No one know what or who they are waiting for — not even those who wait. There is no expectancy in the air.

The Game

They play a game in the inns along Murderers Walk, which newcomers shun when they first arrive. Newcomers are detached and need nothing but themselves. They are either elated or relieved at having escaped the law in their own coun-

237

tries, and for a time this is sufficient to sustain them. The game is played in groups of nine, called 'scaffolds'.

The Rules

Each player draws cards from the pack containing two jokers, until none remain. The players look at their hands and the one holding the ace of spades must commit suicide, by hanging, twenty-four hours later, on the stroke of 8 a.m. It is a simple game, with simple rules, but the winning players recharge those feelings of elation and relief that they felt on first arriving in Murderers Walk. They have beaten death yet again.

The Victim

The players keep all their cards secret until the time arrives to take account. They gather at the inn where the game took place. One of the players will be missing and he or she will hold the ace of spades. The other players then go to the victim's rooms to witness the self-inflicted execution. Victims who are not ready at the appointed time are hunted down by the scaffold and the deed is done for them.

Alternative

There is an alternative to suicide. The victims can leave the city-state and the sanctuary of Murderers Walk to take their chances with the law on the outside. Not many do. It is not fear of death that is responsible but terror of dying in the hands of strangers: a ritual death conceived by a morality since rejected. It is a repulsion stronger than the fear of suicide.

Reprieve

There is however another possibility of escaping death. If a player, other than the victim, holds both jokers — those wild cards of Fortune — in one hand, these may be displayed at the last moment before the hanging. The game is then declared void and the victim is reprieved.

Murderers

Only confessed murderers are admitted to a scaffold. Membership is permanent and quarterly games mandatory for all members. As a new murderer in the walk, you survey the faces of the established population with scorn. 'I shall never become like them,' you tell yourself, as you stroll down the street, studying the apathy, the suppressed desperation. Yet, gradually, over the course of time your contempt dissolves into that same desperation. Inside you, the ghost of your victim begins its slow, insidious possession of your soul. You may relive, time and time again, those moments when you killed, especially if your victim was a former loved one. If you are without guilt, there is the bitterness of discovery and consequently flight. Eventually you sink into the same morass as your fellow malefactors and are drawn into the game out of despair.

Play

You begin the walk along the narrow street to your first game. Eventually you arrive at the inn where you are to play for your life. The faces of the other players register vague anticipation. The cards are dealt. The faces turn to stone.

You play the game perhaps once a quarter at first — then more frequently as the drug takes holds. As one of the eight winners you feel the exhilaration of defeating the spectre of death. The group changes as new members are taken on in place of those who have drawn the death card. The more you win, the more you come to believe in a charmed existence, a superior destiny fashioned partly from luck and partly from the essential ingredient of a special *self*. You are not like the others. You move on a higher plane, god-like in your ability to thwart the noose.

Time

But eventually there comes a time when you draw the death card. At first the ace fails to register. It is tucked partly behind an innocent card. Then, suddenly, you see it. Inside you a silent scream begins. All the moisture leaves your mouth and your brain ferments with terror. You are sure all the other members know already, for how can such inner turmoil not show on your face? You put your cards in your pocket, managing a smile, and call for a round of drinks. Then you slip away, after the first sip of ale, which tastes like vinegar, out into the night air. You begin running. You run north along the street, pausing only to puke.

You run to the edge of the city-state, where the border guards of the neighbouring country stand ready. You turn and run in the opposite direction, to find them waiting there too. Then east. Then west. Finally, you trudge back to your lodgings in order to think, to formulate plans.

Twenty-four hours

There is only one thing worse than not knowing when you are going to die — that is, *knowing*. You sit on the edge of your bed and stare around your room. You envy the cockroach that moves across the floor: you envy its lack of imagination. One minute your hands are dry, the next, damp. The weight of guilt has gone. You are about to atone. You try to tell yourself that what you feel is remorse, but you know that it is only regret for the deed that cannot be undone, the act that placed you in this uncompromising position. Your head turns over a thousand thoughts, but none of them lead to escape. Suddenly you understand why this sanctuary exists. It is a prison as secure as any with high walls and guards. In Murderers Walk, the prisoners try each other, and sentence each other to death.

Death

You wonder what the feel of the rope will be like against your neck. You touch your throat with your fingers. Will the spine break or will you expire slowly? Perhaps your lungs will burst? You try to imagine the pallor of your distended face: purple perhaps? Your eyes, huge balls easing out of their sockets? Your tongue hanging long between blue lips? You weep. Your mind goes numb. Your eyes are dry. Your head is full of a thousand active thoughts, each one a nightmare.

Void game

There is of course the possibility of a void game. It is not so unusual. But the closer the time comes, the surer you are that you will not be granted a reprieve. You have taken life and deserve no mercy. The hours pass quickly, and slowly; time races and stands still, depending on whether it is the pain of life, or death, that occupies you. One thing you are sure of: you cannot hope.

Absence
It is three minutes to the appointed hour. The other players will gather together with their cards. They will know, of course, by your absence, that you are the victim. They will be feeling high, victorious, excited. They will be talking in quick voices. Their eyes will be bright.

Eight a.m.
You drag the chair beneath the beam as the others arrive. You hear their feet on the wooden stairs. These are sounds to treasure: every creak, every hollow footfall. They open the door and enter. Their faces are as ashen as yours had been on witnessing other deaths. The elation has been put aside for the moment. But it has to be done, for without a death there is no game, and without the game there is no life. This is as much an ordeal for them as it is for you — only the standpoint is different.

One of them hands you the rope. You stand on the chair hoping your legs will support you for just a few moments longer. You tie the rope to the beam. Your hands are unsteady. *Then — suddenly — you are ready to die.* In that moment all the terror has gone. You may still tremble, or wince, or blanch, but you are *ready*. It is not the moment of death that is so terrible, it is the preparation leading up to that moment. You are ready. You are ready. Just a moment longer ...

End
One of the party steps forward and waves two jokers in your face. 'Void game,' he cries. 'You live to play again.' They pull you from the chair and jostle you towards the door, down the stairs and out into the street. Inside you the fear erupts again, and that precious moment, the moment when you were ready to die, has gone. They have stolen your death from you and you know you cannot retrieve that state of mind again, without reliving another twenty-four hours of terror.

That is when you dig your heels into the unyielding cobbles and grip a passing windowsill with fingers that would squeeze a rock to powder. That is when your mind flies open like a sprung trapdoor. That is when they drag you along the street, kicking and screaming, like a man being led to his execution.

HOWARD WALDROP

Originally from Mississippi, Howard Waldrop has spent most of his life in Texas, where he says he fishes a lot. He also writes a lot. He sold his first story in 1970, and since then there have been seventy more. His first novel, co-written with Jake Saunders, was *The Texas-Israeli War: 1999* (1974); his first solo novel was *Them Bones* (1984).

But it is as a short story writer that Waldrop has made his reputation. Many of his unique and bizarre stories have been published in the collections *Howard Who?* and *All About Strange Monsters of the Recent Past*. A frequent awards nominee, his story 'The Ugly Chickens' won both the Nebula and World Fantasy Awards in 1981.

1988 sees two more books from Waldrop: a short novel entitled *A Dozen Tough Jobs*; and a book of collaborations, *Custer's Last Jump*. His next collection will be *Night of the Cooters*. (The title story is a 1988 Hugo nominee). As well as writing more unclassifiable stories, he is currently working on a novel called *I, John Mandeville*.

Waldrop was born on 15 September, 1946, which is Wild Card Day.

Wild Card Day? Now read on . . .

THIRTY MINUTES
OVER BROADWAY!
Jetboy's Last Adventure!
by
HOWARD WALDROP

Bonham's Flying Service of Shantak, New Jersey, was socked in. The small searchlight on the tower barely pushed away the darkness of the swirling fog.

There was the sound of car tires on the wet pavement in front of Hangar 23. A car door opened, a moment later it closed. Footsteps came to the Employees Only door. It opened. Scoop Swanson came in, carrying his Kodak Autograph Mark II and a bag of flashbulbs and film.

Lincoln Traynor raised up from the engine of the surplus P-40 he was overhauling for an airline pilot who had got it at a voice-bid auction for $293. Judging from the shape of the engine, it must have been flown by the Flying Tigers in 1940. A ball game was on the workbench radio. Linc turned it down.

"Lo, Linc," said Scoop.

"Lo."

'No word yet?'

'Don't expect any. The telegram he sent yesterday said he'd be in tonight. Good enough for me.'

Scoop lit a Camel with a Three Torches box match from the workbench. He blew smoke toward the Absolutely No Smoking sign at the back of the hangar. 'Hey, what's this?' He walked to the rear. Still in their packing cases were two long red wing extensions and two 300-gallon teardrop underwing tanks. 'When these get here?'

'Air Corps shipped them yesterday from San Francisco. Another telegram came for him today. You might as well read it, you're doing the story.' Linc handed him the War Department orders.

TO: Jetboy (Tomlin, Robert NMI)

HOR: Bonham's Flying Service, Hangar 23, Shantak, New Jersey

1. Effective this date 1200Z hours 12 Aug '46, you are no longer on active duty, United States Army Air Force.
2. Your aircraft (model-experimental) (ser. no. JB-1) is hereby decommissioned from active status, United States Army Air Force, and reassigned you as private aircraft. No further materiel support from USAAF or War Department will be forthcoming.
3. Records, commendations, and awards forwarded under separate cover.
4. Our records show Tomlin, Robert NMI, has not obtained pilot's license. Please contact CAB for courses and certification.
5. Clear skies and tailwinds,

For Arnold, H.H.
ref: Executive Order #2, 08 Dec '41   CofS, USAAF

'What's this about him having no pilot's license?' asked the newspaperman. 'I went through the morgue on him — his file's a foot thick. Hell, he must have flown faster and farther, shot down more planes than anyone — five hundred planes, fifty ships! He did it without a pilot's license?'

Linc wiped grease from his mustache. 'Yep. That was the most plane-crazy kid you ever saw. Back in '39, he couldn't have been more than twelve, he heard there was a job out here. He showed up at four A.M. — lammed out of the orphanage to do it. They came out to get him. But of course Professor Silverberg had hired him, squared it with them.'

'Silverberg's the one the Nazis bumped off? The guy who made the jet?'

'Yep. Years ahead of everybody, but weird. I put together the plane for him, Bobby and I built it by hand. But Silverberg made the jets — damnedest engines you ever saw. The Nazis and Italians, and Whittle over in England, had started theirs. But the Germans found out something was happening here.'

'How'd the kid learn to fly?'

'He always knew, I think,' said Lincoln. 'One day he's in here helping me bend metal. The next, him and the professor are flying around at four hundred miles per. In the dark, with those early engines.'

'How'd they keep it a secret?'

'They didn't, very well. The spies came for Silverberg — wanted him *and* the plane. Bobby was out with it. I think he and the prof knew something was up. Silverberg put up such a fight the Nazis killed him. Then, there was the diplomatic stink. In those days the JB-1 only had six .30 cals on it — where the professor got them I don't know. But the kid took care of the car full of spies with it, and that speedboat on the Hudson full of embassy people. All on diplomatic visas.

'Just a sec,' Linc stopped himself. 'End of a doubleheader in Cleveland. On the Blue Network.' He turned up the metal Philco radio that sat above the toolrack.

'... *Sanders to Papenfuss to Volstad, a double play. That does it. So the Sox drop two to Cleveland. We'll be right —*' Linc turned it off. 'There goes five bucks,' he said. 'Where was I?'

'The Krauts killed Silverberg, and Jetboy got even. He went to Canada, right?'

'Joined the RCAF, unofficially. Fought in the Battle of Britain, went to China against the Japs with the Tigers, was back in Britain for Pearl Harbor.'

'And Roosevelt commissioned him?'

'Sort of. You know, funny thing about his whole career. He fights the *whole* war, longer than any other American — late '39 to '45 — then right at the end, he gets lost in the Pacific, missing. We all think he's dead for a year. Then they find him on that desert island last month, and now he's coming home.'

There was a high, thin whine like a prop plane in a dive. It came from the foggy skies outside. Scoop put out his third Camel. 'How can he land in this soup?'

'He's got an all-weather radar set — got it off a German night fighter back in '43. He could land that plane in a circus tent at midnight.'

They went to the door. Two landing lights pierced the rolling mist. They lowered to the far end of the runway, turned, and came back on the taxi strip.

The red fuselage glowed in the gray-shrouded lights of the airstrip. The twin-engine high-wing plane turned toward them and rolled to a stop.

Linc Traynor put a set of double chocks under each of the two rear tricycle landing gears. Half the glass nose of the plane levered up and pulled back. The plane had four 20mm cannon snouts in the wing roots between the engines, and a 75mm gunport below and to the left of the cockpit rim.

It had a high thin rudder, and the rear elevators were shaped like the tail of a brook trout. Under each of the elevators was the muzzle of a rear-firing machine gun. The only markings on the plane were four nonstandard USAAF stars in a black roundel, and the serial number JB-1 on the top right and bottom left wings and beneath the rudder.

The radar antennae on the nose looked like something to roast weenies on.

A boy dressed in red pants, white shirt, and a blue helmet and goggles stepped out of the cockpit and onto the dropladder on the left side.

He was nineteen, maybe twenty. He took off his helmet and goggles. He had curly mousy brown hair, hazel eyes, and was short and chunky.

'Linc,' he said. He hugged the pudgy man to him, patted his back for a full minute. Scoop snapped off a shot.

'Great to have you back, Bobby,' said Linc.

'Nobody's called me that in years,' he said. 'It sounds real good to hear it again.'

'This is Scoop Swanson,' said Linc. 'He's gonna make you famous all over again.'

'I'd rather be asleep.' He shook the reporter's hand. 'Any place around here we can get some ham and eggs?'

The launch pulled up to the dock in the fog. Out in the harbor a ship finished cleaning its bilges and was turning to steam back southward.

There were three men on the mooring: Fred and Ed and Filmore. One man stepped out of the launch with a suitcase in his hands. Filmore leaned down and gave the guy at the wheel of the motorboat a Lincoln and two Jacksons. Then he helped the guy with the suitcase.

'Welcome home, Dr. Tod.'

'It's good to be back, Filmore.' Tod was dressed in a baggy suit, and had on an overcoat even though it was August. He wore his hat pulled low over his face, and from it a glint of metal was reflected in the pale lights from a warehouse.

'This is Fred and this is Ed,' said Filmore. 'They're here just for the night.'

''Lo,' said Fred.

''Lo,' said Ed.

They walked back to the car, a '46 Merc that looked like a submarine. They climbed in, Fred and Ed watching the foggy alleys to each side. Then Fred got behind the wheel, and Ed rode shotgun. With a sawed-off ten-gauge.

'Nobody's expecting me. Nobody cares,' said Dr. Tod. 'Everybody who had something against me is either dead or went respectable during the war and made a mint. I'm an old man and I'm tired. I'm going out in the country and raise bees and play the horses and the market.'

'Not planning anything, boss?'

'Not a thing.'

He turned his head as they passed a streetlight. Half his face was gone, a smooth plate reaching from jaw to hatline, nostril to left ear.

'I can't shoot anymore, for one thing. My depth perception isn't what it used to be.'

'I shouldn't wonder,' said Filmore. 'We heard something happened to you in '43.'

'Was in a somewhat-profitable operation out of Egypt while the Afrika Korps was falling apart. Taking people in and out for a fee in a nominally neutral air fleet. Just a sideline. Then ran into that hotshot flier.'

'Who?'

'Kid with the jet plane, before the Germans had them.'

'Tell you the truth, boss, I didn't keep up with the war much. I take a long view on merely territorial conflicts.'

'As I should have,' said Dr. Tod. 'We were flying out of Tunisia. Some important people were with us that trip. The pilot screamed. There was a tremendous explosion. Next thing, I came to, it was the next morning, and me and one other person are in a life raft in the middle of the Mediterranean. My face hurt. I lifted up. Something fell into the bottom of the raft. It was my left eyeball. It was looking up at me. I knew I was in trouble.'

'You said it was a kid with a jet plane?' asked Ed.

'Yes. We found out later they'd broken our code, and he'd flown six hundred miles to intercept us.'

'You want to get even?' asked Filmore.

'No. That was so long ago I hardly remember that side of my face. It just taught me to be a little more cautious. I wrote it off as character building.'

'So no plans, huh?'

'Not a single one,' said Dr. Tod.

'That'll be nice for a change,' said Filmore.

They watched the lights of the city go by.

He knocked on the door, uncomfortable in his new brown suit and vest.

'Come on in, it's open,' said a woman's voice. Then it was muffled. 'I'll be ready in just a minute.'

Jetboy opened the oak hall door and stepped into the room, past the glass-brick room divider.

A beautiful woman stood in the middle of the room, a dress halfway over her arms and head. She wore a camisole, garter belt, and silk hose. She was pulling the dress down with one of her hands.

Jetboy turned his head away, blushing and taken aback.

'Oh,' said the woman. 'Oh! I — who?'

'It's me, Belinda,' he said. 'Robert.'

'Robert?'

'Bobby, Bobby Tomlin.'

She stared at him a moment, her hands clasped over her front though she was fully dressed.

'Oh, Bobby,' she said, and came to him and hugged him and gave him a big kiss right on the mouth.

It was what he had waited six years for.

'Bobby. It's great to see you. I — I was expecting someone else. Some — girlfriends. How did you find me?'

'Well, it wasn't easy.'

She stepped back from him. 'Let me look at you.'

He looked at her. The last time he had seen her she was fourteen, a tomboy, still at the orphanage. She had been a thin kid with mousy blond hair. Once, when she was eleven, she'd almost punched his lights out. She was a year older than he.

Then he had gone away, to work at the airfield, then to fight with the Brits against Hitler. He had written her when he could all during the war, after America entered it. She had left the orphanage and been put in a foster home. In '44 one of his letters had come back from there marked 'Moved — No Forwarding Address.' Then he had been lost all during the last year.

'You've changed, too,' he said.

'So have you.'

'Uh.'

'I followed the newspapers all during the war. I tried to write you but I don't guess the letters ever caught up with you. Then they said you were missing at sea, and I sort of gave up.'

'Well, I was, but they found me. Now I'm back. How have you been?'

'Real good, once I ran away from the foster home,' she said. A look of pain came across her face. 'You don't know how glad I was to get away from there. Oh, Bobby,' she said. 'Oh, I wish things was different!' She started to cry a little.

'Hey,' he said, holding her by the shoulders. 'Sit down. I've got something for you.'

'A present?'

'Yep.' He handed her a grimy, oil-stained paper parcel. 'I carried these with me the last two years of the war. They were in the plane with me on the island. Sorry I didn't have time to rewrap them.'

She tore the English butcher paper. Inside were copies of *The House at Pooh Corner* and *The Tale of the Fierce Bad Rabbit.*

'Oh,' said Belinda. 'Thank you.'

He remembered her dressed in the orphanage coveralls, just in, dusty and tired from a baseball game, lying on the reading-room floor with a Pooh book open before her.

'The Pooh book's signed by the real Christopher Robin,' he said. 'I found out he was an RAF officer at one of the bases in England. He said he usually didn't do this sort of thing, that he was just another airman. I told him I wouldn't tell anyone. I'd searched high and low to find a copy, and he knew that, though.

'This other one's got more of a story behind it. I was coming back near dusk, escorting some crippled B-17s. I looked up and saw two German night fighters coming in, probably setting up patrol, trying to catch some Lancasters before they went out over the Channel.

'To make a long story short, I shot down both of them; they packed in near a small village. But I had run out of fuel and had to set down. Saw a pretty flat sheep pasture with a lake at the far end of it, and went in.

'When I climbed out of the cockpit, I saw a lady and a sheep-dog standing at the edge of the field. She had a shotgun. When she got close enough to see the engines and the decals, she said, 'Good shooting! Won't you come in for a bite of supper and to use the telephone to call Fighter Command?'

'We could see the two ME-110s burning in the distance.

'"You're the very famous Jetboy," she said, 'We have followed your exploits in the Sawrey paper. I'm Mrs. Heelis.' She held out her hand.

'I shook it. "Mrs. William Heelis? And this is Sawrey?"

'"Yes," she said.

'"You're Beatrix Potter!" I said.

'"I suppose I am," she said.

'Belinda, she was this stout old lady in a raggedy sweater and a plain old dress. But when she smiled, I swear, all of England lit up!'

Belinda opened the book. On the flyleaf was written

To Jetboy's American Friend, Belinda,
from Mrs. William Heelis ('Beatrix Potter')
12 April 1943

Jetboy drank the coffee Belinda made for him.

'Where are your friends?' he asked.

'Well, he — they should have been here by now. I was thinking of going down the hall to the phone and trying to call them. I can change, and we can sit around and talk about old times. I really can call.'

'No,' said Jetboy. 'Tell you what. I'll call you later on in the

week; we can get together some night when you're not busy.
That would be fun.'

'Sure would.'

Jetboy got up to go.

'Thank you for the books, Bobby. They mean a lot to me,
they really do.'

'It's real good to see you again, Bee.'

'Nobody's called me that since the orphanage. Call me real
soon, will you?'

'Sure will.' He leaned down and kissed her again.

He walked to the stairs. As he was going down, a guy in a
modified zoot suit — pegged pants, long coat, watch chain, bow
tie the size of a coat hanger, hair slicked back, reeking of Bryl-
creem and Old Spice — went up the stairs two at a time, whistling 'It Ain't the Meat, It's the Motion.'

Jetboy heard him knocking at Belinda's door.

Outside, it had begun to rain.

'Great. Just like in a movie,' said Jetboy.

The next night was quiet as a graveyard.

Then dogs all over the Pine Barrens started to bark. Cat
screamed. Birds flew in panic from thousands of trees, circled,
swooping this way and that in the dark night.

Static washed over every radio in the northeastern United
States. New television sets flared out, volume doubling. People
gathered around nine-inch Dumonts jumped back at the sudden
noise and light, dazzled in their own living rooms and bars and
sidewalks outside appliance stores all over the East Coast.

To those out in that hot August night it was even more spec-
tacular. A thin line of light, high up, moved, brightened, still falling. Then it expanded, upping in brilliance, changed into a
blue-green bolide, seemed to stop, then flew to a hundred falling
sparks that slowly faded on the dark starlit sky.

Some people said they saw another, smaller light a few
minutes later. It seemed to hover, then sped off to the west,
growing dimmer as it flew. The newspapers had been full of
stories of the 'ghost rockets' in Sweden all that summer. It was
the silly season.

A few calls to the weather bureau or Army Air Force bases got the answer that it was probably a stray from the Delta Aquarid meteor shower.

Out in the Pine Barrens, somebody knew differently, though he wasn't in the mood to communicate it to anyone.

Jetboy, dressed in a loose pair of pants, a shirt, and a brown aviator's jacket, walked in through the doors of the Blackwell Printing Company. There was a bright red-and-blue sign above the door: Home of the Cosh Comics Company.

He stopped at the receptionist's desk.

'Robert Tomlin to see Mr. Farrell.'

The secretary, a thin blond job in glasses with swept-up rims that made it look like a bat was camping on her face, stared at him. 'Mr. Farrell passed on in the winter of 1945. Were you in the service or something?'

'Something.'

'Would you like to speak to Mr. Lowboy? He has Mr. Farrell's job now.'

'Whoever's in charge of *Jetboy Comics*.'

The whole place began shaking as printing presses cranked up in the back of the building. On the walls of the office were garish comic-book covers, promising things only *they* could deliver.

'Robert Tomlin,' said the secretary to the intercom.

'*Scratch squawk* never heard of him *squich.*'

'What was this about?' asked the secretary.

'Tell him Jetboy wants to see him.'

'Oh,' she said, looking at him. 'I'm sorry. I didn't recognize you.'

'Nobody ever does.'

Lowboy looked like a gnome with all the blood sucked out. He was as pale as Harry Langdon must have been, like a weed grown under a burlap bag.

'Jetboy!' He held out a hand like a bunch of grub worms. 'We all thought you'd died until we saw the papers last week. You're a real national hero, you know?'

'I don't feel like one.'

'What can I do for you? Not that I'm not pleased to finally

meet you. But you must be a busy man.'

'Well, first, I found out none of the licensing and royalty checks had been deposited in my account since I was reported Missing and Presumed Dead last summer.'

'What, really? The legal department must have put it in escrow or something until somebody came forward with a claim. I'll get them right on it.'

'Well, I'd like the check now, before I leave,' said Jetboy.

'Huh? I don't know if they can do that. That sounds awfully abrupt.'

Jetboy stared at him.

'Okay, okay, let me call Accounting.' He yelled into the telephone.

'Oh,' said Jetboy. 'A friend's been collecting my copies. I checked the statement of ownership and circulation for the last two years. I know *Jetboy Comics* have been selling five hundred thousand copies an issue lately.'

Lowboy yelled into the phone some more. He put it down. 'It'll take 'em a little while. Anything else?'

'I don't like what's happening to the funny book,' said Jetboy.

'What's not to like? It's selling a half a million copies a month!'

'For one thing, the plane's getting to look more and more like a bullet. And the artists have swept back the wings, for Christ's sakes!'

'This is the Atomic Age, kid. Boys nowadays don't like a plane that looks like a red leg of lamb with coat hangers sticking out the front.'

'Well, it's always looked like that. And another thing: Why's the damned plane blue in the last three issues?'

'Not me! I think red's fine. But Mr. Blackwell sent down a memo, said no more red except for blood. He's a big Legionnaire.'

'Tell him the plane has to look right, and be the right color. Also, the combat reports were forwarded. When Farrell was sitting at your desk, the comic was about flying and combat, and cleaning up spy rings — real stuff. And there were never more than two ten-page Jetboy stories an issue.'

'When Farrell was at this desk, the book was only selling a

quarter-million copies a month,' said Lowboy.

Robert stared at him again.

'I know the war's over, and everybody wants a new house and eye-bulging excitement,' said Jetboy. 'But look what I find in the last eighteen months ...

'I never fought anyone like The Undertaker, anyplace called The Mountain of Doom. And come on! The Red Skeleton? Mr. Maggot? Professor Blooteaux? What is this with all the skulls and tentacles? I mean, evil twins named Sturm and Drang Hohenzollern? The Arthropod Ape, a gorilla with six sets of elbows? Where do you get all this stuff?'

'It's not me, it's the writers. They're a crazy bunch, always taking Benzedrine and stuff. Besides, it's what the kids want!'

'What about the flying features, and the articles on real aviation heroes? I thought my contract called for at least two features an issue on real events and people?'

'We'll have to look at it again. But I can tell you, kids don't want that kind of stuff anymore. They want monsters, spaceships, stuff that'll make 'em wet the bed. You remember? You were a kid once yourself!'

Jetboy picked up a pencil from the desk. 'I was thirteen when the war started, fifteen when they bombarded Pearl Harbor. I've been in combat for six years. Sometimes I don't think I was ever a kid.'

Lowboy was quiet a moment.

'Tell you what you need to do,' he said. 'You need to write up all the stuff you don't like about the book and send it to us. I'll have the legal department go over it, and we'll try to do something, work things out. Of course, we print three issues ahead, so it'll be Thanksgiving before the new stuff shows up. Or later.'

Jetboy sighed. 'I understand.'

'I sure do want you happy, 'cause *Jetboy*'s my favorite comic. No, I really mean that. The others are just a job. My god, what a job: deadlines, working with drunks and worse, riding herd over printers — you can just imagine! But I like the work on *Jetboy*. It's special.'

'Well, I'm glad.'

'Sure, sure.' Lowboy drummed his fingers on the desk. 'Wonder what's taking them so long?'

'Probably getting out the other set of ledgers,' said Jetboy.

'Hey, no! We're square here!' Lowboy came to his feet.

'Just kidding.'

'Oh. Say, the paper said you were, what, marooned on a desert island or something? Pretty tough?'

'Well, lonely. I got tired of catching and eating fish. Mostly it was boring, and I missed everything. I don't mean missed, I mean missed out. I was there from April twenty-ninth of '45 until last month.

'There were times when I thought I'd go nuts. I couldn't believe it one morning when I looked up, and there was the U.S.S. *Reluctant* anchored less than a mile offshore. I fired off a flare, and they picked me up. It's taken a month to get someplace to repair the plane, rest up, get home. I'm glad to be back.'

'I can imagine. Hey, lots of dangerous animals on the island? I mean, lions and tigers and stuff?'

Jetboy laughed. 'It was less than a mile wide, and a mile and a quarter long. There were birds and rats and some lizards.'

'Lizards? Big lizards? Poisonous?'

'No. Small. I must have eaten half of them before I left. Got pretty good with a slingshot made out of an oxygen hose.'

'Huh! I bet you did!'

The door opened, and a tall guy with an ink-smudged shirt came in.

'That him?' asked Lowboy.

'I only seen him once, but it looks like him,' said the man.

'Good enough for me!' said Lowboy.

'Not for me,' said the accountant. 'Show me some ID and sign this release.'

Jetboy sighed and did. He looked at the amount on the check. It had far too few digits in front of the decimal. He folded it up and put it in his pocket.

'I'll leave my address for the next check with your secretary. And I'll send a letter with the objections this week.'

'Do that. It's been a real pleasure meeting you. Let's hope we have a long and prosperous business together.'

'Thanks, I guess,' said Jetboy. He and the accountant left.

Lowboy sat back down in his swivel chair. He put his hands behind his head and stared at the bookcase across the room.

Then he rocketed forward, jerked up the phone, and dialed nine to get out. He called up the chief writer for *Jetboy Comics*.

A muzzy, hung-over voiced answered on the twelfth ring.

'Clean the shit out of your head, this is Lowboy. Picture this: fifty-two-page special, single-story issue. Ready? *Jetboy on Dinosaur Island*! Got that? I see lots of cavemen, a broad, a what-you-call-it — king rex. What? Yeah, yeah, a tyrannosaur. Maybe a buncha holdout Jap soldiers. You know. Yeah, maybe even samurai. When? Blown off course in A.D. 1100? Christ. Whatever. You know exactly what we need.

'What's this? Tuesday. You got till five P.M. Thursday, okay? Quit bitchin'. It's a hundred and a half fast bucks! See you then.'

He hung up. Then he called up an artist and told him what he wanted for the cover.

Ed and Fred were coming back from a delivery in the Pine Barrens.

They were driving an eight-yard dump truck. In the back until a few minutes ago had been six cubic yards of new-set concrete. Eight hours before, it had been five and a half yards of water, sand, gravel, and cement — and a secret ingredient.

The secret ingredient had broken three of the Five Unbreakable Rules for carrying on a tax-free unincorporated business in the state.

He had been taken by other businessmen to a wholesale construction equipment center, and been shown how a cement mixer works, up close and personal.

Not that Ed and Fred had anything to do with that. They'd been called an hour ago and been asked if they could drive a dump truck through the woods for a couple of grand.

It was dark out in the woods, not too many miles from the city. It didn't look like they were within a hundred miles of a town over five-hundred population.

The headlights picked out ditches where everything from old airplanes to sulfuric-acid bottles lay in clogged heaps. Some of the dumpings were fresh. Smoke and fire played about a few. Others glowed without combustion. A pool of metal bubbled and popped as they ground by.

Then they were back into the deep pines again, jouncing from rut to rut.

'Hey!' yelled Ed. 'Stop!'

Fred threw on the brakes, killing the engine. 'God-damn!' he said. 'What the hell's the matter with you?'

'Back there! I swear I saw a guy pushing a neon cat's-eye marble the size of Cleveland!'

'I'm sure as hell not going back,' said Fred.

'Nah! Come on! You don't see stuff like that every day.'

'Shit, Ed! Someday you're gonna get us both killed!'

It wasn't a marble. They didn't need their flashlights to tell it wasn't a magnetic mine. It was a rounded canister that glowed on its own, with swirling colors on it. It hid the man pushing it.

'It looks like a rolled-up neon armadillo,' said Fred, who'd been out west.

The man behind the thing blinked at them, unable to see past their flashlights. He was tattered and dirty, with a tobacco-stained beard and wild, steel-wool hair.

They stepped closer.

'It's mine!' he said to them, stepping in front of the thing, holding his arms out across it.

'Easy, old-timer,' said Ed. 'What you got?'

'My ticket to easy street. You from the Air Corps?'

'Hell, no. Let's look at this.'

The man picked up a rock. 'Stay back! I found it where I found the plane crash. The Air Corps'll pay plenty to get this atomic bomb back!'

'That doesn't look like any atomic bomb I've ever seen,' said Fred. 'Look at the writing on the side. It ain't even English.'

'Course it's not! It must be a secret weapon. That's why they dressed it up so weird.'

'Who?'

'I told you more'n I meant to. Get outta my way.'

Fred looked at the old geezer. 'You've piqued my interest,' he said. 'Tell me more.'

'Outta my way, boy! I killed a man over a can of lye hominy once!'

Fred reached in his jacket. He came out with a pistol with a muzzle that looked like a drainpipe.

'It crashed last night,' said the old man, eyes wild. 'Woke me up. Lit up the whole sky. I looked for it all day today, figured the woods would be crawlin' with Air Corps people and state troopers, but nobody came.

'Found it just before dark tonight. Tore all hell up, it did. Knocked the wings completely off the thing when it crashed. All these weird-dressed people all scattered around. Women too.' He lowered his head a minute, shame on his face. 'Anyway, they was all dead. Must have been a jet plane, didn't find no propellers or nothing. And this here atomic bomb was just lying there in the wreck. I figured the Air Corps would pay real good to get it back. Friend of mine found a weather balloon once and they gave him a dollar and a quarter. I figure this is about a million times as important as that!'

Fred laughed. 'A buck twenty-five, huh? I'll give you ten dollars for it.'

'I can get a million!'

Fred pulled the hammer back on the revolver.

'Fifty,' said the old man.

'Twenty.'

'It ain't fair. But I'll take it.'

'What are you going to do with that?' asked Ed.

'Take it to Dr. Tod,' said Fred. 'He'll know what to do with it. He's the scientific type.'

'What if it is an A-bomb?'

'Well, I don't think A-bombs have spray nozzles on them. And the old man was right. The woods would have been crawling with Air Force people if they'd lost an atomic-bomb. Hell, only five of them have ever been exploded. They can't have more than a dozen, and you better believe they know where every one of them is, all the time.'

'Well, it ain't a mine,' said Ed. 'What do you think it is?'

'I don't care. If it's worth money, Doctor Tod'll split with us. He's a square guy.'

'For a crook,' said Ed.

They laughed and laughed, and the thing rattled around in the back of the dump truck.

The MPs brought the red-haired man into his office and introduced them.

'Please have a seat, Doctor,' said A.E. He lit his pipe. The man seemed ill at ease, as he should have been after two days of questioning by Army Intelligence.

'They have told me what happened at White Sands, and that you won't talk to anyone but me,' said A.E. 'I understand they used sodium pentathol on you, and that it had no effect?'

'It made me drunk,' said the man, whose hair in this light seemed orange and yellow.

'But you didn't talk?'

'I said things, but not what they wanted to hear.'

'Very unusual.'

'Blood chemistry.'

A.E. sighed. He looked out the window of the Princeton office. 'Very well, then. I will listen to your story. I am not saying I will believe it, but I *will* listen.'

'All right,' said the man, taking a deep breath. 'Here goes.'

He began to talk, slowly at first, forming his words carefully, gaining confidence as he spoke. As he began to talk faster, his accent crept back in, one A.E. could not place, something like a Fiji Islander who had learned English from a Swede. A.E. refilled his pipe twice, then left it unlit after filling it the third time. He sat slightly forward, occasionally nodding, his gray hair an aureole in the afternoon light.

The man finished.

A.E. remembered his pipe, found a match, lit it. He put his hands behind his head. There was a small hole in his sweater near the left elbow.

'They'll never believe any of that,' he said.

'I don't care, as long as they do something!' said the man. 'As long as I get it back.'

A.E. looked at him. 'If they did believe you, the implications of all this would overshadow the reason you're here. The fact that *you* are *here*, if you follow my meaning.'

'Well, what can we do? If my ship were still operable, I'd be looking myself. I did the next best thing — landed somewhere that would be sure to attract attention, asked to speak to you. Perhaps other scientists, research institutes ...'

A.E. laughed. 'Forgive me. You don't realize how things are done here. We will need the military. We will *have* the military and the government whether we want them or not, so we might as well have them on the best possible terms, ours, from the first. The problem is that we have to think of something that is *plausible* to them, yet will still mobilize them in the search.

'I'll talk to the Army people about you, then make some calls to friends of mine. We have just finished a large global war, and many things had a way of escaping notice, or being lost in the shuffle. Perhaps we can work something from there.

'The only thing is, we had better do all this from a phone booth. The MPs will be along, so I will have to talk quietly. Tell me,' he said, picking up his hat from the corner of a cluttered bookcase, 'do you like ice cream?'

'Lactose and sugar solids congealed in a mixture kept just below the freezing point?' asked the man.

'I assure you,' said A.E., 'it is better than it sounds, and quite refreshing.' Arm in arm, they went out the office door.

Jetboy patted the scarred side of his plane. He stood in Hangar 23. Linc came out of his office, wiping his hands on a greasy rag.

'Hey, how'd it go?' he asked.

'Great. They want the book of memoirs. Going to be their big Spring book, if I get it in on time, or so they say.'

'You still bound and determined to sell the plane?' asked the mechanic. 'Sure hate to see her go.'

'Well, that part of my life's over. I feel like if I never fly again, even as an airline passenger, it'll be too soon.'

'What do you want me to do?'

Jetboy looked at the plane.

'Tell you what. Put on the high-altitude wing extensions and the drop tanks. It looks bigger and shinier that way. Somebody from a museum will probably buy it, is what I figure — I'm offering it to museums first. If that doesn't work, I'll take out ads in the papers. We'll take the guns out later, if some private citizen buys it. Check everything to see it's tight. Shouldn't have shaken much on the hop from San Fran, and they did a pretty good overhaul at Hickam Field. Whatever you think it needs.'

'Sure thing.'

'I'll call you tomorrow, unless something can't wait.'

HISTORICAL AIRCRAFT FOR SALE: Jetboy's twin-engine jet. 2 × 1200 lb thrust engines, speed 600 mph at 25,000 ft, range 650 miles, 1000 w/drop tanks (tanks and wing exts. inc.) length 31 ft, w/s 33 ft (49 w exts.) Reasonable offers accepted. Must see to appreciate. On view at Hangar 23, Bonham's Flying Service, Shantak, New Jersey.

Jetboy stood in front of the bookstore window, looking at the pyramids of new titles there. You could tell paper rationing was off. Next year, his book would be one of them. Not just a comic book, but the story of his part in the war. He hoped it would be good enough so that it wouldn't be lost in the clutter.

Seems like, in the words of someone, every goddamn barber and shoeshine boy who was drafted had written a book about how he won the war.

There were six books of war memoirs in one window, by everyone from a lieutenant colonel to a major general (maybe those PFC barbers didn't write that many books?).

Maybe they wrote some of the two dozen war novels that covered another window of the display.

There were two books near the door, piles of them in a window by themselves, runaway best-sellers, that weren't war novels or memoirs. One was called *The Grass-Hopper Lies Heavy* by someone named Abendsen (Hawthorne Abendsen, obviously a pen name). The other was a thick book called *Growing Flowers by Candlelight in Hotel Rooms* by someone so self-effacing she called herself 'Mrs. Charles Fine Adams.' It must be a book of unreadable poems that the public, in its craziness, had taken up. There was no accounting for taste.

Jetboy put his hands in the pockets of his leather jacket and walked to the nearest movie show.

Tod watched the smoke rising from the lab and waited for the phone to ring. People ran back and forth to the building a half-mile away.

There had been nothing for two weeks. Thorkeld, the scientist he'd hired to run the tests, had reported each day. The stuff didn't work on monkeys, dog, rats, lizards, snakes, frogs, insects, or even on fish in suspension in water. Dr. Thorkeld was beginning to think Tod's men had paid twenty dollars for an inert gas in a fancy container.

A few moments ago there had been an explosion. Now he waited.

The phone rang.

'Tod — oh, god, this is Jones at the lab, it's —' Static washed over the line. 'Oh, sweet Jesus! Thorkeld's — they're all —' There was thumping near the phone receiver on the other end. 'Oh, my . . .'

'Calm down,' said Tod. 'Is everyone outside the lab safe?'

'Yeah, yeah. The . . . *oooh.*' The sound of vomiting came over the phone.

Tod waited.

'Sorry, Dr. Tod. The lab's still sealed off. The fire's — it's a small one on the grass outside. Somebody dropped a butt.'

'Tell me what happened.'

'I was outside for a smoke. Somebody in there must have messed up, dropped something. I — I don't know. It's — they're most of them dead, I think. I hope. I don't know. Something's — wait, wait. There's someone still moving in the office, I can see from here, there's —'

There was a click of someone picking up a receiver. The volume on the line dropped.

'Tog, Tog,' said a voice, an approximation of a voice.

'Who's there?'

'Torgk —'

'Thorkeld?'

'Guh. Hep. Hep. Guh.'

There was a sound like a sack full of squids being dumped on a corrugated roof. 'Hep.' Then came the sound of jelly being emptied into a cluttered desk drawer.'

There was a gunshot, and the receiver bounced off the desk. 'He — he shot — it — himself,' said Jones.

'I'll be right out,' said Tod.

After the cleanup, Tod stood in his office again. It had not been pretty. The canister was still intact. Whatever the accident had been had been with a sample. The other animals were okay. It was only the people. Three were dead outright. One, Thorkeld, had killed himself. Two others he and Jones had *had* to kill. A seventh person was missing, but had not come out any of the doors or windows.

Tod sat down in his chair and thought a long, long time. Then he reached over and pushed the button on his desk.

'Yeah, Doctor?' asked Filmore, stepping into the room with a batch of telegrams and brokerage orders under his arm.

Dr. Tod opened the desk safe and began counting out bills. 'Filmore. I'd like you to get down to Port Elizabeth, North Carolina, and buy me up five type B-limp balloons. Tell them I'm a car salesman. Arrange for one million cubic feet of helium to be delivered to the south Pennsy warehouse. Break out the hardware and give me a complete list of what we have — anything we need, we can get surplus. Get ahold of Captain Mack, see if he still has that cargo ship. We'll need new passports. Get me Cholley Sacks; I'll need a contact in Switzerland. I'll need a pilot with a lighter-than-air license. Some diving suits and oxygen. Shot ballast, couple of tons. A bombsight. Nautical charts. And bring me a cup of coffee.'

'Fred has a lighter-than-air pilot's license,' said Filmore.

'Those two never cease to amaze me,' said Dr. Tod.

'I thought we'd pulled our last caper, boss.'

'Filmore,' he said, and looked at the man he'd been friends with for twenty years, 'Filmore, some capers you *have* to pull, whether you want to or not.'

'Dewey was an Admiral at Manila Bay,
Dewey was a candidate just the other day
Dewey were her eyes when she said I do;
Do we love each other? I should say we do!'

The kids in the courtyard of the apartment jumped rope. They'd started the second they got home from school.

At first it bothered Jetboy. He got up from the typewriter and went to the window. Instead of yelling, he watched.

The writing wasn't going well, anyway. What had seemed like just the facts when he'd told them to the G-2 boys during the war looked like bragging on paper, once the words were down:

Three planes, two ME-109s and a TA-152, came out of the clouds at the crippled B-24. It had suffered heavy flak damage. Two props were feathered and the top turret was missing.

One of the 109s went into a shallow dive, probably going into a snap roll to fire up at the underside of the bomber.

I eased my plane in a long turn and fired a deflection shot while about 700 yards away and closing. I saw three hits, then the 109 disintegrated.

The TA-152 had seen me and dived to intercept. As the 109 blew up, I throttled back and hit my air brakes. The 152 flashed by less than 50 yards away. I saw the surprised look on the pilot's face. I fired one burst as he flashed by with my 20mms. Everything from his canopy back flew apart in a shower.

I pulled up. The last 109 was behind the Liberator. He was firing with his machine guns and cannon. He'd taken out the tail gunner, and the belly turret couldn't get enough elevation. The bomber pilot was wigwagging the tail so the wasit gunners could get a shot, but only the left waist gun as working.

I was more than a mile away, but had turned above and to the right. I put the nose down and fired one round with the 75mm just before the gunsight flashed across the 109.

The whole middle of the fighter disappeared — I could see France through it. The only image I have is that I was looking down on top of an open umbrella and somebody folded it suddenly. The fighter looked like Christmas-tree tinsel as it fell.

Then the few gunners left on the B-24 opened up on me, not recognizing my plane. I flashed my IFF code, but their receiver must have been out.

There were two German parachutes far below. The pilots of the first two fighters must have gotten out. I went back to my base.

When they ran maintenance, they found one of my 75mm rounds missing, and only twelve 20mm shells. I'd shot down three enemy planes.

I later learned the B-24 had crashed in the Channel and there were no survivors.

Who needs this stuff? Jetboy thought. The war's over. Does anybody really want to read *The Jet-Propelled Boy* when it's published? Does anybody except morons even want to read

Jetboy Comics anymore?

I don't even think *I'm* needed. What can I do now? Fight crime? I can see strafing getaway cars full of bank robbers. That would be a *real* fair fight. Barnstorming? That went out with Hoover, and besides, I don't want to fly again. This year more people will fly on airliners on vacation than have been in the air all together in the last forty-three years, mail pilots, cropdusters, and wars included.

What can I do? Break up a trust? Prosecute wartime profiteers? *There's* a real dead-end job for you. Punish mean old men who are robbing the state blind running orphanages and starving and beating the kids? You don't need me for that, you need Spanky and Alfalfa and Buckwheat.

'A tisket, a tasket,
Hitler's in a casket.
Eenie-meenie-Mussolini,
Six feet underground!'

said the kids outside, now doing double-dutch, two ropes going opposite directions. Kids have too much energy, he thought. They hot-peppered a while, then slowed again.

'Down in the dungeon, twelve feet deep,
Where old Hitler lies asleep.
German boys, they tickle his feet,
Down in the dungeon, twelve feet deep!'

Jetboy turned away from the window. Maybe what I need is to go to the movies again.

Since his meeting with Belinda, he'd done nothing much but read, write, and go see movies. Before coming home, the last two movies he'd seen, in a crowded post auditorium in France in late '44, had been a cheesy double bill. *That Nazty Nuisance*, a United Artists film made in '43, with Bobby Watson as Hitler, and one of Jetboy's favorite character actors, Frank Faylen, had been the better of the two. The other was a PRC hunk of junk, *Jive Junction*, starring Dickie Moore, about a bunch of hepcats jitterbugging at the malt shop.

The first thing he'd done after getting his money and finding an apartment, was to find the nearest movie theater, where he'd seen *Murder, He Says* about a house full of hillbilly weird people, with Fred McMurray and Marjorie Main, and an actor named Porter Hall playing identical twin-brother murderers named Bert and Mert. 'Which one's which?' asks McMurray, and Marjorie Main picked up an axe handle and hit one of them in the middle of the back, where he collapsed from the waist up in a distorted caricature of humanity, but stayed on his feet. 'That there's Mert,' says Main, throwing the axe handle on the wood-pile. 'He's got a trick back.' There was radium and homicide galore, and Jetboy thought it was the funniest movie he had ever seen.

Since then he'd gone to the movies every day, sometimes going to three theaters and seeing from six to eight movies a day. He was adjusting to civilian life, like most soldiers and sailors had, by seeing films.

He had seen *Lost Weekend* with Ray Milland, and Frank Faylen again, this time as a male nurse in a psycho ward; *A Tree Grows in Brooklyn*; *The Thin Man Goes Home*, with William Powell at his alcoholic best; *Bring on the Girls*; *It's in the Bag* with Fred Allen; *Incendiary Blonde*; *The Story of G.I. Joe* (Jetboy had been the subject of one of Pyle's columns back in '43); a horror film called *Isle of the Dead* with Boris Karloff; a new kind of Italian movie called *Open City* at an art house; and *The Postman Always Rings Twice*.

And there were other films, Monogram and PRC and Republic westerns and crime movies, pictures he'd seen in twenty-four-hour nabes, but had forgotten about ten minutes after leaving the theaters. By the lack of star names and the 4-F look of the leading men, they'd been the bottom halves of double bills made during the war all clocking in at exactly fifty-nine minutes running time.

Jetboy sighed. So many movies, so much of everything he'd missed during the war. He'd even missed V-E and V-J Days, stuck on that island, before he and his plane had been found by the crew of the U.S.S. *Reluctant*. The way the guys on the *Reluctant* talked, you'd have thought they missed most of the war and the movies, too.

He was looking forward to a lot of films this fall, and to seeing them when they came out, the way everybody else did, the way he'd used to do at the orphanage.

Jetboy sat back down at the typewriter. *If I don't work, I'll never get this book done. I'll go to the movies tonight.*

He began to type up all the exciting things he'd done on July 12, 1944.

In the courtyard, women were calling kids in for supper as their fathers came home from work. A couple of kids were still jumping rope out there, their voices thin in the afternoon air:

> 'Hitler, Hitler looks like this,
> Mussolini bows like this,
> Sonja Henie skates like this,
> And Betty Grable misses like *this!*'

The Haberdasher in the White House was having a piss-ass of a day.

It had started with a phone call a little after six A.M. — the Nervous Nellies over at the State Department had some new hot rumours from Turkey. The Soviets were moving all their men around on that nation's edges.

'Well,' the Plain-speaking Man from Missouri said, 'call me when they cross the goddamn border and not until.'

Now this.

Independence's First Citizen watched the door close. The last thing he saw was Einstein's heel disappearing. It needed half-soling.

He sat back in his chair, lifted his thick glasses off his nose, rubbed vigorously. Then the President put his fingers together in a steeple, his elbows resting on his desk. He looked at the small model plow on the front of his desk (it had replaced the model of the M-1 Garand that had sat there from the day he took office until V-J Day). There were three books on the right corner of the desk — a Bible, a thumbed thesaurus, and a pictorial history of the United States. There were three buttons on his desk for calling various secretaries, but he never used them.

Now that peace has come, I'm fighting to keep ten wars from breaking out in twenty places, there's strikes looming in every industry and that's a damn shame, people are hollering for more cars and refrigerators, and they're as tired as I am of war and war's alarm.

And I have to kick the hornet's nest again, get everybody out looking for a damn germ bomb that might go off and infect the whole U.S. and kill half the people or more.

We'd have been better off still fighting with sticks and rocks.

The sooner I get my ass back to 219 North Delaware in Independence, the better off me and this whole damn country will be.

Unless that son of a bitch Dewey wants to run for President again. Like Lincoln said, I'd rather swallow a deer-antler rocking chair than let that bastard be President.

That's the only thing that'll keep me here when I've finished out Mr. Roosevelt's term.

Sooner I get this snipe hunt under way, the faster we can put World War Number Two behind us.

He picked up the phone.

'Get me the Chiefs of Staff,' he said.

'Major Truman speaking.'

'Major, this is the other Truman, your boss. Put General Ostrander on the horn, will you?'

While he was waiting he looked out past the window fan (he hated air-conditioning) into the trees. The sky was the kind of blue that quickly turns to brass in the summer.

He looked at the clock on the wall: 10:23 A.M., eastern daylight time. What a day. What a year. What a century.

'General Ostrander here, sir.'

'General, we just had another bale of hay dropped on us . . .'

A couple of weeks later, the note came:

Deposit 20 Million Dollars account # 43Z21, Credite Suisse, Berne, by 2300Z 14 Sept or lose a major city. You know of this weapon; your people have been searching for it. I have it; I will use half of it on the first city. The Price goes to 30 Million Dollars to keep me from using it a second time. You have my word it will not be used if the first payment is made and instructions will be sent on where the weapon can be recovered.

The Plain-speaking Man from Missouri picked up the phone.

'Kick everything up to the top notch,' he said. 'Call the cabinet, get the Joint Chiefs together. And Ostrander . . .'

'Yessir?'

'Better get ahold of that kid flier, what's his name? . . .'

'You mean Jetboy, sir? He's not on active duty anymore.'

'The hell he's not. He is now!'

'Yessir.'

It was 2:24 P.M. on Tuesday of September 15, 1946, when the thing first showed up on the radar screens.

At 2:31 it was still moving slowly toward the city at an altitude of nearly sixty thousand feet.

At 2:41 they blew the first of the air-raid sirens, which had not been used in New York City since April of 1945 in a blackout drill.

By 2:48 there was panic.

Someone in the CD office hit the wrong set of switches. The power went off everywhere except hospitals and police and fire stations. Subways stopped. Things shut down, and traffic lights quit working. Half the emergency equipment, which hadn't been checked since the end of the war, failed to come up.

The streets were jammed with people. Cops rushed out to try to direct traffic. Some of the policemen panicked when they were issued gas masks. Telephones jammed. Fistfights broke out at intersections, people were trampled at subway exits and on the stairs of skyscrapers.

The bridges clogged up.

Conflicting orders came down. Get the people into bomb shelters. No, no, evacuate the island. Two cops on the same corner yelled conflicting orders at the crowds. Mostly people just stood around and looked.

Their attention was soon drawn to something in the southeastern sky. It was small and shiny.

Flak began to bloom ineffectually two miles below it.

On and on it came.

When the guns over in Jersey began to fire, the panic really started.

It was 3 P.M.

'It's really quite simple,' said Dr. Tod. He looked down toward Manhattan, which lay before him like a treasure trove. He turned to Filmore and held up a long cylindrical device that looked like the offspring of a pipe bomb and a combination lock.

'Should anything happen to me, simply insert this fuse in the holder in the explosives' — he indicated the taped-over portion with the opening in the canister covered with the Sanskrit-like lettering — 'twist it to the number five hundred, then pull this lever.' He indicated the bomb-bay door latch. 'It'll fall of its own weight, and I was wrong about the bombsights. Pinpoint accuracy is not our goal.'

He looked at Filmore through the grill of his diving helmet. They all wore diving suits with hoses leading back to a central oxygen supply.

'Make sure, of course, everyone's suited with their helmet on. Your blood would boil in this thin air. And these suits only have to hold pressure for the few seconds the bomb door's open.'

'I don't expect no trouble, boss.'

'Neither do I. After we bomb New York City, we go out to our rendezvous with the ship, rip the ballast, set down, and head for Europe. They'll be only too glad to pay us the money then. They have no way of knowing we'll be using the whole germ weapon. Seven million or so dead should quite convince them we mean business.'

'Look at that,' said Ed, from the copilot's seat. 'Way down there. Flak!'

'What's our altitude?' asked Dr. Tod.

'Right on fifty-eight thousand feet,' said Fred.

'Target?'

Ed sighted, checked a map. 'Sixteen miles straight ahead. You sure called those wind currents just right, Dr. Tod.'

They had sent him to an airfield outside Washington, D.C., to wait. That way he would be within range of most of the major East Coast cities.

He had spent part of the day reading, part asleep, and the rest of it talking over the war with some of the other pilots. Most of them, though, were too new to have fought in any but the closing days of the war.

Most of them were jet pilots, like him, who had done their training in P-59 Airacomets or P-80 Shooting Stars. A few of those in the ready room belonged to a P-51 prop-job squadron. There was a bit of tension between the blowtorch jockeys and the piston eaters.

All of them were a new breed, though. Already there was talk Truman was going to make the Army Air Force into a separate branch, just the Air Force, within the next year. Jetboy felt, at nineteen, that time had passed him by.

'They're working on something,' said one of the pilots, 'that'll go through the sonic wall. Bell's behind it.'

'A friend of mine out at Muroc says wait till they get the Flying Wing in operation. They're already working on an all-jet version of it. A bomber that can go thirteen thousand miles at five hundred per, carries a crew of thirteen, bunk beds for seven, can stay up for a day and a half!' said another.

'Anybody know anything about this alert?' asked a very young, nervous guy with second-looie bars. 'The Russians up to something?'

'I heard we were going to Greece,' said someone. 'Ouzo for me, gallons of it.'

'More like Czech potato-peel vodka. We'll be lucky if we see Christmas.'

Jetboy realized he missed ready-room banter more than he had thought.

The intercom hissed on and a klaxon began to wail. Jetboy looked at his watch. It was 2:25 P.M.

He realized he missed something more than Air Corps badinage. That was flying. Now it all came back to him. When he had flown down to Washington the night before it had been just a routine hop.

Now was different. It was like wartime again. He had a vector. He had a target. He had a mission.

He also had on an experimental Navy T-2 pressure suit. It was a girdle manufacturer's dream, all rubber and laces, pressure bottles, and a real space helmet, like out of *Planet Comics*, over his head. They had fitted him for it the night before, when they saw his high-altitude wings and drop tanks on the plane.

'We'd better tailor this down for you,' the flight sergeant had said.

'I've got a pressurized cabin,' said Jetboy.

'Well, in case they need you, and in case something goes

wrong, then.'

The suit was still too tight, and it wasn't pressurized yet. The arms were built for a gorilla, and the chest for a chimpanzee. 'You'll appreciate the extra room if that thing ever inflates in an emergency,' said the sergeant.

'You're the boss,' said Jetboy.

They'd even painted the torso white and the legs red to match his outfit. His blue helmet and goggles showed through the clear plastic bubble.

As he climbed with the rest of the squadron, he was glad now that he had the thing. His mission was to accompany the flight of P-80s in, and to engage only if needed. He had never exactly been a team player.

The sky ahead was blue as the background curtain in Bronzino's *Venus, Cupid, Folly and Time,* with a two-fifths cloud to the north. The sun stood over his left shoulder. The squadron angled up. He wigwagged the wings. They spread out in a staggered box and cleared their guns.

Chunder chunder chunder chunder went his 20mm cannons.

Tracers arced out ahead from the six .50 cals on each P-80. They left the prop planes far behind and pointed their noses toward Manhattan.

They looked like a bunch of angry bees circling under a hawk.

The sky was filled with jets and prop fighters climbing like the wall clouds of a hurricane.

Above was a lumpy object that hung and moved slowly on toward the city. Where the eye of the hurricane would be was a torrent of flak, thicker than Jetboy had ever seen over Europe or Japan.

It was bursting far too low, only at the level of the highest fighters.

Fighter Control called them. 'Clark Gable Command to all squadrons. Target at five five zero ... repeat, five five zero angels. Moving ENE at two five knots. Flak unable to reach.'

'Call it off,' said the squadron leader. 'We'll try to fly high enough for deflection shooting. Squadron Hodiak, follow me.'

Jetboy looked up into the high blue above. The object continued its slow track.

'What's it got?' he asked Clark Gable Command.

'Command to Jetboy. Some type of bomb is what we've been told. It has to be a lighter-than-air craft of at least five hundred thousand cubic feet to reach that altitude. Over.'

'I'm beginning a climb. If the other planes can't reach it, call them off, too.'

There was silence on the radio, then, 'Roger.'

As the P-80s glinted like silver crucifixes above him, he eased the nose up.

'Come on, baby,' he said 'Let's do some flying.'

The Shooting Stars began to fall away, sideslipping in the thin air. Jetboy could hear only the sound of his own pressure-breathing in his ears, and the high thin whine of his engines.

'Come on, girl,' he said. 'You can make it!'

The thing above him had resolved itself into a bastard aircraft made of half a dozen blimps, with a gondola below it. The gondola looked as if it had once been a PT boat shell. That was all he could see. Beyond it, the air was purple and cold. Next stop, outer space.

The last of the P-80s slid sideways on the blue stairs of the sky. A few had made desultory firing runs, some snap-rolling as fighters used to do underneath bombers in the war. They fired as they nosed up. All their tracers fell away under the balloons.

One of the P-80s fought for control, dropping two miles before leveling out.

Jetboy's plane protested, whining. It was hard to control. He eased the nose up again, had to fight it.

'Get everybody out of the way,' he said to Clark Gable Command.

'Here's where we give you some fighting room,' he said to his plane. He blew the drop tanks. They fell away like bombs behind him. He pushed his cannon button. *Chunder chunder chunder chunder* they went. Then again and again.

His tracers arced toward the target, then they too fell away. He fired four more bursts until his cannon ran dry. Then he cleaned out the twin fifties in the tail, but it didn't take long for all one hundred rounds to be spent.

He nosed over and went into a shallow dive, like a salmon

sounding to throw a hook, gaining speed. A minute into the run he nosed up, putting the JB-1 into a long circling climb.

'Feels better, huh?' he asked.

The engines bit into the air. The plane, relieved of the weight, lurched up and ahead.

Below him was Manhattan with its seven million people. They must be watching down there, knowing these might be the last things they ever saw. Maybe this is what living in the Atomic Age would be like, always be looking up and thinking, *Is this it?*

Jetboy reached down with one of his boots and slammed a lever over. A 75mm cannon shell slid into the breech. He put his hand on the autoload bar, and pulled back a little more on the control wheel.

The red jet cut the air like a razor.

He was closer now, closer than the others had gotten, and still not close enough. He only had five rounds to do the job.

The jet climbed, beginning to stagger in the thin air, as if it were some red animal clawing its way up a long blue tapestry that slipped a little each time the animal lurched.

He pointed the nose up.

Everything seemed frozen, waiting.

A long thin line of machine-gun tracers reached out from the gondola for him like a lover.

He began to fire his cannon.

From the statement of Patrolman Francis V.
('Francis the Talking Cop') O'Hooey,
Sept. 15, 1946, 6:45 P.M.

We was watching from the street over at Sixth Avenue, trying to get people from shoving each other in a panic. Then they calmed down as they was watching the dogfights and stuff up above.

Some birdwatcher had this pair of binocs, so I confiscated 'em. I watched pretty much the whole thing. Them jets wasn't having no luck, and the antiaircraft from over in the Bowery wasn't doing no good either. I still say the Army oughta be sued 'cause them Air Defense guys got so panicky they forgot to set the timers on them shells and I heard that some of them came down in the Bronx and blew up a whole block of apartments.

Anyway, this red plane, that is, Jetboy's plane, was climbing up and he fired all his bullets, I thought, without doing any damage to the balloon thing.

I was out on the street, and this fire truck pulls up with its sirens on, and the whole precinct and auxiliaries were on it, and the lieutenant was yelling for me to climb on, we'd been assigned to the west side to take care of a traffic smash-up and a riot.

So I jump on the truck, and I try to keep my eyes on what's happening up in the skies.

The riot was pretty much over. The air-raid sirens was still wailing, but everybody was just standing around gawking at what was happening up there.

The lieutenant yells to at least get the people in the buildings. I pushed a few in some doors, then I took another gander in the field glasses.

'I'll be damned if Jetboy hasn't shot up some of the balloons (I hear he used his howitzer on 'em) and the thing looks bigger — it's dropping some. But he's out of ammo and not as high as the thing is and he starts circlin'.

I forgot to say, all the time this blimp thing is got so many machine guns going it looks like a Fourth of July sparkler, and Jetboy's plane's taking these hits all the time.

Then he just takes his plane around and comes right back and crashes right into the what-you-call-it — the gondola, that's it, on the blimps. They just sort of merged together. He must have been going awful slow by then, like stalling, and the plane just sort of mashed into the side of the thing.

And the blimp deal looked like it was coming down a little, not a lot, just some. Then the lieutenant took the glasses away from me, and I shaded my eyes and watched as best I could.

There was this flare of light. I thought the whole thing had blown up at first, and I ducked up under a car. But when I looked up the blimps was still there.

'Look out! Get inside!' yelled the lieutenant. Everybody had another panic then, and was jumping under cars and around stuff and through windows. It looked like a regular Three Stooges for a minute or two.

A few minutes later, it rained red airplane parts all over the streets, and a bunch on the Hudson Terminal ...

There was steam and fire all around. The cockpit cracked like an egg, and the wings folded up like a fan. Jetboy jerked as the capstans in the pressure suit inflated. He was curved into a circle, and must have looked like a frightened tomcat.

The gondola walls had parted like a curtain where the fighter's wings crumpled into it. A wave of frost formed over the shattered cockpit as oxygen blew out of the gondola.

Jetboy tore his hoses loose. His bailout bottle had five minutes of air in it. He grappled with the nose of the plane, like fighting against iron bands on his arms and legs. All you were supposed to be able to do in these suits was eject and pull the D-ring on your parachute.

The plane lurched like a freight elevator with a broken cable. Jetboy grabbed a radar antenna with one gloved hand, felt it snap away from the broken nose of the plane. He grabbed another.

The city was twelve miles below him, the buildings making the island look like a faraway porcupine. The left engine of his plane, crumpled and spewing fuel, tore loose and flew under the gondola. He watched it grow smaller.

The air was purple as a plum — the skin of the blimps bright as fire in the sunlight, and the sides of the gondola bent and torn like cheap cardboard.

The whole thing shuddered like a whale.

Somebody flew by over Jetboy's head through the hole in the metal, trailing hoses like the arms of an octopus. Debris followed through the air in the explosive decompression.

The jet sagged.

Jetboy thrust his hand into the torn side of the gondola, found a strut.

He felt his parachute harness catch on the radar array. The plane twisted. He felt its weight.

He jerked his harness snap. His parachute packs were ripped away from him, tearing at his back and crotch.

His plane bent in the middle like a snake with a broken back, then dropped away, the wings coming up and touching above the shattered cockpit as if it were a dove trying to beat its pinions. Then it twisted sideways, falling to pieces.

Below it was the dot of the man who had fallen out of the gondola, spinning like a yard sprinkler toward the bright city far below.

Jetboy saw the plane fall away beneath his feet. He hung in space twelve miles up by one hand.

He gripped his right wrist with his left hand, chinned himself up until he got a foot through the side, then punched his way in.

There were two people left inside. One was at the controls, the other stood in the center behind a large round thing. He was pushing a cylinder into a slot in it. There was a shattered machine-gun turret on one side of the gondola.

Jetboy reached for the service .38 strapped across his chest. It was agony reaching for it, agony trying to run toward the guy with the fuse.

They wore diving suits. The suits were inflated. They looked like ten or twelve beach balls stuffed into suits of long underwear. They were moving as slowly as he was.

Jetboy's hands closed in a claw over the handle of the .38. He jerked it from its holster.

It flew out of his hand, bounced off the ceiling, and went out through the hole he had come in.

The guy at the controls got off one shot at him. He dived toward the other man, the one with the fuse.

His hand clamped on the diving-suited wrist of the other just as the man pushed the cylindrical fuse into the side of the round canister. Jetboy saw that the whole device sat on a hinged door-plate.

The man had only half a face — Jetboy saw smooth metal on one side through the grid-plated diving helmet.

The man twisted the fuse with both hands.

Through the torn ceiling of the pilothouse, Jetboy saw another blimp begin to deflate. There was a falling sensation. They were dropping toward the city.

Jetboy gripped the fuse with both hands. Their helmets clanged together as the ship lurched.

The guy at the controls was putting on a parachute harness and heading toward the rent in the wall.

Another shudder threw Jetboy and the man with the fuse together. The guy reached for the door lever behind him as best he could in the bulky suit.

Jetboy grabbed his hands and pulled him back.

They slammed together, draped over the canister, their hands entangled on each other's suits and the fuse to the bomb.

The man tried again to reach the lever. Jetboy pulled him

away. The canister rolled like a giant beach ball as the gondola listed.

He looked directly into the eye of the man in the diving suit. The man used his feet to push the canister back over the bomb door. His hand went for the lever again.

Jetboy gave the fuse a half-twist the other way.

The man in the diving suit reached behind him. He came up with a .45 automatic. He jerked a heavy gloved hand away from the fuse, worked the slide. Jetboy saw the muzzle swing at him.

'Die, Jetboy! Die!' said the man.

He pulled the trigger four times.

Statement of Patrolman Francis V. O'Hooey,
Sept. 15, 1946, 6:45 P.M. (continued).

So when the pieces of metal quit falling, we all ran out and looked up.

I saw the white dot below the blimp thing. I grabbed the binocs away from the lieutenant.

Sure enough, it was a parachute. I hoped it was Jetboy had bailed out when his plane crashed into the thing.

I don't know much about such stuff, but I do know that you don't open a parachute that high up or you get in serious trouble.

Then, while I was watching, the blimps and stuff all blew up, all at once. Like they was there, then there was this explosion, and there was only smoke and stuff way up in the air.

The people all around started cheering. The kid had done it — he'd blown the thing up before it could drop the A-bomb on Manhattan Island.

Then the lieutenant said to get in the truck, we'd try to get the kid.

We jumped in and tried to figure out where he was gonna land. Everywhere we passed, people was standing in the middle of the car wrecks and fires and stuff, looking up and cheering the parachute.

I noticed the big smudge in the air after the explosion, when we'd been driving around for ten minutes. Them other jets that had been with Jetboy was back, flying all around through the air, and some Mustangs and Thunderjugs, too. It was like a regular air show up there.

Somehow we got out near the Bridge before anybody else did. Good thing, because when we got to the water, we saw this guy pile right in about twenty feet from shore. Went down like a rock. He was wearing this diving-suit thing, and we swam out and I grabbed part of the parachute and a fireman grabbed some of the hoses and we hauled him out onto shore.

Well, it wasn't Jetboy, it was the one we got the make on as Edward 'Smooth Eddy' Shiloh, a real small-time operator.

And he was in bad shape, too. We got a wrench off the fire truck and popped his helmet, and he was purple as a turnip in there. It had taken him twenty-seven minutes to get to the ground. He'd passed out of course with not enough air up there, and he was so frostbit I heard they had to take off one of his feet and all but the thumb on the left hand.

But he'd jumped out of the thing before it blew. We looked back up, hoping to see Jetboy's chute or something, but there wasn't one, just that misty big smudge up there, and all those planes zoomin' round.

We took Shiloh to the hospital.

That's my report.

Statement of Edward 'Smooth Eddy' Shiloh, Sept. 16, 1946 (excerpt).

... all five shells into a couple of the gasbags. Then he crashed the plane right into us. The walls blew. Fred and Filmore were thrown out without their parachutes.

When the pressure dropped, I felt like I couldn't move, the suit got so tight. I tried to get my parachute. I see that Dr. Tod has the fuse and is making it to the bomb thing.

I felt the airplane fall off the side of the gondola. Next thing I know, Jetboy's standing right in front of the hole his plane made.

I pull out my roscoe when I see he's packing heat. But he dropped his gat and he heads toward Tod.

'Stop him, stop him!' Tod's yelling over the suit radio. I get one clean shot, but I miss, then he's on top of Tod and the bomb, and right then I decide my job's been over about five minutes and I'm not getting paid any overtime.

So I head out, and all this gnashing and screaming's coming across the radio, and they're grappling around. Then Tod yells and pulls out his .45 and I swear he put four shots in Jetboy from closer than I am to you. Then they fall back together, and I jumped out the hole in the side.

Only I was stupid, and I pulled my ripcord too soon, and my chute don't open right and got all twisted, and I started passing out. Just before I did, the whole thing blew up above me.

Next thing I know, I wake up here, and I got one shoe too many, know what I mean? . . .

. . . what did they say? Well, most of it was garbled. Let's see. Tod says 'Stop him, stop him,' and I shot. Then I lammed for the hole. They were yelling. I could only hear Jetboy when their helmets slammed together, through Tod's suit radio. They must have crashed together a lot, 'cause I heard both of them breathing hard.

Then Tod got to the gun and shot Jetboy four times and said 'Die, Jetboy! Die!' and I jumped and they must have fought a second, and I heard Jetboy say:

'I can't die yet. I haven't seen *The Jolson Story*.'

It was eight years to the day after Thomas Wolfe died, but it was his kind of day. Across the whole of America and the northern hemisphere, it was one of those days when summer gives up its hold, when the weather comes from the poles and Canada again, rather than the Gulf and the Pacific.

They eventually built a monument to Jetboy — 'the kid that couldn't die yet.' A battle-scarred veteran of nineteen had stopped a madman from blowing up Manhattan. After calmer heads prevailed, they realized that.

But it took a while to remember that. And to get around to going back to college, or buying that new refrigerator. It took a long time for anybody to remember what anything was like before September 15, 1946.

When people in New York City looked up and saw Jetboy blowing up the attacking aircraft, they thought their troubles were over.

They were as wrong as snakes on an eight-lane highway.

— Daniel Deck
GODOT IS MY CO-PILOT: *A Life of Jetboy*
Lippincott, 1963

From high up in the sky the fine mist began to curve downward.

Part of it stretched itself out in the winds, as it went through the jet stream, toward the east.

Beneath those currents, the mist re-formed and hung like verga, settling slowly to the city below, streamers forming and re-forming, breaking like scud near a storm.

Wherever it came down, it made a sound like gentle autumn rain.

THIRTY MINUTES
_____ OVER BROADWAY! _____
An Appendix

What makes a good story? Why should any story stand out above all the rest? Why does it qualify as one of the 'best'?

The idea. There can be no story without imagination.

Then there's the plot. That's vital, the talent to develop and explore the idea.

The characters, of course. The way they act and react, the way they relate to each other, the way they talk.

The writing is essential. The story must be well written. And well told. Which aren't the same thing.

Style and technique. How the story is narrated. What the author includes is crucial — and so is what is left out.

Observation, the telling detail which makes a scene come alive. That is a far greater test of skill than paragraphs of description.

All these are indispensable, and they can be appreciated simply by reading the story.

But there is more, far more: all the details which aren't noticed, and which aren't meant to be — yet which make all the difference.

As in Howard Waldrop's story.

Waldrop wrote an article to explain all the references in 'Thirty Minutes Over Broadway!' and it is reprinted here.

This was written for an American fanzine, and so perhaps the annotations should be annotated for non-Americans!

Most of it is self-explanatory, however. Even if you don't know what 'off-ramp on I-95' means, you can guess . . .

THE ANNOTATED JETBOY
by
HOWARD WALDROP

Writing is a funny business, but sometimes not nearly so funny as you'd like to think.

The following annotations are for my opening story, 'Thirty Minutes Over Broadway!' in the George R.R. Martin-edited shared world anthology, WILD CARDS.

People have always accused me of researching too much. It was three years between initial conception and the writing of this one — part of the time was working stuff out in the shared world with George and the other writers, but not that much. (With the result that my first draft had a couple of hundred stupidities which — along with four brilliant pages of stream-of-consciousness from inside Harry S Truman's head — I later took out.) The research was to lend what we in the rip-roaring days of Post-modernist fiction used to call *verisimilitude*, but what is now referred to in the Reagan '80's as 'making it seem real-like.'

Some of these were notes to myself, some were things I already knew; most I found in research while writing the story.

I figure if I'm going to work this damn hard I might as well get some use out of it and some credit for it. Whether this adds to your enjoyment of the story, or only clutters up your mind as much as mine. I don't care. Here it (they) are:

page 245 *Shantak, N.J.* H.P. Lovecraft, DREAM QUEST OF UNKNOWN KADATH, others. Also, Bill Wallace and Joe Pumilia 'Some Notes on M.M. Moamrath' NICKELODEON #1, 1976.

page 245 *Kodak Autograph Mark II.* Press camera of the '30s and '40s.

page 245 *Lincoln Traynor.* Link trainers were ground school dummy airplanes in which pilots trained for their instrument ratings. They maneuvered on three axes in response to the controls. Named for their developer.

page 245 *Surplus P-40.* Israel built its air force of surplus P-51s, bought for $500 @, put in crates marked 'tractor parts,' sent to the docks at Jaffa, where a runaway was built. The planes were assembled there and flown to airfields from shipside, a few weeks before Independence. The British looked the other way.

page 245 *Tomlin, Robert NMI.* If you don't have a middle name, the Army puts NMN where it goes. No middle initial, they put NMI.

page 246 *Hangar 23.* See Shea and Wilson, THE ILLUMINATUS TRILOGY.

page 246 *1200Z.* Zulu Time. GMT, Greenwich Mean Time.

page 246 *USAAF.* At the start of the War it was USAAC, the Army Air Corps. In '44 or '45, it was changed to USAAF. On October 2, 1947, it became the U.S. Air Force. (On that day in both the Army and the Air Force, all enlisted men were temporarily given the rank of E-1, buck private: all officers O-1, 2nd looie, until both services decided how many of each rank they needed.)

page 246 *... our records show ...* Orville Wright got his pilot's license in *1940.*

page 246 *Clear Skies and Tailwinds.* The way Robert O. Erisman, editor of G-8 AND HIS BATTLE ACES, used to sign all his letters to Chad Oliver.

page 246 *Arnold H.H.* Chief of Staff, Army Air Corps, WWII.

page 246 *500 planes, 50 ships.* The German *Stuka* pilot, Hans Rudel, had 367 planes and about 100 tanks to his credit when the war ended, mostly on the Eastern Front. And he only had one leg. (And he did most of his flying in a *Stuka* — by the end of the war, this was like going up against a P-47 in a Singer Sewing Machine.) Richard Bong, America's Ace of Aces, had 40 planes to his credit, mostly in the Pacific. He went through the war without a scratch. He was killed in 1946 when the jet he was testing had a flameout 20 feet above the runway on takeoff.

page 246 *Professor Silverberg.* Unless my brain was more burned-out than I think before I stopped using NutraSweet, the names of some of the monks in the monastery where the characters in THE BOOK OF SKULLS go in search of immortality are the same as the monks who raised Airboy, in AIR FIGHTERS COMICS, during WWII.

page 246 *Nazis and Italians and Whittle.* The Germans had an operational jet by 1939 and would have had the ME-262 twin-engine jet fighter in *combat* by 1943 if Hitler wouldn't have been so *stupid*. He made them strap a 500 kg bomb on them, slowing them down by 100 mph. In the last days of the war, the Luftwaffe had 3 operation jets (ME-262, Arado 234, and HE-162 — they were going to give 12-year-old kids two weeks of glider training and then give them the 600 mph jet to go after B-17s with.) and a rocket-powered interceptor, the ME-163. The Italians had the Caproni jet by 1939, the world's first operational jet; like most things Italian, it burned kerosene and flew about *half* as fast as a prop-driven fighter. Whittle made almost all the British jet engines. The Gloster Meteror was the only Allied jet used in combat — but only over England against V-1 buzz bombs. We had the P-59 Airacomet and the P-80 Shooting Star but neither saw combat. The Japanese had two jets, both copies of German designs, the most promising of which made its test flight August 8, 1945. No more *arigato.*

page 247   *6 . 30 cals.* Standard armament for fighters in 1939. By 1945, most fighters had from 6 to 12 .50 caliber machine guns plus one or more 20 mm or 37 mm cannons. The fun was *over.*

page 247   *The Blue Network.* NBC had to divide itself into two radio networks due to an anti-trust suit. They were the Blue and the Red Networks. One later became ABC.

page 247   *Sanders to Pappenfuss to Volstad.* Larry, Darryl and Darryl on the *Newhart Show.* Actually Sanderson, but never stop to check when things are going good.

page 247   *Sox drop two to Cleveland.* See Jean Shepherd, IN GOD WE TRUST — ALL OTHERS PAY CASH. Doubleday, 1966.

page 247   *RCAF . . .* China against the Japs. The war started in '39, America got in on Dec. 8, 1941. Many people went over into Canada and joined the Canadian Air Force, or went to Britain. See A YANK IN THE RAF, CAPTAINS OF THE CLOUDS. The AVG, American Volunteer Group, better known as 'The Flying Tigers' under General Claire Chennault, 1939–41. Like Jetboy, when the war started for the U.S., they were made members of the Air Corps. See FLYING TIGERS, GOD IS MY CO-PILOT.

page 247   *All-weather radar set.* The Germans were the first to equip their night-fighters with radar, though the British had better ground-based ones and some Neanderthal stuff in their Beauforts and Beaufighters by 1940. Most common German nightfighters were converted ME-110s and Heinkel 177s. By the end of the war, they had built a plane especially for night-fighting — the HE-210 'Owl.' So had we: the P-61 Black Widow.

page 248   *Tricycle landing gear.* The most advanced type. You'd be surprised how many WWII planes had two main gear under the wings, and a little bitty wheel, like off a red Radio Flyer wagon, under the tail.

page 248   *4 20mm cannon and a 75mm gun port.* Heavy but not unknown armament. B-25 Mitchell bombers were powered-up and converted to shipping attack planes, the A-25, in the Pacific. They carried 8 .50-cals in the nose, four more on the fuselage, four in the wing roots, four in the top turret which could be fired forward, plus a 75mm cannon. That's 20 .50 cals and a howitzer pointing at you, as the Japanese Navy soon found out. One stripped-down Japanese nightfighter, the *Gekko*, used against B-29s at the end of the war, carried a 90 mm cannon. It only carried two shells. One was *quant. suff.*

page 248   *something to roast weenies on.* The British referred to them as 'toasting fork antennae.'

page 248   *A Lincoln and two Jacksons.* $45.

page 249   *Dr. Tod.* German for death.

page 249   *'46 Merc.* If you had a '46 anything, you had money or a brother in the car business.

page 249   *raise bees.* Like Sherlock Holmes, in Sussex. See THE ART OF BEE-KEEPING, WITH SOME NOTES ON THE SEGREGATION OF THE QUEEN.

page 250   *600 miles to intercept us.* The American P-38s which shot down Admiral Yamamoto in '43 flew more than 1000 miles and came around the end of an island to find his plane flying less than 600 yards away.

page 250   *glass-brick room divider.* Once common, they went out of style, and now cost $20 per brick. In the '40s you couldn't give them away; they were considered Art Deco and old-fashioned for the Atomic Age.

page 251   *Christopher Robin.* Milne, in the R.A.F. in the war, now runs a bookstore in England.

page 252   *trying to catch some Lancasters.* Both sides played this game. We made daylight raids, the Brits and Germans night raids. Our nightfighters got in the formations as their bombers took off; they did the same for us.

page 252   *Mrs. Heelis.* Sawrey. Just like it says. Beatrix Potter died in the winter of '43.

page 253   *modified zoot suit.* The zoot suit came in in '41, was the cause of riots in California in '41-'42. In March '42 the War Production Board declared them to be 'counterproductive to the war effort' as they used too much material, especially the coats. They had been worn mostly by alienated youths, blacks and chicanos. In '46 they had a short renaissance during the be-bop days. See the book THE ZOOT-SUIT MURDERS, and the movies ZOOT SUIT and *1941.*

page 253   *'It ain't the meat, it's the motion.'* Any guy whistling this in 1946 had the wrong kind of friends. Listen to COPULATIN' BLUES, Yazoo Records.

page 253   Pine Barrens. See Wallace and Pumilia, *op. cit.* The place looks just like I say it does.

page 253   *nine-inch Dumonts.* Anyone looking at a nine-inch Dumont in 1946 is either a) rich, b) in a bar, c) in front of an appliance store, or knows someone who is.

page 253   *'ghost rockets.'* A 1946 summer phenomenon in Sweden. Between the 'foo fighters' seen in '44–'45 by Allied and Axis pilots, and Kenneth Arnold's 1947 'flying saucer' sighting, this was the big story. Attributed to Russians testing captured V-2s. They weren't. Not over Sweden, anyway.

page 254   COSH COMICS. A comic book company of the Golden Age, invented for a fanzine hoax, JED-DAK #6, 1965. Paul Moslander, Clint Bigglestone and Steve Perrin made most of it up. I drew the covers they 'reprinted'. A sleazy publisher, according to Moslander's article. We put ads in other fanzines for a year before the article ran — 'Wanted! Cosh Comics, any, but especially CAPTAIN COSH 1–6, 8, 10, 12–14! Will pay top dollar!' In 1965, you could get any comic book ever published, including ACTION #1, for less than $10.

page 254   *Lowboy.* I never realized there might be confusion caused by Jetboy talking to Lowboy. I thought the difference in the first three letters of their names would alert most readers.

page 254   *Harry Langdon.* Silent comedian. Big as Chaplin or Keaton. Sound and total artistic control ruined him. (Sound and lack of total artistic control did Keaton in.)

page 255   *statement of ownership and circulation.* Once a year, in every comic book and magazine, since 1876. These figures, like all, can be doctored, but you Go Up The River for that.

page 255   *no more red except for blood.* Things like this actually happened among the most gung-ho American businessmen, once they saw the Russians were the Enemy. This is the year before the Hollywood Ten trial, and the year Richard Milhous Nixon was elected to congress.

page 256   *Taking benzedrine and stuff.* Read the interview with Harry Harrison, GRAPHIC STORY MAGAZINE #16. Harrison was a comic book art director in the late '40s. He and his friends once did a 52-page comic book; writing, art, covers, separations, etc. in 37 straight hours.

page 257   *U.S.S. Reluctant.* Cargo tub aboard which Ensign Pulver and Mr. Roberts served. Thomas Heggen, MR. ROBERTS, 1948.

page 258 *JETBOY ON DINOSAUR ISLAND.* See both George R.R. Martin's and Lew Shiner's stories and epilogue in WILD CARDS

page 258 *Samurai. 1100 A.D.* A novel-within-a-novel I was going to write once. British kid, Japanese P.O.W., goes with Japanese soldiers to island covered with dinosaur skeletons and rusty samurai armor. Find scroll, which they spend half the book translating. About soldiers, circa 1100 A.D., assigned to take a princess out of danger, being blown off course in the same Divine Wind that destroys the Chinese–Mongol fleet. Ended up on lost island fighting dinosaurs. I was younger then. Then J.G. Ballard wrote EMPIRE OF THE SUN.

page 258 *up close and personal.* Or as we would say today, he's an off-ramp on I-95.

page 259 *Armadillo.* Forty years ago their range was confined to the Southwest. Now that wolves and coyotes have been killed, they are as far east as Florida, as far north as Tennessee and Missouri. They cross the Mississippi River by holding their breaths and walking on the bottom.

page 260 *A dollar and a quarter.* In the days before microchips, weather balloon radiosondes carried half a hardware store worth of electronics with them, and the Weather Bureau used to pay this for their recovery.

page 260 *Only five of them have been exploded.* Trinity Site, Alamogordo July 16, 1945. Hiroshima and Nagasaki, August '45. Able and Baker tests. Operation Crossroads, south Pacific, summer 1946. Large-scale open-air tests didn't start 'til the '50s.

page 262 *Something that is plausible to them.* If you told Harry Truman and the Air Corps you were an alien and were looking for a galactic Doomsday weapon that could wipe out 90% of the people on the planet, they wouldn't believe you. If you told them you were a holdover Nazi in a new kind of plane looking for one of Hitler's Secret Weapons, you'd get their attention.

page 262 *ice cream.* Einstein snuck off every day with two FBI agents to have an ice cream cone in the summertime during the War.

page 262 *book of memoirs.* THE JET-PROPELLED BOY. Never published in full. Excerpts in HARPERS MAGAZINE, April, 1947.

page 263 *Historical Aircraft For Sale.* The JB-1, with these specs, should have those speeds, endurances, etc. Underpowered by 1946 standards.

page 263 *paper rationing was off.* July, 1945. If you could find it, you could print on it.

page 263 *THE GRASSHOPPER LIES HEAVY.* Philip K. Dick, THE MAN IN

THE HIGH CASTLE, 1962.

page 263 *GROWING FLOWERS BY CANDLELIGHT IN HOTEL ROOMS.*
Richard Brautigan, THE ABORTION: A ROMANCE, 1966.

page 263 *Thorkeld.* DR. CYCLOPS, by Will Garth (Henry Kuttner), also
movie, 1940. Actually, Thorkel, but never stop to check when
things are going good.

page 265 *Port Elizabeth, North Carolina.* The Navy antisubmarine
blimp patrol base for the East Coast in WWII.

page 265 *'Dewey was an admiral . . .'* and the others. See JUMP-ROPE
RHYMES, Aldridge, 1966.

page 265 *G-2.* Army or Air Force Intelligence.

page 266 *TA-152.* The Kurt Tank-modified Folke-Wulf 190, with a
longer fuselage, different prop and better engine. A booger.

page 266 *snap-roll.* A tactic used on bombers by fighters on both sides.
The Sperry ball belly turret was designed to discourage such
rude behavior.

page 266 *wig-wagging.* A last ditch tactic — it exposes the whole
bomber rather than the back-end silhouette. You do it when
you're down to just waist-gunners, the tail, top and belly
turret gunners being dead or out of ammo.

page 266 *The whole middle of the fighter* ... Stranger things happen.
Two second looies I knew in 1971 left for Vietnam. They
were back a month later. 'What happened?' 'Well, we were
out in a Huey gunship helicopter with rockets on it. We
looked up and here came a MiG-19 in on us. I pushed all the
buttons to lighten my load, rockets, machine guns, and
headed for the trees. We looked back and there was this parachute coming down. The MiG-19 pilot had run right into our
rockets and shot himself down.' They got Silver Stars.

page 266 *not recognizing my plane.* Even recognizing it. Gunners
popped off at everything. Better safe than sorry. Spitfires and
ME-109s looked a lot alike from the snout, or business, end.
And the only jets in the air over Europe, except Jetboy's, were
German.

page 266 *My IFF code.* Identification Friend or Foe. These flashed a
signal which changed every day. If you didn't flash the right
one back, they fired at you. Better safe than sorry.

page 267 *This year more people will fly in airliners* ... a true statistic for
1946.

page 267 *Spanky, Alfalfa, Buckwheat.* The last OUR GANG comedy
was made in 1944.

page 267 *THAT NAZTY NUISANCE, JIVE, JUNCTION.* Real.

page 268 *MURDER, HE SAYS.* Real, and great.

page 268   *IT'S IN THE BAG.* Remade as THE TWELVE CHAIRS by Mel Brooks, 1969.

page 268   *PRC.* Producers Releasing Company. A studio you rented in Gower Gulch.

page 268   *The way the guys on the* Reluctant *talked . . .* MISTER ROBERTS, *op cit.*

page 269   *rumors from Turkey.* Truman concern during '46.

page 269   *plow . . . M-1 Garand.* True.

page 270   *Major Truman.* One half a comic book writing/art team.

page 270   *General Ostrander.* The other half.

page 270   *he hated air conditioning.* True.

page 271   *Tuesday afternoon, September 15, 1946.* Actually, it was Sunday, but I told Roger Zelazny two months before I began this story to make it a Tuesday. It's also my birthdate.

page 271   *nearly 60,000.* Above the operational levels of most aircraft, and nearly all anti-aircrart artillery in 1946.

page 272   *The number 500.* Five hundred feet above sea level.

page 272   *P-51.* The North American Mustang, the fastest prop-driven fighter of WWII, maybe ever. A *real* booger.

page 273   *They're working on something.* The Bell XS-1, the 'Glamorous Glennis' in which Chuck Yeager broke the sound barrier in October of 1947. I once wrote a story in which Chuck Yeager was the first man on the Moon.

page 273   *The Flying Wing.* The XB-35 was a 6-engine prop-job version, the world's first all-wing bomber. The B-35 was modified by having four jet engines attached outboard on the wings. Then the all-jet version, the YB-49 was tested. Through Congressional and Defense Department graft and corruption, we adopted the B-36 instead. That's why when I looked up in the '50s I saw ugly half-jet, half-prop B-36s taking off from Carswell AFB, rather than the beautiful B-49s. George Pal, no slouch, had a B-49 drop the A-Bomb on the Martians in WAR OF THE WORLDS, 1953. See my 'Love Comes for the YB-49', CRAWDADDY #7, 1970.

page 273   *Navy T-2 pressure suit. The* space suit. It covered the body with all these Bozo rings made of latex and old tires. It had a real space helmet — you wore your oxygen mask and flying helmet inside. It probably weighed a zillion pounds, but it was on the cover of *every sf* magazine, at one time or another, in the 1950s.

page 274   *Bronzino's VENUS, CUPID, FOLLY AND TIME.* Real hubba-hubba stuff in the late 1600s.

page 274   *chunder.* Listen to Men at Work, BUSINESS AS USUAL,

'Down Under.' Aussie for Return Lunch Ticket. Technicolor Yawn. Blowing Beets.

page 274   *Clark Gable Command.* After Carole Lombard died, Gable tried to get in combat. The Air Corps had him flying a desk. He raised so much commotion they had to let him go on bombing missions. Also see COMMAND DECISION, 1948.

page 274   *Squadron Hodiak.* John Hodiak, bad American actor. DRAGONFLY SQUADRON, 1953. ON THE THRESHOLD OF SPACE, 1956. The name of my first bicycle. See 'Hodiak, Son of Battle' PRISM #1, 1973.

page 275   *at least 500,000 cubic feet.* Big for 1946. Small for 1986.

page 276   *'Francis the Talking Cop.'* Dolph Sweet, in Francis Ford Coppola's YOU'RE A BIG BOY NOW, 1967.

page 276   *Sixth Avenue.* Avenue of the Americas.

page 276   *Army oughta be sued.* This happened in the 'Battle for Los Angeles,' late December 1941, when a fake air raid panicked the West Coast, and the air defense artillerymen got so jumpy they forgot to set the timers on their shells. Spielberg's *1941* is based on this real incident.

page 278   *bailout bottle.* Not enough air, thoughtfully provided with early pressure suits. Usually strapped to the leg or back. It was to keep the suit inflated and you breathing long enough to get down to thicker air, or bail out before you passed out or underwent a decompression explosion (your blood boils up there from the body heat).

page 280   *that high up ... serious trouble.* At 50, 000 ft. your chute won't open right, but it will slow you down long enough for you to pass out before you hit air you can *breathe.* Also, it's cold up there — @ —50°F.

page 281   *roscoe.* A heater.

page 281   *packing heat.* Carrying a roscoe.

page 281   *gat.* A roscoe.

page 282   *lammed.* Opting for the path of least Jetboy.

page 282   *'I can't die yet ...'* Larry Fine of the Three Stooges, in one of their 1946 shorts.

page 282   *Eight years to the day ...* Wolfe died September 15, 1938, in Johns Hopkins in Baltimore.

page 282   *Daniel Deck.* Usually called Danny. See ALL MY FRIENDS ARE GOING TO BE STRANGERS. Larry McMurtry, Simon and Shuster, 1972.

page 282   *verga.* The rain that hangs down from the clouds over deserts but evaporates before it hits the ground.

BRIAN ALDISS

At the forefront of British and world science fiction for more than quarter of a century, Brian Aldiss has won almost every sf award there is — and also ones that no longer exist. He started as a prize winner in the 1955 *Observer* science fiction competition; and in 1987 he won the non-fiction Hugo Award for *Trillion Year Spree*. Written with David Wingrove, this is a revision of his definitive history of science fiction, *Billion Year Spree*.

Between these dates, Aldiss has written such novels as *Hothouse Greybeard, Cryptozoic!, Barefoot in the Head, The Malacia Tapestry* and the *Helliconia* trilogy. As well as a novelist and short story writer, he has edited many anthologies, is an astute critic of the sf field and has twice been Guest of Honour at a World Sf Convention.

His latest endeavours have been directed towards the stage. Aldiss has written and appeared in *Science Fiction Blues*, treading the boards with Ken Campbell and Petronilla Whitfield, in what he describes as 'a surreal evening with doom and laughter, in which words don't quite fail us.' The full text of the performance is the first book from Avernus, Aldiss's own publishing company. (Avernus is the name of the satellite which orbits Helliconia.)

His most recent novel, *Forgotten Life,* is not sf; but 1988 also saw publication of *The Best Science Fiction Stories of Brian Aldiss*; the next book will be his *Best Fantasy Stories.*

OPPOSITE NUMBERS

by
BRIAN ALDISS

To have a favourite short story — or at least to have a favourite
short story for very long — is a little absurd. Our obsessions
remain fixed, our opinions change with the times. Still, there's
no harm in being absurd, particularly if we enjoy science fiction.
'L'Etat, c'est moi', declared Louis XIV; 'L'age, c'est nous', we
declare. So we are allowed favourite short stories which we
shuffle like cards from decade to decade, just as if taste were
absolute. We can adhere to these trumps most firmly if we don't
go back to re-read them; re-reading may disclose to our dismay
that those favourites have gone a little yellow round the edges,
just as we ourselves are now trimmed with grey.

These somewhat esoteric thoughts are provoked by the death
of Robert A. Heinlein in May 1988. Because it is a long time
since I re-read it, I may still believe that 'By His Bootstraps' is
one of my favourite SF stories, along with David Masson's
'Mouth of Hell', J.G. Ballard's 'Terminal Beach', James Blish's
'Common Time', and Austin Lundy's 'Law of a Distant City'.

Austin Lundy's name is scarcely remembered, although it is
only five years since he died. For me, however, the opening
sentence of his 'Seven Weeks in a Toy Tomorrow' remains
invitingly in memory: 'Mario Ford had finally achieved the goal
of his life, total incompetence' (the last word translated in the
French version, I was told, as *incontinence*, thereby introducing
an alternative story which no doubt would have amused Lundy).
One may have every confidence that Heinlein's name will last a
little longer than Lundy's, if only because of the large number of
his many books which have been print, still to lie in a world of
which he himself no longer has a share.

Within the SF tribe — that mysterious clan which wanders
the face of the globe looking for new gods — the legend of Heinlein will continue to be related round the camp fires after dark.
Since it is still daylight as I write — a warm May daylight, reduced
to pleasantly confusing patterns at my window as it shines

through the leaves of sycamores disturbed by a slight breeze — I will not join those story-tellers, but rather remind readers of Austin Lundy's enigmatic and possibly emblematic life in SF.

Lundy's first story, 'Back in Breughel's World' was published in 1978, in the short-lived Irish publication, *Uranium-123 SF*. Enthusiasm for SF in Britain was low at that time — unlike our present glorious renaissance — and the story passed largely unnoticed.

Only eight more short stories were to follow before Lundy's death in 1983, and those appeared in non-SF publications. 'In the Eyeball of the Storm', for instance, appeared in the *Mississippi Digest*.

Both 'Back in Breughel's World' and 'In the Eyeball of the Storm' impressed me greatly. So did each one of that handful of stories. I have been asked, Did I think Austin Lundy was a genius? In truth, I thought only that he had genius. Genius consists of more than that renowned infinite capacity for taking pains. It requires an infinite capacity for taking pains *over an extended period*. Irving Berlin had that capacity and lives to be a hundred. Austin Lundy made the mistake of dying young. In some cases, it's psychosomatic.

It was in 1982 that I met Lundy, at a convention in Brighton: our only meeting. He was a pale thin man, dressed in black, in his mid-thirties. An habitual smoker. His manner was listless, he was shy and disinclined to smile; also — a grave disability at a convention — he did not drink. However, he wanted to converse, and he and I took a stroll along the promenade as dusk was falling. He said he was in torment, having just been talked at by a well-known SF writer. The sight of the sea calmed him and he soon became buoyant. He said he could not take the convention and was planning to go home on the morrow; but he showed a considerable knowledge of SF, despite his disclaimer that 'he could not write the stuff himself'. He said he only wrote as he did because he was ill and neurotic. All writers were neurotic, he said, glancing at me slyly.

It happened that we met a couple of pretty and carefree girls on the sea front, and got talking to them. I could see possibilities opening out for the evening, but Lundy was plainly dismayed, and said to me when he got the chance, 'I need to go back to the hotel.'

So we left the two girls. Lundy was furious with me. 'You and I have this precious opportunity to talk together, to talk of things that matter and you'd throw it away for a couple of tarts,' he exclaimed. 'You're one of these enemies of literature who prefers the feel of a girl's tits to the entire works of Thomas Mann.'

When I admitted the charge, he calmed down, eventually saying, offhandedly, 'As a matter of fact, I've no experience of women. To have illicit sexual intercourse with one *at Brighton* would be a cliché of the worst order.' I could not guarantee that 'illicit' was the word he used, but I recall the emphasis he laid on the 'at Brighton' phrase, and the blend of humour and despair with which he spoke. That blend was, I'm sure, very characteristic.

How different was that occasion from my sole encounter with Robert Heinlein in 1969. We were then by a greater ocean than Brighton can boast. We were in that brilliant and nonconstruable city, Rio de Janeiro, attending a science fiction convention with well-known SF writers from all round the globe. This was my first meeting with men I came to respect, such as Frederik Pohl and Harlan Ellison. The temperature in Rio is several degrees above Cooking, the city is dispersed, and we celebrities were shepherded from place to place by young handmaidens in blue, riding in oven-ready Volkswagen buses to entertain the populace.

At one point along the route, my friend Harry Harrison lay in wait for me, with a couple of men lined up behind him, in a parade of two. They stood rigid in the sun as Harry, with a show of showmanship, performed the introductions: 'Brian, this is A.E. van Vogt, this is Bob Heinlein.'

As we climbed together into the little bus, Heinlein talked of his familiarity with Hollywood, and of the ease with which he could once park on Sunset or Vine. Not any longer, it seemed. Later, when I met his wife, she and he were good enough to criticise the English for electing a Socialist Prime Minister, Mr. Harold Wilson. They deplored the fact that England, once so great, was so evidently going downhill. While appreciating Heinlein's patriotism on my behalf, I do not recall his talking about literature. But his assumption, and the assumption of most of the other American SF writers — always excepting van Vogt, who donned no persona, adopted no charisma — was that they had the world at their command or were, at the least, very well, and very well paid. And, unlike Lundy, well laid.

It was in Rio I understood that the difference between American and British SF lay not only in the stories; it was deeply rooted in the personalities of the writers.

I would guess that Heinlein's famous character, Lazarus Long, sums up Heinlein's outlook on life when he says, 'Certainly the game is rigged. Don't let that stop you; if you don't bet, you can't win.' Very admirable in its way. Altogether more positive than Lundy's outlook on life, which might be summed up as 'If you don't bet, you can't lose.' Heinlein went to California, to enjoy the last years of his life. Austin Lundy died in the Isle of Wight, at Ventnor.

It is absurd to attempt comparisons between the two writers. Heinlein was showered with awards and applause, often attained the best-seller lists, and had books written about him, the latest being the most commanding.[1] For almost half a century, he was regarded as one of the leading SF writers on this planet. It is a remarkable record. Lundy, on the other hand, was no one.

Yet Lundy wrote 'Seven Weeks in a Toy Tomorrow', with its inviting first line. Mario Ford is a part of the submerged population. He works in a gigantic food factory in Melton Mowbray. He plays no games, he never visits a pub, he does not read the newspapers. He breeds pigeons. Ford's uneventful life changes when, following a distressing accident in a supermarket — a crate of aerosol toilet fresheners passing overhead falls on him and damages his brain — he finds he can see into the future, as he believes.

Ford goes to a cattle auction, where prize bulls are being auctioned for astronomical figures. He finds he can enter into the minds of the bulls.

Most of them kept their temper, consoling themselves with memories of green fields and buttercups that glowed like farmers' waistcoat buttons. Many of them contemplated suicide.

---

1. Leon Stover: *Robert A. Heinlein.* Twayne's United States Authors Series, Boston, 1987.

Only a certain respect for the good name of bullhood prevented them from dashing out their brains against the metal bars of their pens — that and a realistic consideration of the thickness of their skulls.

'That poor auctioneer!' one of the more Senecan bulls thought. 'What a burden of guilt is his! He'd probably experience nothing but vindication if I give him a good trampling, a proper four-hoof job. Eh?'

'Tush,' said his neighbour. 'The chap may be a vegetarian. Never take too much for granted in this world.'

'Yes, and we may be sold to vegetarians,' said another, sarcastically.

The 'Tush' is well-placed. The thoughts of the bulls are irredeemably old-fashioned.

Many other catastrophes tumble through Ford's injured brain: wars, terrible famines, financial collapse, plagues, revolutions, bloodshed, leaping divorce rates, new diseases: they greet him wherever he goes. When he can no longer endure this future world he believes he is viewing, he visits a leading politician in the Houses of Parliament to warn him of what is to come. the politician sends him, scornfully, to a Jewish psychiatrist. Together, Ford and the psychiatrist discover the truth: he is seeing things that happened seven weks in the past. The future remains obscure. The present remains as the present always was.

Lundy had wit where Heinlein had only wisecracks — and Lundy, I believe, took full cognisance of the continuing catastrophe of the twentieth century.

Little of significance has ever been said regarding the short story as an art form, although we may ponder John Bayley's recent remark that 'The art of the short story must make us feel that the real subject has not been caught in the apparent one, or compromised by it.[2] There remains Frank O'Connor's famous dictum, 'The short story has never had a hero. What it has instead is a submerged population group.' This dictum certainly

---

2. John Bayley: *The Short Story: Henry James to Elizabeth Bowen.* Harvester. Brighton, 1988.

applies to those nine short stories, still awaiting collection, by Austin Lundy. His characters struggle to achieve grandeur or failure (in both cases without distinct success) in circumstances by their nature adverse. Remember 'Law of a Distant City'. The central character, Reg Embole, works in a spaceship factory on Mars. Like most Lundy central characters, Embole has a job involving technology (Lundy himself worked for Rolls Royce in Derby, close to where he was born), and is a lowly cog in a machine, the workings of which he hardly comprehends. In this respect, Lundy is a disciple of Kafka's. Indeed, when we were talking of literature in Brighton, Lundy suddenly cried, 'Kafka and Asimov! Kafka and Asimov! Bloody great!'

It saddens me to think that Lundy has disappeared from view. So have many British SF writers. Their names are not kept in mind, in the way that the Americans, for instance, still remember a minor writer like Terry Carr. Charles Eric Maine? Dan Morgan? Lan Wright? Ken Bulmer? Not remembered, not discussed, not cherished in the way that American fandom cherished Heinlein and the late Clifford Simak.

Of course, Lundy sought obscurity. He believed he could write better without the burden of reputation. That also marks him off from almost any American writer. His name was mentioned once, rather disparagingly, in *Vector*, the BSFA journal, in connection with his appearance on a panel at that same Channelcon I have mentioned. Christopher Priest and I were also on that panel, and Austin Lundy was persuaded to substitute for someone too ill to appear (possibly Robert Holdstock?).

Lundy was almost too nervous to speak. Priest and I were praising Harlan Ellison's *Deathbird Stories*, when Lundy broke in by saying, 'What you have to remember is that people always need to be consoled. I hate to be told everything is possible — it's a lie as far as I'm concerned. That's what's wrong with science fiction. Everything's possible. I want to be consoled by tales of difficulty and woe. Bugger success. Tell me England has been destroyed and I'll enjoy it. So will everyone. Why else would a rotten book like Wyndham's *Day of the Triffids* achieve such popularity? Wyndham never suffered. Ellison suffers. I suffer — but I don't make a fuss about it. In any case, it's probably a grave moral error just to constringe life into a four-thousand-worder.'

Very English. He was in an oblique way boasting as much as an American author. Yet few American authors would allow themselves to rejoice in the destruction of the U.S.A. Patriotism there, in the eighties, is a way of life. How different the ethos here. The British SF short story has never had a hero. Only subversives. And words like 'constringe'.

Frank O'Connor's remark does not apply to the short stories of the typical SF writer of Heinlein's heyday. Their tales have veritable heroes, sometimes supermen, like van Vogt's Slan, who can take in a situation at a glance and become master of it. They kill with aplomb, and the plot allows no backward look. They achieve total competence in the first sentence. The stories are 'optimistic' in a materialistic way; Austin Lundy's stories mingle humour and desperation.

Heinlein and Co were — are — better paid than their British opposite numbers. Is this because they write of successful characters, or is it because they are better paid that they write of successful characters? I must leave the question poised, though I guess the answer is: Both.

Britain is currently, if we believe something of what we hear, enjoying commercial success and international prestige in the business world. Does this volume reflect that new status, or is the spirit of Austin Lundy still with us?

That is another question I will leave poised. You can answer it yourself by observing how many British writers are represented in this yearbook.

JOHN CLUTE

Although born in Canada, John Clute has lived in Britain since 1969. An author as well as a critic, his first science fiction story appeared in *New Worlds* in 1966. His critical articles were also published in the same magazine until its demise, and during the same period he wrote for *The Magazine of Fantasy and Science Fiction* in the USA. His first novel (non sf) was *The Disinheriting Party*; his story 'Eden Sounding' from *Other Edens 2* comprises the first chapters of a new novel, *The Widow Gloss*.

Clute was the associate editor of what is still the basic sf reference work, *The Encyclopedia of Science Fiction* (general editor, Peter Nicholls), and has served as reviews editor of the journal *Foundation* since 1980. He is an advisory editor for *Interzone*, for whom he regularly reviews sf; he also reviews for the *Observer*, *Times Literary Supplement*, *Washington Post* and elsewhere.

A book of his criticism, *Strokes*, subtitled *Essays and Reviews 1966–86*, was published in the USA during 1988.

SCIENCE FICTION
———— NOVELS OF THE YEAR ————
by
JOHN CLUTE

Let us not lament, but the world of science fiction is no longer very neat. There may have been a time, in the morning of the world, before Sputnik, when the empires of our science fiction dreams were governed according to rules neatly written out in the pages of *Astounding*, and we could all play the game of a future we all shared, readers, writers, fans, steaming in the dews of the dawn. But something happened. No longer a game for the members of the club, no longer a secret handshake, the future began to come *true*. The planet of our birth began to over-heat from excessive spin, and that which was past or passing or to come began to merge into one fire, like spokes on the wheel of Juggernaut; science fiction writers began to have to run to stand still, like all of us. Their novels became larger, more worldly, more confused, more cynical, more like any other kind of novel; for good and for ill, the indelible realities of our late twentieth century began to stain the once shiny genre. Which did nothing to stop its growth, in a marketing sense.

Here are some damn statistics. Because they are extracted from *Locus*, an American trade journal which claims to serve every one of us as 'The Newspaper of the Science Fiction Field,' none of them deals with the UK. However, given the size of British publishers' science fiction lists (small), and the extent to which these lists are dominated by books originating in America (not total), the omission of this material from the *Locus* calculations is only modestly unfortunate. The cautionary tale the statistics tell would change by only a few adjectives were British data to be included.

On the face of it, *Locus* tells a tale of relentless cheer, and there can be no doubt that, in a commercial sense, the news is good. In 1977, 445 new titles of all categories were released into the field of fantastic literature, which embraces fantasy and horror as well as science fiction; by 1982 there were 572, the next year 581, then 613, 846, and in 1987 a total of 1026 new titles were published. Sounds triumphant. But put it another way and it may seem less boosterish: Even 20 years after Sputnik, in 1977, an omnivorous reader of independent means could have kept the field within his/her single grasp by mulching a mere 1.2 books per diem. By 1987 this omnivore's diet would have become bulimiacal, amounting to 2.8 books daily, or one book every 8.5 hours. What was once a field had become the Mississippi delta. If pre-Sputnik science fiction could be perceived as a *family of read books* which created (and inhabited) a knowable stage (or matrix) of possible worlds, by 1987 this perception had become deeply nostalgic. No longer could an ostensive definition of science fiction (science fiction is what smells like science fiction) even begin to match the corrosive intricacies of the exploded genre. By 1987, science fiction was no longer a family romance.

That total of 1026 new books of fantastic literature published in America (add a smidgen for the rest of the world) can, all the same, be broken down into more assimilable categories. Of the total only 650 — or 1.8 a day — are novels, a category which excludes the 74 novelizations published in 1987, and of the novels encompassed by *Locus's* remit only 298 are science fiction. The rest — 352 titles — are fantasy and horror novels, which increasingly dominate the field as a whole, much to its detriment. (For this writer, bad science fiction can be seen as a category of trash, and can be junked at sight. Bad fantasy is something else. Perhaps because it transforms archetypal material into sleaze, bad fantasy is *junk-food*, an addictive mockery of the true meal, which sticks to the stomach, and eats it.) Of those 352 fantasy and horror titles, only one or two need mentioning in any overview of fantastic literature in novel form published in 1987. And of the 298 books *Locus* designates as science fiction, 37 are Post-Holocaust Survivalist Adventures, and of the total 123 are series continuations. The task of gaining an overview may be less daunting than it first looked.

It is only polite to begin with dinosaurs. Writers so designated are relics of science fiction's long history as a relatively closed genre (until Sputnik blew the walls down). During that long period of immurement (1926 to 1957) dominant writers tended to acquire a kind of siege significance, rather like the significance accorded bad singers of patriotic songs in times of war. Supercharged and overdetermined by all the signs of meaning that film stars famously bear, science fiction writers, like Doc Smith or Robert A. Heinlein, became the Figures in the Carpet of science fiction, radiating the hot iconic glow of myths of origin, in the flesh. They had the Royal Touch. None of this — need it be said — made them rich. Pre-Sputnik science fiction was too small to support more than a very few adult writers anything like full-time, no matter how deliriously s/he overproduced. After 1960, however, when science fiction began to think of its sacred history as a talisman against the heat-death of the new gigantism, it slowly became evident that the saturated iconicity of these oldsters or dinosaurs had become bankable. It did not much matter that most of them never wrote very well in the first place, and now wrote worse, for they bore Cargo from the mists of time. Some had remained active, and did not now think of stopping; others, who had fallen silent, now returned to active work in the industrial parks of the modern.

Sadly there were mishaps. A.E. Van Vogt decanted a slough of novels in the 1970s, but the oneiric odysseys of his prime had now flattened into stiff-kneed daydreaming, he sold poorly, and fell silent. Theodore Sturgeon remained prey, like Laocoon, to writer's block. Alfred Bester saw his nous appropriated by the snippy wee mammals of the new age, and his own talents peter out. Clifford D. Simak, now dead, kept going until he was past 80, but never seemed to cut a word after the age of 60. Unfortunately, he is now remembered for his unloosed stays, not *City* (1952).

On the other hand, Isaac Asimov (never silent as a writer) returned to fiction like Ozymandias to the desert, determined to salvage for eternity the ad-hoc works of his early primitive years; by recasting his Foundation and Robot series into great rigid novels, he clearly intended to bind almost every tale he had ever written, with ligaments of stone, into a vast megaseries, like death. His 1987 novel, *Fantastic Universe II* (Doubleday), astonishingly rewrites a crapulous 1966 novelization, of which he was properly ashamed, into a long icy guided tour of the human body by miniaturized sub, all limned with numbing dispassion. After several years Jack Vance also returned to science fiction, and in

Araminta Station (Underwood-Miller/Tor) began, once again, to landscape-garden a Big Planet. As always, his characters seemed less colourful than the arbours and grottos they adorn, and which constitute the genuine populace of his topiary (a word this writer has used before) terraforming vision. Arthur C. Clarke continued to pump his indefatigable serenity into fictionalized travelogues of the mind, the latest being yet another episode in a series whose first instalment (*2001: A Space Odyssey*) was hilariously misprisioned into film by the dyspeptic Stanley Kubrick; by 1987 (though the book is copyright 1988 it was available before the end of the year) we had reached *2061: Odyssey Three* (Del Rey).

Of the dinosaurs still active in 1987, one of them, Robert A. Heinlein, is already a late dinosaur. What now seems to be his last novel, and therefore the last instalment in an extraordinary series of valedictory summae, *To Sail Beyond the Sunset* (Putnams) gives off all the greenhouse foetor — all the tropical hypertrophies of narcissism — characteristic of its immediate predecessors. It smells of the inside of the head. By now there can be no novelty in describing Heinlein's late work as solipsistic — the author himself came close to doing so in more than one of the late books — but the distressed camp solipsism of novels like *Sunset* and *The Cat Who Walks Through Walls* (1985) and '*The Number of the Beast*' (1980) may well be their defining characteristic. Ostensibly peopled though they are by enormous casts (almost always made up of characters from the novels of Heinlein's glossy and insinuating prime), these novels are in fact nightmares of a most desperate solitude. At the most visible level of plotting, the elect members of these casts (after butchering the unelect) all turn out to be close relatives of one another, and engage in interminable bouts of gleeful incest on realizing the fact; at a deeper level, they are all aspects of one character, Lazarus Long (who is the author); they are shadows on his wall, and the worlds they inhabit dissolve at his touch. These worlds are skilful travesties of the science fiction worlds created by Heinlein (and others) before Sputnik, and their merciless disparagement in book after book bespeaks an enormity of disgust and rage on the author's part, seemingly directed at a genre grown monstrous. But in the end the disgust and the rage turn insatiably inwards, and in the end *To Sail Beyond the Sunset* reads not as a hecatomb but a mirror.

Of the dinosaurs who remain vigorously alive, Frederik Pohl is by far the most interesting case. The novels of his early career, with the possible exception of collaborations with C.M. Kornbluth like *The Space Merchants* (1953), were far less assured than his shorter fiction; he always seemed a writer too easily distracted from the task to stick to a novel without dithering, shifting his ground, backing off; and for several years he wrote very little in the longer form. But with the publication of *Man Plus* in 1976 he came at long last into his novel-writing prime. Gone was the dither and the demurring. Brilliant and vibrant, *Gateway* (1977) began the Heechee Saga, which concluded in 1987 (way downhill it must be granted) with *The Annals of the Heechee*. *Jem* (1979) was a narration of utopia — a task logically incompossible with the *maintenance* of utopia, but intriguingly assayed, and which pointed to *The Years of the City* (1984) and *Chernobyl* (Bantam), his second 1987 novel, which is not, however, science fiction. *The Annals of the Heechee* (Del Rey) is a baggy monster of a book, full of great lumbering logjams of resume from the three previous volumes of the series, decked out with pages and pages of boiler-factory man-gal backchat a la Heinlein (perhaps designed as an homage), and featuring a first-person narrator whose glutinous coyness about his failures of Competence never manages to keep him from demonstrating his supernormal street-wise powers of lateral thinking whenever the chips are down. The whole lazy farrago, which includes the saving of the universe, could have been told at half the length. It is a shambles which may, all the same, bear perverse testimony to Pohl's continuing savvy, because *The Annals of the Heechee* gives off ample signs of cynical deliberation in its catering to the taste-buds of series addicts. It was very well reviewed.

After the dinosaurs, and before we beard the alpha males of the veldt, an oddment or two might be mentioned. In *The Day of Creation* (Gollancz), J.G. Ballard continued to create work whose utter autonomy glows unscathed by his secondment to the British literary establishment after the success of *Empire of the Sun* (1984); this autonomy is only superficially belied by his use of the same animistic metaphorical substrate that fuels some of the worst fantasies ever written. Avram Davidson, too nocturnal and European to be conceived of as a dinosaur, resumed with *Vergil in Avernus* (Doubleday) his sequence of tales set in a grievous, vulcanism-haunted alternate Naples. James Dickey's enormous *Alnilam* (Doubleday) explored an occult web of affinities linking father and dead son, but with an attention span that extends to mania. In *The Medusa Frequency* (Cape), Russell Hoban made short — indeed truncated — work of a confluence of the Orpheus Myth and Medusa, set in a curiously spastic here-and-now. William Kotzwinkle's *The Exile* (Dutton) dove (once again) into the occult tentacles of Nazi Germany in a tale of possession and paranoia. In *Fiasco* (Deutsch), Stanislaw Lem harshened into a series of cartoon disquisitions — though the final scene is stunning — much of the philosophical substance of *Solaris* (trans. 1961), specifically the doctrine that the human armamentarium of praxis and perception must fail to comprehend the unsayable Otherness of any utter Thing Itself, which may be a sentient ocean, or an alien species (as in this novel), or the Boojum. In *A Child in Time* (Cape), Ian McEwan suggested that a further half decade of Thatcherism would transform England into a factory farm, squalid, eutrophicated, poison to the soul. Keith Roberts composed in *Grainne* (Kerosina) an anguished submission to Woman as intoxicant and succubus, and saviour of these Isles one day. And the rebarbative George Turner finally won something like his due (and more), gaining this year's Arthur C. Clarke Award for *The Sea and Summer* (Faber), a dystopian vision of Melbourne (Australia) some decades hence, after a superflux of disasters has transformed the world into an overburdened slum. But the disasters are too pat, too bullyingly assumed as given, to bear the burden he insists they must, and the complex structures of the tale tend to dry upon the reader. It is, all the same, his best book.

In one way or another, authors like Ballard or McEwan or Lem or Turner stand to one side of the ruined communal theatre of conventional science fiction (as ostensively defined by those who knew what they were pointing at). Their necessary presence in any survey of 1987 is another sign of the demands made by the spinning world upon any writer wishing to portray it, and for whom science fiction imagery may serve as a useful tool in that job of portrayal. It is still the case, all the same, that most of the novels yet to be mentioned come from authors whose origins lie deep in the original field, and whose commercial success must in part depend on the nostalgia value of their continuing loyalty to the pulp *Umwelt* of the old Future History. It is also the case that most of the hundreds of novels which will go unmentioned come from authors whose commercial success depends precisely upon nostalgia value, authors more or less adept at applying mascara to the known; like any entertainment genre, science fiction is predominantly a literature of nostalgia manipulation. Only the greatest novels, after all, ever threaten anyone.

Of the alpha males (there are relatively few women in this cohort) who began to dominate the field around 1965–75, only a handful, like Thomas M. Disch and Samuel R. Delany, fail to emit a nostalgic charm. But neither of these authors published significantly in 1987 (though if it weren't a collection of linked fantasy tales, and if it weren't set in Neveryon, the land of Gongor the Tongue-Locked, Delany's *The Bridge of Lost Desire* might need mentioning). Deep into the nostalgia-realms of Future History with *Great Sky River* (Bantam), Gregory Benford continues to apply chilly intellection (in a style of grey-ish dignity) to material far too thin to merit such Thought. In this instalment of an ongoing saga, humans show their stuff on a planet dominated by several species of thick robots, and at the end of the day escape in a magic spaceship in the direction of some sort of cosmogonic Big Think at the heart of the galaxy (see next volume). *The Secret Ascension* (Tor), by Michael Bishop, gazes inward upon the memory and example of Philip K. Dick, replicating both the man himself (who is a character in the novel) and his deepest literary concerns, in a parody with love, admirably executed. Joe Haldeman, who is far too decent a writer to mean a word of it, has a fine time in *Tool of the Trade* (Morrow) spoofing the Cold War and near-future thrillers and (perhaps) himself. His hero discovers an audio frequency which enforces absolute obedience on those he blows his whistle at, giving him (and Haldeman) every opportunity to run rings around a congeries of official spooks; and the climax of the book depends (if memory serves) on whether or not the Russian premier has cotton up his ears. And the allure of the known future is still potent in *The Smoke Ring* (Del Rey), Larry Niven's solo novel for 1987, full of grippling architectonics but muddily told. With Jerry Pournelle and Steven Barnes, Niven also published, in *The Legacy of Heorot* (Gollancz), quite incredibly, yet another novel about private-enterprise Americans desolating a new planet and destroying its natives and calling the solitude home, just as though Vietnam had never happened — but then Vietnam never did happen to Star Troopers.

Of this cohort, only Gene Wolfe released a novel of the first rank in 1987. But *The Urth of the New Sun* (Gollancz) is less a novel in its own right than a sustained coda to *The Book of the New Sun*, published in four volumes from 1980 through 1983, and all five volumes are best read as one single text, perhaps the finest single work the field has yet produced, though a text far removed from the usual concerns of science fiction. Grave, hermetic, daedal, the *Book* may magisterially sum up all the materials available to the modern science fiction writer (and reader), but at the same time the unremitting religious grasp of Wolfe's vision sea-changes these materials into something utterly strange, sui generis. *The Urth of the New Sun* is a fitting capstone to this vast and inspissate Theatre of Memory, and if Giordano Bruno were alive today he'd wander every niche of it. Severian, who is both Christ and Competent, tells his own story, reversing the usual poles of irony, for he knows much more than we ever can, which can be chilling and uncomfortable. A novella adjunct to the *Book*, and far less taxing, *Empires of Foliage and Flower* (Cheap Street) might give new readers some sense of Wolfe's tone and texture; but only the *Book* will really do.

To separate those writers first prominent in 1965–1975 from those who have only come to notice over the past decade or so may seem more convenient than analytic; but it can be argued, all the same, that some loosening of the bonds of genre can be detected in some of the newer writers, as well as a new parodic freedom in the handling of older material from the time before the stars were torn down. Iain Banks's *Consider Phlebas* may at first strike the reader as an almost excessively loyal homage to traditional space opera; for it is chock-full of galaxy-spanning star wars, Nth generation computers, 'orbitals,' decadent cults, space mercenaries, quests, ancient gods, pachydermatous aliens, nordic behaviour codes, espionage, sex, big bangs. But at its heart the book — despite an overwritten and desultory soft midriff — savagely deconstructs the essence of its ostensible form through a climax that resoundingly demonstrates the utter *uselessness* of all that space opera gear. It may seem unfair to include Neal Barrett Jr among the newcomers, but *Through Darkest America* (Congdon & Weed) has almost nothing in common with his Aldair of Albion fantasies of fifteen years ago, except perhaps for the travel. *Through Darkest America* may or may not have consciously repeated as apocalyptic farce the dawn-to-dark downriver hegira that makes *The Adventures of Huckleberry Finn* (1884) an archetype of the American experience, but the fable-like excesses of the journey it depicts with such monitory ferocity have a revisionary feel. In *The Forge of God* (Tor), Greg Bear had a go at sublimating his own anxiety of influence by radically subverting the kind of story hard-sf writers typically wax triumphalist over. Bevies of aliens bracket Earth, some bent on betraying us, others bent on giving us a hand. Yankee scientists soon work out that what is happening is the planned and irrevocable destruction of the planet, and that there is nothing anyone can do, however Competent he may be. Earth is therefore duly demolished, and a pathetic remnant of humanity hitchhikes (revenge-bound, it must be admitted) into interstellar vacancies (where sequels await). By itself — and may it remain a singleton — it is a savage book.

James P. Blaylock has also made some use of earlier material, and in *Land of Dreams* (Arbor), taking a few lessons from Charles G. Finney's *The Circus of Dr Lao* (1935), he transforms his alternate California into a land of steam-punk bounty, opalescent and emollient, lush and lingering. In the dingy cacophonies of Michael Blumlein's Barea — a term which tellingly conflates San Francisco Bay Area and barrio — a less consoling California comes into view, hierarchical but pastless. *The Movement of Mountains* (St Martin's), an austerely mannered first novel of very considerable stature, takes the obese doctor who narrates it from Barea to an alien planet, where he foments a revolution of the oppressed and becomes commensal, through a shared virus, with the rest of humanity. The last pages of the book may fail to sustain the Wolfe-like secret-passage intricacies of the confessional mode Blumlein crafts for his intriguing physician, but the body of the book burns remorselessly, like dry-ice. A sense of recessive elegy lightly embrocates Richard Bowker's *Dover Beach* (Bantam), whose title derives from Matthew Arnold; mixing together private-eye and post-catastrophe modes, he tells a tale by definition evocative of a demolished past, but the aptness of this particular marriage of modes generates a wry elan; nostalgia is kept in check. From David Brin came another fairy tale in wolf's clothing; *The Uplift War* (Phantasia), an exercise in space-operatic wish-fulfilment, bares its biceps like the strictest of hard-sf, but the magic machines, the magic FTL, the magic neo-chimps and magic Progenitors whose magic secret lore unlocks the magic secret of the magic universe all give the game away: That in hard-sf country the triumphs of the good guys come as easy as Alice. In the stricter world of Octavia Butler, xenophilia and exogamy govern the behaviour of the aliens who dominate *Dawn* (Warners), which is the first of a potentially impressive series about the enlisting of post-catastrophe humanity into a brave new marriage; the style is cumulatively gripping, and the tale hardly begun.

In *Mindplayers* (Bantam), which is her first novel, Pat Cadigan bashes together a railroad flat of linked stories about a young gal on mind drugs cornered into going legit; as a trained therapist (or tinker) specializing in pathos, she enters sick minds for pay, setting off redemptive psychomachies in the theatres of their conveniently addressable souls. In the world of this novel, anguish is a *glitch*. But because Cadigan has found no tale to hang her beads on, there can be no real testing of this strange presumption, and the book soon trails into doodle. Orson Scott Card's *Wyrms* (Arbor) — an exceedingly ramshackle premise couched with all the glitzy skill its author has at beck — was given an unduly civil reception from the science fiction press; but *Seventh Son* (Tor) deserved its praise. Set in an alternate version of America's past in which magic works, and the first of several planned titles, *Seventh Son* does occasionally suffer from

Card's shiny swift slippery way with words, but the tale of Alvin the Maker, and of the Earth he knits within his hands, may grow and grow. (Or not.) On the other hand, John Crowley's *Aegypt* (Bantam) must either grow or dissolve utterly. As a sequence of doors opening into doors in the Theatre of Memory, it is a text of unparalleled and superb complexity. But just as the mouth of narrative opens to say the first words of the Story hidden within the stories told and told again in this first of four integral volumes, *Aegypt* snaps shut, like an amphitheatre echoing with sounds not yet laughed. It is an intensely frustrating moment; we can only await the outcome, a great novel, it may be.

Take Sam Spade, who digs the past. Take Marlowe, whose name is buried under centuries. Or take the archaic Archer. They are the haunted archaeologists, curators of the western slope of latterday America, deciphering the past that calls the tune for the mayfly offspring of the dead fathers, delving through the catacombs of the mean streets of LA for hieroglyphs and papyrus that will reveal the crimes that fix the meaning of the world; the essence of the American thriller genre is contained in one title by Ross MacDonald: *The Underground Man* (1971). Spade and Marlowe and Archer also have this in common, beyond the smell of Egyptian Incas in their clothing: By the end of the book they will have unpacked the scroll that reveals the name that propitiates the risen ancestor, and the scales will balance, and they will survive to scour again the Aztec middens of the West. As will the hero in any book by William Gibson, who did not publish a novel in 1987. Cyberpunk (as he — and others — have written it) shares with the thriller genre not only superficies of style and plot and cast and pacing, but more tellingly an obsession with brand-naming the governors of the world, the voodoo ancestors who call the tune of LA, or cyberspace. The tactile modernity of cyberpunk tends to conceal its deep structure, which is one of propitiation, so that its profound consanguinity with the literatures of nostalgia (that is, with all genre literatures) has been obscured.

Two cyberpunk novels of interest were published in 1987, or three, if one wishes to include William Burroughs's *The Western Lands* (Viking) for its conflation of America with the Egyptian land of the dead; but that might be lese majeste. George Alec Effinger's *When Gravity Fails* (Arbor) dumps its mean-streets hero into an almost indecipherable Middle East, sometime in the distant near future, where for much of the book he refuses the technology of plug-ins that will open the secrets of the world to him. It may be the case that Effinger loses control of the book when he finally manages to plug his hero into it, but neither author nor his shadow really had much choice. An archaeologist has got to do what an archaeologist has got to do. Michael Swanwick's *Vacuum Flowers* (Arbor) carries its heroine down the gravity well from the asteroids to Earth in a constant buzz of information codes, the most important of which, and the secret of the past which shapes her, being the genetic 'integrity' her mother (buried off-stage) has implanted into her; and it is this Integrity she must decipher or lose the game. By applying cyberpunk riffs and overloads to his material, Swanwick manages, in this deftly crammed novel, to give to the dervish masquerade of his solar system a lived-in tarnish, a potent sense of the governing interweaves of the past.

Of novels published in 1987 by writers recently prominent, only a few remain. Mary Gentle's *Ancient Light* (Gollancz), which is a sequel to *Golden Witchbreed* (1983), and which is designed to terminate the series, dots every i for innumerable pages, finally to, come somewhat phosphorescently to life in its final hundreds, when the author gets properly aroused by her task of demolition, about which she is very thorough. No more Witches, no more books. Richard Grant's *Rumours of Spring* (Bantam) must be read as fantasy, which is also true of Jonathan Carroll's *Bones of the Moon* (Century), and Colin Greenland's *The Hour of the Thin Ox* (Unwin), and K.W. Jeter's *Infernal Devices* (St Martin's), and Tim Powers's *On Stranger Tides* (Ace), and Terry Pratchett's *Mort* (Gollancz), and William P. Vollmann's *You Bright and Risen Angels* (Atheneum). But that was also arguably the case with several books already feted, and these strong cousins should be at least mentioned; most readers of science fiction could take any of them on without bends. Perhaps fatally to any poll success, Lisa Goldstein's *A Mask for the General* (Bantam) gives short shrift to nostalgia in her rendering of post-catastrophe California; it is a world which has no secrets to tell Goldstein's protagonist about any magical Integrity within her that will unlock the secrets of the past and make her super, and in that sense the novel must be seen as Humanist. Alan Moore's graphic novel, *Watchmen* (Warners), as illustrated by Dave Gibbon, depicts a film-noir alternate America distinguished from our own dear Land of Dreams mainly by a passel of 1930s and 50s vigilantes who were allowed to prosper and to become costumed heroes; it is a Matter drenched in iconicity, and in crafting an adult comic from this rich mulch Moore has generated a superb tale of apocalypse at midnight. There is a Dying Earth in Paul Park's *Soldiers of Paradise* (Arbor), with Helliconian seasons and a gnarled permafrost of Wolfean theology substrating the whole, whose narrative vigour belies the fin-de-siecle codswallop its protagonists sport; the erotic melancholia that infuses this brilliant first novel has a welcome adult tone. Finally, Lucius Shepard's *Life During Wartime* (Bantam) may have disappointed those readers who forgot that *Green Eyes* (1984) was very clumsy in the joints, despite the brilliance of its scene-setting; so with this book, which is, all the same, a far more ambitious text, and in its phantasmagorical portrait of the new Vietnams south of Texas (or America below the belt) manages something of an imperial conquest (of the pen).

Of 300 or so novels on show from 1987, it has been possible to mention fewer than 50 samples of a genre in the throes of change. Most of the unmentioned titles may ply strict genre routes to conclusions carved in stone by the ancestors, but still we have come a far piece from the old family of read books, as shown by the work of many of the younger writers, far more of them women than the texts of 1987 permitted one to demonstrate. The dinosaurs of the genre may continue to lay their giant pellets, and the alpha males to hatch them, but the future must lie in the delicate mad paws of the changeling creatures who roam the last years of the century, which is beginning to shut. May their bright eyes continue to reflect the omens of the dark.

FOREVER CHANGES
by
DAVID S. GARNETT

Into the Future, via the Past

Year by year, science fiction is becoming better and better. There are always new authors appearing on the scene, developing and expanding from what has gone before. At one time, almost every author served an apprenticeship by publishing stories in the magazines before graduating to novels. Now, it is more common for a writer first to appear in print with a novel. Those authors who have written for the magazines will inevitably move towards the longer lengths, and they are replaced by the next generation.

Good short stories are much more difficult to write than novels. Word for word, page for page, their creation takes far more time and effort — which is what makes a volume such as this so rewarding for readers. But short stories are less rewarding for the authors, who have to write novels in order to make a living.

This is why the names of short story writers are usually not so familiar as those who write novels: they are the newer authors. Only five of the writers whose stories are included in this *Yearbook* — Gotschalk, Kilworth, Tuttle, Waldrop, Wilhelm — are listed in the *Encyclopedia of Science Fiction* (1979). Of these, only Kate Wilhelm has been publishing for any great length of time. Her first story appeared in 1956; the other four writers first saw print during the seventies. (As did Marta Randall, whose first two novels were both published in 1976, although she wasn't mentioned in the *Encyclopedia.*) All the other authors in this book are the product of the last decade, or even the last few years.

Often authors write their best work when they are young. They explode onto the scene with a handful of superb stories or a couple of brilliant novels, then vanish with equal swiftness. Others keep on writing for decades, churning out novel after novel until they die — even though they may have been brain dead for years. Between these two extremes are those who have built up a solid reputation over the years and can still be relied upon to produce fresh and imaginative work.

A useful way of calculating which 'big name' authors are still worth reading is to look at the magazines and anthologies. Those who still care enough to write short stories, instead of taking the simple route of churning out megabuck trilogies, are those who are still at the forefront of sf. Like all such sweeping generalisations, there are exceptions; but the names of a few authors who fit this description immediately spring to mind: Pohl, Silverberg, Aldiss, for example.

Every year produces a fresh crop of authors, stunning debuts by unknown writers; or else new names which will keep appearing again and again, writers who are slowly but surely establishing themselves as 'tomorrow's brightest stars' — as the publishers' blurbs love to proclaim.

Despite the increase in the number of books each year, as new sf authors appear, so must old ones disappear. ('Old' has nothing to do with biological age.) Because of the small amount most authors earn, some give up writing completely. Some may become literary agents or editors, and others may turn honest and become insurance salesmen or estate agents. Others write different forms of fiction to pay the rent: hack books and novelisations, ghost work and horror novels — which aren't the same — or even television scripts, returning to the field with the occasional novel or short story. Until recently, few authors could make a living from writing only science fiction. Those that did had to be very prolific: the survival of the fastest.

This is the way of evolution, and science fiction is living proof of Darwinism. Each sf writer develops his, or her, own ideas from what has gone before. Science fiction evolves out of science fiction. It is more than incestuous, it is cannibalistic.

For every life there is death, and in sf the mortality rate is very high. For every author who is remaindered, there is room on the shelves for another; for every one who stops writing short stories, there is space in the magazines for fresh talent.

Some authors can feed off their own ideas, and reputations, until they become zombies with word processors. But as well as intellectual death, the ultimate sanction is physical death — not that this has prevented a recent series of 'bestsellers'.

In the beginning was the word. And, in the end, that is all that remains of any author.

The Ultimate Rejection Slip

Modern science fiction has existed for about as long as there have been 'year's best' collections, and many of the most famous names in the genre began their careers during the previous decade. This means that many of them are still alive — or were until very recently. Clifford Simak and Robert Heinlein died within a few days of each other, early in 1988, while this book was being prepared.

The most famous author to die during 1987, however, and the greatest loss to the field, was Alfred Bester (1913-1987). Because of publishers' hype, the word 'classic' has become devalued into a synonym for 'reprint', but Bester was the author of two of sf's true classics: *The Demolished Man* (1953) and *The Stars My Destination* (1956, also known as *Tiger! Tiger!*). The former won the first ever Hugo Award for the best novel of the year, and time has not dulled the brilliance of either of these novels; he was also the author of several equally adventurous and memorable short stories. Although away from science fiction for many years, three more novels were published between 1975 and 1981, which inevitably suffered when compared to his previous work. Bester was to have been a guest of honour at the World Sf Convention in August 1987, but was too ill to travel to Britain; he died a month later.

'James Tiptree Jr.' was another casualty of 1987. 'Tiptree' was the real name of Alice Sheldon (1915-1987), who rose to fame with a number of well received and award-winning (two Nebulas, two Hugos) stories. The first Tiptree story was published in 1968 and 'his' real name wasn't revealed until 1977; she was at first believed to be a man. Although she began writing only twenty years ago, there were very few women authors in science fiction at that time. (Compare that with the contents list of this *Yearbook*.) Under another pseudonym,

'Racoona Sheldon', she wrote more stories — and won another Nebula. In a suicide pact with her invalid husband, she shot him and then herself.

Other deaths during the year were those of Richard Wilson (b.1920), who won a Nebula for his 1968 novelette 'Mother To The World'; Theodore Cogswell (b.1918), author of a handful of notable short stories; Gardner F. Fox (b.1911) who wrote several unexceptional novels — one of which, *Escape Across the Cosmos* was plagiarised twice, becoming *Titans of the Universe* and also *Star Chase*; and Terry Carr (b.1937) who made his name as an editor, for which he was awarded a posthumous Hugo in 1987. He edited the Ace Special series in the sixties and the eighties, which produced many famous novels; and he also edited two series of short fiction: *Universe*, which contained new short stories, and *Best Science Fiction of the Year*, which needs no explanation.

Everyone a Winner

Throughout this book, reference has been made to the Hugo and Nebula Awards. At one time, these were about the only prizes in the science fiction field. But as the genre has expanded, so have the citations and scrolls, the trophies and other glittering honours that are available.

Since 1966, the Nebula has been given annually by the Science Fiction Writer of America (SFWA) in four categories: best novel, novella, novelette, short story. (At one time 'best dramatic presentation' was another category; but good sense prevailed, and this was dropped. All it had meant was authors voting for their 'favourite movie' — and the film industry didn't care. Lately, there has been some pressure for a 'best screenplay' Nebula. Considering the number of science fiction screenplays each year, this seems ridiculous — except to screenplay writers. There has also been a suggestion of a 'best comic' Nebula. Guess whose idea that is . . .?)

In 1987, the members of the SFWA voted the Nebula Awards (for first publication in 1986) to:

Best Novel:	*Speaker for the Dead* by Orson Scott Card.
Best Novella:	'R&R' by Lucius Shepard.
Best Novelette:	'The Girl Who Fell From The Sky' by Kate Wilhelm.
Best Short Story:	'Tangents' by Greg Bear.

And Isaac Asimov was given the 'Grand Master Award', for lifetime achievement in writing sf.

Because this *Yearbook* is going to press very late, the 1988 Nebulas (for original 1987 publication, awarded in Los Angeles, May 1988) can also be listed:

Best Novel:	*The Falling Woman* by Pat Murphy.
Best Novella:	'The Blind Geometer' by Kim Stanley Robinson.
Best Novelette:	'Rachel In Love' by Pat Murphy.
Best Short Story:	'Forever Yours, Anna' by Kate Wilhelm.

The Grand Master Award for a lifetime's work went to Alfred Bester — who would have appreciated it more if it had been awarded during his lifetime.

The World Sf Convention used to be as global as the American 'World' Baseball series. The first such convention was held in New York in 1939, but (apart from an excursion to Toronto in 1948) it wasn't until 1957 that Worldcon was held 'overseas' — in London. Since then, it has also been held in Germany (Heidelberg, 1970), twice in Australia (Melbourne in 1975 and 1985) and on three more occasions in Britain (London in 1965, and Brighton in 1979 and 1987). By the time this *Yearbook* has been published, the 1988 Convention in New Orleans will be over. In 1989, the World Convention will be in Boston; and in 1990 it returns to Europe — The Hague, in the Netherlands.

The August 1987 convention was the 45th World Sf Convention. For many attendees the only problem was caused by British licensing laws, which meant that the main hotel would not serve alcohol in the afternoon. Licensing hours have since been altered, although the timing is probably a coincidence.

The Hugo Awards are voted on by each year's Worldcon membership. (The Science Fiction Achievement Award, to give the award its full title, somehow became named after Hugo Gernsback, founder of the world's first sf magazine *Amazing Stories*; and Gernsback himself was given a special Hugo Award in 1960.)

The 1987 awards were as follows:

Best Novel:	*Speaker for the Dead* by Orson Scott Card.
Best Novella:	'Gilgamesh in the Outback' by Robert Silverberg.
Best Novelette:	'Permafrost' by Roger Zelazny.
Best Short Story:	'Tangents' by Greg Bear.

The Hugo for *Speaker for the Dead* represented a unique double for Card. The book had already won the Nebula, and was the sequel to another volume, *Ender's Game*, which also won the Nebula and Hugo the previous year. Lucius Shepard's 'R&R', which won the Nebula novella, came third in the Hugos despite winning most first-place wines. (Instead to having only one vote, the system allows voters to rank the nominees in each category; second and third preferences can often make a difference to the ultimate result.) The award for Silverberg, however, broke a very long drought. He had been nominated for, but lost, twenty-one Hugos since he'd last won in 1969 for another novella, 'Nightwings'.

Kate Wilhelm's Nebula winning novelette didn't make it to the Hugo ballot. (And, through a mistake by the company counting the SFWA nominations, it almost didn't make the Nebula ballot either.) Roger Zelazny, who did win the Hugo novelette award, has been collecting such trophies ever since 1966, which was also the same year that he won two of the first Nebulas. Greg Bear was to repeat Zelazny's achievement by also winning two Nebulas and one Hugo in the same year, 1984; and in 1987, his 'Tangents' won both the Nebula and Hugo for short story.

The Hugo Awards are more comprehensive than the Nebulas, and for the sake of completeness the other results were:

Best Non-Fiction:	*Trillion Year Spree* by Brian Aldiss, with David Wingrove.*
Best Dramatic Presentation:	*Aliens.*
Best Semi-Prozine:	*Locus*, edited by Charles N. Brown.
Best Professional Artist:	Jim Burns.*
Best Professional Editor:	Terry Carr.
Best Fan Writer:	Dave Langford.*
Best Fan Artist:	Brad Foster.
Best Fanzine:	*Ansible*, edited by Dave Langford.*

Brian Aldiss had last won a Hugo in 1962 for his 'Hothouse' stories. Winners marked * (above) were British. (There were only two British nominees for the fiction Hugos: *The Ragged Astronauts* by Bob Shaw came second in the novel category; and some guy called David Garnett was fourth in the short story category.) It has been a long time since a British author — with the exception of Arthur C. Clarke, who has lived in Sri Lanka for over thirty years — won one of the major fiction awards, either the Hugo or Nebula. The only other British authors to win the Hugo are Eric Frank Russell in 1955, and John Brunner in 1969. And only Brian Aldiss and Michael Moorcock have ever won a Nebula — over twenty years ago.

Also on the same ballot as the 1987 Hugos was the John W. Campbell Award for best new writer, which was won by Karen Joy Fowler. Campbell was undoubtedly the most significant editor in the history of magazine sf, editing *Astounding/Analog* from 1937 until his death in 1971.

This prize is not to be confused with the John W. Campbell Memorial Award, for the best novel of the year, which in 1987 was given to a *A Door into Ocean* by Joan Slonczewski. From the same source (a panel of judges, and the University of Kansas) emerged the first Theodore Sturgeon short story prize, which was for Judith Moffet's story 'Surviving'.

Another memorial award, given every year for the best book to have originally appeared in paperback, is the Phillip K. Dick Award, which was won in 1987 by James Blaylock for his novel *Homunculus.* Phillip K. Dick (1928-1982) should need no introduction to most sf readers. If you haven't read any of his novels, do so — you won't regret it. Dick wrote many of the great sf books of the sixties and seventies, and was one of the most influential authors in the genre. The movie *Bladerunner* was based on his novel *Do Androids Dream of Electric Sheep?* He won a Hugo for *The Man in the High Castle.* (An alternative world novel, in which there is a book set in the 'real' world entitled *The Grasshopper Lies Heavy* — see Howard Waldrop's story in this *Yearbook.*)

The World Fantasy Awards were given out at the World Fantasy Convention in Nashville. The main awards were: Best Novel, *Perfume* by Patrick Suskind; Best Novella, 'Hatrack River' by Orson Scott Card; Best Short Story, 'Red Light' by David J. Schow.

All these awards are usually in the form of some kind of trophy or other. Although nice to win, they don't pay for groceries or printer ribbons. But then, in 1987, came the first Arthur C. Clarke Award. Clarke donated £1000 as the prize, to be given to the best science fiction novel published in Britain during the previous year.

Arthur C. Clarke was born in Britain and is probably most famous as co-author of the film *2001*, but his best novels are *Childhood's End, A Fall of Moondust* and *Rendezvous with Rama.* For many years he has been one of the 'big three' of world science fiction: Asimov and Heinlein are the other two, but Clarke was the one who was still worth reading. He has won more Hugo and Nebula Awards than all other British authors combined. (Three Hugos, three Nebulas — four, if the Grand Master is included.)

The judges for the Clarke award decided that the 'best' novel was *The Handmaid's Tale* by Margaret Atwood, a Canadian author. This seemed an odd choice in view of the fact that Atwood had claimed her book wasn't sf; and she had already made comments which indicated her hostility towards science fiction. From an outside perspective, it appears that awarding the prize to Atwood was more of an attempt to honour the award, by associating it with a 'literary' novel, than it was to honour the book. The judges were put in their place, literally, by being relegated to the back of the audience when the presentation was made. Less than overwhelmed by the award, Atwood was probably equally unimpressed by the £1000 — because the U.S. paperback rights to the novel had already sold for $605,000.

In 1988 the Arthur C. Clarke Award was given to the Australian author George Turner's for his novel *The Sea and Summer*. This was Turner's fourth sf book — although, as with the Atwood, it was not published as science fiction.

It would take too much space to list all the other minor prizes, and all the various foreign awards — French, Swedish, Spanish, Australian, German, Canadian, Japanese, Dutch, Argentine, Yugoslavian, and maybe Sri Lankan, etc. — but the other British awards should also be mentioned:

The two main British Fantasy Awards for 1987 went to Stephen King for *It* (Best Novel) and Dennis Etchison for 'The Olympic Runner' (Best Short Fiction).

And the major British Science Fiction Awards for 1987 were given to Bob Shaw for *The Ragged Astronauts* (Best Novel) and Keith Roberts for 'Kaeti And The Hangman' (Best Short Fiction). These awards are voted on by members of the BSFA and those who attend each year's Easter convention, the main British sf convention.

Because of the publication date of this *Yearbook*, it is also possible to list the 1988 winners, for fiction published in 1987, which were presented at Follycon in Liverpool. Best Novel was *Grainne* by Keith Roberts, and Best Short Fiction was 'Love Sickness' by Geoff Ryman. (Ryman beat Garry Kilworth by the narrowest of margins, one point. Kilworth was on the ballot for his 'Triptych', one story of which is reprinted in this volume. And Kilworth beat yours truly, David Garnett, into third place by a much greater margin.)

*Born in the USA: from Pulp to Paperback to Limited Edition
on Acid-Free Paper*

When Bleiler and Dikty edited their first annual collection, the majority of science fiction appeared in magazines, either short stories or serials; there were very few sf novels published in book form. Forty years later, short sf can be found in various original anthologies and the occasional non-genre book or magazine, as well as the traditional magazines. There are very few magazines still in existence, and each year more new novels are published than short stories.

The magazines with the longest history, and the only ones which survive from forty years ago, are *Amazing* and *Analog*.

Amazing is published bi-monthly, and since 1986 has been edited by Patrick L. Price. It emphasizes that it has existed since 1926 — the first sf magazine, founded by the immortal Hugo Gernsback — and from its appearance, it is doing its best to recreate that era. It seems to be printed on very cheap paper and publishes numerous awful illustrations — which might look a lot better if they were reproduced more accurately. (Or maybe they wouldn't.) *Amazing* also includes several poems and various articles in each issue, although it is the only magazine not to include regular book reviews. There is less room for the stories because of these features*, which is a pity because some of the fiction is quite interesting. (None of it is reprinted here, however, although one of last year's stories, 'Kid Charlemagne' by Paul Di Filippo — whose story 'Agents' appears in this anthology — made it to the Nebula short list.)

A magazine should be more than merely a collection of stories, but this latest incarnation of *Amazing* hasn't yet found its identity. A further indication of the way that *Amazing* is trying to recreate the past is that if offers new writers a booklet on how to write 'scientifiction'! With the lowest circulation of the American magazines, *Amazing* probably couldn't survive if it weren't owned by the people who market Dungeons and Dragons.

---

*Unlike this volume, of course ... Here, all the non-fiction is extra. There would be no more stories even if these articles were not included.

Analog is another magazine apparently determined to boldly leap into the past. It changed its name from *Astounding* in 1960. Then in May 1987 the cover started to announce that the magazine was 'Formerly *Astounding*', and in October it began proclaiming 'Since 1930 *Astounding*'. Leaving aside this amendment, the full title of the magazine is *Analog Science Fiction/Science Fact*, which means that every issue includes an article such as 'Nanotechnology' or 'Moonbase Orientation Manual' (in two parts — *Analog* is fond of serials) or 'A Memoir Of Nuclear Winter'. (There was even an apology when the May 1987 issue published no 'science fact' and extra fiction had to be included.) All of this is fine if you need to read this kind of stuff in an sf magazine — which plenty of people seem to do: *Analog* has the highest circulation of the four American magazines.

Analog's fiction tends to sound like non-fiction; one of the 1987 serials, for example, was enticingly entitled *The Report on Bilbeis IV*. Almost every issue contains part of a serial, taking up valuable space where shorter fiction could be printed. This seems a self-defeating process, because most of *Analog*'s novels will later be published as books. (Although maybe they shouldn't be.) People who buy novels don't need the magazines, but readers — and writers — of short fiction do.

Analog has been edited by Stanley Schmidt since 1978. Schmidt is also an author, whose latest novel is called *Tweedlioop*.

There are no stories from *Analog* in this *Yearbook*.

But one magazine is doing its best to keep up with the times. With its 38th anniversary issue, in October 1987, *The Magazine of Fantasy and Science Fiction* (*F&SF*) underwent a change in design. Edward L. Ferman has edited *F&SF* since 1966, which probably makes him the most experienced editor in the entire genre. He, at least, knows that we are far nearer the twenty-first century than the nineteenth, and he has taken steps to maintain his magazine's reputation as the most reliable in the field. *F&SF* has always seemed more mature than its rivals, and it is still the only magazine not to use interior illustrations. (Paperbacks don't have illustrations, so why should the fiction magazines?) Instead, however, *F&SF* publishes some really awful cartoons.

And what was the major design change that occurred in October? The fiction is no longer printed in two columns per page. Such typesetting has been good enough for Isaac Asimov's science fact column for years, and now finally it's spread to the rest of the magazine. (*Analog*, perhaps not surprisingly, is the only magazine which still prints in two columns.)

Although no longer the top magazine in the field, *F&SF* can be depended upon to publish more than its share of imaginative, literate fiction. The non-fiction content is usually interesting — the regular Asimov feature, the occasional film column by Harlan Ellison, and in depth reviews by Algis Budrys. (Lately, Orson Scott Card has also begun reviewing for *F&SF*, presumably because, as the years go by, Budrys devotes the same amount of space, issue by issue, to analysing fewer and fewer books, while using, as is his habit, increasingly, more and more commas.)

There are more stories in this *Yearbook* from *F&SF* than any other source: Paul Di Filippo's 'Agents', Jonathan Carroll's 'Friend's Best Man' and Felix C. Gotschalk's 'Ménage à Super-Trois'.

The newest of the magazines is *Isaac Asimov's Science Fiction Magazine (Asimov's)*, which celebrated its tenth anniversary during 1987. Since 1985 this has been edited by Gardner Dozois; he is also an author and has won two Nebula Awards for his short stories. (And according to rumour, he edits another 'year's best' series ...) Without a doubt, *Asimov's* is currently the best of the American sf magazines. Dozois has brought a new sense of excitement to the magazines. The newest authors and the latest themes are most likely to be found here ... which is completely at odds with the title of the magazine.

Isaac Asimov seems to have little to do with the magazine which bears his name, apart from commenting on the letters and contributing a regular editorial — often on his favourite subject: Isaac Asimov. Asimov's own fiction is rooted in the past. His recent novels and stories could easily have been published twenty or even thirty years ago, and no one would know the difference, whereas much of the fiction in *Asi-*

mov's is at the cutting edge of contemporary sf. (And much of it isn't; but we can't have everything.) Each issue of *Asimov's* also contains informed and informative book reviews by Baird Searles, or else an article by Norman Spinrad.

I — and having avoided the personal pronoun for so long, it's time to use it again — I must admit that I've long been an Asimov fan. He stands as one of the cornerstones of modern science fiction, essential reading for each new audience. But it's been quite a time since I've been able to read his latest fiction, because he seems content to keep on repeating what he has done for years without progressing. Asimov, however, recognises that contemporary sf must change to survive, and he is prepared to lend his name to a magazine whose contents are totally different from the fiction he himself writes. (Although *Asimov's*, perhaps to justify the title, does contain the occasional Asimov story; there were two during 1987.)

Asimov's is published by the same company that produces *Analog*. Five years ago, both magazines had the same circulation. *Analog* has maintained its readership; sales of *Asimov's* have declined twenty percent.

'The Sun Spider' by Lucius Shepard and 'Rachel in Love' by Pat Murphy were both first published in *Asimov's*.

These are the four American science fiction magazines. Most of their sales come through subscription. They are almost impossible to find on sale in Britain; even the sf bookshops carry very few copies.

Omni is also difficult to find on sale, one reason being that the shops don't know where to put it on their shelves. This is the American popular science magazine, which usually includes one or two sf stories per issue. And, considering how few stories it publishes per year, *Omni* maintains the highest standard of all. This may have something to do with the fact that Ellen Datlow, the fiction editor, offers the highest payment for stories and so has first refusal on the best — and worst — manuscripts. But having access to the material is only the start of an editor's job.

'Forever Yours, Anna' by Kate Wilhelm and 'E-Ticket To Namland' by Dan Simmons were both originally published in *Omni*.

As well as the magazines, several anthologies containing original stories were published in the U.S.A. during 1987. For many years Damon Knight edited a series called *Orbit* (no connection with this book), while Robert Silverberg edited *New Dimensions* (Marta Randall was co-editor of the final two volumes), but the only continuing series was Terry Carr's *Universe*. Volume 17 was the last one to be edited by Carr, because (as mentioned earlier) he died in 1987. The series will continue, however, appearing every other year under the editorship of Robert Silverberg and Karen Haber.

Marta Randall's 'Lapidary Nights' was first published in *Universe 17*.

Two new series began during 1987. The first of these was *Synergy*, edited by George Zebrowski. This is evidently meant to be a high class collection, because it comes from a publisher not normally associated with science fiction and costs twice as much as most other U.S. paperbacks.

The other new series is *New Destinies*, which published two volumes. Edited by Jim Baen, and published by Baen Books, this reads like a paperback version of *Analog*. Even the blurb says so — 'The Paperback Magazine of Science Fiction and Speculative Fact.' But at least it doesn't have illustrations, although the first issue does contain the second half of a serial, the first part having appeared in another paperback series. This is *Iron* by Poul Anderson, and the synopsis of the first section concludes with: *The kzinti captain to whom they appeal finds the very notion of risk-laden rescue of enemies yet another example of monkey grotesquerie. They are trapped. Soon the shuttle will be eaten through, and the molecule will begin to digest their suits.* Monkey grotesquerie . . .?

Baen Books also published the third in their *Alien Stars* 'series' edited by Elizabeth Mitchell. The 1987 volume was entitled *Under the Wheel*, which consisted of 'three visions of tyranny', a loose theme to link three stories by different authors. According to the cover, these were *Three Short Novels Never Before in Print*. But the first story, Gregory Benford's 'As Big As The Ritz', had previously been published by *Interzone* in a shorter version — where the annual readers' poll placed it in next to last position, 21st out of 22 stories. This was probably unfair — unfair on the story that took last place.

One of the other stories in *Alien Stars*, however, made it to the Nebula ballot. This was 'Fugue State' by John M. Ford. Mitchell also edited another three-story anthology for Baen during 1987, *Freelancers*. According to the covers of the books, however, she did not edit them — they were 'created by' her.

The 'created by' phrase has evolved from the 'shared world' anthologies which have been published for some time in America. Usually these are fantasy collections, in which different authors write short stories set in the same imagined backround, and they have been profilerating at an alarming rate.

The idea has even spread to novels. It is now possible to buy 'Isaac Asimov' books written by other authors. This series is know as *Isaac Asimov's Robot City*. Instead of writing their own novels, other authors are churning out formula books using a background created by Asimov. In science fiction, this notion probably derives from the success of the *Star Trek* series, the latest volumes of which regularly make the American bestseller lists.

Other such series are *Arthur C. Clarke's Venus Prime* and *Roger Zelazny's Alien Speedway*. The possibilities are endless. Unfortunately.

The latest 'shared world' series, in which different authors contribute stories to the same book, derives from a science fiction premise: *Wild Cards* edited by George R.R. Martin, which published three volumes during 1987. This begins with the idea of an alien virus being let loose on the Earth and turning various people into superheroes — the kind of characters who have populated comic books for the last half century. Superheroes have always seemed a particularly American wish-fulfilment fantasy, and many of the stories don't rise much higher than this level. The very first story in the first volume, however, contains no such superhero and is far superior to what follows. This is Howard Waldrop's 'Thirty Minutes Over Broadway!' reprinted in this *Yearbook*. (The first *Wild Cards* was published in January 1987, which explains the 1986 copyright date.) *Wild Cards* has also been nominated for a Hugo, in a new category — 'Other Forms', which seems to cover screenplays and comic books.

The most ambitious American sf anthology of 1987 was *In*

the Field of Fire edited by Jeanne Van Buren Dann and Jack Dann, a collection of stories on the theme of the Vietnam war. Although this consisted mainly of new material, the best stories were written and published when American forces were still in Vietnam, stories as effective now as they were then: 'A Dream At Noonday' by Gardner Dozois (from 1970) and 'The Village' by Kate Wilhelm (1973).

Vietnam was more than merely an American experience — it had an infinitely greater effect on the people of Vietnam, a fact which has been largely ignored — it was the first 'world' war, in the sense that the whole world could switch on their television sets and watch what was happening. Without a doubt, if the war hadn't been shown on TV every night in America — and elsewhere — it would have lasted much longer and cost far more lives. This lesson wasn't lost. During the Falklands 'conflict', the British media were only able to report what had happened long after the event. The same was true when the Americans 'liberated' Grenada. But as I was saying . . .

Vietnam was more than an American experience, but the only non-American represented in the Dann anthology is Brian Aldiss. In his story 'My Country 'Tis Not Only Of Thee', the VC are the Ventnor Commies: it is Britain which has been invaded by the Americans. This could almost be taken as an allegory of contemporary science fiction.

Stars of Albion: from Mary Shelley to H.G. Wells to Austin Lundy

Interzone is the only British science fiction magazine. Founded in 1982, it is edited by David Pringle and Simon Ounsley. Although only published quarterly (becoming bi-monthly in August 1988), *Interzone*'s influence is far greater than can be measured by its circulation and frequency. At a time when other magazines are stagnating, it has both ambition and drive, is never afraid to experiment. To keep up with contemporary short science fiction, and ahead of the novels, *Interzone* is the magazine to read. (A sample issue is highly recommended: £1.95—£2.50 overseas/$4 U.S.A. — from 124 Osborne Road,

Brighton BN1 6LU, U.K. End of commercial.) This is not to say that the magazine doesn't have its failures: as mentioned earlier, for some reason it published Benford's 'As Big As The Ritz'.

It is frequently Americans who have taken the lead within the pages of *Interzone*, and the only story reprinted in the *Yearbook* is by an American, Richard Kadrey's 'Goodbye Houston Street, Goodbye'. During 1987, *Interzone* published fewer stories than it might have done, because half the year's issues were monopolised by the Geoff Ryman serial 'Love Sickness'. (Which, as earlier noted, was to win the British Science Fiction Award in 1988.) And I decided not to reprint the story which *Interzone* readers chose as the best of the year — because it was by me. (It can be found in *Interzone: the Third Anthology*.)

1987 was a good year for British anthologies. There were three books containing original stories. The first of these was the *Gollancz/Sunday Times Sf Competition Stories*. Garry Kilworth won the first competition in 1974, and a mere twelve years later the second competition was held. The book included stories by the two winners and the runners up, a total of twenty-five stories by new authors.

A second collection was *Tales from the Forbidden Planet* (named after the sf bookshop in London), edited by Roz Kaveney: fifteen stories of science fiction, fantasy and horror. This was a handsomely produced volume which demonstrated that maybe illustrations do have their place in books and magazines, if properly executed and printed.

The best of the three, however, was undoubtedly *Other Edens*, edited by Christopher Evans and Robert Holdstock. (I must express an interest here: Chris and Rob are both friends of mine, and it was my suggestion that an anthology of new British sf stories should be published to coincide with the World Sf Convention being held in Britain.) *Other Edens* has since developed into a series, and the first volume contained stories by most of the top British authors.

Lisa Tuttle's 'The Wound' is reprinted from *Other Edens*, as is Garry Kilworth's 'Murderers Walk'.

With Richard Kadrey's *Interzone* story, this means that three stories in this *Yearbook* are reprinted from British sources —

but only one author is British: Garry Kilworth.

This book originates in Britain , from a British publisher and a British editor. It should not bother you, the reader, where the stories come from — whether they first appeared in Britain or America, Tahiti or Tierra del Fuego. But it bothers me.

Throughout the world, science fiction is dominated by authors who write in the English language. Germany and Argentina, Japan and the Soviet Union, they all publish books which originally appeared in English. But when did you last see a book by a Japanese or German author? (Nor does this book include any stories first published in another language, because few — if any — are ever translated into English.)

And just as the English language dominates world sf, so books by American authors overwhelm the British scene. This is to be expected because the U.S.A. is a much larger country, therefore statistically there should be five times as many American authors as there are British. But from John Clute's reviews of the 1987 novels, it is easy to see that the percentage of books by American authors is far greater than this.

I feel oddly ambivalent about this situation, because I grew up on American sf. I was attracted by and enjoyed the paradox of a fiction which emerged from a culture so similar to that of Britain, yet also so different. The aliens in science fiction were the Americans!

During the mid-sixties, Britain was setting the pace in contemporary sf, thanks to Michael Moorcock, *New Worlds* and the 'new wave'. That was almost a quarter of a century ago, however, and science fiction has advanced and developed since then. (With one or two exceptions, of course.)

Although they didn't quite make it, two or three other stories by British authors were considered for inclusion in this volume. But *Interzone* will produce more fiction during 1988 (although the most popular story in the year's first two issues is by an American author); *Other Edens* continues, and there are new collections on the horizon. So maybe there will be more than one British author in the second *Orbit Science Fiction Yearbook*.

Find out next year. Whatever their origin, already there are some great stories lined up for inclusion ...